D0043641

ALSO BY PATRICE NGANANG

FICTION
Dog Days

POETRY
Elobi

MOUNT PLEASANT

MOUNT PLEASANT

PATRICE NGANANG

TRANSLATED FROM THE FRENCH

BY AMY BARAM REID

FARRAR, STRAUS AND GIROUX

NEW YORK

Farrar, Straus and Giroux
18 West 18th Street, New York 10011

Originally published in French in 2011 by Éditions Philippe Rey,
France, as *Mont Plaisant*
English translation published in the United States by Farrar, Straus and Giroux
First American edition, 2016

Library of Congress Cataloging-in-Publication Data
Names: Nganang, Alain Patrice. | Reid, Amy Baram, 1964– translator.
Title: Mount Pleasant : a novel / Patrice Nganang ; translated by Amy Reid.
Other titles: Mont Plaisant. English
Description: New York : Farrar, Straus and Giroux, 2016.
Identifiers: LCCN 2015035418 | ISBN 978-1-250-11841-7
   ISBN 9780374713089 (e-book)
Subjects: LCSH: Cameroon—Colonization—History—20th century—Fiction. |
   France—Colonies—Cameroon—History—Fiction. | BISAC: FICTION /
   Literary. | FICTION / Historical. | GSAFD: Historical fiction
Classification: LCC PQ3989.2.N4623 M6613 2016 | DDC 843/.92—dc23
LC record available at http://lccn.loc.gov/2015035418

Designed by Jonathan D. Lippincott

Our books may be purchased in bulk for promotional, educational, or business
use. Please contact your local bookseller or the Macmillan Corporate and
Premium Sales Department at 1-800-221-7945, extension 5442, or by e-mail at
MacmillanSpecialMarkets@macmillan.com.

www.fsgbooks.com
www.twitter.com/fsgbooks • www.facebook.com/fsgbooks

P1

For Nyasha, of course,
and to C. K. Williams,
who went, and came back as a butterfly

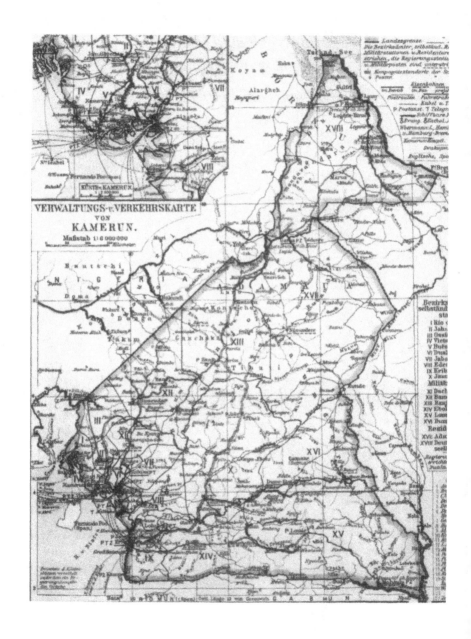

VERWALTUNGS- U. VERKEHRSKARTE
VON
KAMERUN.
Maßstab 1:6 000 000

A Few Notes on Cameroon's History

Cameroon comprises 238 ethnic groups who speak as many different languages, in addition to French, English, and Camfranglais (an urban patois that combines French and English). The principal groups include the Ewondo, in the region around Yaoundé; the Bamum, around Foumban; the Bamiléké, around Dschang; the Mankon from Bamenda; the Douala along the coast; and the Fulani in the north.

In the fifth or sixth century: The Carthaginian explorer Hanno, in the description of his travels along the coast of Africa, mentions a "Chariot of the Gods": this may be the first historical reference to Mount Cameroon.

1472: The Wouri River is named Rio dos Camarões (River of Shrimp) by the Portuguese navigator Fernão do Pó. The word *camarões* will evolve into "Cameroon."

July 12, 1884: Douala chiefs sign a treaty with German traders; two days later the German governor will declare German sovereignty over the territory of Cameroon, which they call "Kamerun."

June 28, 1914: Assassination of Archduke Franz Ferdinand and the start of World War I. Battles also take place in Africa, in the colonies of the belligerents, including Cameroon.

August 8, 1914: Rudolf Manga Bell is hanged, along with Adolf Ngosso Din, his secretary, and Martin Paul Samba, each accused of treason by the German authorities. This event marks the birth of Cameroonian nationalism.

1916: Germany loses the battle for Cameroon. German Cameroon is divided in two and placed under French and English occupation. Foumban is initially occupied by the English, while Yaoundé falls to the French.

July 10, 1919: The League of Nations gives France and England a mandate to administer Cameroon as two distinct territories, thereby legitimizing the de facto occupation of the colony.

1920: Charles Atangana, paramount chief of the Ewondo, is exiled to Dschang, in western Cameroon. There he meets and becomes friends with Njoya, sultan of the Bamum.

1921: Yaoundé is chosen as the capital of French Cameroon, in the eastern part of the country; Buea, the former German capital, becomes the capital of the British Cameroons in the west.

1921: Njoya is exiled from Foumban, the capital of his sultanate, by the French authorities. He finishes writing his book, the *Saa'ngam*, better known by the title of its French translation: *Histoire et coutumes des Bamoum: Rédigées sous la direction du Sultan Njoya* (The History and Customs of the Bamum, compiled under the direction of the Sultan Njoya).

October 22, 1922: The Catholic prelate François-Xavier Vogt arrives in Cameroon. Two days later he announces his intention to reside in Yaoundé.

January 30, 1933: Adolf Hitler becomes chancellor of Germany.

May 30, 1933: Njoya dies in exile in Yaoundé.

September 1, 1939: Hitler invades Poland. In response, Britain and France declare war on Germany. World War II begins.

September 1, 1943: Charles Atangana, paramount chief of the Ewondo, dies in Yaoundé.

July 13, 1955: L'Union des populations du Cameroun (UPC), a nationalist party calling for the independence and reunification of Cameroon, is banned by the French authorities.

January 1, 1960: French-speaking Cameroon gains independence.

October 1, 1961: English-speaking Cameroon gains independence. The southern part of the formerly British-controlled territory, known as Southern Cameroons, and the French-speaking Republic of Cameroon are reunited under the name of the Federal Republic of Cameroon.

Here is the story of Njoya, of Charles Atangana,
and of Sara, her mother's daughter.

SARA AND BERTHA

卍 彐

The one duty we owe to history is to rewrite it.

—Oscar Wilde

1

Conversations One August Afternoon

She was already a boy, Sara was, when she arrived at Mount Pleasant, the royal residence in exile. That is the simple truth of it. She was only nine years old, and yet she had been offered to Njoya, the sultan, when he arrived in Yaoundé. Offered as a sign of friendship, "friendship and brotherhood." The paramount chief of the Ewondo, Charles Atangana had convinced the monarch to leave Bamum land and take up residence in the French protectorate's capital. The least he could do was to make his guest's stay comfortable; custom required no less—ah, yes, our famous customs!

It was the dry season; according to the calendar, the year was 1931. The trees said it was August, even if the day was clothed in the colors of refusal: Sara's refusal (she was called Sara ever since a Catholic priest had miswritten her actual name, Sala) because she did not want to leave her mother. The sultan's refusal, for he did not understand how coming to the heart of the region under French control would lessen their mistrust of him, evident ever since his difference of opinion with their local representatives some ten years before in Foumban.

"Isn't that just stepping on the snake's tail?" Njoya had asked one day when his friend pushed him for an answer.

"What can I say?" Charles Atangana replied, playing distractedly with his bowler hat. "It's just a change of scenery."

Like Njoya, he knew that if the French feared them, it wasn't for their words or their power, but for the good relationship they had enjoyed with the former German colonizers.

"Don't you know that France is a very jealous woman?" the chief added. "And with all your wives—"

"And what about you," the sultan interrupted with a sly smile. "You have only one wife, and yet . . ."

What could Charles Atangana say to that? He and Njoya still bore the scars of events from before the war, traces they could not erase. "I'm like a woman, and the whites are like men," Njoya had written in the *Saa'ngam*, his memoirs. "What can I do except obey?" He was referring to the English, who had come before, but it was the French who, by ordering his banishment, had left him without a voice; yes, without a voice. And yet that's just how Sara felt, too: without a voice. For very different reasons, of course. She had uttered her last words the night of her departure. Her mother hadn't given her a moment to rest after waking her, and Sara's whispers had been lost in the night, muffled by the bamboo frame of her bed, which bore the marks of all the times she gnawed on it in silence.

That same morning, the house had awoken to the sound of her mother's hollow voice crying out in a nightmare. The little girl's pale face was a blank that no one wanted to look at too closely. Especially not her mother, a sensible peasant who the previous night had made her peace and furtively wiped away her tears. Not this mother who had mortified her own flesh for days on end after accepting her daughter's bitter fate, for she had seen men cut the knot of women's destiny many times before. So she pulled a pagne tightly around her waist, girding herself to speak as the inescapable shadow in which her daughter would now live closed in around them. Uncle Owona, the girl's godfather, kept quiet. He had wished so hard to put this moment of pain behind him that he had nothing else to say. He knew it was his fault, and that was enough.

As for Carl, Sara's brother, he was too young, so no adult found it necessary to explain to him why he would now have to spend his days without his sister.

And what about Sara? She had been informed of her "good fortune"—yes, that's how her mother put it—her good fortune to answer the call of destiny, even though she was still a child.

"If I were you," her mother added, "I'd be happy."

Happy? That's the question that sounded in the mute child's head as her eyes scanned the silent room, trying to understand the flutterings of her misfortune.

"I would have danced."

Danced?

No, Sara couldn't dance, even if her mother sketched a few steps and started to sing a familiar song, a lullaby that swaddled her warmly in her praise names.

"Daughter of the panther," said the song.

"Child of the river," it added.

"Flower of the night."

"Mother of groundnuts."

For this rustic woman, singing was a way to calm her burning tears. Yet she knew it was useless to hide from her daughter the truth of the woman's life that was about to begin for her. Later, much later, Sara would hear her mother's voice calling for her in songs of praise. Sometimes she'd hear other voices calling for her in the night, voices both familiar and unknown. She'd hear the syllables of her name ricochet off Yaoundé's seven hills and then roll through the mud of the valley before they were lost in the heart of the rain, in the joyous laughter of the girls her age. Sometimes it would be the voice of her younger brother, whom she would see only once more after that morning. Her brother, who, although just eight years old, already held the gourd of *arki*—excuse me, I mean alcohol—between his legs, and called her "woman," as if he were a husband calling for his wife.

Of course Sara would also hear the gruff voice of Njoya calling for her from the depths of his deathbed, calling for her, much to the stupefaction of the six hundred and eighty royal wives. Oh, Sara would hear all of these voices spreading out endlessly over the green hills of the part of town known as Nsimeyong; she would hear these cries, these calls, these shouts, these songs of destiny. For her story is, in truth, a song: a song so poignant and so profound that it can find its echo only in the silence of the father, who, on the day of her departure, was himself absent. All her life Sara would search for the voice of this father—all her life long. The solid voice of this unknown father, she would catch hints of it even in the echo of dogs barking impatiently or in the nocturnal yowling of cats.

I'll come back to this later in detail.

When I met her, all she remembered of the sultan were his eyes. How could she forget them? Njoya's face was as captivating as an abyss, she confessed.

"An abyss?"

"Yes."

"How?"

"You would have thought he could swallow a soul."

She smiled. Though Sara was ninety, she still revealed traces of the child she had been at nine: she was astonished. I asked her if she had ever looked at herself before in the mirror.

"No," she replied. "How could I have?"

I couldn't believe that it was through Njoya's eyes that she had seen herself for the first time.

"No," she corrected me. "The chief's."

Who she meant was Charles Atangana.

2

The Abduction of Someone Else's Daughter

Because the paramount chief's envoys had arrived too soon, Sara's mother made them wait. They had the threatening look of men on a mission. One of them, his chest and back covered with thick hair, was wearing the cap of a colonial soldier. A purple pagne was tied around his hips in a flowery knot that hung loosely at his side. His demeanor was that of a colonial guard or a swindler, maybe both.

It was he who demanded "the girl."

"She's not going to run away," Sara's mother snapped back, exasperated.

The man turned to his companions, who burst out laughing.

"We know," said the swindler-guard after a pause. "We know."

His men signaled their agreement with one voice.

"We know."

"Yes, we know."

Sara's mother gave them something to drink and eat, and they sat down in the dusty courtyard. They smoked cigarettes and told dirty jokes that only they found funny. Their leader, the man with the cap, made no effort to hide his impatience. Three times he asked Sara's mother, and three times she replied: her daughter wasn't ready yet. The fourth time, the man got mad.

"We must leave," he said, pulling his pagne more tightly around him, as if girding himself for a fight.

"We must . . ."

"Leave."

"Please, just five more minutes," Sara's mother implored. "Just five more minutes, please."

The man stuck his fingers in his ears and gestured to his companions, who all rose, dusted off their behinds, and stretched their legs. A couple of them spit on the ground. The seconds ticked by; the men were well aware that a mother's love could force a chief to wait forever on the road of lost time.

"Woman!" the man in the cap exploded, raising the back of his hand. "We do not have the time."

"Just two more minutes," Sara's mother begged.

But the man knew that the paramount chief would turn a deaf ear to a request for even one more minute.

"We need to take the girl," the guard continued, scanning the dark entryway of the house.

He emphasized the word "girl" as he scratched his testicles through his pagne. His men, standing behind him and looking on with approval, repeated "Yes" in unison.

"The girl."

"Yes, the girl."

"And then what?" her mother shot back suddenly.

"The sultan is waiting too," the man in the cap replied, as if that made all the difference.

He swallowed his spit; the mother's rather violent retort had unsettled him.

"Yes," his men insisted, "the sultan is waiting, too."

"He is waiting."

"Too."

The comedy they played out failed to mask their fear of making Njoya or the chief wait.

"One minute, that's too much for you?" Sara's mother shouted. "My God, don't you have any children? What do you want from me? To hand over my child just like that? What kind of men are you?"

The unexpected burst of violence from the woman made them fall silent. The chief's men looked around at one another.

"Are you animals?" she continued.

She stood with her fists on her hips as her mouth spit bile. She called the man with the cap a slaver, the shame of all the Ewondo, assassin, son of a rat. She let loose with a whole dictionary full of vile names, but his companions stopped her before she reached the end of her foul-smelling litany. They knew that the mouth of an Ewondo woman can cut as sharply as a colonial soldier's whip. One of them headed into the house and came back out running, with Sara hoisted on his shoulder and crying for help. The chaos of this abduction was brutal, but the chief's men managed to carry it off.

Later Sara would remember that of all the men who came running at her cries, only her uncle held back her mother's arms, pleading with her to let things run their course.

"This is life," he said. "It's just life."

Maybe Uncle Owona knew that a mother's pain is a door no man wants to leave open for too long.

"What he didn't know," Sara added, "is that I would never see him alive again."

Her face clouded over. On that day she understood that if she wanted to escape from her captive body, she needed to become someone else. Why did she decide to tell me her story? I would learn that soon enough.

•

Several years ago, when I returned home to do some research, a writer friend of mine told me that I should go see a house he had heard about. We drove along toward Nsimeyong, losing ourselves on all the endless tracks. The quarter had nothing to show me—just the familiar faces of a city weaned off its own future and suffocating in the dry season, where young girls bet their future on the Internet, on the chance of flying off to meet some hypothetical "white man," and where young men quickly ran over when I beckoned because I had the look of someone newly arrived.

When I mentioned the sultan's name, a dozen faces suddenly appeared around me, each of them swearing that they bore his name, were his direct descendants. There are, as I already knew, as many Njoyas in Cameroon as there are leaves on a tree. In fact, in this neighborhood, there were an equally limitless number of Atanganas. Yet none of these proud namesakes could tell me where to find the place I was looking for. My friend had been quite clear: the site contained the ruins of a vibrant community of artists that had flourished in the 1930s on a vast tract of land perched on the summit of Nsimeyong, where the Sultan Njoya had lived in exile. It was known as Mount Pleasant.

One voice rose up from the group of agitated and bewildered young people: "I know what you're looking for."

The one who had spoken had big eyes and an ironic smile. His name, I'd soon learn, was Arouna, and before long I'd discover, too, the rapacious breadth of his dreams. His dreams were quite simple, really: "The United States, since France is done for." And of course he hoped that I would reward his efforts by helping him get a green card—that is if I didn't just marry him to speed up the emigration process. For the moment the scope of our conversation was narrow, since he had raised my hopes . . .

"You're looking for the doyenne, right?"

"The doyenne?"

. . . only to dash them right away.

"The thing is, she's mute."

"If I could just meet her . . ."

"She doesn't talk to strangers."

"Or even see where she lives."

I knew that this roundabout conversation was a way for Arouna to raise the price on the information he had. The confidence of his voice imposed silence on those around him. He became my guide by default and, at the same time, the voice of the young people of Nsimeyong. It was he who led me into the courtyard of a house built of clay and introduced me to an old mama.

And that is how I met Sara, the doyenne of the neighborhood, as Arouna put it, meaning that she was the eldest person in the community. Sara didn't contradict him—on the contrary.

"It's just," she said, weighing each of her words carefully, "that the house she's looking for burned down a long time ago."

Shocked, Arouna and his friends exclaimed that they thought she was mute. They explained that the old mama hadn't spoken for some "eighty years," and they wanted to know what I had said to untie her tongue. My desire to know what had sealed the lips of this venerable woman was fanned as much by the length of her silence as by the fire that had brought down the artists' residence. Only two bricks of Mount Pleasant remained, but after this first visit I hoped that Sara, who had finally found her voice, might know how to shape words strong enough to replace the walls that hadn't survived the deaths of their builders. As it turns out, she had another story to tell.

The Face of Sara, the Old Woman

It wasn't the astounding reappearance of Sara's voice, but rather the look on her face that made me put aside my research into the origins of Cameroonian nationalism to listen to the doyenne's stories. Who could have known that from her very first words, I would be caught up in the net of her testimony and that it would take me weeks, months even, to sort it all out? And who could have known that by the time we were finished, she would give me the key to understanding the very period I had come back to Cameroon to research? Clearly not Arouna. No—especially not him. If he were to see me out of breath and struggling, like a catfish caught in a net, he'd probably laugh! And caught I was: getting Sara to keep telling her story from where she'd left off the night before was no small task.

When I came by the next day, her scrunched-up eyes made it clear that she had nothing more to tell me. Faced with her exasperated brow—so typical of the women where we're from—I didn't push it. I just sat down on a bench and offered myself up to her silence. It was simple: Sara was a monument. Even sewn tight, her mouth was an event. Her eyes didn't show their age. Like two bright lamps, they lit a pathway through the wrinkles of her sagging skin. Only her hands seemed to have been dried out by the years, a network of sinuous blue veins popping up beneath their cracked skin.

Overwhelmed by life's floodwaters, Sara was sitting on the ground, wrapped in her *kaba ngondo*, the loose-fitting robe often worn by women in Yaoundé, with a red scarf wound tightly around her head, her feet crossed in front of her. She sniffed softly at her tobacco and occasionally looked up to toss a few grains of corn to her hens, who eagerly picked at them. From time to time she cleared her throat and spit into the distance.

I realized that she loved chewing tobacco, and so I brought her a good supply, which she didn't refuse. She stuck out her tongue and put a pinch on it, then opened her eyes wide with youthful pleasure.

"It comes from Virginia," I told her, "from the United States."

Arouna had already told her that I came from "America," so I was only repeating what she already knew.

Oh, every day I would find Sara in this position, her favorite: dressed in a *kaba ngondo*, a different color each time, her head covered in a scarf of yellow, blue, or red. Soon she took root in my mind as distinctly as the statue of Charles Atangana in Yaoundé, or the one of Njoya that stands in Foumban, in the western part of the country, marking the spot in the center of the city where once a large baobab grew. With one short phrase she had revealed herself to me: living proof of a forgotten time. For Sara's body—a castle of a thousand hushed voices washed up on the shores of time—spoke even when she remained silent. There in the middle of her courtyard, even in her moments of quiet, she told me that each of us carries on our shoulders the whole of the age in which we live. The gift of time is memory, yet Sara seemed instead to live in expectation. In expectation of what? I'd learn that soon enough.

Sara's Eyes Are a Tale
That Begins with a Question

"What's your name?"

"Your name?" Arouna repeated the old woman's question.

He had explained to Sara that I loved Nsimeyong and wanted to learn about its history. I hadn't contradicted him, even if almost everything he said about me was the product of his own imagination. He looked at me and smiled as he spoke. As for me, I knew that he was presenting me in the best possible light now so that he could negotiate a better price for his services later. I must admit, it was a while before I could take this boy seriously. How could I have guessed that there was still some critical insight left beneath his pronounced fascination for everything American—for dollars above all?

What made me change my opinion about these young people from Nsimeyong was how suddenly they silenced their chatter as soon as Sara opened her mouth. At first Arouna was the only one who asked questions. I couldn't do anything to change that. Sara had known him since he was a boy. I told myself that she must think I was just another of his "clients," one of those people from the university who often come around with a tape recorder to collect the true stories of the elders, which they then label as literature.

"Your name?"

"Bertha," I replied.

Sara's eyes lit up, and her gaze shot right through me: "Ah!" Just then she burst into a laugh I could never forget, a laugh that silenced the universe. The old woman's voice echoed in the courtyard, sending chickens scattering.

"But you're nothing like her," she added.

Her laugh turned into a racking cough that made her repeat the word "her" in a rush, as if she wanted to slow down the sudden emergence of a memory buried deep in her mind.

"Like who?" I asked.

Arouna looked perplexed.

That's how Sara began to tell me her story. Bertha was the matron into whose care she'd been delivered, as a child, by the chief's men. A slave, that's what Bertha had been: a slave entrusted with training Njoya's future wives, a job she held for most of her years. Though she'd been eaten up by life—left with a wide scar across her neck, a reminder of violence long ago—Bertha was not just another version of the Sara who sat before me, no. She had been aged, yes, "very old," even, but still younger than the doyenne was now.

"What a coincidence!"

When Sara laughed, her whole body laughed, and her laughter drew her eyes out from the depths where they hid. That's how I discovered that she had lost none of her teeth. Sara was laughing because finally, after eighty years, Bertha had finally come back; and now she was ready to listen, to listen to the story she hadn't had ears for all those years ago. All her life Sara had been waiting for this reunion.

"It's too funny, isn't it?" she said at last.

None of the young people from Nsimeyong understood why the old mama found this so funny. Neither did I, in fact. It took me several sessions to understand that Mount Pleasant, the house Sara entered as a child after leaving her family, was in fact a labyrinth, as disorienting as the coincidence of names that finally untied the old lady's tongue. And it was in this House of Stories that Bertha took the place of Sara's mother and became the most important person in the young girl's life.

"I never liked Bertha, you know," she told me, "but you're not like her."

I sighed quietly.

"Listen to me," she repeated. "You are not like her."

What could I say in response to this unexpected show of confidence? One thing was clear: I had become an important part of Sara's life. With time, another thing became clear: since I had found a way into this story, I wouldn't be making my exit anytime soon. I wanted to know what happened, wanted to know it all. I was prepared to swallow up Sara's life, her whole world. The depth of her silence was an urgent invitation, and my questions were polite knocks at her door.

"So what was Bertha like?"

Sara cut to the chase.

"She was a witch."

What could I say after that? It seemed to me that Sara had escaped from a story, from a myth. Her deep, trembling voice evoked for me the telling of age-old tales. Was I to believe that she hadn't spoken at all during the eighty years she had been waiting for Bertha? Or was this just another trick of Arouna's, designed to raise the price of his services?

"Don't worry," Sara continued. "Later she'll become my mother. Can you imagine that?"

Then I burst out laughing, too. "The world is really something!"

While she again saw Bertha the matron, I was looking for Sara, the nine-year-old child hidden somewhere in the body of this ninety-year-old woman who was laughing at life's ironies. I wanted to know why that child had decided to stop speaking. What hell had made her keep silent for so long?

Soon I would find out. Sara would find the words to tell me. Together she and I would replay the scene of the prodigal mother: I would listen, and she would speak. We played this game so long that over the course of our exchanges, the doyenne relived her whole life. Yes, it was a *bayamsellam*—an exchange of confidences among market women—that allowed Sara, word by word, sentence by sentence, to reconstruct the House of Stories, to reconstruct Mount Pleasant. It was in a burst of laughter that Sara rediscovered her words. That's the long and short of it. Laughter, yes, what more to say?

"I'm sure she lied a lot," she went on, swatting at a mosquito on her neck. "How could she have really known everything she told me?"

If Sara had asked, "Do you know who I mean?" I would have quickly replied "Bertha." And yet how could I be sure that Sara herself wasn't just making up the stories she told me? It's just that I never found the courage to interrupt her—never. The idea that a ninety-year-old could lie struck me as simply outrageous. I shuddered at the thought of grabbing hold of her hands to interrupt her: "Come on, Grandma, aren't you exaggerating just a little?" I could see her face falling, its cavernous beauty fading, a lamp's flame snuffed out by a sharp breath. Yes, I could see her mouth closing up again for all eternity. The old woman would take her story to the grave, leaving me the assassin of her voice. One skeptical word is all it takes to kill off both the storyteller and her tale.

5

Bertha and Her Shadow

"Do you have any children?" Sara asked me one day.

"A daughter."

I showed her the picture I kept in my wallet.

"A very beautiful child, isn't she?" she said after gazing at it for a few minutes. "How old is she?"

"Nine years old."

"Hmm," murmured the old mama thoughtfully. "Nine years old, too. What's her name?"

I told her. She smiled, slapped her leg, and put the photo down so she could get a pinch of tobacco.

"At least her name's not Sara."

We both laughed.

"That would have been too much, huh?"

"What do you mean?" I asked.

"What a good girl," the doyenne continued, picking the picture of my daughter up again and staring at it intently, her eyes ablaze. "You must be a happy mother, am I right?"

Only later would I understand that this was her way of distancing me from Bertha: I was the happy mother. When she said it, Sara closed her eyes, as if to drop the curtain on a scene that might have been glimpsed, mirrored in her eyes. She had seen my face tracing thoughtful questions that my stammering mouth couldn't ask, and she refused to reach out to me in my timid silence.

Ah, Sara!

Didn't she know that it is harder to listen to the truth than to tell it? Oh, she certainly knew that! Sara wanted me to listen to her story, that's all; and I would soon understand that her story was cobbled together from disparate pieces, each piece an echo of the many lives she held within her and joined into contrapuntal destinies. It was when her voice burrowed into my brain that I could see her eyes burning like coals in the hollows of her wrinkled face.

"Good tobacco," she said after a long pause. "At your daughter's age," the old mama continued, "I was already Njoya's wife."

"At nine years old?"

"Nine years old. He taught me to write."

Once again I looked at Sara in surprise: I had thought she was illiterate. My reaction amused her. How she loved to see me confused!

"Yes," she repeated simply, "to write."

There were moments when Sara was again the mischievous child she had been at nine: playful. I could see her sitting in a courtyard; perched behind her on a bench, her legs spread wide, Bertha, her matron, braided the young girl's hair, holding the strands between her teeth, forcing Sara to sit up straight. She'd quietly sing a lullaby to distract her from the pain.

"Do you also do your daughter's hair?" she asked me one day when I was watching a mother braiding her daughter's.

"No," I said.

"How come?"

"I take her to the hairdresser."

"Bertha never braided my hair either," Sara told me that day. "She always cut it."

"Why?"

Sara looked at me, as if surprised that I didn't know her story already. First, she demanded that I scratch out the image of the mother doing her daughter's hair from my notes: just a cliché. Her life in Mount Pleasant wasn't the life of a typical child, she told me. Once again I was the happy Bertha. Sara preferred to bury the sorrowful Bertha, that long-suffering figure, in the twisting pathways of her silence. I agreed to her strange game of avoidance, for as she played it out, I saw her rediscover the scent of ancient words even as she chose to shut her ears to their music, to feel the weight of stories untold even when she didn't want to taste them, and, most of all, to lose herself in the whispered phrases and nervous rhythms of the bodies she felt deep in her own flesh. The community she discovered in the sultan's courtyard was strange, for sure; and stranger still the matron, Bertha, who was charged with turning her into a woman.

The chief's men brought her into Mount Pleasant through the back door. One or two stifling corridors, one or two trembling voices, one or two surprised faces—and Sara found herself before the red eyes of this woman, as tall as a man and with the features of a Fulani, wrapped tightly in a pagne—blue, the color of widowhood. A woman whose sleepy breasts were like two flat mats hanging in front of an emaciated body, her haughty head covered with thick, closely shaven hair. She was a true temple of despair. Her eyes were those of a woman who has seen her husband fall dead several times. She wore her widowhood as if for all eternity, the sublime face of endless mourning.

"So that's the girl?" Bertha asked the men.

She untied her pagne and adjusted it under her armpits, revealing as she did another pagne in bright colors beneath her austere garb.

"Yes," replied the man with the colonial cap, "this is her."

The woman bent down to speak, for she was taller than her interlocutors. She barely concealed her natural impatience.

"Her name is Sara," the man in the cap continued, his eyes scanning the scene.

"Sara," his men echoed, as usual.

"Don't you have something for us to drink?" the leader of the group blurted out. "Nothing to drink?"

Bertha disappeared into the house, dragging a silent Sara behind her. She returned alone, a gourd of palm wine in her hands. The man with the colonial cap poured a bit of the wine on the ground, then drank down the cupful Bertha held out to him.

"No beer?" asked one of the others, sounding disappointed.

"No German beer?" added another.

The leader cut off their chattering complaints.

"Shut up and drink."

One after the other, the men swigged down the cups Bertha poured for them, then wiped their mouths with the backs of their hands. One after the other they said, "Not too bad, huh?"

Bertha seemed to look right through them. They could have been shadows, these wicked clowns who shook the courtyard with their raucous laughter. Had she even glanced at Sara when she dragged her into the house, she would have seen the tears on the child's face, heavy tears.

Sara would soon learn that the actions of the old captive, who seemed oblivious to the young girl's suffering, were habits of blind obedience; each of Bertha's gestures reflected her eternal servitude. Sara would realize that the deep scar injustice had left around the matron's neck was the cause of her stony heart. As the doyenne would tell me later, Bertha had already seen it all.

6

Bertha's Shame

Clearly Sara wasn't the first! Bertha had prepared dozens of girls for their royal nuptials with the sultan. Still, she seemed to avert her eyes when she went about her work; the matron had no confidence in these young girls she was responsible for transforming into royal wives. Her bruised heart even shut her ears to the girls' stories.

Why had Bertha lost her faith in her girls? Was it when first one, then two, then three arrived, their faces dripping with tears for a virginity washed away by rivers they couldn't even remember? After five, six, or seven of them began inventing unbelievable stories in which the sultan played no part, though he should have? Or when dozens of girls she had trained disappeared into the forest and were soon spotted working as prostitutes in the city?

Or maybe it was years ago in Foumban, back in Bamum land? Bertha would remember this until the very end. It was when one girl, named—and this was the best part—Njapdunke, after the queen mother, hopped into bed with a certain Lieutenant Prestat, the local French official; she slept in his bed and then got right out and accused Bertha's own son, yes, Nebu, Bertha's son, of raping her. Ah, Bertha never did get over that old betrayal of her school of chastity: Sara would learn that soon enough, along with all the details of the infamy that was obviously still eating away at the matron's soul.

"She was still bleeding from it," Sara told me. "It was plain to see."

To tell the truth, the whole Bamum sultanate never really got over that business. Even if its fall from grace had actually begun long before, on the sixth of July, 1902, to be exact, when the first whites, three German representatives—Lieutenant Sandrock and Captain Ramsay, accompanied by the Swiss merchant Habisch—knocked at the southern gate of Foumban and Sultan Njoya asked his archers, who were ready to kill them, to lay down their arms.

Let me clarify, if I may: the fall of the Bamum sultanate formally occurred on the April 13, 1903, when Njoya himself, carrying a plate of eggs, greeted a certain Lieutenant Hirtler—how could anyone forget that awful name?—at the gate of his capital city. Ah! Did the sultan even realize that he was opening his court to a never-ending slew of calamities? First, the lieutenant had the eggs boiled and shared them with his men; second, when he arrived at the royal court, the stupid officer actually went and sat down in the sultan's own chair, the Mandu Yenu, which had been waiting all this time for his colonial behind, or so he seemed to think. Of course, Sara couldn't have known all the ins and outs of this shameful history—1903, 1914, 1931 . . .

It was now 2000. How could she have known what happened back then?

Yet Sara discovered that all these wounds that cut so deep into the back of the Bamum people were quite personal to the matron. The violence of her grip, just like her refusal to listen to the litany of complaints from her girls, was proof that she no longer believed that others felt pain. The scar on her neck revealed enough of the violence she had suffered—of which she never spoke—even if it failed to explain her cruelty. As for the car that back then stood dead in the courtyard of Mount Pleasant, it didn't even answer the songs, shouts, and tears of the children who pretended to drive it, trying in vain to get it back on the road: *vroom, vroom!*

1914, 1931 . . . The car's engine gave a little leap, as did the history of the Bamum—and that of the world itself. Whatever Bertha had lived through, it was terrible. One day Sara would realize the same could be said of her own life.

1931. Her day began early in the sultan's compound, at an hour when the sun's rays were still timid. How could Bertha not see that that alone could make a girl smash her head against the wall?

"Your mother spoiled you," that's all the matron had to say about it.

That was what she thought of all the girls who came to her: spoiled children. She hadn't had a daughter, but a son, Nebu, about whose tribulations Sara would soon learn. Still, Bertha considered the girls she trained, and the babies that they in turn offered to Njoya, as her own.

Training the sultan's wives was no small task, oh, no! Even back in Foumban, the work had eaten up her life, although she could only glimpse that truth reflected in the eyes of others. Sara became her eyes, though it did her no good. Now in Yaoundé, Bertha never imagined anyone had a past outside the walls of Mount Pleasant, and it is no exaggeration to say that she lived as if she had no future: that was the price paid for the right to see the sultan naked.

Then one day the matron read that same absence of a future in Sara's frantic, unfocused eyes. How could they have been friends? If the girl had opened her lips, her mouth would have spoken words the matron couldn't understand. It was already bad enough that Sara hadn't passed the virginity test she had been forced to undergo. But when Bertha saw the layers of silenced stories spread out before her eyes, questions she had previously thought necessary only for Bamum girls were unleashed.

"Who did you sleep with, you hussy?"

Followed by: "Just one man?"

Girls from Yaoundé don't have enough fingers to count the number of men who have been between their legs. How sad that virtue is lost so quickly! Sara flinched at each of these remarks, especially since Bertha screamed them in her ears. Yes, the matron was shouting, convinced that that was how to get through to a person who didn't speak her language. The girl's frightened eyes sought refuge in the dark from the thousands of images that haunted her past. The matron shouted, and Sara kept quiet. For the girl more than for anyone else, the beginning was also an end.

7

A Mean Woman

"Didn't you try to escape?" I ventured.

"Of course I did. And not just once," Sara confessed. "I always wanted to go back to my mother."

One day she left the matron's rooms and set off down the corridors of Mount Pleasant. She walked on and on, passing sleepy-faced guards, family homes with their whispered secrets, happy invitations to come play in the sultan's dead car. She walked on and on. She didn't run, so as not to attract the attention of the men sitting on the ground in the inner courtyards, busily playing *ngeka*, the mathematical game so popular among the Ewondo. Finally she found herself back in front of Bertha, who was standing in her doorway wrapped in her blue pagne. Bertha, whose anger was evident in the fists propped on her hips.

"Where did you think you were going?" the furious matron shouted.

Sara kept silent. Even on that day Bertha couldn't wrest one word from the girl. Not one! The matron turned away from Sara, who thought the episode forgotten; she would soon learn the price of her refusal to speak. Bertha disappeared into the main courtyard and quickly returned, a stripped eucalyptus branch in her hands. She tested the elasticity of the whip, bending it in front of the terrified little girl before grabbing her by the arm. The old woman grimaced as she raised the whip. But then her hand froze. She couldn't seem to make her body inflict the punishment. Again she raised her whip, and again she froze, her body thrust forward, her hand above her head. Tears ran down her face.

"Where were you, you miserable child?"

Sara didn't answer. The matron tried again.

"Never run away again, or I'll really have to show you!"

"I want to go home to my mother!"

These words reduced the woman to silence. She threw down her whip and walked away in defeat. Another time, she got so angry she sent Sara herself to the courtyard to pick the whip for her punishment. Some of the children from the compound helped the girl to complete her absurd task, reveling in the opportunity to turn from their simple games to actual violence. But once again the matron was unable to mete out the threatened punishment.

Later she admitted, "I looked everywhere for you, did you know that?"

Her voice grew gentle, and she asked, "Where did you go?"

That day Sara realized that Bertha's anger wasn't just surprising—it was strangely inconsistent. After each of her attempted escapes the girl would find herself once more in front of the blue silhouette of the matron, who stood waiting in the doorway of her house of suffering, hands on her hips. Flabbergasted, Sara would let herself be dragged into the bedroom by a Bertha who raised an impotent whip—a Bertha whose mouth spit out angry flames but whose hands only waved the whip and never used it. Once, at the sight of Bertha's seething face, Sara began running backward, terrified by the lady's silent defeat. "I am tired of chasing after you," Bertha exploded. "I am worn out, do you hear me? Don't make me chase after you ever again!"

"Didn't you ever ask her why she couldn't . . . ," I started to ask one day, regretting the phrase as soon as it was begun.

"Why she couldn't what?"

Sometimes Sara dreamed that a woman was coming through the shadows to take her away. The woman would open a door leading into the forest and Sara would rush right after her. But soon all the paths would fade away beneath the little girl's feet and she'd stop dead. She'd watch the woman disappear in the distance. Once or twice she ran to catch up with the elusive woman. Sara ran but soon grew tired. Although she never saw the face of the woman in her dreams, Sara was convinced it was her mother. This faceless woman haunted both her nights and her days for quite a long time. Sara never saw her mother again, except in her dreams. These became moments of real torture, from which she'd awake screaming in terror.

"Why do you cry out in the night?" Bertha scolded her. "You should speak during the day, not at night."

"I thought she had sold me," Sara admitted, her voice filled with despair. "To think how I hated her for that!"

No, her mother couldn't have sold her. Looking deep into her empty eyes, her deep wrinkles, and her enigmatic silence, I told her so: "That's just not the kind of thing a mother would do."

Sara seemed to accept what I said.

"You're right," she replied distractedly, scratching her feet, lost in her own thoughts.

I breathed a sigh of relief.

"I always thought," Sara confessed another day, her hands spread open to include me, "that my mother was a prisoner of her woman's body, too."

Even the loss of her virginity hadn't opened the doors of freedom for Sara. Had she first met Bertha in Foumban, the situation would have been dealt with differently: shame would have sealed the girl's fate, and she would have been sent back to her mother's house, her body bearing the scar of rejection. A cousin or some other young girl in the family would have taken her place; Bertha would have bribed the Tangu, the chief of the sultan's police, and the whole thing would have been resolved quietly. If her impurity had been discovered on the eve of her introduction into the sultan's bed, chicken blood, instead of the girl's own, would have stained the royal bed . . .

The archival documents wax eloquent about this period of Njoya's life, although they are quiet about the ins and outs of his bedroom and antechambers. Colonial modesty? I have found notes from bureaucrats, as well as from priests, botanists, veterinarians, and even anonymous travelers who had spent no more than one night as Charles

Atangana's guests, but who still found the words to fill page after page of their notebooks. Yet about Njoya's intimate relations, these scribes said precious little.

Still, isn't it interesting to know that the chief, Charles Atangana, never failed to furnish these colonial travelers with a girl for the night, just as he did for Njoya? Only one of these mad scribblers mentioned the "sinfulness" of the night he'd spent "in the valley of the Ewondo, which only a miracle could save." The author of these lines was a Catholic priest! I'll come back to him soon enough. Of all of these men, however, not one seemed indifferent to the charisma of Charles Atangana.

In the records, the differential treatment accorded to Njoya and to the chief didn't stop at the bedside. Charles Atangana had redefined his relationship with the French in a twist that even the sultan found difficult to understand. And how! Atangana is still mentioned in history books as the only person in the protectorate who, between 1914 and 1920, right in the middle of the war, was able to change his name, to shed the Germanic Karl and become the English Carl and then the French Charles without any uproar from the colonial public. The few scattered documents in the French archives that do draw attention to his hypocrisy, his duplicity, and above all his humble origins—they actually use the word "slave"—hardly count.

When Sara arrived at Mount Pleasant, Charles Atangana had just returned from a trip to Paris, where he was the guest of President Gaston Doumergue and attended the opening of the Colonial Exhibition in the Bois de Vincennes. Oh, but Paris wasn't the first European capital he had visited! He already had seen Madrid, where he had spent two years, and also Barcelona and Rome. So he could gauge his opinion of the French capital by what he had seen elsewhere in Europe, just as he could compare the French president with the German kaiser, the Spanish king, and the pope. Of course, for obvious reasons, he didn't ever make these comparisons when he was in Cameroon.

The friendship between Charles Atangana and Njoya dated from the period of the chief's disgrace when, in 1920, after his return from Spain, he was stripped of his title as paramount chief by the French, who were then administering Cameroon. He was sent instead to work on the construction of roads in the region around Foumban. That's how he found himself in the city where Njoya was struggling to maintain his former authority in the face of a new and overly capricious political force. One little word would soon rewrite the chief's destiny, restoring the powers that had been his under the German and British administrations: the word was "cocoa."

I'll come back to this later.

Njoya's trajectory, on the other hand, would follow the path—first torturous and then shameful (not to mention tragic)—of those who put all their eggs in the Germans' basket: the path of collaboration. Sometimes I think that Charles Atangana, a professional translator, had relied for survival on his tongue's gymnastics when the whole world turned topsy-turvy. Initially he had put himself squarely in the Germans' camp, for they had named him an *Oberhäuptling*, a paramount chief, and he had acquired a taste for giving orders. He had followed them to Europe after the war, had testified for them before all the tribunals, where, at the end of the conflict, German colonizers sought restitution for their lost plantations. Yet the chief hadn't hesitated to change camps, for he understood that it was the only way for him to get back home to Cameroon.

For Njoya, colonization had been simply a game of chess, one he hoped to win with a final flourish. Yet, and this I swear, he never could have imagined that Sara, the nine-year-old child who had been offered to him by a friend, would be the one to trace a path through the labyrinth of his colonial redemption. But again, on this point the colonial archives remain silent. And that is why the doyenne's words must pick up the slack, although the little girl who entered Mount Pleasant, shivering as she passed through the corridors of the compound, could never have imagined that she'd come to play such a role.

How could Sara imagine it, especially when, in the matron's darkened room, she spread her legs and discovered that her vagina would swallow up an egg that was supposed to be too big for it? When she got up afterward, she met Bertha's glowering, shame-filled eyes. There are falls from which no one expects to recover. Happily, the world also holds the secret of bounces.

8

Girl-Boy

Here are the facts: if Sara hadn't swallowed her tongue, she might have found the words to express her emotions. Every time Bertha's hands touched her legs, she bit her lips. She stomped her feet. She tore at her skin. She felt as if a hand were going right through her flesh. Oh! She didn't cry out, but her eyes just filled with tears all the faster.

If Bertha had shown a little compassion here; if she had asked one or two questions; if, in short, she had opened her own ears, she certainly would have opened the floodgates of this most frantic of silences: the silence of Sara's uncle Owona when the chief's men came to drag the girl away from her mother; the silence of that shadowy man who hadn't held on to his niece, but had instead used his hands to trap Sara's mother's, to keep her from protecting her daughter.

And what of her father?

What father? Hadn't Uncle Owona become Sara's father after her own father died? Hadn't he inherited Sara's widowed mother? Ah, let's forget about this father for a moment: it would have taken just one word, one step, one move—yes, with one simple move Bertha could have discovered the depth of Sara's trembling silence. But *all girls are liars*: that was her opinion. Only a mother's ravaged face could have understood the horror Bertha was unable to comprehend. It wouldn't have cost Bertha a thing to get to know her girls a little more, that's what the doyenne told me.

And yet, and yet:

"What did anyone really know in those days?"

There are families that offered up their youngest born to the sultan in the hopes of a reward. For whom a daughter was merely a step on the ladder of their slow ascent to power, a tree that grew in order to protect them with its generous shade. Fathers who dreamed of moving closer to the palace, whatever the cost, certainly advocated most eloquently in defense of this convoluted logic. Sara's story, however, differed from the classic scenarios someone like Bertha could imagine among the Bamum in Foumban, for the girl was from a different ethnic group—a different world. She was Ewondo. And the sultan's matron, who had grown old watching over and judging the Bamum girls who were brought to her on the basis of their potential alone, would have benefited from being just a tad more curious in this specific case, from pushing a little harder on the locked gates of the girl's whispered words, from, in short, asking questions in the past tense.

"People are strange, but that's an argument with very short legs, isn't it?" Sara said to me, shaking her head.

Because Sara went from silence to wild convulsions, the matron was forced to pay closer attention to her. Soon her eyes began to follow the girl along the corridors of the house. And often Bertha's voice was heard calling Sara's name through the passages. When the old woman let go of the girl's legs on the day of the infamous egg test, Sara ran and hid, naked, in the first open room she found. Only a mother is able to cover up a shameful story under a cloak of love. And so the boy, yes the boy whom Bertha dragged from the room where Sara had disappeared would soon understand that the reason for the matron's increasingly labored breathing was that she had suddenly, and unexpectedly, rediscovered her maternal instincts.

Oh, was there any way to explain what had suddenly misted Bertha's pale cheeks and filled her sleepy breasts, except to say that he had been recognized by a mother's body? Had he shown just a little more curiosity, this boy would have discovered in the body of this maternal latecomer the tortured story of a loss, the story of a life linked to the end of his own.

Bertha asked the only question possible in this situation. "What's happening?"

She furiously wiped her hands on her rear end, as if she had just touched excrement.

"Who are you?" she demanded.

The boy whose gaze had frozen her own asked no questions. He stared at Bertha silently, desperately.

This is what happened: Sara had gotten confused. In the darkness where she sought refuge, she had put on clothes that didn't belong to her. Her mind was filled with thoughts of escape: escape from the matron, from Uncle Owona. Escape. Obviously, in her panic, she hadn't realized what she had become. But Bertha saw the boy she was from then on, and she immediately recognized him as her son. Yes, the matron recognized the young girl struggling in her arms as the son she had lost in the far-off, swirling mists of her life in Foumban. Her face turned to clay. Covering her mouth with her hand, she smothered a cry; she wanted to be sure of what she was seeing.

"Who are you?"

Bertha took a step back but stopped in the doorway, thus blocking out the light that could have revealed the truth.

"What's happening?"

She pressed hard on her belly to calm the kicks she had never expected to feel again.

Bertha shivered with cold, squeezing her dripping breasts and pushing on her aching belly. She knew her questions were of no use. Sara wouldn't answer any of them. The matron stripped this accidental boy with the violence of a disappointment felt by her alone. She raised her hand to strike but let it fall, having finally understood the limits of her anger. She didn't ask the girl to go get the whip for her punishment. On the contrary, her eyes were filled with tears when she finally managed to stammer, "Why?"

On that day, the relationship between Sara and Bertha was radically changed, retreating ever further into the labyrinth of lies. The matron, who for an instant had seen her son come back to her, wiped her eyes and discovered instead a terrified Sara. The shadows held nothing more for her than a mute and disoriented young girl. From then on, Sara noticed that Bertha eyed her suspiciously, looking for something only a mother can see.

Poor Sara. She had no idea about the crazy plan beginning to take shape in the mind of a matron whose maternal instinct had been abruptly awakened. She was truly dumbfounded when, after her attempted escape, Bertha burst into tears and stood frozen in front of her, holding a whip she suddenly lacked the strength to wield. The matron's lips were murmuring the words "my child." Like a butterfly caught in a spider's web, the girl collapsed against the mats of the old woman's chest. Bertha cut the girl's hair, leaving only one lock on the top of her head, like a boy.

Since the Bamum prefer boys to girls, Sara had no trouble wending her way through Mount Pleasant's courtyards in her new apparel. Only the children on the sultan's car gave her any trouble: she distracted them from their games with the stationary automobile. As Sara passed by, they'd shout out invitations to play, but when she turned away, they'd taunt her with this annoying rhyme that hit the mark each time:

> *"Cluck, cluck, cluck! went the hen! Oh my!*
> *See the little boy come by!*
> *Tonight is the night I'm gonna die!"*

Happily, the little devils were taken in by the cross-dressing. Nothing about Sara alarmed them. And in any event, Bertha quickly set them straight: children couldn't make fun of the sultan's shadow like that. As for Sara, she was happy to be left in peace at last, although she would have liked a chance to play with kids her own age.

"If walking around with a shaved head was the price to pay for being free from the matron's whip, that was a good deal," the doyenne added, her grandmotherly pragmatism reflected in the set of her jaw.

But that wasn't all: Bertha also ran hot stones over Sara's chest to delay the development of her breasts. To tell the truth, this routine was no surprise to the girl: her mother had done it to her several times, too. Except that the matron wasn't trying to slow down the rapid growth of a woman. She wanted to bring her son back to life. She wanted to turn Sara into the boy she had become by chance: Nebu.

"Why did you go along with it?" I asked the doyenne.

Sara told the saga of her life without losing her smile; she took another pinch of tobacco, as if there were nothing strange about her story. She was thrilled that she had tricked the omniscient Sultan Njoya, and she still laughed about how a simple garment had changed the life of a little girl.

"Even the witch was completely taken in by it," Sara told me. "I was a perfect little boy."

"And did you like that?"

"What do you think?"

Her transformation into a boy had freed not just one but two women from the tragedies of their lives. If the tears that streamed down the matron's face each time she raised the whip to hit her allowed Sara to guess what was going on, only later would she really understand what it meant for Bertha to call her, forever after, "my son."

9

The Labyrinths of Childhood

The exquisite pleasure of being someone else, that's what finally freed Sara from her suffering. The girl entered into a house, excuse me, into a life, where she didn't meet any children her own age, but where her ears were filled with a thousand stories. She entered into an existence where a specific task was assigned to her. Sara entered, in fact, into a house of mystery, a house of a thousand whispers, where silence was always menacing, filled with invisible ghosts. By an absurd stroke of luck, the sultan was in need of a shadow—the previous one had quit, preferring to live out his exile in the city's poorer quarters.

The little girl had to get used to the name Bertha gave her. Happily, her entrance into Njoya's inner circle was facilitated by her decision to remain silent. The sultan's secrets, along with her name, would remain buried in her mouth as if in a tomb—just as Bamum tradition required.

"Ah, I was only a slave," Sara told me. "Nothing but a slave!"

Was she serious? I could have replied that since slavery had been abolished in the protectorate by colonial decree, her status was rather ill defined. There are questions that must be asked, especially if one has spent time in America.

"Tell me," I asked her, "what did it mean to be a slave in those days?"

"I was the sultan's property. Only," she added, raising her finger to emphasize her point, "he wasn't my master!"

Did Sara realize I didn't understand her answer?

"Your silhouette doesn't belong to you, does it?" she continued with a smile.

"No."

"But it follows you everywhere."

"Yes, it follows me everywhere."

"Except that," she added, giving a quick look around, "sometimes you don't see it. Well, that's the kind of life I had. The life of a shadow."

Sara might have saved herself a lot of trouble had she answered Bertha's calls with less impertinence. The matron was exploring the unexpected consequences of her renewed motherhood. Breaking with tradition, Bertha insisted that the sultan's shadow spend his nights "at home." What a strange demand! Yet there were ears to hear it, and hands willing to make it so. I had some trouble, I'll admit, imagining a woman who had been introduced as a witch suddenly shedding a mother's tears.

Sara reminded me of this simple truth: "Bertha always called me Nebu."

The matron insisted, "I want the right to see him."

The right? You have to understand how affection grows in the belly of a woman when she belatedly discovers the child that could have been her own. Could anyone have imagined that after her breasts' sudden reawakening, Bertha would vow to give birth to her son once more? Could anyone have suspected the pains she felt in her belly whenever her *boy* left for Njoya's chambers? Was there anyone who didn't hear the cries of a woman in labor coming from her room each time he did?

Only Nebu could have known it had all started the day Bertha took in a girl given as a gift by the chief. If a boy was seen leaving her house every day, who could swear it was a girl who had entered? As for the chief's men, they had come there only once and then disappeared, lost in the endless mystery of colonial violence.

"Nebu!" Bertha called. "Nebu, come here!"

Everyone found it funny to see her chase her boy with the shaved head through Mount Pleasant's courtyards. Everyone laughed when, out of breath, she called the child by his full name: "Nebuchadnezzar!"

But call she would, until her son's face appeared at her door.

Sometimes an adult offered a helping hand and brought the recalcitrant child back to her: "Here he is!"

Bertha also tried flattery: "Do you know that when you were a child, you ate a lot?" That's how Sara knew that Nebu hadn't died in childhood, but when he was an adult. She understood that ultimately, Bertha dreamed not just of giving birth again to the child she'd lost, but of giving him an entirely different life. Bertha thought that life would be possible if she could just tell her newfound son the full story—bit by bit, anecdote by anecdote—tell him all the twists and turns in the life of the one she had lost; if she could just breathe into this miracle child, word by word, the life of the one who had fallen on the path through hell. It wasn't a problem for her that Nebu was the sultan's shadow. No, far from it.

From the doyenne's story I deduced that the matron needed her son back in order to love the work to which she had sacrificed her life. A mother's love has no limits, right? But Bertha rediscovered her purpose the moment she no longer had any girls to care for. Sara was the last one entrusted to her. She didn't want to dwell on that. Like all the others, that girl had failed the virginity test—and in the end, she'd just as soon forget that, too. Her son, Nebu, on the other hand, gave her back an energy she thought she had lost for good. She told him all the details of the other one's life: "Do you know that . . ."

Here's how it went. Sara would sit on the ground, with Bertha on a bench behind her, as if she were going to braid her hair. The matron would squeeze the little girl's body between her knees and hold her head with her hands. She would speak directly into her ears, whispering and singing. She would tell her about Nebu's life, all the details of his remarkable epic, his life in Bamum land, his travels in and around Foumban. She spoke to the child, but it was really one long monologue. She spoke until her voice gave out, until her words were emptied of life and burned her lips. She spoke as a mother speaks to her child, nourishing him with words and milk. At the end of her tale, it was as if suddenly someone else began to move within the little girl's body, in her limbs. The long-lost Nebu had come back to life, and suddenly a new destiny opened up for Sara. Hard to believe that Bertha's son was just one of the faces of the thronging crowd I discovered under the shell of Sara's face!

10

Symphony of a Colonial City

In the 1930s Yaoundé wasn't a city, but a town with a population of barely 150,000, whites and blacks included. In those days, the high commissioner's palace, the central post office, the police stations, the French bakery, the café La Baguette de Paris, the church in Mvolyé, and the palace of the paramount chief were the only signs of the capital city that Yaoundé has since become. These touches of European-style urbanity let everyone know they were in a colony. The many shops that spread out along the main road, including a pharmacy and even a pet store, gave the area—already known as Ongola—the feel of a place where things were looking up. Mount Pleasant, with its ornate bamboo walls and its raffia roof, adorned with geckos and two-headed snakes, stood out starkly, even among the disparate architectural styles. There were some compounds built in the Fulani style, especially in Briqueterie, the Muslim neighborhood, but they were becoming less common.

The truth is that the group of native Ewondo families that today claim the history of Yaoundé as theirs and theirs alone was already outnumbered by the Fulani shepherds who had settled in the valley, on both sides of the Mfoundi River, and by the Bamiléké who had immigrated to Yaoundé from the western plateaus or from Nigeria. The Bamiléké weren't yet talking about putting down roots. Their peregrinations across the Ewondo swamplands dated back to an invitation from Charles Atangana himself: he had needed workers for his cocoa plantation. I'll get back to that later. If the town didn't yet have the shops run by Indians found elsewhere in Central Africa, it's because the French administrators had placed their bets on the Lebanese they'd brought to the region. There was a rumor that Yaoundé's "Lebanese" were actually Indians—that is to say, decommissioned British colonial soldiers who had settled there at the end of the First World War. Some even claimed that they were actually Egyptians, but what does it really matter?

Among the whites, several different nationalities were represented: the French, of course, but also Englishmen and Greeks (actually, the Greeks were Cypriots who owned trading companies), and even Germans, almost all of whom had "gone native" under the leadership of a collector of flowers, birds, and butterflies named Zenker. This eccentric, who hid away in the depths of the forest with his compatriots, had refused to return home and, no joke, insisted on being called "Cameroonian." Most of the white colony was made up of Frenchmen who owned the best stores in the city, as well as the bordellos, which were off-limits to the black population.

Despite its two-tiered cosmopolitanism, Yaoundé kept traces of its original seven villages; these had been transformed into neighborhoods, some might even say slums. Most of the natives' houses had mud walls and roofs covered with palm fronds, despite an order from the French high commissioner banning the use of such materials in the city and insisting on cement-block houses with corrugated metal roofs. Was this order followed? Hmm. The authorities had no means of enforcing their decrees save the force of the law, as always. But, well, the law . . .

Even then it was impossible to live anonymously in this city, especially if, like Nebu, you were the sultan's shadow. The child's red pagne made him stand out, as did his shaved head. To think that the boy was the only person in Foumban who could have stripped bare and become an entirely different person, yes, a girl who could come down the hill from Nsimeyong and disappear!

So what kept him from going back to where he was born? Yes, what made Nebu stay among Njoya's men? Bertha, or rather . . . Ah! that's it! It was Uncle Owona's eyes—Sara could never forget them—the wild flames in those treacherous eyes that, even when she was ninety, she still described as horrifying.

"He gave me to the chief to forget."

"Forget what?"

The voice of the doyenne was again that of a young girl. "His crime."

No, she'd never gotten over it.

"There are things that even a whole life can't erase," she added in a muffled voice.

"Did your mother know?"

"She knew my uncle went crazy when he was drunk."

She paused thoughtfully before continuing.

"My mother knew Uncle Owona did things he would regret for the rest of his life and that he kept drinking more and more to forget."

"Like every drunk," I added tentatively.

Was agreeing to incarnate Nebu the young girl's own way of escaping Uncle Owona's grasp? Of getting rid of him once and for all? Even after all these years, her uncle's face still burst violently through her words as she told me her story.

11

What a Man!

"What a man!"

Yes, what a man! That's how many German and English texts speak of Njoya—with repeated exclamations. Though French texts usually do tend to minimize his genius. Some call him a "Negro king." Of course, Nebu couldn't know what the colonial chroniclers had written, much less grasp the implications of what they said. How could he have? Thankfully, before my trip to Cameroon I had visited the Library of Congress in Washington, D.C., and then the German Staatsarchiv in Berlin. The Cameroonian National Archives came to my rescue in moments of doubt, spreading before me the totality of the words, the mountains of correspondence that the monarch exchanged with the colonial authorities of his day.

From this unending supply of confidential reports and books filled with admiration and hatred, I was able to reconstruct an image of Njoya as he invented the writing system that had fueled his dreams, as he toiled away in flickering lamplight for twenty years to perfect it. I saw him, Njoya, dressed in his caftan, awake at five in the morning, already eager to get to work. I saw him standing in front of his table in the half-light of his workshop, imagining model pictograms, then moving on to phonograms, and then to phonemes. Making calculations and sketching drawings of his printing press with Monlipèr, the master blacksmith he had brought with him into exile so that the traditional Bamum heraldic banners might keep flying high. I saw him crumple up his designs and start again. I saw him poring over his plans for his new palace, the "Palace of All Dreams," which he wanted to finish building as soon as his exile ended and he was allowed to return to Foumban.

I saw Njoya examining the sketches, despite the painful distance of his banishment, and finding them lacking. Assessing disdainfully these manuscripts that Western archives now guard so jealously, wanting to tear them up, and staying his angry hand because of a noise behind him. "You must maintain control of time," he said to the man who had just entered, focusing his anger on him. "You are always late, *Mama*."

And Nji Mama would bend his head in shame. He was the sultan's closest collaborator. The occasions when Nji Mama angered the sultan were rare, for after all, it was he who had built Mount Pleasant. He had done it in just one month, though he didn't brag about it too much. In his haste he had reused sketches drawn up for the old palace in Foumban that he had constructed in 1917. Njoya's arrival in Yaoundé had caused some turmoil. The vast entourage that accompanied the monarch needed to be housed somewhere. That Nji Mama had had to copy his own sketches was humiliating for a man who took such pride in his art. And yet, who was unaware of his talent?

Here are the presumed plans for Mount Pleasant:

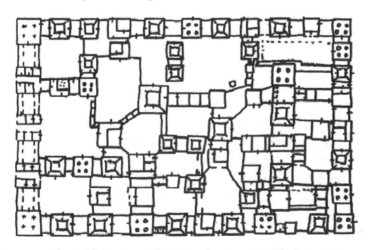

Copy of the plans of the former palace in Foumban,
drawn in 1917 by Nji Mama

Nji Mama included distinctive design elements in his sketches, patterns of snakes and geckos above the doors, for example. He surrounded the windows with five rows of bamboo rather than the two typically found in Foumban. As for the entryways, he decorated them with buffalo heads instead of human faces. More important, he replaced the seemingly infinite rooms found in the former palace with a more modest number (sixty), and had the interiors painted with yellow chalk, the color of the sun. For the exteriors he chose the color of the earth in Foumban. As for the windows and the doors, they were white.

Even if these decorative features contributed to the building's originality, it was nothing compared with what Nji Mama had already built. He was the one who had worked with the sultan on a topographical map of Bamum land in 1913, before the war. In 1920, with a team of thirty assistants, he had drawn the map of Foumban. He, again, was the architect of the Palace of All Dreams in Foumban and oversaw its building as well. His many achievements were not limited to the domain of construction: he taught in Njoya's schools, and he was responsible for the *muntgu*, the palace police, as well as for the collection and transcription of Bamum folktales. And he was credited with collaborating on—or perhaps inventing—the writing system officially attributed to Njoya. Yet the master was a deeply humble man and, I might add, too respectful of the sultan to boast of his own genius. Chief architect—that was his title, and it suited him.

"You must maintain control of time, Mama!"

For the moment, humility was the only possible response to the sultan's anger; Njoya grumbled and banged his cane on the ground, showing little concern for his interlocutor's expertise.

"Things can't go on like this!"

"Yes, Alareni!"

Even the most respectful forms of address failed to calm the sovereign's anger. It had become clear that Nji Mama was lost in Yaoundé without the assistance of his younger brother Ibrahim, who was a master craftsman as well as a Muslim, and whose hours were measured by the rhythm of his five daily prayers instead of by a watch. Ibrahim had stayed behind in Foumban, managing the sultanate's assets in Njoya's absence.

"*Donnerwetter!* Damn it all!" Njoya cursed in German. "I have been working all night, and look when you arrive!"

"Yes, Fran Njoya."

Even his praise name had no effect . . .

"This just can't continue!" Njoya railed.

Here I can imagine Nji Mama risking a subversive phrase, something along the lines of "Perhaps you are working too much, Mfon Bamum?"

He couldn't really have said anything of the kind to Njoya, even if it was cushioned by a respectful expression of gratitude. There are things that no man—other than the colonizers—ever dared say to the sultan. Besides, Njoya had always worked too much. He walked in a dreamlike state; work was his refuge, the garment in which he clothed his wounded soul. For Njoya had to protect himself from many different furies. The period of time I'm discussing actually produced abundant documentation describing Njoya's intellectual pursuits, things of which Sara had no inkling. Why? Nebu was illiterate, yes, but good God, let's drop the speculations! I am just the mouthpiece for the dusty archives, for the documents eaten away by roaches. Still, I'll admit that sometimes, carried away by the scent of the leather-bound pages of the *Saa'ngam*, the sultan's memoirs, I abandon myself to the flow of my dreams . . .

That said, I have no right to lose sight of the goal of my efforts: to explore the building that is the life of an old lady. Sara's life.

So why not just listen to her?

"What a man he was," said the doyenne. "What a man!"

12

The Primer of Love

"You are a good boy."

Bertha's voice was insistent. With one hand she held Nebu's head while she ran a wet razor over it with the other. The child didn't complain.

"You'll be a handsome man."

She filled the child's silence with her resonant voice.

"A very handsome man."

If Nebu had spoken, Bertha would have expected to hear words in Shüpamum, the Bamum language. That's because the matron was a pragmatic woman. This child had come back to her, and she didn't want to waste her second chance. She wanted to show this prodigal son the best life had to offer, and like anyone offered a second chance, she knew exactly what she had to do.

"You'll speak better," she added.

Her eyes plunged into Nebu's to erase any trace of Sara in them. Did the other boy have a stutter? That's something she wanted her new son to get over. Did he wet his bed? That, too, he needed to get over. Bertha didn't want a mute son, either; she wanted to overcome death. Her son's tightly shut lips gave her the opportunity she needed to slip in words of her own choosing. Yes, it was up to her to coat this child's lips with words of love that would replace Nebu's tragic story. Bertha knew it: her son would speak not just to say something, but to conquer his former destiny. He would need a dictionary

filled with a new kind of beauty. And what of Sara? Ah, the girl
retreated into her own flesh, where she spun about in silence until,
little by little, she built the vocabulary of her survival. She would
take as her own the boy's phrases, which Bertha whispered to her;
patiently, she would learn the language of a redefined existence.

"I will teach you the words you need," Bertha said. "Better words.
Pure words."

Bertha was carried away by her own enthusiasm. One day, she
undid her pagne and offered her full breasts to Sara, as Bamum
women would do for a prodigal son! "Do you want to eat the stars?"
Her hands pointed at the nipples while her eyes expressed the perfection of her happiness.

"Crazy, isn't it?" Sara summed it up for me. She was smiling.

Even the young men from Nsimeyong were stunned.

"So did you . . . eat . . . the stars?" I asked the old lady. "Did
you?"

I waited, bemused, expecting Sara to reply, "Of course not."

But what she said was "Of course I did."

"What?"

"Would you have refused if it were you?" the doyenne asked,
showing me her nine-year-old face.

That's how Sara came to suckle at Bertha's breasts and swallow
the matron's new words. Bertha insisted that the pronunciation be
perfect, the tone sweet. "That is what makes a sentence exquisite,"
she said, "for how could a virtuous soul reside in a filthy belly?" She
remembered her son; she remembered how Nebu called some women
"whores." Such awful, slavish words, Bertha eradicated them from
her respectable language.

"Butterfly," she said, pointing at her own eyes.

She had realized that Nebu would turn away during his lessons—
in other words, that her new son was in the grips of an undefinable
shame. For the matron, however, moral integrity was measured by
how well one chose one's words.

"Butterfly."

The truth is that Bertha wanted no more filthy words around
her. She would have loved never to pronounce them again. She
would have preferred that that sort of ugliness had never existed. It

was the same for all the parts of the body: words she repressed, buried deep in the cellar of her vocabulary.

"Music," she said instead of "heart." "Gourd" for "buttocks." And for "girls"? I just don't know.

The hardest part was what to call the genitals, which had no place in the matron's duties. Maybe her trembling hands, her stammered words, the whole arsenal of Bertha's sanitized world revealed to Sara the tragic depths that hid behind the colorful butterflies. Ah, why do children always keep quiet about the essence of things, even though they see it so clearly?

"Sky," the matron continued. "Dance." That was her word for "love."

One day Nebu awoke, and everything around him was covered with words: the sky, the birds, the clouds. That's what Sara told me.

"A universe of love, then," I replied, amused.

"Yes."

"You know," Bertha said to her, "you always loved to eat." And Nebu suckled at the matron's breast as tears ran from Bertha's eyes. He ate up Bertha's words hungrily, and his full belly illuminated his delicious intelligence. He came to differentiate more and more clearly the unique faces of the identically dressed artists and artisans. It was as if the key to this busy royal court was found in the gluttonous grammar of his suckling. In his belly, Njoya's world seemed liquid. In no time he had digested everyone's name, but Mount Pleasant never became a place he could really call home.

The doyenne still remembered vividly the day she was first introduced to Nji Mama. Bertha saw the man walk by and greeted him with a whisper. The architect turned around. He had a graying goatee and deep, thoughtful eyes. His boubou, a flowing wide-sleeved robe, was made of cloth woven from bark and cut in the style traditionally worn by artisans. There was no pretension about him. No one would have guessed he was a master craftsman. The way he replied to Bertha reflected his humble dignity. The matron, on the other hand, had practically thrown herself onto the ground to salute him, uncovering the nobleman's finely made sandals.

Later she confided to Nebu, "That was Nji Mama."

The architect was an especially striking figure. He was present in Njoya's chambers every day and at all hours, drawing maps, making sketches. People said he was working on a watch. When he wasn't with Njoya, Nebu would see his silhouette moving quickly through the corridors, suddenly appearing right next to the boy, lost in thoughts he did not share. Other times Nebu would hear his sandals scuffing along. Who didn't recognize him? Who had never passed by his dreamer's face?

"Ma-ma," that was the first word Nebu said in Shüpamum. Bertha, who had waited so long to hear it, was speechless. But for an entirely different reason: by speaking to his elder like an equal, before he had been spoken to, the child had broken a taboo.

"Pay no attention to what he is saying, master," she beseeched the architect, at whom Nebu was pointing. "He's only a child."

"He's a good child," said the architect.

Bertha added, "His name is Nebu."

"What a coincidence!" he exclaimed, visibly grasping for a distant memory. "He has the same name as your son, doesn't he?"

Nji Mama's thoughts were elsewhere; otherwise he would have heard Bertha's whispered reply. "He . . . is . . . my . . . son!"

At this turn in Sara's tale, I could only smile, for I knew something about the interweaving of names, lives, and destinies. Weren't we, after all, and after eighty years, still caught in the web of this game that had first made the doyenne burst out laughing and then open her lips to tell her story? Even if our roles, unsettled by the secrets Sara and Bertha kept, were no longer the same, we were still enmeshed in a very strange love story.

"Yes, what a coincidence!" Bertha replied to the chief architect, this time out loud.

"What a coincidence!"

The man moved on, the echoes of his steps retreating along the corridors of the house.

Like a schoolmaster, Nji Mama always repeated what people said to him. Lost in his thoughts, he hadn't noticed the happiness written on the face of this reborn mother.

13

A Hell of a Car!

It took a while to get over a visit from Charles Atangana. It wasn't Nji Mama who would announce the chief's arrival, but the commotion triggered by the appearance of his car in Mount Pleasant. He came to pay his respects to the sultan, as he regularly did, but this time he obviously also wanted to introduce the yellow-and-black Cadillac, the Golden Car he had purchased at the Colonial Exhibition. Charles Atangana wasn't the first person in the city to have a car. There were a good number of whites who had them. Everybody recognized the high commissioner's black Peugeot—or had at least heard of it. Njoya also had one; its skeleton, sitting there in the courtyard, had, through life's twists and turns, ended up as a plaything for the children. For them, there was nothing trivial about hearing the roar of a real engine—*vroom!*—nor about seeing an automobile appear in the distance and slowly make its way into their lives. When its horn set the universe in motion, even the adults stopped dead, dropped what they were doing, and ran after the machine, shouting and clapping, their bodies clothed in a cloud of dust.

The artisans, servants, even the animals of Mount Pleasant followed the chief's vehicle into the sultan's courtyard. This was just the start of a long-standing fascination, for even after cars had become banal, the Cameroonian government would choose yellow as the color for taxicabs, as if to remind everyone of the chief's mythic Cadillac.

This event gave Nebu his first real chance to leave Bertha's house. How so? The boy just gaily followed the crowd, mesmerized by the machine's magical movement; that was how he learned to navigate the corridors and gardens of Mount Pleasant. Neither Bertha's breasts nor her calls could hold him back. No more than could Nji Mama's threats rein in the children dancing around the miracle. Not to mention their parents, who stood there gaping. When the chief emerged from his infernal machine and stood in front of everyone, a long cigar in one hand and his foot on the running board, the collective frenzy reached a crescendo. Decked out, hat to socks, in the same color as his car, it seemed as if he were waiting for someone to take a picture. The sultan himself couldn't stay away.

Charles Atangana's explosive laughter wasn't enough to silence the din caused by his arrival. Faced with such a technological marvel, the sultan, too, was like a child with new sandals. The chief glowed with pride as his friend walked around the machine, silently examining it piece by piece. Then he opened the door wide, as if inviting the whole breathless crowd into the secret realm of the gods.

"Aren't you coming?" he asked Njoya, who had come out without his cane.

Charles Atangana's voice rose above the crowd's chatter and took hold of the sultan, who still hesitated to get into this Car of Light. It was a far cry from Njoya's old red pickup truck, you have to admit. Luckily, he hadn't been caught totally off guard, for he was dressed in his best.

"*Donnerwetter,*" he said at last. "God damn!"

His daughter Ngutane was the first to get into the vehicle of temptation. No one who knew her was surprised. Ngutane, oh Ngutane! The way she walked was an artistic manifesto. No one could imitate how she swayed her hips from left to right! Years earlier in Foumban, she had been the first to wear a brightly colored fabric that was all the rage in Berlin—a gift from the German schoolteacher, Fräulein Wuhrmann. Afterward she had ordered her tailors to make her a dress fashioned after the boys' clothes she'd seen in the *Quelle* catalogs her Swiss friend collected.

In the Basel archives there are two photographs of her in fashionable outfits. I was able to interview people in Foumban who remembered seeing her coming down the Artists' Alley in Foumban, wearing a broad red hat and high-heeled shoes, like some showgirl right off the stage of the Winterpalast theater in Berlin. She wasn't known as Nji Mongu—the first daughter—for nothing. So she got into the car first and asked her father to follow her, as no one else would have dared to do. Njoya had never refused her anything. I don't need to tell you that she would also be the first woman in Cameroon to drive a car—the very same one, in fact, that she had just gotten into. Yes, she'd convince the chief to teach her to drive! For the moment, she was glowing—not because of her audacity, but out of sheer happiness. She adjusted her outfit and waved goodbye to everyone through the window.

"Next time," the chief said, "we'll all go on a tour of the city."

This time, he added, he just wanted to *show* the sultan his new acquisition.

"Show? What a joke! Then he started the engine, supposedly on account of Ngutane," the doyenne stressed. Ngutane was the only woman who dared to be so presumptuous in the company of these powerful men. Oh, I know, maybe Sara exaggerated her character. But that's not what's most important, for one fact remains: the chief was always filled with a joy that had deserted Mount Pleasant. Ngutane's rush to get into his car was just a response to the melancholy that inhabited her father's chambers. The sultan had opted to bury himself in his scientific experiments. He had traded the responsibilities his position previously imposed on him for the comfort provided in exile by his machines. He still allowed his daughter to read him the newspapers, because he couldn't give them up. Ngutane relished this duty, for it kept her up-to-date with the changing fashions of the European capitals.

This child's tastes (Njoya called Ngutane "his child," even though she was already married and a mother herself) drew her to the *Journal illustré*; its pages of pictures fed straight into her dreams. The only drawback was that she often had to wait months for her copy. At least the French hadn't outright forbidden Njoya to read European magazines, a habit of his that dated back to his friendship with the missionary Göhring.

Göhring was the first to write an article about the sultan. That was how the friendship started. The Swiss missionary had had to translate and read the article to the sultan, who then wanted to know what else was in the magazine, *Der evangelishe Heidenbote*. Narcissistic curiosity is at the root of many an extravagance. After reading all the magazine's pages, the missionary thought to continue by reading the Bible, starting with the Old Testament. When the unbelievable stories of that book failed to whet the monarch's appetite, Göhring moved on to Thomas Mann's massive novel *Buddenbrooks*, which he used both to kill time and as a pillow. And wouldn't you know, that exemplar of German literature, a bestseller in its day, captivated Njoya, who valued family above all else.

But let's get back to Ngutane, who, after completing her studies at the German school, took on the role of her father's reader, a function Göhring had held till then. Only a truly shortsighted colonial officer could have written what I saw in the archives: that Ngutane's love of European clothing was a reflection of her vanity. How could anyone forget that she would also become Cameroon's first woman of letters? Ah, it seems the French colonial chroniclers dismissed these reading sessions, for there is no mention in their records of a reader named Ngutane, although they made repeated reference to the "grandiloquent dreams" of the sultan's daughter.

"A spoiled child," that's what they wrote about her when they weren't expressing their exasperation at this "overly pretentious Negress." News that she had a copy of *Madame Bovary* would, I think, have spread like wildfire through the colonial ranks and certainly led to the classic being banned for a second time, now in France's overseas territories. Of course Ngutane would have sympathized with "poor Emma," as had many others before her in Paris and the other European capitals. For the moment, however, Ngutane's dreams weren't hitched to a swallow's wing, but rather to the sweetly scented seats of a Golden Car. No lover: it was her father who sat beside her. Once around the courtyard—*vroom!*—and the surrounding crowd broke out in hymns of joy. One more time—*vroom! vroom!*—and the crowd went wild, lost in ecstasy and a cloud of dust.

Sara began to see the sultan differently because of the car, for after this, the heartiest laugh heard in the corridors of Mount Pleasant was Njoya's. The sultan was happy, yes! How had Charles

Atangana done it? That evening Charles was telling jokes—about his car, his life, everything. As usual, he seemed to be talking to everyone at once. This time, however, he also talked about his trip to Paris for the Colonial Exhibition. Ah, will this story ever end? Everyone in the lively room could clearly envision the fat woman he described, "an overly perfumed countess, with red lips" who was left speechless when he told her that he wasn't polygamous. The chief imitated the countess: "Not polygamous, really?"

Carried away by his own comments, he forgot that the man to whom he was telling this story had more wives than anyone else in the protectorate.

"A Negro and not polygamous!" he continued, then changed voices once again and, bowing aristocratically, added, "And Catholic, my dear lady, Catholic!"

He was the only one laughing, of course, for none of the men listening were Catholic or even Christian, and certainly not monogamous. But who would have thrown cold water on the chief's pleasure when he had a story to tell? More important, who would have reproached him for his lack of tact? After all, he was the only real friend Njoya had in Yaoundé, the one who understood best the sultan's weaknesses. He was also the only one in the protectorate's capital who could tell jokes like that! That's surely why his last words were met with polite laughter. But maybe it was also because Njoya had responded to his friend's anecdote with a quip of his own: "Well, if you ever want to become pagan again, just call on me . . ."

14

Friendship's Twisted Secrets

What was it that had thrown these two men into each other's arms? They had so little in common! Collaboration, according to some evil tongues; a similar position of authority in the protectorate, according to others. But when he was driving that infernal car of his, Charles Atangana, a committed monogamist, always had his "very dear Juliana," his wife, by his side. Njoya, on the other hand, might have chosen a favorite from among his six hundred and eighty-one wives—except that his impatient daughter would never have given him the chance. So, was it their similar temperaments?

Well, maybe not. The chief's voice and his alone always dominated the conversation, for he had a way with words . . . or rather, he talked a lot. Even if his title of paramount chief was only a flattering translation of the German *Oberhäuptling*, he owed his power to the force of his voice alone.

As for Njoya, who had a low voice and was more of a listener, it was his family's hegemony over the Bamum (a note: the colonial archives make mention of "the criminal intrigues of his mother, Njapdunke") that was the basis for his authority in Foumban. The chief had seen the world, and not just what lay beyond the borders of the protectorate. He had toured all around the colony with the Germans. By contrast, Njoya's only trip, in 1908, had taken him no farther than Buea. His exile to Yaoundé was the biggest move he had ever made, and merely his second excursion outside Bamum land.

So what had drawn these two men together? Let's see. Their love of fine, expensive clothes? The fact that they were both, without a doubt, the best-dressed men in the protectorate? Njoya's collection of sculpted canes was on a par with his friend's cigars and brightly colored outfits, I can vouch for that. Except that vanity doesn't draw men together; on the contrary, it divides them. Maybe what made Njoya and Charles Atangana friends was the feeling that "they had been through it all." They had seen the faces of all the colonizers.

Or maybe it was their playful habit, which they never lost, of speaking to each other in the first language that came to their lips. A strange game, one that amused those who heard them. The chief would say something in Ewondo and his friend would reply in Shüpamum, then continue in German and be answered in French. Ah, how did they understand each other? Even today, how do Cameroonians, with their two hundred languages, understand each other? The fact remains that their friendship began in Mantoum in 1920 with a burst of laughter. Charles Atangana had paid a visit to Njoya in the residence where the sultan was spending the first months of his exile, and their conversation turned, seemingly of its own accord, to the colonizers who had spent time in their respective cities, and who had been on opposite sides of the war.

"So," Charles Atangana began, "which are the best? The French, the Germans, or the English?"

"That's not fair!" the sultan protested. "You can't ask me such a thing."

"Believe me," the chief continued in a conspiratorial tone, "never compare a Frenchman to a German."

"Or a German to an Englishman."

"An Englishman to a Frenchman."

"A Frenchman to anyone at all."

The chief thought for a moment about what Njoya had said.

"You are right," he said with a great guffaw. "Whites are such tribalists!"

Then Njoya burst out laughing. It was so true!

Cameroon, such as we know it today, wasn't yet born. For Sultan Njoya, the word had for so long referred to a city, Cameroon City, the present-day Douala, that it couldn't mean anything else. As for Charles Atangana, this country—if one could speak of it as a country—would only be important once his hometown, Yaoundé, where he had convinced the Germans to set up a camp, had become the city of his dreams: the Cameroonian metropolis.

That, at least, was his reputation: he wanted Yaoundé to become a second Rome. According to some, his plan was insane for one simple reason: the land itself was too poor. Only groundnuts grew there—although in abundance, it's true. People snickered and said that the only thing the chief could trade on to realize his wild dreams was the future. A visionary without the funds to make his dreams come true, Charles Atangana knew he had to make compromises and, above all, to make as many friends as possible. He invited everyone to Yaoundé; Njoya was only the last of a long list. The Germans were the first to let themselves be convinced, mostly because of the friendship between the chief and their hero Dominik. The French came along later because he had sworn he would transform the forests of Southern Cameroon into endless cocoa plantations. In terms of megalomania, it was a plan so wild it even amused the French high commissioner, Marchand. But Marchand was too astute a politician not to recognize this chief, with his steady gaze and his quirky habits, as a kindred spirit. "This guy is a genius," he told his colleagues. "No joke, he has dreamed my dream."

Thanks to Charles Atangana's ability to dream the colonizers' dreams, in 1921 the Cameroonian capital was moved from the mountains of Buea to Yaoundé, and he was chosen to supervise its construction. Ongola, the city center, was his home base. What more could he ask? Still, it wasn't enough for him; he spread his arms and told the streets of his hometown—bush tracks, really—that he imagined a "City of Seven Hills." Those who still share his dream have clung to the nickname he gave it, trying to keep the chief's fantasy alive in our poor neighborhoods, to invent a different future for this stupid, chaotic city that is, in reality, so sad and so dirty. Mount Pleasant was itself a name plucked from the chief's flamboyant vocabulary. Curiously, over time, people forgot it. I'll come back to that. (Yes, I promise.)

Charles Atangana and Njoya? Whatever it was that made the

men cross paths—the coercive borders of a nascent country or the intrigues of a chief who invited both local and colonial authorities into his hometown to secure his own place in the heavens—it was friendship that exploded in the sultan's chambers each time Charles Atangana was there. There was laughter, raucous voices, a whole rosary of debates—too many to number, and yet never too much for the chief. It was life at its best.

Still, it was always the chief who had the most to tell: how hard it had been to get a license plate for his car ("Do you know why? Because it's an American car!"), his trip from Yaoundé to who knows where ("But not on horseback, like when I traveled to Kousseri with Hans Dominik, you know . . ."), and so on.

Finally, late at night, the car disappeared, leaving behind it unlikely tracks, words that bloomed in phosphorescent dreams.

15

Talking About Hell . . .

After the chief's departure Nebu couldn't close his eyes. He was entranced, and far into the night, the symphonies of Lisbon and Hamburg rang in his ears. That evening he hadn't had to help undress the sultan. Two of Njoya's wives, Mata and Pena, his current favorites, had stayed with him. So the child headed back to the matron's, whistling as he went. He lay down on his mat and covered his eyes with the palms of his hands, the better to see far-off places.

The day had left a smile on his lips that he couldn't quite explain; a taste of happiness surged sporadically through his veins. Bertha was already asleep. Her rhythmic breathing filled the room. Nebu thought about what it meant to be a slave. He wondered why the joy of two powerful men came at the cost of a little girl's damnation. He also wondered what would have happened if the sultan had refused to come to Yaoundé. Would Sara have had a different life?

Would Yaoundé have been different?

And history? Would its course have changed?

Ah, history! Is it inevitable? A series of knots in the weaving of a gigantic braid, isn't that what it is when all is said and done? Terror flooded his mind. He saw Uncle Owona's dark eyes again and understood that he would have to accept the truth of his life: Sara. Nebu heard the little girl crying. A shout. He felt his uncle's hot breath in his ears and suddenly opened his eyes. What was it? One thing was certain, it wasn't Sara who was screaming. The boy shut his eyes again, but the cry kept coming: strident, scattered. Then there were hurried steps. And someone calling, "Ngosso!"

It was the sultan's voice. It kept going: "Ngosso! Samba! Manga!"

Nebu jumped from his bed and ran outside. In Mount Pleasant's main courtyard he met a terrified Pena. Her head was bare and her face panic-stricken. She ran toward the house of Mount Pleasant's chief doctor. The boy immediately understood that something awful had happened. Without even thinking, he suddenly found himself in Njoya's bedroom. The monarch was stretched out on the ground, one hand clutching his chest. His breathing was labored.

"Manga!" He was yelling, his eyes like milky ghosts.

Two men were working away at his body. They were holding him, repeating incantations Nebu didn't understand. Their frantic actions didn't drown out Njoya's confused words. "Samba!" Njoya shouted, his hands and feet spread out, his mouth open wide in the chaos of the room. "Ngosso!"

Standing beside him, Mata looked lost and helpless—each frantic gesture canceling out the one that had come before. Nebu ran back to his room. Bertha wasn't there. She must have joined the other servants who, alerted by the noise in the sultan's room, were running around or forming groups of curious onlookers in the hallways. The image of the fallen sovereign filled Nebu's mind with every imaginable horror. He suddenly took off backward and bumped into a man coming from the courtyard: it was Nji Moluh, Njoya's son and successor.

"What's going on?" asked Nji Moluh, who was still pulling on his clothes as he ran.

No one answered him, because no one knew.

Njoya's cavernous voice broke the silence.

"Manga! Samba!"

"Alareni!" A voice in the darkness repeated this flattering title, chanting it like an incantation. "Alareni!"

It was Nji Mama.

Nebu kept walking backward. He knew the path out of Mount Pleasant well. He didn't need to search for his way through the labyrinth. In the courtyard there was only the skeleton of the sultan's pickup truck to answer the sky's song. There were no children, no one at all. Even the heavens were empty. Soon the boy found himself outside the compound. He ran between the trees of a misty forest. He hurtled down Nsimeyong's hill as if he had wings. He made his way along the rocky paths. Dogs barked. He cut a path through the brush. Voices cried after him, describing a destiny he didn't recognize as his own. In his mind, the grimace on the face of the fallen sultan revealed the disaster he was fleeing: the face of his father as he fell. Nebu ran to escape those misty visions of the fall, to escape Sara, to escape Bertha.

In the distance, a light let him know he had reached the church in Mvolyé. He was out of breath. He beat on the door with both hands.

Silence was his only reply.

He knocked again, and finally a feeble voice asked, "Who's there?" A woman's scared voice.

Nebu banged on the door even louder.

"Who is it?"

A white man opened the door. He held a wavering lamp in his hands. His face, lengthened by a beard, identified him as a priest, even if he was wearing pajamas. His voice was familiar.

"Who are you?"

Yes, it was the priest. His outfit made him look strange. Seeing the child standing there, he responded in a fatherly way.

"Come in, my son," he said in Sara's language.

Nebu moved toward him, then stopped. The heads of two women appeared behind the man. Maybe the priest thought it was another dramatic case of a native child fleeing the clutches of paganism. Isn't that how so many girls came to him—in the night, fleeing forced marriages, pursued by bloodthirsty spirits, ancestral traditions, and curses, by abusive uncles or violent husbands? The church was a refuge and Catholicism a heaven for these hopeless souls. No need even to attract them with candies; it was easy to convince them to become nuns, to offer their lives to God.

This time, however, it was a boy. And this boy—although the bearded man didn't know it—suddenly thought of Njoya, abandoned, covered in his own spit, his two favorites, who had no idea how to save him from death, by his side.

"Come here and tell me what's wrong," the priest repeated.

Instead of obeying the man of the cloth, Nebu backed up, waving his hands left and right, tripping over himself in his confusion.

"Wait," the prelate cried, for he had guessed what the child couldn't say. "Wait, I'm coming!"

He didn't even pause to get appropriately dressed. He raced off after Nebu. What good luck that he was a doctor in his heart, even if a priest by vocation! He had come to Cameroon to escape the constraints of a small Alsatian village where no one told any stories he didn't already know. That was ten years ago. Before he perfected his strategy for hunting down pagans, he had already run out of people to whom to distribute his circulars. Since he had decided to found a little church on the spot in the forest that the chief had graciously allotted him, miraculous events kept happening, one after the other. He refused to believe that the sweets he gave the children had anything to do with it. He summarized the situation with a phrase that has since become famous: "Faith is exploding in Ewondo land!"

One word said it all: "Miracle!"

He couldn't walk down the street without crowds of children at his heels. Sometimes he was seen coming down the hills on his bicycle, followed by dozens of kids who thought the Catholic Church was a kingdom, a kingdom where they could eat nothing but sweets. They were enthusiastic about becoming catechumens. Most did so against their parents' wishes, which didn't bother the priest; his goal was to separate the good seed from the bad.

Still, he could see the fear in the eyes of a child who knocked on his door at night. That's how he saw all Cameroonians: children waking him so that they might free themselves from the darkness of night. He heard their knocks as a call to his faith. Hadn't he come here to find an answer? That's the story I found in a circular signed by the man I can now identify by name: Father Vogt. Yes, the very one whose name now adorns a school in the capital, and of whom the Ewondo still speak with reverence. If Father Vogt's pajamas contributed to his reputation as a saint (the two nuns who were with him that night made sure to note to the Catholic hierarchy how he was clothed—a significant sign of his zeal), on that night his outfit also made it easier for him to make his way through the dark corridors of Mount Pleasant and into Njoya's room.

"The doctor!" many voices shouted when he appeared. "Let the doctor through!"

Servants cleared a path for him. Njoya's wives stopped crying. Nebu's footsteps guided the priest, who was deaf to the premature keening.

"Let him through!"

That was an order from Nji Moluh. His father's medical team moved back. Oh, I can't imagine how the people of Mount Pleasant would have reacted if the bearded man had come dressed in priest's robes to the bedside of the sultan they thought was at death's door. From then on, Father Vogt was known as the doctor who saved Njoya's life.

"Make way," he ordered. "He needs air."

He demanded all sorts of things, none of which were refused. The news of the sultan's fall echoed across the city's hills, although the name of his illness remained shrouded in mystery.

When Sara told me this story, she still wasn't convinced that the bearded man she had awoken wasn't polygamous.

"You know how Catholic priests are," she added slyly.

I asked her why she had run to him, since I remembered her telling me that she didn't like this hunter of pagans, and why she hadn't taken advantage of this opportunity to run away from Mount Pleasant. She smiled and, once again, contradicted herself.

"Where would I have gone?"

I was about to say, "Back to your mother's," but the doyenne continued on and confessed, "Maybe I went to him because I knew he could perform miracles."

"You believed that?"

She burst out laughing.

"I was just a child," she explained. "But I didn't stay in his church. Just between you and me, it was far better to be Bertha's son than one of his nuns, don't you think?"

Really?

16

The Song of the Red Earth

As the proverb says, the past is a path that only those with ears can see. I don't know if it's Bamum, Ewondo, or Bamiléké. What I do know is that I'd have said the opposite: "That only those with eyes can hear." Sara had long since ceased suckling, but the matron's breasts hadn't stopped producing milk. Nor had her language lessons come to an end. The rug woven by her love had grown into an unparalleled syllabary. Her vocabulary bordered on poetry. Sometimes she was so caught up in her newfound maternity that she began to sing and occasionally even danced a few steps.

In fact, what she told her son in a series of perfect words was a love story. A song a mother sings to her little boy so he'll fall asleep smiling, and also to warn him about the heartaches sure to come. A song people whistled in their gardens and in their rooms, sometimes whispered like a prayer by girls in love. A song of calamity, of deep suffering, despite the beauty of its words; a song so sublime and poignant, I must say, that Bertha had tears in her eyes each time she sang it. With a few small exceptions, her song told of a lost land.

For the matron, this song blazed with an incandescent memory. A memory swathed in purple. Clearly, Bertha couldn't continue to hum her heartfelt song after the drama that took place in the sultan's room. The inhabitants of Mount Pleasant wouldn't allow it. It made the walls of the house shiver, for its verses roused the memory of the red earth of Bamum land that, when it rains, holds tight to your sandals to prevent you from abandoning it.

"Do you want to kill us with that song of yours?" a woman asked one day when she heard the matron singing in her room.

"Stop!" ordered another voice.

"Enough is enough!"

"Shut up, woman!"

Thankfully, amidst the angry chorus of voices, some conciliatory words were heard.

"Why don't you sing a different song, Bertha?" one woman suggested.

The echo of the names—Ngosso! Manga! Samba!—that Njoya had cried out in his suffering still rang in everyone's memory, especially the elders. It was out of the question that the matron intone a song describing how she'd lived as a slave before the exile:

"No more bad memories!"

The prohibition was total:

"No more sad songs!"

"A joyful song!"

"A hymn to joy!"

"To life!"

To put an end to the list, someone suggested, "Say, Bertha, do you want us to hang ourselves because we're in exile?"

"Because we're so far from Foumban?"

"Because we're in Yaoundé?"

Someone else added, "Do you want the sultan to kill himself because he fell?"

Sultan Njoya's agony wasn't something to make light of. Scenes describing the fate of slaves when monarchs died flooded the matron's mind and shut her lips. She thought of her own fate. Then the fate of the royal wives. This made her angry, for she wanted to think only of her son, of Nebu, of life in Foumban. Maybe she was trying to defend herself against the unexpected turns life had taken when she decided to describe her son as a young man and to tell Sara the story of his adolescence. After all, Nebu's life was just another version of her own!

One morning Bertha declared, "Nebu killed his own father."

Her voice was calm, as if she had uttered that shocking phrase many times before.

"Yes, he killed his own father."

Was this some sort of joke?

No. She continued: "But the Dog deserved to die!"

Sara had to get used to hearing the matron call her husband "the Dog." Bertha's deranged voice and her conspiratorial glance were enough to catch the girl's attention, despite the feeling she occasionally had that she was back in the sewer she thought she had escaped the day Uncle Owona's eyes had disappeared. Her ears recorded all the details of Nebu's story. And Bertha described her son, for wasn't it important that the girl listening know whose place she had taken?

"What a kind boy he was," she said. "An angel!"

Sara tried to get ahold of herself as the matron continued.

"A good boy, really."

The matron's eyes filled with tears when she repeated, "Good boy."

And then she added, "But he was possessed by the Devil."

She spit out the word "Devil," and her tears turned into lines of fire, which she hoped would protect Sara.

"Like his father, that Dog!"

This is what Sara could understand of the matron's tale, so often interrupted by curses and tears: Bertha had nursed a feeling that could only be a luxury for many women in Foumban—jealousy. Of what? She couldn't stop imagining her man—the one she'd been given to—off in the company of other women. As she saw it, her husband had married her, "so she deserved his love." Outrageous words, especially when spoken by a woman of her lowly status among the Bamum. Still, Bertha, a slave, concocted many schemes to attract and hold on to "her man."

Once, she staged a suicide. She certainly didn't lack imagination! A few drops of goat's blood on her and the Dog would be the most infamous man on the planet. Because she was an intelligent woman, however, the matron realized that since her husband already had enough saved up to buy a new wife, the suicide of his first one would only give him more freedom.

"A woman is the remedy for a woman": that's the treacherous wisdom men circulate among themselves, and the Bamum are no exception. At the same time, it's impossible to keep faking suicide. Bertha's husband hadn't even asked her why she wanted to die; he had already closed the chapter of his life in which she was his only wife. One could conclude that a sinful longing had surged through his manly flesh, reminding him that while he was still making do with a monogamous life, all the other members of his cohort, the men of his clan with whom he had come of age, were already surrounded by several wives. To say that this gentleman had to make up for lost time is to underestimate the pressure he endured in the company of his fellows. He was a scribe, of course, and intellectual work pays very little. He might not have been innately inclined to polygamy, but he felt obliged by peer pressure to take another wife.

Every man wants more than one wife, he told himself. He just doesn't know it yet. This phrase, which wasn't his own but belonged to one of his friends, was soon his favorite. The problem is that he came to this decision quite late in his life. His son Nebu's voice had already changed, and now he was showing signs of a beard. To be blunt, Nebu had also begun to look at women with a gleam in his eye. Nebu knew, of course, that he couldn't lay claim to a girl, for, as the son of a captive mother, he had no rights. But still, his eyes, and especially his penis, refused to abide by the rules imposed by his condition. They each reacted quite independently when a girl passed by, his left eye in particular. Sometimes his loincloth seemed to catch fire. Then his tears flowed and his face grew hot. He felt something hard between his legs; thankfully, no one else knew about this insurgence of his flesh.

"What's wrong?" Bertha asked whenever she happened upon Nebu in those moments of searing pain.

Nebu kept quiet.

"What's going on?" his mother insisted.

"It's the onions," he'd say, even though his mother wasn't cooking. "Onions."

In those times, many slaves turned to animals. Often a cow or a dog would be heard crying out in the night. Nebu preferred to dream of women he couldn't have. One day Bertha caught him lying in the fields, waving his arms and crying, alone but for the sun overhead. That day her maternal heart grew light, for after all, she told herself, the earth is an acceptable substitute. But she didn't want to catch her son indulging in that way twice. She warned him never to forget that he would be doubly punished if he was caught lusting after a woman promised to a free man. The Bamum laws were very clear about what would happen if a male slave made love to a free woman. Still, it was even more dangerous to do it to animals. Just the thought of such things made Bertha sick.

Perhaps Nebu's desire was fanned by knowing that if caught, he would be stoned. Bertha couldn't ever be sure; male logic is so strange. She told her son that the flames felt by slaves—who, like him, couldn't stop looking at other men's women—would be with them when they were hanged. It's true; there were many free women who slowed down on their way back from the river whenever they reached groups of slaves working along the path. Some shook their behinds slowly before the captive audience, the calabashes balanced on their heads highlighting their shapely bodies. Ah, there are moments, Bertha's son said to himself, when the stoning promised by proverb-spouting elders doesn't amount to much when compared with a man's unquenchable desire. Other women would let their pagnes fall—oops!—as they settled a container of water on their heads, displaying their nudity for all to see. A slave would run to help the indiscreet woman with her impossible burden and her independent-minded garments, but gallantry was all he was permitted. Nebu's body showed such evident signs of virility that the expert hands of many women lost their assurance in the middle of tasks as mundane as drawing water, and they'd spread their legs, which had already been offered up against their will to old men.

Let's turn back for a minute to his mother, Bertha, the jealous woman who already couldn't bear the idea of sharing her husband with another woman; yes, let's imagine what she was like then. That she suffered sleepless nights, overwhelmed by the fear of seeing her son castrated right in the center of town or stoned because he had touched a nobleman's woman: Wasn't that the worst? Let's imagine Bertha, already torn apart by her suffering, finally confronting her fate the day a noble girl came knocking at her door, tears streaming down her face, and told her, between exaggerated sobs, that she had been raped.

The girl's name was Ngungure.

"Raped?"

Bertha stood up in her kitchen and automatically retied her pagne, tightening the knot under her arm. The day she feared had finally come, she was certain of it. She looked closely at the girl she'd been expecting since the birth of her son's desire; she examined this "ugly face" and smiled, for it was all too evident: in Foumban, only an accusation of rape could open the doors of matrimony to such an ugly woman.

"By whom?"

"Nebu."

17

Red Is the Western Soil

A mother is her son's first advocate. It goes without saying that Bertha defended Nebu all the more vigorously since the charges were serious. Faced with this girl who wanted nothing less than her boy's head, she felt maternal love squeeze her heart tight, grab onto her throat, her hands, her feet, and transform itself into an enormous burst of laughter that sent her flying out of her kitchen and into her courtyard, where she said the very phrase that every mother the world over would have said in her place: "Not my son, no way!"

She was categorical.

"Not Nebu!"

She clapped her hands to underscore her certainty, then covered her lips with the palm of her hand, bent her head, and let loose with the traditional cry of Bamum women: *"Woudididi!"*

Does idiocy know no limits? No. Bertha had seen it all before, for God's sake, but this time she had seen right through the plot. Behind the flowing tears of *that girl*, she had caught sight of cold calculation inspired by a raw desire for cock.

"Why didn't you go to the palace?"

The girl stood in the kitchen doorway biting her nails. Nebu's mother understood that the bitch preferred the implacable justice of a woman to the proverbs of old men.

"What do you want me to do?" Bertha asked.

The girl sucked her thumb.

"Kill my own son?"

"No," she replied.

Bertha was furious. "So just what do you want?"

Why does love always come hand in hand with suffering? That's a question Bertha would ask herself only much later. For the moment, what she felt flowing through her veins was desire: the desire to strangle this girl, to cut off her childish fingers, to tear out her tongue. Yet the matron's trembling hands did nothing more than reach out and slap Ngungure's quivering mouth just as the girl was opening her lips to conjugate a verb Bertha could not bear to hear.

"I love—"

"Stop sucking your thumb," Bertha cut in, "you hussy!"

Ngungure couldn't finish the sentence as she had wanted. ". . . your son . . ."

Ah, this is the end of Foumban, Bertha thought. There was a time when a girl, and a noble to boot, never would have come into the courtyard of a slave to conjugate the verb "to love" so brazenly! Love? Bertha was a more than reasonable woman. She remembered her son's face, scrunched tight, that time she'd caught him in the yam field. Then her face brightened at the thought that if he had finally found the woman who wanted nothing more than to touch him all she could, so much the better. She bought the girl's silence with a few cowrie shells and then lectured her son. Of course, she neglected to tell her husband the details of this exchange. For her, it was over, a done deal, old news, and she could move on to something else.

When her husband informed her that evening that he had fallen in love, Bertha couldn't help but burst out laughing a second time.

"You too?" she said.

She again covered her lips with the palm of her hand: *"Woudidi-dididi!"* She made a couple of jokes about this epidemic of love that had taken over Foumban and then told her man he should be ashamed of himself. He should be getting ready instead for their son's wedding. That's when she began to hate the Dog. The borders between love and hatred are porous, as we all know, especially for a jealous woman. Bertha knew her husband wasn't talking about her when he confessed he was in love. There are things one just doesn't ask. But what wouldn't the matron have given to know what hussy was responsible for this trick!

Things moved ahead rather quickly.

A few months later the Dog announced he had decided to get married again. Bertha couldn't believe her eyes when he introduced her to the woman he had chosen—"a good girl," he said. Yes, Ngungure, the very same one who had knocked on her kitchen door, a grotesque accusation against her beloved son on her lips. So when the Dog moved into a new house, the House of Passion he had built for the "Devil" (that's what Bertha, who was Christian, called her), the matron saw a weed sprout up in her courtyard. Never had a silence been so strongly imposed, nor so accursed. "She really got me," Bertha said, and she slapped herself for having underestimated the machinations of that hussy. "She really got me good!"

But that's not all. She blamed herself for underestimating girls. "I would have killed her," she went on, her eyes growing red. "I should have killed her."

She couldn't hide the powerlessness of her empty hands to commit the crime she desired. Her husband was so much in love that he went to Habisch, the local Swiss merchant, to buy himself some European clothes: a green jacket, a black belt, and white gloves. He also bought black shoes with white trim. The merchant advised him on what to buy: this is what Europeans wore when they got married. He invited his first wife to his wedding. Bamum law required it. The poor woman, whose love had already turned to hatred, thought of the many stupid things she could do to destroy this Europeanized joy that had planted its accursed roots in her courtyard. She could have started scabrous rumors: that the Dog's wife was polyandrous, for example. But she restrained herself: as a co-wife, her opinion counted for nothing and would only make people laugh. Bertha also thought about shouting that the wedding was scandalous, shouting it so everyone could hear, but she remembered that it was in her best interest that the ceremony take place as planned. She didn't want to have to flee because she was accused of witchcraft. Nothing worse could be said in Foumban!

Suspected of jealousy, Bertha would have lost all her standing, and like any other man taking a second wife, the Dog would have just laughed off her warnings. "Ridiculous!" That's what he would have said. The jealous woman could feel the words dissolving in her mouth, but she still refused to keep quiet. And then there was her son. He offered no consolation: Wasn't that Nebu she saw sidling along the walls to sneak into the House of Passion when his father was in the fields? The boy was so determined that only the threat of a curse from his mother slowed his steps—and then just for an instant!

"What are you doing over there?" Bertha demanded. "Do you want to die?"

She soon realized her questions were lost on the puzzled face of a boy who no longer knew what to do about his raging penis. Nebu could see no farther than his own erection.

"So curse me then," he told his mother. "What difference would it make!"

"It's your father!"

"He took my woman!"

If Nebu forgot he was talking to his mother, he remembered that Bertha had once before given her tacit blessing to his relationship with Ngungure. But because Nebu's spirit was on fire, he forgot that Ngungure was now his father's wife. He was already cursed! His mother saw that he was engulfed by the flames she had first seen light up his eyes.

"Let them stone me!" the son said.

He meant the *muntgu*, the sultan's police: they would stone him. And he imagined this horrific outcome over and over, even as he was screwing his father's wife. Love? Oh, Nebu was already stoned, stoned! He didn't need to die again. He was already dead, and his laughter in his father's bedroom made his mother bleed again and again, bleed herself dry.

"Burn down the house," he added. "Burn us with it!"

"You are my son," Bertha replied.

The mother's dilemma wasn't the same as the son's.

"I am a man."

"You are my child." Bertha took his hands, pulled him in toward her chest, and pulled out a breast for him to suckle. "My son."

There is an age when a mother's milk becomes bitter for the child.

"Leave me alone!" Nebu shouted.

He would rather his thirst be quenched by the flames of a fire than do his mother's bidding. He would have preferred to express openly his love for his father's wife, his girlfriend. In Foumban, many first wives had set fire to their co-wife's house, but their jealousy never succeeded in bringing their husbands home. Nothing—not even being a mother—could protect a woman from the rage of a mob of men determined to avenge the humiliation of their fellow. It was always the woman who was exiled from the sultanate. That's what the law said. So Bertha squelched her motherly fears and her wifely pains. There was already suffering enough.

Had she set fire to Ngungure's house, she would have said, "I did it for my son," and all the men would have burst out laughing. "Find something more original, woman."

Bertha could already see her son being stoned. She pulled back in fear. Tears ran down her cheeks. Tears of love for her son on her right cheek and tears of hatred for her husband on the left. For the first time since Nebu's birth, her womb contracted, as if in labor, as if she were again giving birth to this son she already saw dead.

According to the doyenne, when the matron told this story, she kept hold of her belly, so unbearable was her pain. As Sara took in the terror provoked by the matron's revelations, a look of compassion appeared on her face. I want to be Nebu, she thought, the son so beloved.

She knew that a story once told can't be untold; in that, it is similar to life itself. Bertha's voice cracked under her pained cries— "*Woudidididi*"—as she sought to bury the wail she had repressed in Mount Pleasant as well as in far-off Foumban, as she sought a place to hide her defeated eyes from her unlikely son. That was only the beginning of a long and shameful story from which she hoped Sara would save her—the seventeenth chapter of a humiliation that had first left its mark on her neck and stained her hands with the horrific brutality of a crime before stealing her faith in the girls entrusted to her care. Still, she insisted, "The Devil stole my child."

She hadn't stopped calling Ngungure the Devil.

The start of this story left no doubt in Sara's mind. Now she knew why Bertha had been so happy at her son's return, and why she wanted to give birth to him once more.

"Strange that she didn't censor her story," I commented. "You were only nine years old."

"She had been through hell," the doyenne explained. "Regardless of the words she chose, her mind could only be dirty."

Sara's eyes gave me an idea of this hell.

"The poor woman was spitting flames without realizing it; she was eating shit and couldn't even smell it anymore."

Sara was telling Bertha's story—this was clear to me after just a few sessions—in order to escape from the furnace she had kept burning for eighty years, to put out the fire that had been set all around her. Bertha, meanwhile, kept inventing new words, the wounded flowers of her sublime vocabulary, to make up for the filth of her macabre existence. Listening to the matron's suffering ate up Sara's childhood day after day, one chapter after the other. As for me, I couldn't keep from wondering: Was it better to transmit such stories to a child or to let a little girl disappear in the obscure chambers of a sultan's life? In a way, it seemed to me that there wasn't much difference. A story can also rape a soul.

With her tales, the matron made Sara painfully aware of the hell she had lived through herself and gave her a glimpse of the paradise of a love Sara wanted to hear more about. I opened my ears like one might open an engine's valves. The spoken word was the only connection between those two souls, those two worlds, but that only made the depth of their shared silence more evident.

Life is a story as much as it is a destiny.

18

A Decidedly Scattered Story

Each of us is a kaleidoscope of our times. Events that take place in the most far-flung corners of the earth must have repercussions in the world's capital; delusion alone lets us believe it's possible to live in isolation on this globe. To love is to accept the unexpected that knocks on destiny's door. Maternal love is a metaphor for the strange relationship that links us to beings who have always been there and who are, in the end, as unknown to us as a newborn babe who has his whole long life before him to surprise us. In thread after thread of the doyenne's tale, I discovered the infinite knots of a soul's testimony; the old mama revealed the world of a woman whose name I shared and who was so far removed from me, so different!

"I know that you didn't speak," I began one day, "but if you had asked Bertha questions, what would have been the first one?"

Sara looked at me for a moment.

"I knew you'd come back to that."

"To what?"

"The scar on her neck."

The old mama was wrong. I wanted to get back to Samba, Ngosso, and Manga, to know who they were and above all why Njoya had their names on his lips the day of his collapse. She didn't give me the time to ask. She took a pinch of her tobacco and opened wide both her eyes and her mouth, as if she wanted to swallow me up; then she froze in that position. She didn't sneeze, no. We both laughed when I admitted that she'd scared me. Truthfully, it was hard for me to adapt to the zigzag rhythm of her narrative, to melt into the multiple lives she spread out before me. She alone controlled the tempo of her tale.

So I settled myself into the tale she chose for me.

"So, did she get that scar from her husband?"

That would have made sense, right? But no.

"Stories can wound us as well," was Sara's reply. "Don't you know that?"

"Yes, I do."

I would have liked a more direct answer to my questions, but I couldn't find the words to make her understand that. I wanted her to respect the logic of her tale and to slake my greedy thirst for it with a series of goblets. The more I opened myself up to take in her stories, the more I got lost in Mount Pleasant's corridors, and the more simple questions bubbled up in my mind: Who was Sara? Who were her parents? Yes, who was her father?

"Why are you so impatient?": that's how she would have replied. Her tale had shown me a museum of the colonial era, introducing me to unknown figures, like Nebu, and to luminaries, like Njoya and Atangana, as well as to history's illustrious martyrs—Ngosso, Manga, Samba—and who else? There are stories that don't need a plot. Sooner or later they rise above the confusion and untangle their mysteries in a series of sentences.

Sara was carried away by Bertha's story. And since the end is, in some ways, also a beginning, Sara realized that the matron's suffering was only just beginning on that day when she reached the bloody borders of her madness. If Bertha had taken little Sara's tale seriously, she would have heard echoes of Nebu's tale in the soft barks this girl with the enigmatic past made each time Bertha shaved her head.

"No," the doyenne continued, somewhat irritated. "It wasn't her husband who gave her the scar. We're just at the start of Nebu's story."

Sara took another pinch of tobacco. Once again she didn't sneeze, but before continuing, she tucked her snuff back into her cleavage and opened her eyes so wide it was as if she were opening the Book of Life.

"You're just not going to believe what's coming next."

Sometimes even the most attentive listener needs to take a break. Bertha knew that. But life is a tobacco seller whose stand you just keep coming back to. Like the wandering imagination of an old lady. Sara, or rather the boy she had become, had to set aside the story of Nebu's adolescence before it was done, because there was work to do. There was the sultan. And in his coma, the monarch couldn't wait. If you recall, he had turned all of Mount Pleasant upside down. Apoplexy is no joke, even today. And in the 1930s? In colonial Yaoundé, where the central hospital hadn't yet been built? Ask me about it—or let's ask Sara. Or the archives.

There are many explanations for Njoya's survival. For example, the medical priest, Father Vogt, wrote in his circular #37 that it was the Hand of God that performed the healing. I can easily imagine that in his methodical heart, the prelate thanked the Lord for this miracle obtained without the usual candies, which was sure to pay real dividends soon. Weren't the rooms of Mount Pleasant the places in the city where the resistance to his hunt for pagans was the greatest? On the other hand, Njoya's doctors attributed their sovereign's survival to the ancestors, to Nchare Yen, the founding father, in particular, and to the titular spirit of Rifum, the motherland of the Bamum. Yet these learned men couldn't say why the sultan had come through his unhappy night but remained captive in an inexplicable sleep. Of course, no one asked young Nebu what he thought about it. But if someone had, he would have voted for a miracle. He remembered the collective sigh let out by the compound when Father Vogt, who'd been listening to Njoya's heart, declared to all those around, "He's still breathing!"

The phrase had been quickly repeated, echoing through the palace's many courtyards and corridors.

"He's breathing!"

"Thank God," everyone cried. "He's breathing!"

Clearly the worst had been avoided, even if no one could say what the future might hold.

The sultan's apartments soon became the destination of a never-ending pilgrimage, although during the first days of his illness very few people were allowed into his bedroom. Thankfully, Nebu was among them. His duties had kept him there. So the boy was present when Chief Atangana came back to see his friend, this time keeping a low profile. Nebu was there as well when Marchand, the French high commissioner, paid him a visit. Since the events in Foumban with Lieutenant Prestat, the French had always preferred to work through intermediaries rather than with Njoya himself: first with Fompouyom, the sultan's official representative in Foumban, then with Nji Moluh, another of Njoya's sons, with whom they believed they were building a future.

"I was there," Sara told me, "when the white man came."

The high commissioner's visit was a political event and was treated as such. If for some, such as Nji Mama, the man had no other reason for coming than to "see with his own eyes" that the sultan wasn't already dead, for others, including Ngutane, this visit was more of an opportunity for diplomacy. With that in mind, she wore her finest garb, a *ndop* in the Bamum style, made of cotton with a pattern in indigo.

She was making a statement. Ngutane had not forgotten that the French had refused her father the help he needed, not only to repair his truck, but to get his life back on track. And when his family arrived in the capital, the colonial administrator had looked at the vehicle that had carried the sultan over the most dangerous pathways of his exile and said, "Well, it's junk now!" How could she forget that? That her father had opted to let the truck rot in his courtyard was no surprise. Njoya's truck had become the most visible symbol of the deterioration of the relationship between the royal family and the French.

The French official didn't stay long. He held his tongue, well aware that his mere presence was potentially explosive. Or maybe he finally understood that the Bamum were covering their shame with proud apparel. He brought several books, novels, as gifts for the sultan. They were accepted as marks of his humanity. After he left, Ngutane was seen reading aloud in her father's room the pages of a French newspaper that the high commissioner had added to his list of gifts. There was no better way to soothe that woman's wounded heart, for it was an edition of the *Journal illustré*.

Njoya lay quite still when she read. The sultan was shut off in his own private conversation with death. His daughter held his hand

and, under the glow of a lamp, read the news of the world for an hour before getting up to dry her tears. Never before had she seen her father so weak. But she didn't flinch. What precisely did she read during those dark hours? In the boxes where Njoya's things are stored, I found copies of papers, the *Nouvelles coloniales* and the *Gazette de Paris*. But also a book by Hugo, *The Art of Being a Grandfather*. Because Europeans tend to frame everything in terms of their own reference points, I can imagine one of the sultan's French visitors (a colonial clown, shall we say) giving him that book in hopes that the sultan would, in exile, become like Hugo, a sort of "Guernsey patriarch." And—why not?—the official could invoke Njoya's triumphant return from exile, a return that would coincide with the end of French colonization. Still, there's no better way to saw off the branch on which one is seated!

It was probably the priest who brought Njoya the French Bible I found among the sultan's things. It's hard to believe Ngutane would read pages from the Bible to her father; this man of science had not been very impressed by the stories of Jacob, Noah, and the others, which Göhring had translated for him back in 1913. Ngutane was clearly aware that her father, shocked by the excesses of the Christian God, had decided to write his own Book of Faith—his famous *Nuet Nkuete*, which he filled with stories the average Bamum would believe. More than biblical stories and their promises of eternal life, it was the joy of hearing tales told by his descendants that would give him a reason to live, wasn't it?

"Ngutane knew that for Njoya, words were like an intravenous injection," Sara affirmed.

"And Nebu?" I asked.

Nebu? There was a different story ringing in his ears. A story of the flesh that consumed him entirely at the very moment he arrived home.

Bertha didn't even give him a chance to undress.

19

What Begins in Foumban Ends in Foumban

Foumban, 1913. The question really wasn't *if* but *when* Nebu's father would see through the chaos of his House of Passion; that's what the boy told himself. His mother was also sure it would happen soon, even if her wildest nightmares couldn't predict the outcome of his story. As for the Dog, his friends were just waiting for the juicy details of the nights in his second wedding bed. Impatiently waiting! He knew that his spicy bedtime tale would finally put him on the pedestal they had left empty for too long. After two or three months of wild passion, fueled by all the *mbitacola* and the other aphrodisiacs he ingested, he decided he had enough stuff to tell his story.

His mouth full of words, he ran to the raffia-wine seller, where he hoped to find his friends waiting with open ears. Rubbing his hands, he couldn't imagine that his friends, tired of waiting, had headed off in search of other entertainment. Or that maybe they'd found something to distract them that was not merely a repeat of the stories of their own second weddings, even if they were told by an excited new convert. All he would have needed was a bit of common sense, but that was the first thing he had thrown out the window, along with his loincloth. Bertha could attest to that! Like any smitten man, her husband believed his story was unique. So when, dressed in his European finery to make a real impression, he arrived at the place where he usually found his friends, no one was there. Even the wine seller, who was usually surrounded by a crowd of loud customers, was nowhere to be found. The Dog was dumb-founded. He searched all around Foumban before finally giving up at noon. "To hell with the jealous bastards!"

So he headed back to the House of Passion. The thought of finding Ngungure and picking up right where they'd left off gave wings to his feet. In the song on his lips, she was the most beauti-ful woman on earth. He stopped dead when he arrived in front of the house. He could hear frolicking going on inside, and he wasn't there. He concentrated hard to be sure of what his ears were telling him. Aie! Cries coming faster and faster, the sound of a repeated effort, rising higher and higher, and then? And then? A song of si-lence burst into a loud chorus.

The Dog froze in his tracks. He watched the walls of the House of Passion shaking, shaking, shaking. Horrified, he put his hands on his head. *"Woyo-o!"*

As if possessed, he burst into a wicked cackle. *"Woyo-o!"* But even a laugh like that couldn't relieve the tension building up inside him. His hurried steps brought him to the door of the house, out of breath but sure of himself, mouth agape but full of words: in short, a shattered man. What he saw was beyond belief. What he saw was unnameable. His feet, his head, his hands all moved to grasp his cutlass. Deep within he felt an urgent need to kill what he couldn't even name, to silence the wicked laughter of the House of Passion, laughter that could come only from lips open in betrayal.

"Schwein!" he shouted in German. "Pig!"

What stopped the Dog's advance was his son's face, which sud-denly appeared in the cloud of his madness. He closed his eyes and opened them to behold a truth his entire body refused to acknowl-edge. He saw the flash of a man jumping out the window. Now he was alone in his room with his wife. Ngungure was naked, just as he had imagined on his way home, but this body he had so clearly sketched in his mind's eye evoked nothing but disgust. He felt a call to murder ricochet off the woman's eyes and glint on his cutlass. He took a step, raised his arm. Ngungure, realizing that demons had taken possession of his soul, just burst out laughing.

"Shut up!" he screamed.

She couldn't stop laughing. She wiped her mouth with her right hand, then with both hands, and still she kept chuckling, like a person who knows they're done for and wastes their last minute, their very last minute, pointing at their assassin and laughing because he is holding his gun in his left hand when he's right-handed. Like someone, in short, who is just wasting his time. Ngungure laughed, and for the first time, the Dog wondered why he loved her. He had shut the door of the house behind him. Even if he'd left it open, no one would have distracted him from his madness, as everyone else was in the fields.

"You really thought I loved you?" said the girl, holding her sides. "What a joke! Me, love you?"

She went on the offensive, knowing her end was near.

"Shut up!"

"Have you even looked at yourself?"

"Shut up!"

"Bent-necked old man!"

"Shut up!"

"Dirty dog!"

There are words not worth repeating. "Dog," for example, reminded him of his first wife.

"Shut up, woman!"

Ngungure didn't give a damn about his words or their terrifying, explosive power.

"Do you really think I came here for you, you dirty old man? Do you really think my body belongs to you, you dried-out old fish?"

The dried-out old fish suddenly saw the humiliation that covered him. The Dog opened his mouth, took in a gulp of air, and barked, trying to save the man from the assassin within.

"I love . . ."

"I said, shut up!"

Ngungure's head, sliced off in one fell swoop, landed at the man's feet like a catfish tossed onto the shore. The poor girl hadn't even had time to finish her sentence—though clearly it would have ended with "your son."

Her mouth was stopped just as it conjugated the verb "to love" in the first person singular of the present tense: "I love . . . I love . . . I love!" The verb named the very act the man had interrupted with his scandalized arrival. Ngungure's mouth could conjugate it infinitely: she needed to say it, to pronounce that verb in all its bloody fullness, to give sense to the tragedy that had to be played out to its end. What did the Dog think in this moment of profound solitude about that head, spitting purple and bouncing at his feet, repeating endlessly, "I love . . . I love . . . I love!"? An inexpressible thirst burned his throat; yes, his throat was parched.

The man needed to slake his rage. His hands needed to kill again. He shook because the fateful call would not be silenced. On the mattress that was supposed to attest to his own love, he could see sperm stains that weren't his, and his penis shriveled. His hands trembled, and his bleary eyes could not focus. He grabbed his tie, as if to strangle the woman he'd already beheaded, and then threw it over a beam holding up the roof of the house. This man, whose anger spilled out from his body, whose head was offered up to the roof of his House of Passion, and at whose feet lay the head of that bitch, his wife—he just stood there, thinking about the unimaginable game fate played with mortals. Then he climbed up on the first stool he found.

Yes, I'll admit it. What I've just told you is perhaps nothing more than a tall tale of Sara's creation, a fiction, a carpet of lies. But the story didn't stop there. Bertha arrived in time to cut the tie the Dog had used to hang himself. But she was too late to know precisely what had happened. If she had been there, the drama would have played out differently. Whatever may have happened, here's the thing: Bertha arrived at her co-wife's house and found her husband dancing from the ceiling, all decked out in his best clothes. An outfit she knew he had purchased to give himself a new lease on life. How could she have imagined he'd be buried in it?

But the Dog didn't die. Bertha arrived in time to save his last breath. As his first wife screamed in panic, he landed on the ground, right on top of Ngungure's lifeless body, in a pool of the blood that stained the woven mat in his House of Passion. Bertha had been alerted by the brutal echo over the fields of a verb rarely used here: "I love . . . I love . . . I love!" She had a premonition that it was less a question of life than of death. And her fears were confirmed by the shadow of a naked man she saw running to hide in the forest.

Bertha wasn't fooled for a minute. The fleeing man was her son. How could a mother not know? She didn't follow him. No. She hurried off to confirm that the drama she hadn't been able to forestall with her rumors and plots had reached its conclusion. She had the presence of mind to rewrite the ending of her choice. She used the cutlass her husband had killed with to save his life. The Dog awoke in a pool of blood and realized he wasn't dead. In his crazed state, he had never thought he might survive, for that meant waking up in a world devoid of love and filled with shame. He shut his eyes to be sure: no, that wasn't Bertha's face he saw, and all of Foumban hadn't come to see the show. He opened his eyes: his first wife was still there, and so was the crowd.

"Damn me," he begged.

"It was your son," Bertha replied.

The Dog's wild eyes fell on the cutlass in the woman's hand, and his soul exploded in a thirst for blood.

"Kill me!"

The fiery words made Bertha step back in horror. But the man who craved death followed her, his beseeching hands held out before him like a sleepwalker.

"Cut me into pieces!"

Bertha leaped out of the accursed house.

"Burn down the house!" shouted her husband, hot on her heels.

He didn't stop begging her to kill him, whip him, cut open his belly. He used her praise names and cajoled her, swearing that she alone could fulfill his need: not for love, but for death. The Dog didn't let her sleep all night.

Bertha was forced to flee her home and take refuge in the sultan's palace, for only Njoya's doors could keep her safe from such madness. Arrested by the sultan's police and then released because he had been declared crazy by the palace judges, the Dog found himself wandering the city streets, drunker and more menacing than ever. He was still wearing the suit he had bought from the Swiss merchant, Herr Habisch, but now he stank like an old goat's fart. His bloody tie hung around his neck and he asked passersby to help string him up.

This love story played out long after Lieutenant Hirtler's arrival in Foumban, when, as we know, he was so foolish he sat on Njoya's throne. Still, there were only a few Germans in Foumban, and they hadn't yet set up their colonial court. I would like to know how they would have judged this affair. For a long time, different versions of the story circulated in the city's houses, chambers, and drinking holes, but I found no trace of them in any of the colonial accounts. I've been told that there are detailed records written in Shümum of the judgment handed down by the judges in Foumban. But this precious document is part of the archives of Mose Yeyap, the sultan's rival, who—yet another twist to this plot!—died several years before my arrival in Yaoundé. And his sons refuse to open the boxes he left behind, supposedly because they're filled with accusations against Njoya.

We'll soon learn just what Mose Yeyap was capable of.

For the moment, however, it's enough to know that Bertha didn't tell the judges the name of the man she saw running naked through the fields; this gives us a clearer sense of the unending chain of love that unites mother and son. "I don't know who it was," she said.

"She said it with her most honest face," Sara told me, "I swear."

Bertha told everyone that Nebu had left for Bamenda, a nearby town, right after the tragedy, adding that it was the right thing to do, since "a child shouldn't see his father covered in shame." This was the first time her maternity filled her with a pain she couldn't express and the second time she refused to betray her son. As for Ngungure, sadly, Bertha saw her features on the faces of all the girls entrusted to her in the sultan's antechambers. The matron could lie to everyone, but not to her own hands. The death of "that girl" had left her longing to cut out her tongue, wring her neck, and, yes, kill her herself. And this strange thirst, this macabre thirst that had already made her husband's eyes cross, it turned her grip to steel and trapped her voice in a song no one in Mount Pleasant wanted to hear.

There are stories that must be told for the satisfaction of the storyteller—just for the storyteller.

For a moment, let's forget who was listening.

NGUTANE AND NGONO

𝌡 𝌬

For many that were once great are now unimportant . . .
—Herodotus, *The Histories*, 440 B.C.E.

1

Sara's Memory

Isn't writing history just following the evanescent perfume of someone who has departed? You sense their presence at the end of the trail; you follow the scent left by their footsteps in the dust; you rely on your own memory. But like a shy boy who scribbles a love note and counts on his younger brother to deliver it, how can you find the courage to speak up without embarrassing yourself? And what about the messenger? Irresponsible as a butterfly, he zigzags along the paths; he disappears down impassable trails and then somehow arrives at his destination, a fragile bit of truth held in his hands like some smiling promise. From the start of our quest for the girl-boy she once was, Sara's pounding words held me captive, left me thirsting for more. There were moments when Nebu's body suddenly appeared in the middle of her ramblings, but much of the time, the vague images I gleaned of the young man only made me skeptical.

It wasn't just the old lady's penchant for contradicting herself that made me wary. Mostly, it's that there were mistakes in so much of what she told me, as my research easily revealed. I didn't expect her to have a steel trap of a mind, far from it. But even the words for everyday things seemed to get confused by her wandering tongue. Sometimes she described events she certainly hadn't lived through, that she couldn't have witnessed herself. But just what constitutes a witness? Who gets to be a witness, and what does it mean to testify? The faulty memory of a ninety-year-old woman put an end to my questions, of course. I preferred to blame her memory—we all forget things. But nothing shocked me more than the day she undid her scarf and asked me to braid her hair.

I was equally amused and touched. You see, she barely had any hair left on her head.

"What hair?" wondered the young people from Nsimeyong, staring as they imagined the scandal that would result from the intimacy created by our exchange of words. Thankfully, Sara understood their sarcasm.

"Don't tell me," she quipped, "my hair is a mess."

Her laugh sounded across the veranda.

"It's just that . . . ," I began.

"What?"

All I could do was give in. I grabbed a bench and sat down behind her as she leaned back against my knees.

"You're looking for a comb, right?" she asked with a smile.

"Yes, and some string, too."

In truth I was grateful that even at her age, Sara still had moments of vanity. She described in great detail how she wanted her hair braided. She would have needed a huge Afro to reach her dream, but why should I tell her that with her sparse hair, all I could do was make *motobos*, those little braids that mothers do to make their daughters' hair grow more quickly. The young people from Nsimeyong snickered silently, seeing me caught in this trap. Arouna covered his mouth with his hands to keep his laughter from exploding all over the courtyard. That Arouna. Terrible!

"Stop laughing, fool!" I barked at him. "Bring me a comb!"

"Let them be," Sara interjected. "What do they know?"

She settled her head between my legs and smiled. One of the girls in the group brought me a wooden comb.

"Bertha could never wipe her mouth clean, you know," Sara went on after a long pause. "She was just a poor woman with a dirty mind."

How could I ever forget the disdain with which Sara said "poor woman." Well, I wasn't that Bertha. Feeling reassured, I gently braided the old woman's hair. And I kept my ears open to hear the rest of her matron's story. For the other Bertha hadn't stopped there. Between phrases, Sara bit off pieces of string and handed them back to me. I'll admit, the more I listened to her talk, the more I wanted to dive into the archives—that was the only way I'd be able to temper the glint of her sentences and stop her words ringing in my ears.

"Don't wiggle so much," I told her.

She winced from the pain of my braiding. But was that the only reason? Sara's story was also twisting itself into knots, following her mood or the judgmental perspective that came with old age. When I finished her hair, I handed her a mirror. She was pleased with what she saw, turning her head this way and that to admire her beauty. Then she said, "You've turned me back into a young girl."

I'll never forget her beaming face.

"That's what you wanted, isn't it?" she added.

What could I say? I opened my mouth, but all that came out was a question.

"Do you know who your father was?"

Though caught off guard in her moment of happiness, Sara didn't hesitate. "He was called Ngono."

Then I asked, "Do you know his name? I mean, his Christian name?"

Here the old woman grasped my hands. Their warmth spread through my body.

"I never called my father by his first name," she confessed. "I wasn't that badly brought up."

That wasn't what I meant. She stopped me from trying to make excuses.

"Just maybe—" I stammered, "you might have known . . ."

"Joseph," she cut in. "But I didn't really know him."

She patted the top of her head, as if trying to get used to the *motobos* and their scattered tufts, or maybe to ease her aching scalp.

"Joseph Ngono, the political activist?"

A historian's skepticism flooded over me: this was just too perfect. You see, where we come from, it's practically a custom to fabricate illustrious genealogies. For example? you ask. Well, the number of children Njoya is supposed to have fathered makes it impossible to come up with a realistic estimate, and at any rate, he is considered the father of all the Bamum. Still, everywhere you looked around Mount Pleasant, people were trying to cash in on his name. Arouna's own family name was Njoya! So I wouldn't have been surprised if Sara had revealed that she was actually the paramount chief's illegitimate daughter. Who would be stupid enough to question an old woman's family tree? Or foolish enough to believe that Charles Atangana's offspring were limited to the single boy and girl that his "dear Juliana" bestowed upon him, children who were baptized by Father Vogt, the first fruit of his church? Go on, open up a Cameroonian phone book! Look for "Atangana," and you'll see what I mean.

Even the most naïve historians would never believe that the pants of such a flamboyant man had been kept zipped up by threats of damnation—and Catholic threats at that. What we know is that Charles Atangana was married twice. After the death of his first wife, he wed his "dear Juliana," with whom he'd been in love since his tender childhood. But that's beside the point. If Sara had announced that the chief was her father, I wouldn't have been surprised. It would have explained why she, of all Ewondo girls, had been offered as a gift to his friend. Wasn't it a common practice among the people of the equatorial forest to give one's own daughter in marriage to a friend?

But *Joseph Ngono*? No, I couldn't get over it. The reason I had come back to Cameroon was to research the tumultuous history of our independence, a movement set in motion by this man we'd all forgotten. By a sort of lucky coincidence I had once run across his name in the Library of Congress, tucked away in a folder labeled "The African Colonial Diaspora in Germany." The erasure of his life from the Cameroonian collective memory had awoken the historian in me, and the promise of a truly original dissertation had led me to Berlin. And now, somehow, at the end of my travels, I found myself sitting in the courtyard of his . . . daughter? Who would have believed it! Sara just smiled; she was too busy admiring the beauty of her new hairdo to give much thought to this new coincidence. Even my friends from Nsimeyong couldn't understand why I was so excited. But on this vast sea where I alone was able to chart a course, the scattered knots of the old woman's tale were growing tighter. Was it really just a coincidence?

If Sara was the daughter of Joseph Ngono, the cursed companion of Charles Atangana's European travels, then the old woman's tale was unfolding in directions I never could have imagined when I wandered into her courtyard, followed by a troop of adolescents from her neighborhood. And now this revelation of the chief's secret political machinations. Like any man with a strong personality, Charles Atangana's anger knew no bounds. Many times he had rattled the chains of the colonial administration and had had a rival put away: Should I be surprised by this new betrayal of trust?

"So giving you to the sultan was an act of revenge?"

Sara looked at me as if I were a child, no older than the young people from Nsimeyong who were drinking up her tale—that is to say, as if I were an idiot, as if I understood nothing about men. She quietly took a pinch of snuff and asked, ever so quietly, "What do you think?"

I knew she was teasing me, and yet I was reassured by her words. I was even more at ease when, after I told her about finding her father's name in the American archives, she gave a start and stared at me with that same hungry expression I had seen when I told her my name was Bertha.

"My father?" she asked. "Really?"

"You'll have to tell me."

And that was true, for the revelation of her paternity suggested the twisted outlines of a friendship that clearly had ended with her brutal separation from her mother. The next day, Sara began to call me her daughter, or her granddaughter.

"You are my granddaughter," she said, "don't you know?"

I was truly honored to be able to reveal to this fountain something of her own sources, to tell her about the circumstances leading up to her birth: events that had taken place on a continent, Europe, and in a country, Germany, and in a city, Berlin, where Sara never could have set foot. And so she became the eager audience for the story of her own gestation. The beginning is an end, isn't it? For the moment, however, I had just one brief mention of an enigmatic name in the documents I had found, along with a few notes jotted down in my files. Ah, Sara was far enough removed from the story of Joseph Ngono that she could wait, like a child eager to hear an amazing epic tale. But what about me?

2

Time Regained When You Least Expect It

What a trove of information to be found in the observations of colonists! What an immense contribution colonialism made to African historiography. No more sifting through idle chatter: real books, the written word, firsthand accounts, actual facts. I needed to restrain myself in the name of science, or else I would have shouted with joy, ecstatic at the sight of those piles of official accounts, biased ethnographic studies, missionaries' circulars, and the administrative reports in which the lives of the natives were buried. The vast colonial archives laid out Joseph Ngono's life before me in minute detail. And what's more, I could draw on photographs and even films, not to mention the Internet. What I had previously found in the Library of Congress and in the German Staatsarchiv also came to my rescue. The colony is fixed in our memory in black and white; all I needed to do was to wipe off my glasses and give free rein to my Technicolor imagination to see it all play out before me. With a little effort, I came up with enough details to please Sara, who was waiting for me, ears open wide.

The young people of Nsimeyong would tell me that these comments are not politically correct "for any *good* Cameroonian." But if I wanted to stitch together Sara's confusing ancestry, if I wanted to tell her her father's name, I needed to draw on all my sources, all of them. It was thanks to colonial-era films that I was able to see Joseph Ngono walking through the streets of Yaoundé in 1911, from

Nkomkana—the neighborhood where his family had a compound—
to Ongola, the city center. I saw him as a child, holding his little
sandals in the rain to "save them"; I saw him with his schoolbag on
his head to keep off the sun; I saw him carrying his slate under his
arm and hurrying to make it to the mission school on time. Because
I saw him go about his business so clearly and carefully, I could tell
Sara that her father was a true flower of the colony. I found Ngono
again several years later, working as a clerk, politely answering the
questions of a German officer, just as he'd been taught. At times he
laughed, and occasionally he got angry.

But what I couldn't tell from the archives was what Ngono did
when he wasn't with the whites. Although he clearly spent most of
his time with his compatriots, he seemed to have lived a good part
of his life—the most important part for his daughter's story—in the
shadow of the whites, in and around their settlements. The reasons
behind his unpredictable behavior were beyond me. In a certain
sense, his life was the mirror image of Charles Atangana's, even though
Ngono's had unfolded in Germany's sordid underbelly, its stinking
bars, and Atangana was received by emperors and kings, even greeted
by the pope. Wouldn't that have been enough to make the most
honest of men lose his footing?

A temperament can change radically over the course of a life.
The more police reports, anthropological articles, and greeting cards
from German citizens I read, the more obvious it became that Ngono's
decision to quit his job at the Institute of Colonial Studies of the
University of Berlin was the real start of his wanderings. Charles
Atangana, on the other hand, zealously fulfilled his mission at a
similar institute in Hamburg, where he was posted: he copied folktales from his homeland, provided the vocabulary necessary to
produce an Ewondo-German dictionary, recorded his voice for
phonetics exercises, and gave endless Ewondo conversation classes.
And unlike his compatriot, he was rewarded for his efforts. As for
Ngono, after several months of work, he knocked on the door of the
institute's director and, after being invited in and without even taking a seat—as etiquette required—abruptly declared, "I quit!"

Of course, this scene isn't recorded in any document; still, it is
just as true as any of the reports of the vice squad, who were soon

instructed to follow him across Berlin. For the first time, this man—
who had, for too long, dreamed only of the sunny future laid out for
him by colonists—felt how hard life could be. Ngono quit just before the start of the Great War, that's a fact. Up till then, his life had
been a pale copy of his friend Karl's, for that's how the chief was
known at the time. Roped in by promises of an endless supply of
candy, they had both started at the missionary school and converted
to Christianity together. Thanks to the rudiments of their European education, they quickly embraced the future that colonialism
held out for men of their precocious intelligence.

In reality, the possibilities open to them were quite limited. Just
two years after the end of his studies, Ngono realized that he had
already gone as far up the colonial ladder as a native could go. I am
sure that somewhere in the archives there is a report where a German
officer, let's call him Lieutenant Rectanus, describes his visit to
Kribi, Douala, or Yaoundé and wonders who had swept the streets:
the person responsible for this is clearly destined to do great things
for the colony! Or maybe a description of another officer, Killmann,
let's say, eating his red sausage off a plate so clean he wants to know
what local hands have washed it. "The future of this country is in
these hands," he shouts, greedily swallowing his sausage. "What attention to detail!"

Of course, my years of remove from the situation give me the
advantage of perspective. I know now that the future evoked by this
colonist never came to be; these colonial officers—so amazed by
the hands of their subalterns who washed their plates, swept their
streets, took care of their every need—they could do anything they
wanted in the tropics, and yet they still couldn't predict an African's
future. Whatever the outcome of the conflict ahead—a conflict
moving ever closer, although they couldn't see it coming—Joseph
Ngono seemed destined for success, just like Charles Atangana. It
couldn't go any other way. Weren't the two friends the cream of the
colony's crop?

"Attention," the administrative regulations declared, "colonialism
provides professional mobility for the natives." Yes, according to the
system's logic, you could leave a job as a houseboy to become a
clerk or even a translator. But for the translator to become a lecturer

of Ewondo—and in the fatherland, to top it off—that was a step that no colonized subject would have dared to dream of in 1913. This dream assumed that this colonized subject would teach classes of future colonial administrators, all sitting politely in rows and listening to a black professor. It would have turned the whole colonial order upside down.

Because a black professor in Germany would, of course, grade the exams of his white students, requiring the less assiduous among them to amend their work, it goes without saying that his position would be untenable. The mediocre students of the professor in question (who, following the tenets of colonialism, certainly think themselves smarter than the professor) would sometimes have to repeat a course, and perhaps even abandon their colonial dreams. These same students would give themselves permission to stop by the professor's office to ask that he let them retake exams or that he *adjust* their grades—by which I mean falsify their report cards to save their careers.

Sometimes the Ewondo lecturer would watch his students— especially those most certain about their mission to civilize the colonies—and he would start to laugh, a ferocious laugh, deep in his chest, that he would have a hard time stifling. Why? Ngono had just discovered European poetry, and these human specimens working so hard to scale the steps of conformity made him uncomfortable, for in the verses of their compatriots he had discovered the hymn of futility.

In the Staatsarchiv I actually found—no joke—a note written in the margins of the minutes of a meeting by the famous Professor Baumann, doctor of philosophy (then the director of the Colonial Institute and Ngono's boss), that mentioned a book the illustrious doctor had found on his lecturer's desk: Rilke. This theoretician of Bantu languages, including the one spoken by Ngono, burst out with a laugh that echoed down the halls and through the classrooms of the whole university; he was amused by the scandal of someone like Ngono reading Rilke, a logical reaction if measured against the colonial mentality that so blinded him.

Dr. Baumann wrote a paragraph about this affair in his annual report of the institute's activities, although he neglected to mention which book of Rilke's Ngono was reading. This lapse really says something about the esteemed professor's poetic tastes, or about the commotion his discovery provoked in the institute (too much laughter for a German research institute!). It also taught me why, just a few months after Ngono arrived in Berlin, the Ewondo lecturer suddenly began to feel uncomfortable in his role as colonial educator and cut off from his colleagues. It's a fact: he had started to separate himself from his shadow—or rather, to think independently of it.

Sara willingly accepted this image of her father, adding that she knew him to be a dreamer.

"But you weren't even born yet," I remarked.

What did it matter? In the end, such details weren't important to her. That Ngono was clearly the father she preferred, the one she would have invented herself if necessary.

"He was a poet," she repeated.

I was amazed by her lack of pretension as I described her father to her, and nothing entertained me more than that look of hers, which reduced me to silence in a flash. "You're joking, right?" she seemed to ask.

"He's crazy, isn't he?" she sometimes said about her father, interrupting my story. "He's really crazy, isn't he?"

At other times she said, "Tell me the truth."

3

A Sultan's Smile Can Change
the Face of the World

But I wanted to hear the rest of Sara's story. The one she was telling was as tumultuous as her father's, no doubt about it. Several days after the events that shook up Nsimeyong and condemned Njoya to lie in bed in an unending coma, Nebu found the sultan's apartments abuzz with activity. Ngutane came running out of the bedroom, her hair a mess, tears in her eyes. Her voice echoed through Mount Pleasant's corridors and made everything in the main courtyard fall still. Njoya had opened his eyes! It wasn't his daughter's faithful reading sessions alone that had given him the will to live once more. Ngutane had brought his grandchildren to his bedside, asking each of them to sing happy songs and recite joyful verses.

That's what had roused Njoya.

At the end of the last poem, something strange had happened: all of a sudden the sultan smiled. He felt heartbeats speeding up in his chest. The smile was still on his lips when Nebu came into his bedroom. Ngutane was outside crying, whether in disbelief or happiness. At first she had taken her father's grimace for the start of a mad dash to the doors of eternal absence. Oh, had she stayed by his bedside, Ngutane would have seen the extraordinary signs of a man's victory over fate. But perhaps she wanted to hide the shock of her unexpected joy from Njoya's keen eye.

It had taken him so long to wake up that the idea of a miracle was hard to swallow. Still, Father Vogt didn't miss the chance to appear at the bedside of the newly awakened sultan; he even found a way for his future flock—meaning all of Mount Pleasant—to know that the hand of his God had made it so.

"He smiled?" he asked the overexcited artisans.

"Yes, he smiled," a chorus replied. "He smiled!"

"God," Father Vogt said simply, "God is great."

Father Vogt kept asking the same question and always got the same answer: "Yes."

Only a few voices—exceptions in the crowd—ignored his enthusiasm.

"In faith," the father insisted, "we are all God's children."

"*Amin*," said the Muslims.

"Amen," said the others.

When the prelate made the sign of the cross, no one followed suit. Even the energetic professional pagan hunter inside him could understand that the bedroom of someone brought back from the dead is not the place for a conversion. But he wasn't a man to show restraint when a miracle just needed a little bit of help. Instead of looking for Bible verses that would back him up convincingly, he reprised his role as doctor. And what Father Vogt the medic did then will forever be engraved in Mount Pleasant's memory. He took apart his bicycle and asked that someone bring him a chair. Even Nji Mama was startled.

"A chair?"

"Yes, I want to make a chair for the sultan," he answered, rubbing his long beard and smiling.

"I don't understand," interrupted the chief architect. "You want a chair to make a chair?"

The artisans looked at one another in amusement, and with good reason. Ah, these white people!

"Yes," the priest continued, carried away with his idea. "A special chair."

He stressed *special* in his most convincing voice.

"A special chair," old Monlipèr repeated, closing his eyes the better to see how special the chair would be. "Yes."

"A throne, if you will," Father Vogt added. "But I need a chair to build it."

Monlipèr was in charge of all the tools and materials in the palace. The prelate's surprising proposal was crossing a line, but since he had made his way into Mount Pleasant, Father Vogt basked in the prestige of his medical talents. No one refused him anything, even if it would have been unthinkable for anyone else. He wanted a chair? Here's a chair! He wanted to make a throne? Well, let him do it! Mount Pleasant's artists would judge his work on its merits; that's really all the man was asking.

Father Vogt worked all afternoon. Under the compound's watchful eyes, he attached the wheels of his bicycle to the chair they'd provided; then he stood up, stretched his legs, and looked around at the skeptics he knew he had won over. He sat down on the chair and made it roll, turning the wheels with his hands. When he stopped, his broad smile faded quickly under the glare of Ngutane's eyes as she burst onto the scene.

"My father will walk," Njoya's daughter declared tersely.

Father Vogt quickly fell back on his double role as doctor and priest.

"Of course he will walk," he said, standing up. "By the grace of God, he will walk."

Ngutane didn't listen to what he had to say. The bright colors of her robe were a symbol of her certainty; she disappeared into Njoya's chambers. Father Vogt turned back to the gathered crowd.

"This chair will help him to walk again."

What Father Vogt didn't realize was that Ngutane was the least of his problems. In fact, the talents of the community assembled around him were insulted by his audacity; up till then, they had refrained from reacting, out of respect for the sultan. Just who did he think he was? Did he really think Njoya would sit on that thing, even if it did roll? Or that the artists, blacksmiths, and carpenters—whose hands had sculpted the sultan's seats their whole life—would just accept this? These thousand questions silenced those who had gathered around the priest, but he, blinded by his faith, had no idea and just showed off his handiwork, taking their silence as an open invitation.

"It's a rolling throne," Father Vogt repeated.

The priest caught Nji Mama's eye. The chief architect was calmly stroking his beard.

"A rolling throne, yes," Monlipèr murmured, his face breaking into a smile. "Not bad. Not bad."

4

Black in Berlin

Sara had interrupted her own story because she was afraid for her father, and rightfully so. She was caught up in Ngono's tale. Being unemployed in 1913 Berlin was no small problem, especially if you were black. He really was a poet, the doyenne said, or else her father would have thought long and hard before quitting. Sara, however, would soon learn that Joseph Ngono just followed his impulses, unlike the chief, that master of careful calculations. When the Ewondo lecturer left the institute, he didn't realize that he had become the centerpiece of one of the vice squad's special dossiers, nor that his boss had made the call to put the police on his trail. This dossier, fifteen pages long, can still be consulted in the Staatsarchiv. It's a monument of detective work, spiced up with satirical comments that say a lot about the sort of people Sara's father was dealing with.

Once the doors of the institute had closed behind him, Ngono suddenly found the German capital inspiring. He meandered through it for one, then two hours, heading no place in particular, lost in his thoughts, his hands stuffed into his pockets. In the neighborhood known as Wedding, he went into a bar where German workers stopped for a drink. It was his first time in such a place, but he really needed a strong one. He sat at a table in the corner and waited for a waitress. Patting the pocket of his jacket, he realized that he had left his copy of Rilke behind (once again, the archives don't tell us what book he was reading; whose fault is that?). The book had been left on his desk. He got up to go back and get it, but he stopped at the bar, where men were trading drinking stories.

"*Darf ich bitte um Bier ersuchen?*" he asked.

Yes, Ngono actually said, "Beg your pardon, might I request a beer?"

Surprised, the bartender looked him over from head to toe. Because of his clothes, perhaps? It must be said that Ngono was dressed like a Prussian civil servant of the day. The lecturer realized that all the faces at the bar were locked on him. As if they had just discovered a scandal.

"What did you say, comrade?" asked the heavyset man beside him as he put his hand on Ngono's shoulder in a friendly gesture.

"*Ersuchen?*" added the man next to him, who was missing two teeth.

"*Darf ich bitte um Bier ersuchen?*" Ngono repeated, feeling less and less sure of his German.

Sara's father thought the chuckling workers were trying to start a fight, but the laugh that shook the bar was a welcoming one. The labyrinths of ignorance hold many surprises. These dapper gents appreciated the flavor of his words, so different from their usual call for "*n'Bier.*"

How could they have imagined that the lecturer had memorized that phrase after reading *Buddenbrooks*, which he finished right before he started on Rilke. And how could Ngono have known that at the very same moment when he, in his bedroom on the Koloniestrasse, was flipping through Mann's pages and enjoying the characters' banter, in the green mountains of Foumban, a missionary named Göhring was reading the same pages to Sultan Njoya, translating as he went.

Amused by this learned black civil servant, the man with the missing teeth offered Ngono a beer, which he didn't refuse.

"Can you say it again, comrade . . ." he pleaded. "*Er . . .*"

He couldn't even say the word without bursting into laughter. "*Suchen?*"

This was a kind of German these men never heard in this red part of town. To think it was an imperial subject who brought it into their dusty bar! The African had awoken in them a paternalism they never would have expected to find in their Communist hearts. One after the other they bought him a beer, and surprisingly, Ngono never said no. Did he have that many worries to drown? Did the memory of the job he'd quit hurt that much? Probably not. No, it was more likely a sudden wave of homesickness, a longing for a certain type of liquor, a certain dish, a certain smell of the earth. Ngono knew that bottles of German beer wouldn't fill his need, for he couldn't even name what he was missing without bursting into tears. Was he already as drunk as the men he was talking to? If he was laughing with them, it was because laughing lifted his melancholy. If he drank all those bottles offered by his newfound friends, it was for a very simple reason: it was the cheapest way to get drunk.

"Comrade," said the men.

And he answered, *"Jawohl!"*

That night's police report ended with a simple question: Had Ngono become a Communist? Nothing proved he had read Marx as enthusiastically as Mann and Rilke. So let's set that aside. When the bar shut its doors behind him, the lecturer found himself once more on the painful path he thought he had drowned. His furtive shadow scurried away like a black cat. Ngono was too far gone to follow it. And yet he knew the far-off place where his torment hid. He looked at the stars, smiled at their nightly dance, then recited poems by Rilke to bolster his courage. His mother tongue brought to mind a certain Ewondo song from his village, which he whistled and sang through the streets of Berlin. It was a counting song, and it warmed his heart. When the song faded in his mouth, he started talking to the lampposts in Ewondo. And just maybe, thanks to all he'd had to drink, the lampposts answered, bending down to tip their hats and swathe him in their satiny glow.

"Comrade!" they said.

He was clearly drunk, but Ngono was sure of what he heard. He was so convinced of the good manners of Berlin's lampposts that when a voice behind him called out "Nigger," he knew it wasn't a lamppost that had spoken, but a stranger.

"Hey! You, nigger!" the voice shouted.

Another voice added, "Don't you hear us?"

What Ngono heard were footsteps, hurried footsteps coming from a dark alleyway. He started to run.

The footsteps ran with him.

5

Love's Apprenticeship

Still in 1913, but thousands of kilometers away. It is impossible to flee your mother's welcoming breast! Nebu, then a young man, learned this at his own expense when he jumped out the window of the House of Passion, raced through the forest, and realized that his steps were leading him inexorably back to his mother's house in Foumban.

"Here's what happened," said the doyenne.

She was telling this story in such a way that I would have sworn she had lived it herself. It was as if Nebu's life had taken possession of her. She let her soliloquy flow, her eyes fixed on a past that came back to her in spurts of blood. She had become Nebu, yes, and what's more, I could hear a new intonation in her voice. Once again, eighty years later, Bertha's son reappeared in her volcanic flesh. But she was also Sara, the little girl disguised as a boy so that the stories of far-off men and women might find their resolution. Sara relived the stages of her metamorphoses; she became Ngungure, the girl starving for a body. Her voice changed again; she barked and shrieked because she needed me to know all the details of what had happened in the House of Passion . . .

"How do you know all this?" I asked again and again.

Sara just smiled, then replied ironically, "And you, just how do you know what you're telling me about my father?"

"The archives," I explained. "The German archives."

"My body is an archive," retorted the doyenne. "It remembers stories that I don't know."

Where should I put my trust? In the capricious memory of an old lady or in the colonial archives? In the written lies of Berlin's vice squad or in the faded image of Foumban's courtyards, where, by all accounts, Sara had never set foot? Should I just put my faith in the heartbeats around me, searching Nsimeyong's winding pathways, looking for the truth of a story that had taken place in the most forgetful neighborhoods imaginable? There are choices I would have preferred not to make—that's for sure!

All around us, life spread out in wild abandon. My mind searched for a bit of calm in the tornado. Music from the bar next door shook the walls. A two-year-old child crawled around in the dust and the adults paid no attention. He picked up a clump of earth and ate it absentmindedly. Like him, I would have liked to eat the earth, to let Foumban's history move through my body, coursing through my veins and rising up to my nostrils like alcohol. Sara chewed silently on a kola nut, her eyes seeking mine. She offered me a piece of the bitter fruit and chuckled at the grimace I made. My neighborhood friends chewed on their pieces of kola with a childlike pleasure, which reminded me how estranged my body had become from the city where I'd grown up. How our own past becomes like a stranger to us all.

Sara's story had the bittersweet taste of a kola nut. We were in 1913, I told her. When Nebu left the House of Passion, he knew his game of hide-and-seek was over, even if, till the very end, he'd insist to his mother that he was right. After all, his father had stolen his girlfriend. Bertha's son had understood that the game was up long before its bloody climax. The day Ngungure told him that she had the right to do what she wanted with her body, Nebu knew that she wasn't a woman to marry and that, with her, he was taking on a whole set of problems—just as his mother had warned him. He was reassured when she confided that she was "giving her body" to him. Honestly, he was so in love he would have agreed to anything. "Because I love you," she added, "because I love you eternally. Eternally."

As a slave, Nebu didn't have the money to buy a wife, but Ngungure didn't mention that. No, she talked about love, and love has no price. Bertha's son had no other choice than to let his girlfriend define love as she pleased. Oh, if only he had realized what lay hidden beneath Ngungure's words. When his mother told him that *that girl* was going to marry his father, Nebu couldn't believe it. He remembered Ngungure's words and slapped his leg.

"Women!" he exclaimed. "Why?" he asked his mother. "Why would she do that?"

"Because she's the Devil, my son, don't you get it?"

Nebu then asked Ngungure herself.

"Why?"

"Why?" the girl echoed.

"Yes, why?"

"Because I love you eternally, my dear, eternally."

It made no sense.

"I love you so much," Ngungure continued, "that I want you by my side twice, ten times, a thousand times: eternally at my side."

Nebu did not understand this mathematics of love.

"I love you so much," Ngungure added, "that even your shadow is precious to me."

"Then is it still love?" he asked.

Was it that love that had pushed her into his father's bed? A wave of nausea overcame Nebu, his ears ringing with a mad hymn. Death—two, ten, a thousand deaths—whistled a song in his ears.

But Bertha's son soon retraced his steps, took back his words, and gave back his body, drawn in by the girl's scent; he was addicted to her. He returned to her, unaware of what he'd done until he woke up and found Ngungure naked at his side. Was this madness? Yes, of course, only madness could have propelled him back between the legs of that woman, that girl, in the bedroom he knew was his father's. It was madness that made him believe, there in the paternal bed, that a solution could be found.

Nebu had attended Njoya's school, where his father taught writing. His father found only rational solutions to life's problems—he made no allowance for superstitions, none at all. He had worked as a copyist for the sultan for five years. Father and son could have talked it out themselves, there was no need for a judge. But good God, where we come from, where can a father talk to his son about love? So for Nebu, it was clear: there was no bar, no room, no place where he had the right to speak to his father's wife without addressing her as "Mother." Besides, with him lying there in his father's bed, it was already too late for them to talk. Moreover, he knew that the oral tradition was lying in wait, with its curses and its proverbs. And if necessary, the elders would invent new proverbs that would justify killing him.

Njoya had done away with many of the laws that would have justified stoning the boy. But when this story took place, the sultan was still writing the first version of his "Book of Love," the *Lewa Nuu Nguet*, in which he describes the one hundred and seventeen positions that will allow a man and a woman to reach multiple orgasms. So Nebu was wise to escape out the window when he awoke to the sound of his father's voice. He ran and ran until he realized that his treacherous feet had led him into a forest with no way out. When he saw a glimmer of light between the trees, he had no idea it was the streets of Foumban. And yet he soon found himself standing at his mother's door.

There's no question that Bertha had heard her son calling her in the woods. When he appeared at her door, she opened her arms and shut her mouth. Nebu was as naked as the day he was born. His eyes were unfocused. Only one question echoed in the boy's head: "Was it love?" How could she answer? Love had stopped Bertha from chasing her crazy son. Love had made her check, frantically, that no one had seen Nebu knock at her door and be let in. Love had made her lie to the palace police when they came asking questions, made her maintain that her son had left for Bamenda the day before. It was love that hit her right then in the chest and made her tell Ngungure's whole sordid story to her disbelieving son. But he didn't believe her! Oh, no!

Nebu listened to his mother going on about a mad love—his father's—with gestures seasoned with tears. And in his mother's song, the son saw his lover's head bouncing at the Dog's feet, bouncing and shouting, "I love! I love! I love!"

Of course it was love, Nebu thought, that had caused his beloved's death—what else could it be! It was love's throbbing that had kept Ngungure's heart beating even after her death, kept her body writhing sadly as it danced on the ground.

Nebu was suddenly filled with fear at the thought that he hadn't loved his mother as she deserved, and that he hadn't loved Ngungure as she had hoped. His rage exploded, forming a question that lashed at his soul: Didn't I love you enough?

Even today, as I transcribe Sara's words, I carefully weigh my own because I still see the flames that lit up a mother's eyes. I still hear my friends from Nsimeyong voicing their disgust. Lost in the forest, prevented from being anything but a witness, Nebu hadn't been able to stop the unfolding of the story set in motion by his love. In Bertha's arms, the young man opened his ears, the better to understand the twists of his own fate, his eyes lost in his mother's as she told him the incomprehensible story of his life.

How strange are the paths of love! When Foumban awoke one day, shocked to hear the town crier announcing that no longer would anyone trouble the city's inhabitants by begging for his own death, there were some who smiled. The Dog had been found hanging from a tree, his feet swinging in the air, his tie having finally served its purpose. The sultan sent his police to find out who had fulfilled the wishes of the madman whose life on the city's margins had been protected by one of the sultan's official decrees, but, since no reward was offered for turning in the guilty party, and especially because a death penalty awaited whoever had done what was generally deemed a public service, no one stepped forward.

"Would you have stepped forward?" Sara asked me.

Her question tore me from the madness of Nebu's tale and from Bertha's bitter hands.

"Me?"

Ngungure's story disappeared into the whisperings of the raffia-wine drinkers, reappearing as that bit of wisdom that advises men to love by small drops, one woman after the other. Some breathed more easily, released by the death of Nebu's father, but no one asked what Bertha felt. It's true that the Dog's death meant nothing to her, really, nothing. And with good reason.

"Not even hatred," Sara stressed. "Nothing at all."

She spit out the bitter kola juice and declared, "She always wore a brightly colored pagne beneath her *ndjutchu*, her widow's robe."

In a culture that has no word to describe the suffering of a mother who has lost her only son, or any other child, but that devised hundreds of rituals to inscribe a husband's death on a woman's body, Bertha had to hide her feelings of joy beneath a widow's blue. She shaved her head and wore the obligatory *ndjutchu*, but none of the rituals held any real meaning for her.

Nebu, however, felt entirely differently. He realized that he missed something about his father, but he couldn't put his finger on it. Perhaps his gruesome epileptic fits? The seductive power of abjection? One month and thirteen days after the Dog's death, Nebu went to Herr Habisch's shop, where, with the money he had saved, he bought a black tuxedo, a tie, gloves, a white shirt, and shiny leather shoes. The Swiss merchant assured him, too, that this was how gentlemen dressed in Berlin when they were happy. Nebu refused to let his mother shave his head, as tradition requires after the death of a close relative—especially a father. No. He asked his mother to shave two parts into his hair, Bamum fashion. Bertha was dumbstruck!

"If I do anything to your hair, I'm cutting it all off!"

Bertha didn't care about Herr Habisch, what he said about fashion and all the European gentlemen. Her pain—the flip side of love—was the only measure of her actions. To put an end to the conversation, Nebu went back to the Swiss merchant and bought a top hat. When his mother saw him "dressed like a madman"—those were her words—she didn't think of cursing Herr Habisch and all his kind, but rather her husband. She also thought about Ngungure and that girl's evil tricks.

"What has gotten into you?" she asked her son. "What are you trying to prove?"

"Nothing, Mama, nothing at all."

"Don't say 'nothing.' Do you think I don't know what's going on?"

"Well, if you already know . . ."

"The Devil has gotten into your head, too," Bertha insisted. "He's still here, I'm sure of it."

Like all mothers, she looked at her son and remembered the suckling infant he had been, how he had refused to be born because he was afraid of being overwhelmed by the force of his mother's love. Nebu was hiding something from her, she was sure. She instinctively held him all the tighter, loved him even more—just like the baby he had once been—and tried to make him spit out the secrets of his soul.

The Temptation of the Final Solution

It's a fact: no one can escape his fate. Hide beneath your bed and she'll toss a venomous snake in after you. Stand under a tree and she'll have lightning grill you alive. Hide under water and she'll send you a starving crocodile. All these thoughts whipped through Ngono's mind as he ran onto the Frühlingstrasse. He thought of his parents, his ancestors, his childhood in the missionary school. He saw his friends, especially Charles Atangana. He thought of all the children playing in the streets of Yaoundé, and suddenly he felt hope. Berlin's lampposts were transformed into spirits sent by his faraway hometown to guide his feet. He knew they'd protect him, yes. He remembered the day when lampposts had been installed in Yaoundé.

"They're the spirits of the dead," people said, and also "of the unborn." Ngono thought of his father, who just laughed at all this silliness. He also thought of his mother, who believed it. He saw her face on one of the lampposts. She begged him to run, to run and keep running. He saw his brothers and sisters, who also asked him to run and keep running. Lampposts. Ngono thought about those who loved him: the women, men, and children who lived in his family's compound in Yaoundé. All of them—uncles, aunts, nephews, grandparents—asked him to run and save his life: "Run, Ngono, run!" They reminded him that he was the first of his ethnic group to go to the white man's land. "Run, Ngono, run!"

Really, the stupidest thing a black man can do is let a racist kill him. It's simply not worth it. Ngono knew this. So he listened to the voices of his kin. Especially his father's: in Ewondo his father called him a coward.

"What are you running from, huh?" he asked. "Don't tell me you're running from those sons of rats! You don't run away from mosquitoes, do you?"

His father burst out laughing. "Whites aren't men, is that what you think? Are you such a coward that you run away from men just like you?"

"I'm not a coward!" Ngono protested.

He didn't turn around to confront the shadows that were chasing him, forcing him to run through the night. Suddenly the refusal to live like a coward slowed his steps. He stopped and turned to face his assailants; he went at them, even, determined to prove to his father that he wasn't a coward, no, not him, Ngono junior. No Ewondo had ever lived like a coward, and he wouldn't be the first to break the rule. The police report is clear: it's the "nigger" who struck the first blow. Alas, there are no other documents about the affair. So I'll just have to take it as truth: Ngono wasn't the victim.

"I'm not a coward!" His voice echoed in the depths of the night. He spoke in Ewondo because he was talking to his father, his ancestors, his tribe. His cry echoed in the far reaches of 1913 Berlin like a declaration of tribal war.

"I'm not a coward!" Ngono shouted again, and threw himself at his pursuers. He head-butted one, hitting him hard in the jaw and sending him flying. Later he'd recall that the man had a mustache. But then he just saw him fall like a tree. Ngono's sudden offensive, his war cry, his "call for tribal warfare," the madness of it all stopped his assailants in their tracks. They hadn't expected Ngono to react so savagely. Ngono himself was unaware that deep inside his head hid a warrior just waiting to smash the face of a German racist.

"You want to play cat and mouse?" taunted one of the men, putting up his bare fists.

"Let's get out of here," suggested another. "It's not worth it."

"No," said a third. "Let's stay here!"

"Let's civilize him!" said the one with the smashed face.

Ngono heard the trio of his sad fate. He remembered his father's lessons: "Go after one of them, just one, and make him rue the day he was born."

"Cowards!" the lecturer shouted. "*Imperialistische Feiglinge!* Imperialist cowards!"

The man with the bloody mustache said to his friends, "He's calling us cowards? Did you hear that?"

He pointed at Ngono and laughed.

"Cowards?"

"Us?"

One of the three, a small guy with a large bald spot, dove at Ngono, hitting him right in the stomach. The police report had no words to describe the chaos that followed. Ngono was hit in the stomach, on the back, on the head; feet, words, and fists all came at him. He was hit with chunks of asphalt and slurs; he saw blood. Ngono took a thousand blows; he was abandoned by the polite lampposts and by the moon herself, who shut her evil eye when his assailants left him for dead. His father's words filled his mind, contradictory bits of advice offered in both Ewondo and German at once.

"Did my loins produce this coward, this *Feigling*?"

"Cowards!" Ngono shouted in German.

The one with the mustache stopped dead.

"A coward, me?"

He brought his hand to his mouth and spat out blood.

"Adolf," said the little bald one, "let him be, he's just a nigger."

"A monkey," said the third.

Clenching his fists like a boxer, Adolf came at Ngono, who was barely able to stand.

"Are you insulting me?"

Just then, Ngono thought of his father's words: "Go after one, just one, and make him regret that a woman ever gave birth to him! Make him wish his mother was a whore and regret that his father had balls."

Ngono answered his father, and in his language, his words sounded like a magical incantation: he kept asking his father to "let him finish off the bastards." His assailants stopped, speechless. The old man of the night kept spurring his son on: "Make that son of a bitch eat through his own asshole! Make them all fuck chickens!"

The Ewondo lecturer danced to the rhythm of his father's angry words, and he pointed his fingers at each of the three faces, one after the other.

"One by one!" he said. "I'll take you on one by one, that is if you are men!"

The men stared at him in amusement, unable to believe their eyes.

"One by one!" Ngono repeated.

Laughing, the three lined up, the one with the mustache in front. But they didn't laugh long. Ngono picked up a rock and threw it at them. He missed the bald spot of the little fat one, and a shout rang out. It was the cry of an animal, a dog or maybe a man. The rock landed on the asphalt in the distance. The men stepped aside.

"He is crazy," one said.

"*Ilang nuazut!*" shouted Ngono. "Your asshole! Come one at a time and I'll make you fuck your own cat!"

"Let's finish him off!"

As he spoke, the mustached man covered his bloodied mouth.

"What are you waiting for, *belobo lobo*?" shouted the lecturer in the dark. "Invaders! Come and finish me off!"

This was his death dance, and he knew it.

"I'm going to civilize you!"

Ah! If words were all it took! The fat bald one struck the first blow. They surrounded him, attacking from all sides. Ngono didn't seem to care. Should he have? All traces of the ensuing fight have disappeared in the German police archives, lost among the thousands of brawls that broke out in prewar Berlin. Ngono defended himself valiantly, oh yes! He protected his gut but left his face open. He doubled over, leaving his back exposed. He bit someone's ear, whacked another's shin, broke Adolf's balls, but all to no avail. He couldn't hold up against the horde and was soon left for dead.

"*Ilang nuazut!*" the lecturer stammered in the hollow silence.

He took another blow to the head. It was Adolf.

"*Schweig!*" he cried. "Shut up!"

"*Feigling!*" Ngono replied.

"*Schwein!*"

The mustached one hit him in the eye. But even with just one eye, the lecturer refused to shut up. "Son of a rat!" he spat.

"Let's get out of here," a voice shouted. "Let's just leave him and get out of here!"

But Adolf couldn't stop. Maybe his aching balls were screaming for revenge. Or maybe an evil spirit had melted away his brain and turned his eyes and his voice red, telling him that this monkey tale needed a final solution. Maybe he'd never before been called a "son of a rat" by a "nigger." There was no end to his anger; he'd become a vampire, a Nosferatu who, with his own teeth, bit two fingers off the lecturer's hand and spit them out in the gutter. The shriek from Ngono's lips shattered the darkness, sent a black cat scurrying away, woke up the whole street. Sirens were heard in the distance.

"The police!" a voice called out from the corner. "Hurry!"

They had to drag Adolf away.

"I'm going to burn him alive!" he yelled, searching his pockets for matches. "I'm going to burn him!"

"*Mensch, die Polizei!* Let's get out of here!"

Ngono was the only one arrested. How could he have hidden? Even if he had fled, in those years all the blacks living in Berlin could have fit into one phone booth. Still, the German civil servant didn't get a ticket on a boat back to Cameroon, as the law required. No, he was released the day after his arrest. Later he learned that it was because a certain Dr. Mult, who preferred to remain anonymous, had stepped in and paid the fines necessary to free the "imperial subject who was wandering around drunk in the night."

"You're really lucky," said the officer as he opened Ngono's cell.

Ngono couldn't believe it either.

"*Weg damit*, get the hell out of here before I change my mind," snickered the policeman. Berlin is unbelievable, isn't it?

In his report, no mention is made of Adolf. That name wouldn't have led the police anywhere anyway. Adolf, Rudolf . . . all those sorts of names were very popular at the time. And German men really liked their mustaches, too, because they made them irresistible to the ladies, or so they thought. So there's no way I can check out what Sara added to round out the story or her description of an

"Adolf with a mustache"—"the cannibal who didn't even have the courage to fight like a man, but who left my father with a shameful scar on his heart."

"Is he the man who . . ." Arouna asked. His friends wanted to know, too. "Adolf?"

What to say? The archives, and especially the fact that I had gotten my information from Germany, gave me such authority. There are details that would change a story entirely. I admit it: I wish that the blow Ngono gave Adolf on the chin had left his irascible mustache mute. We all know that this would have spared all humankind from a savagery that the Ewondo lecturer didn't live long enough to see. Would anyone blame me for going a bit too far? It's true, faced with the dusty silence of the colonial archives, I let the historian in me get carried away. Good sense requires that we opt for the cold, hard truth. So let me hurry back to the chambers of truth, to Mount Pleasant, you understand, because now it's the doyenne's turn to talk. And what she told me next, she had lived through from start to finish.

7

The Art of Being a Sultan

Yaoundé, 1931. Ngutane decided to ensure that her father awoke each day in a bed of words, because listening to stories was giving him back his strength. Tucked into bed with the world's surprises, Njoya glowed with newfound health. Ngutane also wore her most elegant clothes, "to stimulate his eyes," she said. Her fashion show caught everyone's attention and made them smile. People wondered what she would wear the next day. Her wardrobe ranged from Bamum styles to those of the Fulani and the Bamiléké, not to mention styles popular in Germany, France, and England. She even wore retro styles, yes, Retro Ngutane, just to keep everyone guessing.

One might have thought she was trying to seduce the most handsome man in the world. She knew her father hated dreariness most of all, that he sucked greedily on the mangoes of happiness. The man was never badly dressed, because, as he loved to say, "life is too short to not be stylish." Njoya's good humor was his true gift to his court, and he warned his advisers that he didn't want any sullen faces around him. So his daughter put pots of flowers in the windows of his room, and a ray of sunshine spread over his face each morning. Ngutane assigned one slave to care for the flowers and another to pick fresh ones in the fields around Mvolyé every other day. That's how she kept her father's room in a continuous state of exuberance. "Happiness is the true essence of the world," she declared—this was, in a few words, her life's philosophy—"it keeps us alive."

Ngutane forbade European visitors from taking photos of her ailing father. Njoya had been the colonial photographers' favorite subject, their star, and his voice had been recorded, too. But it was out of the question that his misfortune be turned into a spectacle for those who, she was sure, had pushed him into this stupefying lethargy. One day Nji Moluh's son shocked them all by reciting a poem—"Waterloo"—in a language no one understood, but which was thought to be English. The kid had marched like a soldier around Njoya's bed as he declaimed the poem, his hands spread out before him. To conclude, he clenched one fist behind his back and pushed his stomach out, striking a pose that made everyone laugh. After that, Ngutane had all the children of the house, including Njoya's grandchildren, come and recite poems at his bedside.

From then on, each child—often egged on by their zealous parents—had their minute in the limelight at the sultan's bedside. Ngutane wanted them to recite the most beautiful verses they had learned. Ugliness would kill their grandfather, she warned. After that she brought in the cousins, and then the Nji, the heads of the most illustrious Bamum families. She enlisted the scribes, the copyists, the illustrators, the miniaturists, the sketchers, the hagiographists, the potters, the ceramicists, the weavers, and, of course, the blacksmiths. Everyone had a turn and, in the end, all of Mount Pleasant paraded before Njoya.

Yes, everyone.

Why? Well, because no one wanted to be forgotten! Everyone dressed in their finest, did their best to impress the sultan. The shimmering *agbada*—a robe in the style of the Yoruba of Nigeria—that one woman showed off one day certainly got the most attention. More than the scarf another woman tentatively wrapped around her head in what the whispering gossips judged to be a poor imitation of the more artistic Fulani fashion. There were outright failures as well. How could anyone forget the long tresses sported by a woman from Douala, recognized as a wig by the chattering noblewomen. Ngutane, whose braided hair made everyone stare, mouths agape, called it simply "disgraceful." The women who appeared in Njoya's chambers were so well dressed—no, let me use Sara's own words—they were so *mami nyanga-o*, so cute, that one might have suspected that all the women were trying to compete with the mistress of ceremonies, and even outdo her on her home turf.

Njoya's daughter had too many other things to worry about to get caught up in such nonsense. All too quickly the visitors at her father's bedside began to gossip about their neighbors. They turned from telling pleasant stories to tragic tales and grievances. That's why Nji Mongu called on singers, drummers, bards, and town criers. Their memories contained all the stories of the sultanate, or so she thought. She soon realized there were limits to their resources. Oh, Ngutane didn't waste time bemoaning the death of the spoken word; she just summoned the heads of Yaoundé's seven original families. She would even have invited all the most important chiefs in the territory if they hadn't, in some sense, already invited themselves when they'd first heard "the awful news."

The chiefs had come running; they'd arrived out of breath. They told the sultan the stories of their families and their animals, stories of life and death, sometimes more fiction than fact, but who cared? The sultan already knew some of the stories, but how could these enthusiastic storytellers have known that? And really, it didn't matter, because each gave the story his own personal twist. Bowing down on bended knee, Ngutane welcomed them all; her gratitude was all she could offer them in return.

"Do you have peace? " she asked.

The storytellers always replied in the same way: "Peace only."

They adjusted their *gandoura*, their caftan, whatever garment they had chosen especially for the occasion, and began to speak.

"And your children, do they have peace?"

"Peace only."

Then they'd start talking about their children.

"And your wives?"

"Peace only."

Then they'd talk about their wives.

"And your servants?"

"And your animals?"

Stories about animals always went over the best. These storytellers transformed Mount Pleasant into a House of Words. They turned the sultan's court into a marketplace of wonders. With his illness, Njoya's home became a compendium of humorous and serious tales, the site of a storytelling competition that went on from morning to night. It became a chain of anecdotes, where men and animals shape-shifted and were remade, where plants and things, dreams and lies were combined—a logorrhea in multiple languages, something even the sultan's daughter never could have anticipated. Some added unexpected spice to their tales. Knowing that the sultan's senses were foggy, they told their stories backward, juggling with reality and having a good laugh. Ngutane, though, kept an eye on her father; his expressions were, for her, the only way to measure a story's success. She judged the tales by Njoya's appetite for more.

One day, before the first storyteller had arrived, Ngutane said to Nji Mama, "The world's secrets are medicines that allow life to be more than a defeat."

"Sometimes you have to face your own suffering head-on," the master architect replied. "Suffering makes us strong." There are invalids who have regained the use of their legs just by listening to the story of someone in worse shape. This idea fueled Ngutane's optimism, but she would have preferred that her father hear only stories of greatness. Nji Mama should have known that Njoya's memory was as long as that of an elephant in a field of calabashes. In her despair at seeing her father locked in an endless coma, Ngutane had turned to the chief architect, certain that he would help her find the right path. He knew her father better than anyone. But Nji Mongu didn't yet know how exile had changed Nji Mama. He had never been a simple man, that's for sure.

After reading Hugo's *The Art of Being a Grandfather* to her father, and then a detective novel brought by a British officer (in the archives in Yaoundé there's a copy of Agatha Christie's *The Mystery of the Blue Train*, but we can't be sure it was that one), Nji Mongu turned to comedies. In her rather pragmatic mind, since her father had regained his breath (after Father Vogt's miracle) and his smile (thanks to his children's and grandchildren's poems), not to mention his powers of logical deduction (the joys of reading a detective novel!), all that remained was to make him laugh. So she asked the French high commissioner to find her a good book. But his bookshelves, filled with administrative tracts and studies about educating the natives, were of no use. For a moment Ngutane thought about contacting Madame Dugast, her French friend who had stayed on in Foumban. The schoolteacher had, on her own initiative, reopened one of the sultan's schools in Foumban after they'd all been shut down by Lieutenant Prestat, the local colonial official. Ngutane had thought about asking her, "What is the funniest European novel?"

Ngutane would have happily taken Madame Dugast's advice on many things; she was, after all, the only person who still called her by her Christian name, Margaretha, after her conversion to Islam. Ngutane also called her friend by her first name, Idelette. Our Nji Mongu was not unaware that this question was one wiser minds would have avoided, a question that would not fail to provoke endless debates in educated circles. On top of that, she wasn't sure about her friend's state of mind. Ngutane knew that Madame Dugast was a voracious reader. The Frenchwoman had a collection of every book written in the sultan's workshops. In her passion for all things Bamum, her friend would certainly suggest that the ailing sultan be told fantastical stories from his own culture rather than read chapters from a witty book. Madame Dugast would draw from her own immense library of Bamum tales and from the stories that praised Njoya's illustrious family. As if Ngutane hadn't already run through all of those. And it went without saying that our Dugast would surely have intoned a hymn to the griots and the oral tradition, as if the sultan had anything to learn about that!

Because those newly convinced of the grandeur of African civilizations are difficult to cut off once they start talking, Madame Dugast would propose stories that Njoya himself had dictated to his scribes. She found them delightful, she who considered herself a Bamum specialist. Ngutane had no doubt that her father would have suffered a fatal heart attack if he had to hear his own story from a French colonial mouth, even if it was the kindest in the sultanate, or that of a very friendly lady. So Ngutane decided to forgo Madame Dugast's advice.

That's when she remembered that Njoya had written a history of the Bamum, the *Saa'ngam*. She recalled all those folks (some very strange characters among them) who had come to the house where he'd lived back in the twenties, when he'd been banished for the first time, to the House of Exile in Mantoum. Ngutane had been only a kid back then, but she remembered all the visitors from far-off places, from cities she'd never heard of whose names set her dreaming: Ouagadougou, Dakar, what names! And also Cairo, Khartoum, Timbuktu. Or even nearby Yaoundé, the home of a very likable man—although he wore too much perfume—whose name she'd soon learn: Charles Atangana. She couldn't forget how these strangers would sit around the sultan and tell him about the world's highs and lows. Later the palace scribes had compiled these first-hand accounts in a book that Ibrahim, the chief calligrapher, had illustrated with his most beautiful designs. Ngutane thought again about how happy her father had looked when he held in his hands the brand-new compendium of all their words, the *Saa'ngam*. And most of all, how the chattering breadth of all those destinies, melted into one book, had erased all traces of his own misfortune from his face. It was the memory of those happy days that convinced our Nji Mongu to transform her father's chambers in Mount Pleasant into a House of Stories.

8

Coincidences Here and There

On December 12, 1913, a young man is attacked in Berlin by unknown thugs whose names posterity would have done well to learn. At the same moment, another young man is coming down a busy street in Foumban, looking for his father, the laughingstock of the city. The young man has a knife between his teeth; his heart has been split open by shame. On the same day and at the same time, but years later, in 1931, a young girl dressed as a boy is staring, hoping to glimpse some signs of an awakening consciousness in a sultan who was stricken but now grows stronger as he listens to life's unbelievable stories. The story of the monarch learning that his own lot isn't the most tragic one that can befall a colonized man has taken root in one of the protectorate's most powerful families.

Question: What do these three stories have in common other than being brought together by the pen of a historian, a woman just arrived from the United States? My friends from Nsimeyong were speechless. Even Arouna, I could see, had fallen silent. History is more than mathematics, he was probably thinking. Well, yes, I went on, listen to these other apparently disparate episodes: June 28, 1914, a young man pulls a gun from under his suit coat, shouts an insult in his mother tongue, and empties his gun into the heart of Franz Ferdinand, who clearly did not understand what the man said, but who belonged to one of the oldest and most powerful families in Europe.

"Scheisse!" shouted Franz Ferdinand before he died. "Shit!" Nothing more.

At the same time, in Leeds, England, a young worker makes love to his girlfriend. The girl's father, coming home from work too early that day, opens the door to his house and freezes at what he sees.

"Son of a bitch!" he shouts.

He dives into his things and pulls out a rifle. The worker is able to jump out a window, leaving behind the disappointed father and the naked, humiliated girl.

And again, at the same time, in Casamance, in Senegal, a seventeen-year-old fisherman returns home empty-handed after a day fishing.

"What a damned day!" he says to his father.

The old man bursts out laughing. "Because you didn't catch any fish?"

"Well, I guess the father of the fisherman isn't a fish," Arouna began with a laugh, "or else this whole thing is kinda fishy . . ."

Why did I suddenly lose patience at this quip from my friend?

Tell me, I cut in, could the father of the fisherman see the net in the unfathomable, shifting depths of the ocean that links all these people together? His son, the young worker in Leeds, and Franz Ferdinand didn't know each other. They had nothing in common but their humanity. And this humanity was certainly relative at that time—is there any way that the heir to the Hapsburg monarchy could compare himself to a young Englishman without a future who has to get his girlfriend knocked up before he can marry her? And their humanity seems to have even less in common with that of the Senegalese fisherman, who is, after all, nothing but a native.

And yet, the death of Franz Ferdinand will start World War I. Exactly one year after his assassination, which sank the whole world into an abyss, the young Englishman signed up to escape fate's stranglehold and take on a role admired by all: a hero. As for the young fisherman, back in his village he was enrolled as a *tirailleur*, his eyes aglow at the promise of his first salary. These men, however different they may have been, all died in a slaughter they never even understood . . .

"It takes more than a fish to curse a day," the father had said to the sad young fisherman, his son. But the boy hadn't understood. He didn't get it at all. "What besides a fish?" he asked.

"Yes, what besides a fish?" Arouna asked. "Tell us."

Listen, I replied, the fisherman respected the wisdom of his father, the proverbs that rolled off his tongue. But the old man had no answer to that very simple question. As for me . . .

9

What Else?

Sara didn't want to hear about coincidences. The question posed by the young fisherman was the key. That day would be damned, in fact, history tells us as much. Damned thousands of times over by the millions of young men from around the world whose lives would be interrupted by a bullet. And yet neither Arouna nor my other friends from Nsimeyong plugged their ears. It was Sara who didn't want to hear about history's perverse twists of fate. Life in Mount Pleasant was historic enough for the old woman, and Njoya's life held the last possible hope for life's upheavals. She was counting on Ngutane to usher in a day of blessings.

So I let Sara take it from there. Nothing could be more disappointing to the sultan's daughter, she went on, than the man who came to tell his story that day; as soon as he stepped into his friend's room, it was clear that the paramount chief had decided to demolish the castle of rumors that had been built there.

"That's the kind of man he was," added Sara sarcastically. "Egotistical to the bitter end."

Charles Atangana wanted to do what he thought was right, that's all. But he had a way of hiding his multidimensional ego beneath a neatly framed philosophy. In short, he wrapped his bullshit up in flowers.

"Sometimes, silence is a good remedy," he said after hearing the story of his predecessors' successes on Ngutane's stage.

And he added, "Especially for a sick man."

His wife agreed. Charles Atangana sat down beside the bed and took his friend's hand. That day he was humbly dressed, although he still cut an elegant figure. Maybe the chief remembered that his friend had fallen into this stupor after one of his flamboyant visits. Maybe he felt a tad guilty.

"I am speechless," Charles Atangana repeated. "Speechless."

That said it all.

After a while he got up and started working the pedal of the gramophone in Njoya's room. The machine played a waltz, even if it skipped a few notes. The flight of an invisible orchestra filled the space. The chief stood there nodding his head, keeping time to the music with a tap of his foot and a click of his lips. The music was vaguely familiar. What mattered most was that his friend liked it, he said. Njoya had brought the gramophone back with him from his trip to Buea in 1908. It was a gift from the former German governor, Ebermaier. A large blue blossom opened up, and as soon as the apparatus began its miraculous sputtering, everyone froze in their tracks. The sultan once danced to the sound of this marvelous flower at the ball given by the governor to mark the kaiser's birthday; since then, the gramophone had graced Njoya's room.

Sometimes Njoya would set the pedal in motion and play a piece, especially when he was in the right mood. The music machine had become part of his daily routine, just like those little things, the biscuits Herr Habisch had brought to Foumban when he opened his shop there.

"Can you waltz?" Charles Atangana asked. He stood up, ready to dance but needing a partner. He had asked the question of Ngutane, but she only smiled; it wouldn't have been proper for her to fill her ailing father's room with such exuberance. The madness of the chief was no excuse. Even his wife declined. Yet Charles Atangana would not be deterred. He took a few steps, his arms held out in a circle in front of him, as if holding an imaginary woman. And he began to dance, yes, to dance with his cigar. The women looked on in amusement, unmoving but jealous of the invisible woman who brought such joy to the chief. He led the invisible woman, going faster and faster with the music, caught up in the whirlwind, just like at a fancy ball. It wasn't only the chief dancing; it was his jacket, his hat, his handkerchief that floated like a butterfly. His shadow danced, and the lamplight fluttered to the rhythm as well.

Juliana Ngono was the first to see Njoya move, and she shouted in her language, "He's dancing with his fingers!"

The chief stopped mid-step. The invalid, lying in his bed, was moving a finger, a hand, his head to the rhythm of the music.

"Well, then!" the chief exclaimed, breaking the stunned silence that met the sultan's indomitable spirit. "Well, then! He really likes it!"

Then Charles Atangana caught Ngutane's hand and pulled her to him. The sultan's daughter didn't protest; how could she? She began to sway to the music, following her partner's lead. Once around the room, then the chief released her and took hold of his wife by the waist. Perhaps he remembered the two waltzes he had danced when he was an Ewondo lecturer, or the waltz he was always talking about—when a prostitute on the Reeperbahn, Hamburg's red-light district, danced with a dying man who promised to give her anything she wanted, eternity even, if she'd give him "one last dance." Or then again, maybe he remembered the balls thrown by the German emperor. The chief felt a devilish surge of energy as he led more and more invisible women in his dance.

Outside the sultan's chambers, tree branches bobbed, their leaves falling to the sound of the magical gramophone. The music spread beyond Mount Pleasant's corridors, through the city, and down Nsimeyong's hills, like the scent of an enchanted flower. Yaoundé's lampposts swayed, and if you looked carefully, you could have seen them take each other in their arms and kiss. The city's rare vehicles zigzagged along the streets. Even the children were caught up in the enthusiasm of this unfamiliar song. Colonizers and locals, whites and blacks, even dogs and cats were dancing. Even the fish in the Mfoundi River gave in and were carried away by the swiftly churning waters. The doyenne remembered that she, too, had been seduced by the sublime power the paramount chief exercised over everyone and everything. She wasn't the only one. All of Mount

Pleasant's artisans stood and stared like children at the universe's dance, their mouths agape.

"I had never seen anything like it," Sara told me, still under the music's enchantment. "Never."

That day, Charles Atangana showed Mount Pleasant why the city referred to him as a magician. They said that he could stop the rains, that there was a Yellow Room in his palace: anyone who entered came out without his shadow. They said he kept the keys to that room in the right pocket of his jacket, on the end of the golden chain that always hung from it. They also said that it was his magic that had made all the Europeans who came to Cameroon—the Germans, the English, the French, and even the Spanish—his closest friends. His greatness, they said, came from how he combined African magic with the Western science he had learned in Europe.

What didn't people say about him? In any event, the chief woke up the cursed sultan with a dance. Even after the universe had settled down, Njoya still held his hand aloft, tracing arabesques in the air.

"He wants a slate," shouted Nji Mama. "Bring him a slate! He wants a slate!"

"A slate!"

"A slate!"

A copyist soon brought him a notepad and ink.

"I said a slate," Nji Mama insisted, "you idiot!"

The architect's anger put a stop to the music. But Njoya wanted it to go on. He spoke, yes, he spoke in an unfamiliar voice.

"Dance," he whispered. "Dance!"

Nebu saw tears of joy run down the sultan's cheeks. A joyful face never before seen. A monumental silence fell all around.

"You should have seen him," Sara insisted, her face still lit by the miracle of that awakening long ago. "It was . . . It was . . ."

The old mama's lips searched for the right word, her fingers snapping to mark the holes in her vocabulary, or perhaps keeping time with the long-silent music. Still today, yes, still today in Nsimeyong the legs of an old man can be set in motion by the rhythm of a magical waltz. The man rises in the middle of his courtyard, puts his arms around the waist of his wife or the nearest woman, and they dance. Sometimes the sound of an accordion accompanies them. That dance is called *le bol*, clearly a deformation of the French *bal*: there's no doubt that after all these years, Yaoundé is still dancing at the ball that the paramount chief Charles Atangana opened that long-ago evening.

10

Even the Animals . . .

Yes, people talked about the dancing city for a good long time.

"For days on end," Sara told me.

The sultan's marvelous waltz brought a new wave of visitors to Njoya's bedside, she added. If Africa had been made aware of the fall of a great man, the whole universe showed up after the mythic dance. They came from unheard-of places, from unknowable cities, drawn in by the allure of this far-off miracle. The visitors never failed to dress as if they were going to an imperial ball. It started with one peacock who appeared, lighting up the corridors of the house with his iridescent tail feathers; even the animals were caught up in the mad dance. And they all met on the way to Mount Pleasant.

At night, masses of butterflies gathered around the sultan's bed to tell him the story of their transformation, how ugly maggots became beautiful. They danced dreamily around the hurricane lamp, moving to the sounds of a symphony played by dogs and cats in the distance. The cats led the moon in a joyful hymn. Sitting on the roof of the house, they sang poems of love and despair. The sultan's household awoke to strains of birdsong proclaiming the glory of the newborn day in rhyming couplets.

A colony of northern birds flew down from Europe, no joke, to sing of the beauty of winter for Njoya's ears and to tell him how lucky he was to live in the warm embrace of Africa's eternal sun. Ducks crossed the city to bring him the tale of their collective death on life's starving streets. Slaves had to use flaming branches to sweep away the lines of ants marching to Njoya's bedroom, where they hoped to tell him how, by working together, they had transformed dust into a golden mountain. What to say of that animal—what is it called? Sara struggled to find the right name—that swore he was too busy to dance? No one, the animal went on, "not even the sultan of the Bamum," suffered as much as he. He grew angry when Ngutane told him that her father's curse was the same as had befallen Sisyphus.

"What?" he shouted. "Just who is this Sisyphus?"

"A Greek god."

Njoya's daughter told him the story.

"Me, I have to push balls of poop with my feet," the animal complained. "Did your Sisyphus have to do that?"

Ngutane didn't answer. She understood the poor animal—he would have filled her days recounting the gloomy twists and turns of his incomparable hell had Ngutane not chased him away. Another day, slaves killed a boa as it zigzagged along the walls of the House of Stories. It was coming to tell the sultan how it had swallowed an antelope. Yes, Sara confirmed, the whole mad world met at Njoya's doors, wanting to share its wondrous tales.

After the boa incident, no one had the courage to get the magical gramophone's pedal going again. Still, the sultan's happiness remained in everyone's memory. The universe would never be the same, and everyone knew it.

11

Coffee and Cake on a Hot Afternoon in Berlin

Although Sara had broken with our normal routine and told two stories in a row, I hadn't interrupted her. After all, I was there to listen. And yet I had some good news to share. It was connected to Franz Ferdinand and the drama that followed his assassination. The Germans reacted as if it were their own kaiser who had been killed, and they weren't the only ones. Most European nations already had a declaration of war signed, sealed, and ready to deliver to their enemies long before a bullet pierced the chest of the Hapsburg heir. If that bullet hadn't been shot, no doubt they would have found another pretext.

For Sara's father, on the other hand, World War I was a blessing. We'll never know how he felt in those moments of collective hysteria, or what he was thinking. Nor will we know who he was with and what he was doing the day war broke out. Did he join the excited crowd and dance with joy in the streets of Berlin? Was he even in a crowd?

I found just one note in the archives of Berlin's Anthropological Society, dated May 1914, that mentioned her father's name.

"About my father?" the old lady asked, unable to speak.

"An official document bearing his signature," I confirmed.

It was a document donating his body to science in the event of his death. A better fate than that of the many unknown soldiers who fell as the war started. Still, this bit of information horrified the doyenne. I suspected that perhaps it was a bargain he struck with the famous Dr. Mult, who had bailed him out of jail. Alas, I wasn't able to find a picture of him in the anthropology museum's collection of photographs of Africans, each one taken of a naked subject and noting the measurements of his or her skull. But some of the snapshots didn't give the subject's name. I was, I'll admit, relieved by this shadow of doubt, for I wouldn't have dared show those pictures to Sara, who had made it clear that she didn't want just any old guy for a father. If only she knew what a poet is capable of doing to survive.

Joseph Ngono had lived through those painful, leaden years, I could prove that, and that was enough. I could also reassure her that while the mud and rain of the trenches of the Marne and Verdun provided the world with ample memories of savagery, the domestic front offered her father a seemingly limitless freedom. He was lucky that the war had taken thugs like Adolf off the streets of Berlin— that they were much happier at the thought of fighting in the Great War than brawling with Communists and blacks.

"To war!"

In their drunken zeal, they shouted across the city. They threw their hats into the air and kissed girls.

"To war!"

"Thank God!"

"To war!"

Their noses had ferreted out new species of prey. They raced frantically to join up.

"To Paris!" they cried.

"To Paris!"

"To Moscow!"

History books overflow with their demented cries, their demands for vengeance; their hysteria fills the archives of Europe through 1918. Amidst the chaos of this loud descent into hell, I'll keep asking my question: Who then took over the streets of Berlin? Ngono had never seen himself as a hero, that I knew for sure. I bet that if they could talk, many of the cities, many of the houses and beds of those absent heroes, could have told stories of Ngono's volcanic passage. I could see Sara's father traveling from the north to

the south when Germany was at war, a pack on his back and nothing else to offer but his love, hoping for just a little warmth in return. I imagined him sleeping under bridges when necessary but
preferring to find shelter for the night in the secretive beds of tem-
porary lovers. He felt free, free and carefree, for the first time in his
life. He feared only the thunderous quarrel that was playing out far
overhead.

His fate wasn't the worst, if you compare it to what happened to
others. THE FRENCH ARE DONE FOR read the headline of the *Saar-
brücker Rundschau*. "They're recruiting niggers to fight for them!"
Thank God, Ngono could say, thank God the Germans don't think
I'm worthy of dying for them!

In Leipzig, he met Ludwig M'bebe Mpessa, a compatriot, built
like a boxer, who worked as a bartender and dreamed of starting a
black theater troupe. Later Ludwig Mpessa took the name of Louis
Brody, better suited to his dreams of grandeur. Sadly, his film career
was limited to playing crazed tribal chiefs caught in the nets of racist plots.

Ngono became his companion. Together they founded the
People's Theater. Ngono excelled in the role of the African, which
paid rather well. The Germans liked it; the domestic front was
starved for entertainment. Wives and single girls, who feared their
husbands or lovers would come back missing their essential parts,
took their minds off their worries in the company of these black men
who were playing at being actors.

This was the first time Ngono worked together with other
blacks. Had the reader of Mann and Rilke undergone some sort of
change? Had he gained what could be called "race consciousness"?
Only the outcome of his story can tell us that. What is certain is that
belonging to the People's Theater made it easier for him to travel.
At the same time, it was the first way he'd found to earn money
since quitting the institute; in short, it freed him from the kindness
of bosses who were too happy to put the police on his trail.

In 1917 he married a woman from Saxony, but I've found no record of any children. Luckily, that is, because I would certainly have
had to tell the doyenne that her siblings had been arrested and
sent to concentration camps, where they disappeared. *Endlösing,*

the Final Solution. But I'm getting ahead of myself. Sticking to her father's story, the vice squad's records indicate that in 1918 he belonged to a League for the Defense of the Negro Race, founded along with "a certain Louis Brody."

This league, with only a handful of members, was classified along with the groups of radical ex-soldiers who were cut off from the blood and action, shunted into the unemployment line when they returned from the front, and kept political activism alive in postwar Berlin. A rather dubious analysis, for how could one seriously imagine the few blacks who could be found in Berlin meeting in a cellar to plot a Bolshevik-style revolution? Maybe some of them had read Marx, their ears abuzz with what had happened in Russia in 1917, and maybe there was a poster of Lenin on their wall as well. But all the same, let's not exaggerate.

Yet it was in the notes left by these young men, notes peppered with rage as well as optimism, that I found Ngono's trail: for the first time, he found a way to give meaning to that sense of emptiness that had once made him laugh and cry and rush into the first corner bar he found for a strong drink. Alongside his new friends, he formulated a few ideas that would play an important role in his life back in Cameroon.

"Run, black man, run!" It was no longer his father's voice or the lampposts that urged him on, but his joyous friends from the People's Theater. Maybe it was the league's forceful resolutions or daring quotes culled from books that swayed his mind; clearly, the echo of the brawls that burst out in the streets of Berlin in 1918 played their part.

And Joseph Ngono would rebel once again: "I am not running anymore!"

Like many others during those dark years, the Ngono who emerged from the war was a changed man. But the question that keeps coming up in the police notes—Did he become a Marxist?—misses the point. Alas, a subsequent war destroyed the documents that might have provided an answer. I read that Sara's father was in Berlin on November 9, 1918, when the Republic was proclaimed. Perhaps he was part of the crowd of ecstatic young men who, just as in 1914, threw their hats in the air, kissed girls, and screamed, "Long live the Republic!"

"Socialism!"

"Democracy!"

"The Socialist Republic!"

"The Democratic Republic!"

Maybe, sickened by this collective madness, Ngono turned back to his friends, Brody for example, who dreamed of being a movie star after the war, and who in 1918 was impatient for change. Maybe together they calculated their chances of finding happiness in the Germany of the future, imagining that the new life afforded blacks in that Germany could only "be better," as Brody the optimist put it. For Ngono, it would have been enough that the streets of the capital were rid of thugs like Adolf. That would have sufficed to make him happy, yes. How to think otherwise?

Maybe Sara's father ended up instead in the home of Mandenga, the Landlord, as he was known in Berlin's black community, because he was the oldest and most established. The ex-lecturer told him the story of the brawl he'd been in, about his assailant's crushed testicles and bloody mustache.

"I can't even lift my hand to eat without thinking of that idiot—"

"The real problem," someone interrupted, "is that you can't wave at the ladies as you'd like. Come on, tell us the truth!"

"Whoever did that to you . . ." Mandenga started, but a wave of nausea kept him from finishing his thought.

Everyone understood and nodded in agreement.

Whatever may have happened, on that ninth of November Ngono certainly listened to his friends talk, eating cakes and drinking coffee as the Landlord's children played around him; meanwhile, out in the street, the mad world grew calmer. In one corner of the living room some compatriots were in a heated debate.

"A republic?" one said.

"Not one, two," replied Theophilus Wonja. "Two republics, my dear."

Wonja was another Cameroonian soul lost in the winter.

"You're joking!"

"Check for yourself."

"The same day?"

"The same day."

"What a country!"

Ngono swallowed a bite of cake. "So what?" he said, exasperated. He had underestimated the Landlord's political drive.

"So what?" Mandenga shouted. "It should mean something to us, shouldn't it? That's the problem for us Africans. Nothing that happens ever matters to us! How can Africa have a future if nothing ever matters to us? If we have no faith in our actions, can anything really happen on our continent? If we Africans don't do anything, will anything happen to Africa other than what the Europeans decide?"

And that was the start of another endless discussion, just like always in this House of Exile, a discussion where the people of the diaspora ripped into one another. Did these exchanges send lost black souls flying out of Mandenga's door? Ngono felt empty; he had no more arguments to make. He was tired. Or was he suddenly disappointed by the futility of these gatherings? In any case, he decided to go back to Cameroon. With no tam-tams, and far from Berlin's inflamed crowds. There, holding a cup of coffee and a piece of cake in the home of Mandenga the Landlord, who was talking about "action" and "political action," but who stayed in his seat.

Just like that.

12

Arabesques of Times Gone By

I broke off my story about Joseph Ngono because Sara had begun to draw in the dirt. I hadn't noticed sooner, I was so caught up in her father's story. She was tracing small figures with her fingers. I felt an unfamiliar sense of self-doubt. Was it the self-doubt of the historian before the eyewitness? That was my daily fare. Or maybe the old lady didn't want to listen to my story any longer.

Sara had her own way of interrupting my story, and I knew, yes, I knew that she'd never fail to tell me what kind of father she preferred. I watched her trembling hands and read:

Which means, *Now I see my father.*

I tried to be circumspect. It was as if, by some sublime necromancer's trick, Sara had turned the father I had discovered under a pile of papers into the child she said she'd never had. Her maternal need to protect that child in his darkest hours had burst forth from her belly in arabesques of love she traced on the ground. As much as her assertion, the way she wrote it left me speechless. It was Lewa writing, Njoya's very first alphabet, invented by the sultan between 1895 and 1896, before the whites set foot in his territory.

I looked at Sara in surprise, for it had taken me a lot of work and five years to learn to read these pictograms that no other Cameroonian still understood. It was an American friend who taught me, a professor in New York who was researching precolonial writing systems—"those that aren't just oral literature," as he put it.

And there we were, half-illiterate me sitting in the dirt in front of the remains of Mount Pleasant while the doyenne scribbled on the ground signs that would have remained cabalistic were it not for my American friend! Happiness lit up our faces. I was certain that we had reached the chthonic knot of this jumble of disparate stories that bound us together. Tears rolled down our cheeks. Sara reached out to me and I clasped her hands. She was trembling. For a moment we were both the happiest, most transparent people on earth.

"He survived," Sara murmured, "after all."

"He survived," I said in turn, but I was thinking of Njoya.

Sara understood and told me how the sultan had regained the use of his hands and taught her to write.

"Step by step," she insisted.

I could see the monarch waking up from his death, lying in his bed, a visitor behind him telling a story to keep him from falling back asleep. Njoya opened his eyes in surprise, and greedily entering this miraculous world, he let the story flow into his ear and flood through his body; he opened his mouth the better to eat it up. Little by little he regained his strength; little by little he built up the strength in his hands so he could write down what he wanted to remember on the slate Nji Mama had brought him, as if his slate were the memory of a long-lost butterfly. Njoya wrote, without knowing that behind him a silhouette watched every move of his fingers, committing them to memory!

Ah, memory is an archive!

"It's too bad he didn't write during all those storytelling sessions," Sara said, sighing. "Then I would have learned even more."

I imagined Njoya struggling to follow the stories that came out of his translators' mouths, our country's two hundred (and more) languages bursting out in an unending shower of tales. Wasn't he disgusted, since he had in fact combined the languages spoken in his kingdom—Shüpamum, Fufulde, Haoussa, Bali, along with elements borrowed from French, German, and English—to invent a new language, Shümum, that was spoken in his palace? He who had wanted a language that incorporated all the earth's languages, a truly global language—how could he not be disgusted by this backsliding, despite his lifelong efforts?

Sara recalled that day long ago when he had sent his principal master artists, Nji Mama, Ibrahim, Nji Kpumie, to the home of that polyglot teacher Fräulein Wuhrmann, to "steal the white man's words," as he put it. His advisers described for him how the woman pronounced such words as "*schwimmen*," "rainbow," "flour," "mission," and "*Ordnung*," among others. "It was as if she owned these words," Nji Mama said.

How surprised the lady was when they returned two days later, accompanied by Njoya, to show her the first "Bamfranglais" dictionary, as they called it, where Njoya had given new meanings to the colonialist teacher's words!

" 'Mission'?" she asked.

"In Shümum," Njoya explained with a smile, "that means 'to see.' "

"And 'flour'?"

"We say *farinsi*, which means 'to spend the night.' "

" 'To have'?"

"*Awar*, or 'full.' "

" '*Kommst du*'?"

" 'Tree.' "

Miss Wuhrmann seemed disoriented. Njoya went on, " '*Links*' means 'children.' "

She couldn't believe her ears. The sultan had turned her universe upside down, just to suit himself. He had made parallels between her words and his own understanding of the universe. He thought it was funny.

That's when he gave her back a letter she had written to him that he had reinterpreted in ways she never could have imagined. Ah, our Wuhrmann!

And what about the day Njoya read her pages from the Bible, which he had rewritten using words from the Koran so that it fit the religion he wanted. What a scandal! The missionary's face made it clear that as far as she was concerned, there was a Christian limit to this kind of language game. She turned for support to Nji Kpumie Penu, who was sitting next to the sultan. Nji Kpumie Penu didn't have a chance to open his mouth.

"In Shümum, his name is Monlipèr," Njoya stated simply.

"Which means?"

This time Monlipèr answered, "Professor."

Old Monlipèr was proud of this name, you could see it in his face, and from then on he asked everyone to call him just that. Fräulein Wuhrmann turned to another artist, the carpenter Nji Shua.

"Laponte," Njoya said.

When she looked at Nji Mama, Njoya announced, "He is still Mama."

The woman was almost disappointed.

"Why?"

Yes, why not continue the game? But our Wuhrmann didn't suspect Nji Mama's rebellion.

"And what about me?" she asked. "What is my new name?"

Njoya had thought about that, yes. How to forget the shock on our dear Wuhrmann's face when he replied, "Fräulein Wuhrmann, your name is Lasisvenère Pristenawaskopus."

"A little long, don't you think?"

Later she'd shorten it to Lasisvener.

This took place in 1911. That's what Njoya did when he was still young and agile. Was it now up to him, there in the bedroom of his exile, to combine all the protectorate's languages and come up with Camfranglais? Or all the languages of Africa and of the world, just so he could understand the madness of the universe that the storytellers had laid out before him? It was a daunting task, especially since he was sick.

NEBU AND NGUNGURE

♮ 1

But the truth is so dear to me, *trying* to *create something true . . .*
—Vincent van Gogh, letter to Theo, February 12, 1890
(translated by Sue Dyson)

1

The Artist Revealed

There was a time in Foumban when princes, freemen, and, of course, the nobles who served the court—the Mbansi, palace pages—had the right to take whatever they wanted from the back of a slave. Walking up the Artists' Alley dressed in his black European suit coat, a handkerchief tucked in his breast pocket, a top hat on his head—all of which he had purchased from Herr Habisch—Nebu caused a bit of a stir, and he knew it. Still, not one noble moved a muscle. Only their amused eyes followed him as he went by. One of the sultan's magistrates would soon place limits on the greed of the Bamum ruling class, but on that day, what mattered was a young boy provoking whispers as he passed and staying the nobles' hungry hands. Murmurings followed him to the end of the alley, where he entered the darkness of a blacksmith's shop.

"I want to become an artist," he said with determination.

He emphasized "artist."

The master blacksmith stared at Nebu, noting that he was dressed just like his father, that madman who until recently was begging for death in the city's streets. He smiled. Nebu removed his hat respectfully, as a Bamum child was expected to do.

"Are you trying to blind me, son?" Monlipèr teased.

Monlipèr's smile revealed teeth reddened by kola nuts. Behind him, dozens of boys working with gold and bronze lifted their burning eyes to stare at Nebu and whispered jokes to one another. He seemed to have come straight from the moon.

But on that day it just so happened that Monlipèr needed day labor to fill a number of pressing orders. Besides, a master craftsman would never have sent a young man so eager to learn the trade away from the Artists' Alley.

"To become an artist," the old engineer began, "it does no good to dress like a Christian . . . Just be faithful to your own truth."

When Nebu undressed in front of Monlipèr, the old man understood the wild stories that circulated about him in the city. Bertha's son was a handsome young man, well shaped, with impressive muscles, virile, but with a hint of femininity because of his thick hair, his beardless face, and his smooth chest. Oh yes, he was handsome. The old man, whose hands knew how to create beauty, was not mistaken. Nebu had the body of a clever wrestler, an imaginative hunter, a spiritual soldier. The top hat, still perched on his head, made the apprentices burst out laughing.

"Take off that damned hat," Monlipèr ordered.

"Peasant . . ."

Nebu heard this coming from the furnaces, but he just closed his ears.

He was transformed when he put on the blue pants and the flowing boubou worn by artists, but the boy was still better dressed than the master, who styled himself with the respectable carelessness of a sage.

Before setting off down the Artists' Alley, Nebu had thought about joining Njoya's army or his police. He had even considered signing up for the German army, yes, of becoming an *askari*. The *askaris* were the only ones who could wander through Foumban's streets and not be stripped bare by the nobles. Nebu had watched their entrance into Foumban, following behind the whites, dressed in beige uniforms, with red *chechias* on their heads and menacing weapons on their backs. Enough to make any adolescent go pale with envy. Many slaves had joined their ranks, moved by dreams of taking revenge against the nobles.

His mother alone had made him change his mind. Bertha threatened to slit her wrists if her son got mixed up with those "guys in poop-colored uniforms." Nebu understood that the *askaris* went wherever the whites told them to go to kill their enemies. But he also decided against it because he had heard the accusations of rape that followed the soldiers, like flies chasing a boy who's just taken a crap. No one in Foumban really liked the *askaris*. People sneered at them, especially the women, who called them "cockroaches." They were all slaves, mostly from Dahomey. Nebu had suffered enough when his father's saga had made him the target of all kinds of gossip. So he had hidden when the palace called out for a hundred volunteers to accompany a German prospector who was heading north "to meet the emperor of the Sokoto." He had hidden in the bush and hadn't come out until a week after the white man with the hippopotamus-tail whip had left.

Choosing the Artists' Alley relieved him of the fear of conscription. A special order from Göhring had put Njoya's artists under protection, keeping the hundreds of young men who worked there safe from the rapacious colonial administration. But Nebu didn't know that yet. He had come straight from the fields, where his hands had never produced anything but yams. He had occasionally met artists, whom everyone admired. How could he have believed he would have a talent for producing anything other than muscular yams? But he didn't want to spend his life working the earth, that's for sure. He was horrified at the idea of ending up on one of the coffee, cocoa, or banana plantations that the Germans were setting up all over. The earth was the wealth of the Bamum, but Nebu despised peasants.

In his heart and in his mind he felt the need to better himself. Love gave him an idea of the magic mountain he was searching for. After making love to the first woman to seduce him (yes, it was the woman who had seduced *him*!), he had closed his eyes and seen strange figures take shape in his dreams. Like letters falling from the sky. After his second tryst he again closed his eyes, and the letters from the sky had become pictograms in the shape of a lion. This vision of a sky filled with letters captivated him for quite some time; the meaning of the universe's words still eluded him.

Since he wanted more than anything to explore the realm of his dream vocabulary, to walk along the paths of his enchanted body, he began to examine the spice market intently. He would wait for girls, then follow and seduce them. He discovered that a dream following lovemaking is different from a sleeping dream: after lovemaking, he could experience the same captivating dream again. "I want to dream my dreams right to the end," he decided. "I want to repeat the same dream again and again."

Of course this was before he met Ngungure and began to dream of her shape and hers alone. Ngungure did not match any of his familiar pictograms; on the contrary, she chased them all away. She was a free woman who didn't fit any of Nebu's prejudices about noblewomen. For example, he could not guess how old she was. Much to his chagrin, he lost all his wits when he saw her. He searched in vain for the most common of words, always coming up empty. He stuttered, and were it not for his fingers, he would have been mute. The figures he drew for her were usually quite simple—just a lover's mumbling. Ngungure was the one who taught him how to make love. Sometimes he missed her body so much that he dreamed of her fingers, the palm of her hand, the flesh that clothed her, although he, like any other slave in Foumban, still walked around naked. "I want my body to become your clothes," Ngungure told him. "Then you won't need to wear anything else."

She undid the belt of his loincloth and dressed him as she desired: with her lips she dressed first his toes, then his knees, and finally his belly, his chest, nose, ears, and eyes. Then she undressed him once more, piece by piece.

"Your turn," she said. And Nebu undid the red pagne wrapped around her chest. He uncovered her heavy breasts. He removed all her necklaces, the bracelets on her wrists, the jewels on her fingers, toes, and ears. He played with each of these accessories to her beauty, especially the golden ring attached to her belly button. But he left that ring there in the hollow of her belly. That's just how Ngungure wanted him to love her: bit by bit, she insisted, like an artist.

She was the one who first spoke of him as an artist. She described something he could aim for with his lovemaking, something he could attain through love, the glowing promise of happiness. Yes, she gave him the gift of her body so that he could squeeze it and create a work of art. His nerves were on fire as he touched her toes, then moved on to her knees and her hips. He never would have believed how he would love looking between her legs, but she asked him to do it, saying that the pictogram he sought in the far-off sky of his dreams was traced right there.

"Don't just dream about it," she told him. "Draw it again yourself."

And his fingers moved closer to the place he had seen.

"Wait, first draw on my body."

Nebu traced an invisible tattoo around her belly button.

"Now on the bottom of my feet."

He sketched figures on her hips, her thighs, kissed her from the bottom of her feet to her knees.

"Now here, between my legs," said Ngungure's voice.

He created shapes there.

"On my lips."

He did.

Nebu obeyed until he could no longer feel his legs, till he lost his mind, until Ngungure opened up and pulled him in with every part of her body. When he penetrated her, she moved her limber hips so he could go deeper inside her. He went further, and she kept moving her hips, grabbing hold of his cheeks with both hands and pulling him into the deepest reaches of her body. He was searching for the lost pictogram, the one he had drawn on her belly—the shape of his own bewilderment. He reached into each part of her body, touched every nerve of her skin, each section of her veins, each drop of her blood, each note of her scent, and suddenly he felt Ngungure's nails scratching his cheeks, her hands gripping his behind, her head buried in his neck, the bite of her teeth. Deep within her he felt something squeeze his cock tight—one, two, three, four, five times. Ngungure's voice shattered his mind, but in her cries he heard one word murmured again and again, a sob from the innermost rooms of the house where he had finally found her, a verb conjugated in the present: "I love."

He didn't let Ngungure finish the conjugation. He knocked repeatedly at the door of her secret spot. More than her stammered word, more than anything—ah!—he loved to see her glowing face, the transformation of her features. Love leads to bliss, which is the realization of true love. Nebu made love to Ngungure again and again, just to see her face. He would have wanted to hold it in his hands forever, to capture it at the height of its most intense sensations. But this ardent face was fleeting! Elusive like a perfume. In its flight, a sudden line, a shapeless shape, a featureless face, a fevered bliss. Ngungure didn't allow him time for quiet contemplation, no. She breathed deeply and lifted him up so high he thought he was a panther, a lion, an elephant. Tears fell from his trumpet, then he shattered into a thousand pieces and fell back on the mats of the woman he had just loved. Already Ngungure's face had disappeared. She put her clothes back on.

"I want to be a sculptor," he said.

Ah, Nebu had dressed scandalously when he appeared in Monlipèr's workshop because he wanted to be free from the loss he felt after making love, a loss without end since Ngungure's death. He wanted to re-create his girlfriend's evanescent face and, through art, make it eternal.

2

Let's Talk About the Devil . . .

Nebu's adventure was a classic coming-of-age story. People said Ngungure was a happy widow who found pleasure in vice, but that wasn't all: in fact, she was a polyandrous nymphomaniac. Had he even asked these gossiping women for their opinions? But Nebu heard much more; snide comments dropped as he passed by, oozing all around like duck poop. Without realizing it, he began to pay some attention to these gangrenous rumors. He learned that before him, Ngungure had seduced twenty-seven young men in Dschang, in Bamiléké territory, inviting them one after the other to the House of Passion that a rich trader had built for her in a field.

There, unbeknownst to her rich lover, she made love to her men as only a free woman can. No! Nebu couldn't believe it—all those piles of whispers, silences, and laughter. He heard the echoes in the looks and smiles cast his way each time he walked up the Artists' Alley. The tale-tellers made fun of him because Nebu was the son of a man whose misfortunes were of mythic proportions, who had been seduced by a female spirit, a Mami Wata, then forced to buy a tie and beg for death on the streets in order to join her in her watery realm. "The bullshit of slaves," he told himself. "They're just jealous."

Why would Bertha's son have given any weight to such nonsense? But then a storyteller, who suggested he was one of Ngungure's "closest neighbors," started in, as if he had seen with his own eyes what went on in the aforementioned bush house.

"That man," the storyteller wondered, perplexed, "didn't he know that she was the Devil?"

So now his own mother's foul words followed him right into the artists' workshop! Nebu knew that the guy who was asking about the Devil was referring to his father. That jerk was surely looking for a fight, yet Bertha's son paid him no mind. He focused on his art. No one had ever heard his side of the story. No one knew that he had first sketched the shapes he was so carefully composing in Monlipèr's workshop on the skin of the wicked woman everyone kept talking about. And that was all right because had they known, never again could Nebu have walked calmly along the Artists' Alley.

If his mother's lie had saved his life, his artistry let him move quickly from day laborer to apprentice. Still, all the nonsense kept stripping him bare. They kept reinventing new lovers for Ngungure—there were thousands and thousands of them now, and with each telling, new names were added. Nebu's silence gave the chatterers free rein to reinvent her life.

"*Djo, djo,*" whispered a voice, "brother, brother, have you heard? They screwed her together."

"You mean one after the other."

"No, *djo*, together."

"They were slaves," added another voice.

"Slaves?"

"Yes."

The yes was immediately challenged.

"No, they were freemen."

"Freemen?"

"Only nobles could do a thing like that, I swear."

A boy with the menacing look of an off-duty soldier had spoken. He had short legs and the round cheeks of a newborn. The skin on his head was yellow with the workshop's dust, and chickenlike eyes peered out from his greasy face. His name was Ngbatu.

All the apprentices turned toward him. He backpedaled. "Listen, listen, I'm not going to tell you who they were."

The faces moved in closer all the same, and the guy who had sworn himself to silence struggled to excrete the sleazy story blocked up inside him. It took one minute—just one minute—before the workshop heard his incendiary mouth list off the names, carefully, as if reciting a prayer, although his brow was dripping with sweat. With a final wave of his hand he swore all the artists to secrecy.

"You see," the distraught conspirator went on, revealing in a whisper the last drop of the awful secret he had only begun to share, "they were all Nguri."

Never before had anyone dragged the Nguri, the noble princes of the Bamum, through such shit, but there was nothing Bertha's son could say to refute the insult. Ah! The boy's voice filled the workshop. "That guy must know," he said, pointing.

All faces turned toward Nebu, who disappeared into his work.

"Didn't your father work in the palace?"

"*Djo*, why not tell us?" urged the chatterer. "Your father was one of them, right?"

And that wasn't all.

"You think we don't know?"

He emphasized the *we* and then added, "You know the truth."

And then, "Your father killed her, didn't he?"

There are truths that cannot be kept silent. Nebu realized that, but still he didn't speak.

"The *muntgu* killed your father, admit it!"

A story of palace intrigue turned into the full-fledged exposé of a perfect crime. The fourth time he was called out about his father, Nebu jumped up. His veins were bulging, his fist clenched. He thought an artists' workshop would be a place where he could forget his manly troubles. But then the images of his violent passion came flooding back, taking hold of his hands, his body, setting off explosions of exasperation in his mind.

Thankfully, a voice intervened.

"Leave him alone!"

Such a scene could take place only when Monlipèr was absent. The master engineer was at the palace too often—getting new orders and delivering the pieces his artists had finished—to maintain the order Nebu would have liked in the workshop. The boy looked at his fellows and clenched both fists. He needed to control his mouth. He needed to restrain his body. Because he knew. Had his companions insulted his mother, he would have reacted differently. He would have dumped a cauldron of molten gold on the head of the loudest of the big talkers, namely Ngbatu.

"Say anything about my mother, Ngbatu," he mumbled, "and you'll wish you'd been born from a whore's ass."

Were these boys who were always pushing him to the edge even ready to hear the truth?

"You want to know the truth, you sons of rats?" Hearing that question, they would have plugged their ears! Nebu learned that truth is only one version of reality: "My father and I," he could have said, "we fucked the same girl, one after the other." His friends would have taken off, flabbergasted. "Yes, and then *I* killed my father, not the *muntgu*." They would have said he was crazy. "It's the truth, motherfuckers!"

Nebu couldn't even own up to his crime! But it was better that way. He learned that in every work of art an unbearable truth is buried. He learned to sink his story deep into his art, leaving it to others to interpret, to refract it through the forms and features of their will—their imagination and their intelligence—with words that reflected their own morality, giving no consideration to the truth that had initially inspired him, the artist. He accepted that his story be told in the words of the first person who happened to pass by in Foumban. That was the only thing he could do if he wanted to escape death: accept it. So he accepted the image the artists soon evoked of a man running naked through the bush, and he became that ridiculous character he caught wind of when they made fun of him behind his back. The artisans laughed so hard that one of them bashed his own finger with a hammer.

"His penis was still standing when he took off running."

Nebu looked at the boy who had just told his version of the story. He was pretty tall, with a chiseled, triangular-shaped face. He wasn't dressed like an artist; all he wore were dirty pants, a reminder of his noble origins. Two strands of cowrie shells hung on his chest, and there were bangles around his wrists and ankles. His name was Muluam.

"In fact," Muluam added, "he needed to hold on to his penis with both hands so he could run faster!"

Muluam spoke with the calm confidence of someone sure of

what he knew. Nebu let him go on, and the boy started to act it out, holding an imaginary penis in his hands. "Like this."

Ngbatu wanted more details. This guy was over the top, maybe that's what caught his interest. He wanted to see just how far a twisted imagination would go, just as Nebu wanted to study the contortions of his most pointed critics. Muluam went on, his hands held in front of him.

"His *bangala* stayed hard for a whole week!"

"Is that why he couldn't come out of the forest?"

"Yeah, he was so hard he finally had to take care of it himself, I swear."

"Lies!"

"It was two weeks!"

"Let me tell you," a confident voice broke in, "he screwed animals to find some release."

"He screwed monkeys."

"Antelopes."

"Birds."

Sometimes Nebu laughed at these monumental fabrications, but he couldn't tell his version of his father's death. The image of a son following his father through Foumban's neighborhoods, down streets, passages, and dark paths until he finally cornered him behind a house and gave him the fatal love he'd been begging for all over the city: that certainly wouldn't make this crowd laugh. And what about a son wiping his bloody knife on the grass, a knife red with the same blood that flowed through his own veins? That was just disgusting!

"*Djo*," Nebu heard behind him, "brother, we feel sorry for your father."

"We feel sorry for him, we do."

Bullshit, he thought. More nonsense from slaves.

Nebu learned a lot by listening when he couldn't respond. It taught him to control his rage. Taught him to keep it, like burning metal, at a safe distance from his body and his eyes. Taught him to strike it with a hammer, striking, striking, and striking again until it grew malleable, until it took on the shape he wanted to give it: flat like a knife, oval like a bird's body, triangular like a lion's head. It taught him to heat up his rage, to dilute his rage, to polish his rage; to file it, yes, to file it down and wipe it clean, like the metals he worked with. And Nebu polished his rage, blowing on his over-heated fingers, blowing on his heart to keep it from exploding, blowing on the embers of his incandescent soul. Art is an antidote to madness.

3

The Depths of Friendship

Oh, Nebu still had no idea what lay at the bottom of the volcanic abysses that fed Muluam and Ngbatu's stories. Only once he had plunged into their gutters did he understand who those fools really were. To think how they sidled up to him, almost becoming his friends. The furnace needed fuel, and as usual, Muluam and Ngbatu were chosen to bring some back from neighboring Bamiléké land. They would have gone alone, as always, but since a new recruit had joined their master's workshop, the devils sensed an opportunity for new mischief. Smiling, they bowed down at old Monlipèr's feet.

"Couldn't Nebu come with us?" Muluam asked.

The master surely had other plans in mind for the new apprentice, but lost in the clouds that were always hidden beneath his closed eyelids, he had no idea of the malice lurking in his interlocutors' eyes.

"Nebu?" he asked simply. "Yes."

Muluam and Ngbatu knew that as distracted as he was, dear old Monlipèr's yes wasn't really an answer.

"He can help find the path," Muluam reasoned.

"Who knows, maybe the next time . . ." Ngbatu added.

"And see the market as well."

"So he can learn about the prices."

The most pensive of all the Bamum bowed under the weight of these twinned arguments. As the newcomer, Nebu didn't say a thing. But he saw the trap being set. The artisans were given two donkeys because three would have made them the target of bandits. Since the new apprentice didn't have a mount, the three would take turns riding, although Bertha's son opted to start out on foot. He walked for hours, following his colleagues as they rode on ahead, laughing at his stubbornness.

"Don't be so stubborn," they told him from time to time, especially when they reached a valley. "Don't you see the mountain ahead?"

Their ugly words from the day before were still echoing in Nebu's ears. He used his endurance to show them that he wasn't just any old fool, much less a coward they could laugh at all they wanted. But he couldn't go on forever, torturing himself to defend his dignity. Walking to Dschang would take several days. The first night, Nebu lay down far from his friends, despite their warnings: "The forest is full of wild animals!" The second, he still refused to speak to them, just let them keep on laughing at their own stories. After the second day, however, he could no longer avoid the complicity inevitable on such long trips without being ridiculous.

It all started with hunger. The travelers' provisions had run out too soon: Nebu and Muluam learned too late that Ngbatu ate like an elephant. Thankfully, he was an amazing hunter. In the evening he headed into the bush and soon returned, an antelope slung over his shoulders.

"There you go," he said, laying his still-struggling prey out on the ground. "That should do it."

And it did! Nebu learned that Ngbatu was the son of a well-known hunter who had turned to farming after the German administration had forbidden all the Bamum from carrying weapons. Of his four brothers, Ngbatu was the only one who'd escaped conscription, and only because he'd found shelter in Monlipèr's workshop. Give or take a few details, Muluam's story was the same; he was the son of a soldier turned farmer.

When the defrocked hunter and soldier confided their stories, why didn't Nebu admit that he was the son of a scribe, a peasant only because he was a slave? Bertha's son didn't want to remember his father. He learned many other things about his comrades, although his silence made him look like a snob in their eyes. When he awoke the next day, they were already long gone. He found them an hour later, hidden behind some bushes. He was ready to let loose with a mouthful of insults.

"Shh!" Ngbatu cut him off.

Muluam put a finger to his lips. Nebu tiptoed up and was dumbstruck by what he saw his friends were watching: a girl washing clothes in a stream. They held tight to their genitals so they wouldn't explode. Bertha's son was paralyzed by the sight. She was a dream caught mid-flight, the static perfection of a vision he thought he had conquered. There was no doubt: it was Ngungure.

"She must be Bamum," Ngbatu said.

"What about the tattoos on her shoulders? She's Bamiléké, no doubt about it," Muluam disagreed. "After all, we are in Bamiléké territory."

Ngbatu cut to the chase. "Bamiléké or not, I don't give a damn. She's mine."

"No," Muluam snapped back. "Mine."

"Why?"

When Muluam stood up to go join the girl, a firm hand grabbed his leg and pulled him back behind the bushes. He swallowed an insult.

"Let me go," he grumbled, spitting out the grass from his mouth. "Let go of my foot, you sad fool!"

A few years or even a few months earlier, Nebu would have been the first to want to seduce the girl by the stream. Today, however, what he said came as a real surprise.

"Leave her alone!"

His two companions really would have laughed if they'd known the reason behind this change of heart.

"Well, if you don't have any balls . . ." Muluam started to say.

"What, is she your woman?"

When the young men lifted their determined heads, the girl had already disappeared. Muluam and Ngbatu looked for her up and down the riverbank but eventually gave up. They came back to Nebu, united in their anger against him.

"It's your fault," they declared.

"No, it's yours," Nebu retorted.

All three burst out laughing, for each was pointing at another's face. They talked about the girl for quite a long time, although of course Nebu didn't tell them that in her fluid shapes, he had suddenly recognized a face he knew very well. He didn't even have a chance to explain. The girl in the stream soon faded from his friends' memories, replaced by two opulent prostitutes they treated themselves to that evening in Dschang—"a bit of consolation."

Nebu also tried to forget the fleeting face of the girl from the riverbank. Art gave him the clay he needed to transform life's ugly miasmas into a dazzling sky. He threw himself into his work with a will made stronger by his desire for revenge, and he cut himself off from the faces of those who wanted to make him miserable. He learned the ins and outs of the sculptors' ancient craft from the hands of his master, finally accepting that gold was nothing more than the material with which he could realize his artistic dreams. He wanted to move closer to the sun's bright light.

Nebu learned how to fill the eyes of an antelope with gold and polish a lion's teeth. Soon he knew how to inject an illusion of truth beneath the skin of a gilded leopard. He knew how to make an immobile lizard zigzag through the dust, and even how to make geckos cock their heads. He deftly re-created all the animals from memory. He knew that surprise is the silent expression of truth, and he suffered less when Muluam and Ngbatu got caught up in their endless critiques of his work. He knew, yes, Nebu knew he still had a lot to learn in Monlipèr's workshop if he wanted to erase, once and for all, the shameful story that had brought him there, if he wanted to realize his vision with his own hands. Art is a corrective for a life that's become unlivable. Art can transform a life. Art can become life. Art can be the whole of a life. Finally, he understood that.

"You take everything too seriously," Muluam said one day.

"Art is my life," Nebu replied.

The possibilities are limitless, he could have added, but instead he just said, "Don't you get it?" No, his friend didn't get it yet. How could he? Lost in the gilded park his hands had created, amidst the animals transformed by his talent, Nebu was always searching for new forms while his friends were content to repeat the same old things. He sought out unknown figures and unimagined visions. He sought animals he had only dreamed of, but never seen. Yes. Those he had imagined, even if just in his dreams, he wanted them, too. Soon he moved on to more abstract symbols, for he had deconstructed spiders enough to make the connection to birds, and he had dived deep enough into serpents to recognize their relation to dogs.

One day, to the stupefaction of the whole workshop, especially his two chattering companions, he sculpted a two-headed dog. Nebu had progressed far ahead of them. He added his visions to Monlipèr's vocabulary of Bamum symbols, and soon there were five-footed dogs coming out of the old engineer's workshop, horses with human heads, winged men, and even, yes, even unicorns. Since Nebu never claimed credit for the forms he created, his master presented them to the sultan as his own discoveries. Still, the old blacksmith gazed at his new apprentice in amazement. More than anyone, he understood the call of innovation that burned in Nebu's fingers. In all his years as a master artist, he had never met a young man who worked with such intense focus, who constantly found new expressions for his vision.

"You'd think the Devil had possessed your hands, my son," he commented one day.

And that was very close to the truth!

4

Workshop Conversations

Nebu's dreams were intense. He saw all the details of Foumban's streets. He saw the House of Passion he had set aflame in his vengeful anger. He saw her room, and in her room, sitting on the bamboo bed, Ngungure. He was sitting on the ground, between his girlfriend's legs. He felt her knees against his shoulders, her breath on his neck. She was wearing a red pagne that covered her breasts. She was carefully, meticulously, braiding his hair, for Nebu's hair had grown thick. She divided the mop into little sections that she combed and twisted between her fingers, one by one. At the same time, she sang in his ears a melody that made him feel stiff and weak. He woke up drenched in sweat. Ngungure was nowhere to be seen. Trembling, he touched his head. His hair was braided, and to his great surprise, he had a red pagne wrapped around his hips. He was so excited he had to take care of his erection with his own hands.

Why was he suddenly ashamed? His whole life he had walked naked across the city, never imagining that one morning his own nakedness would cover him with shame. He had seen dozens of women's pagnes fall at his feet and never would have thought that he'd feel such a need for the hands of the woman whose garment now covered him; that he would need her hands to awaken his body; that he would need to hear her voice whisper in his ears to come back to life. He was ashamed because he suddenly realized that he felt sick. He was stunned by the shocking discovery of his capricious desire and aggravated by his inability to control it. Still, he couldn't believe that Ngungure had braided his hair during the night only to disappear at dawn. Were it not for his workshop fellows, who were making his life even more miserable, he would have spent more time pondering the mysteries of his night!

"You braided your hair?" Muluam piped up as soon as he saw Nebu walk by the door to the furnace.

"Good day to you," Bertha's son replied coldly.

"Good day to you, Monsieur Bamiléké!"

Ngbatu was on the same antagonistic wavelength as his companion, but Nebu's dream had left the sculptor listless. If he had thought their escapade had been left behind back in the bush, the unstoppable logorrhea of these guys was there to prove him wrong.

"*Djo*, you must be in love," Muluam shot out. "Still that girl by the river?"

"She's Bamiléké, isn't she?"

"No, Bamum, I think."

"So when's the wedding, *djo*?"

"Or are you interested in Bamum girls now?"

"The revenge of the Bamum."

Ngbatu and Muluam shared a sly laugh.

"Bamum girls are good lays, aren't they?" Muluam asked, suddenly calm.

What do they know? Nebu thought, shaking his head. Assholes!

He didn't even tell his mother who had braided his hair, especially because Bertha had warned him against "wild hairstyles," advising him to not overstep the limits set for slaves in Foumban.

"What about artists?" he replied simply. "I am an artist."

Slaves had to keep their heads shaved. That wasn't the most important thing, though. Bertha didn't insist, because Nebu stood before his mother dressed just like an artist. The matron forgave him his choice of hairstyle because being an artist not only kept him close to the palace—or rather, close to her—it also kept him safe from the colony's greedy clutches. Nebu added three pearl necklaces and earrings to his outfit. They were the only signs of his fingers' talent, except for his artist's uniform, of course.

He didn't share his nocturnal dream with his master, but rather asked him about the nature of truth.

"Truth?" Monlipèr replied, lost in his far-off thoughts. "Truth needs to be hidden. Or else it'd blind us."

"Blind us?"

"Yes, yes. We are like butterflies, my son, and truth is a lamp."

Nebu had to keep repeating those words. Truly his mother's son, he had never looked his master in the eyes. For the first time, the man seemed old to him. Very, very old. Monlipèr was an old man weighed down by multiple responsibilities and many years of work. Nebu noticed that his master closed his eyes when speaking about the arts. Maybe it was a habit from spending long days in his suffo- cating, smoke-filled workshop. His voice seemed to come from the grave, from a mystical workshop, from the forges where blacksmiths had worked for millennia. He spoke in a whisper, but each of his words had the force of a steel stamp. The sculptor took in the words gratefully. If he'd had a notebook at hand, he would have written them down so he could reread and ponder over them later. He wanted to digest them slowly.

"If the butterfly comes too close to the lamp," Monlipèr contin- ued, "it burns its wings, doesn't it?"

And Nebu repeated, "Yes, it burns its wings."

"So the lamp must always be covered to protect the butterflies," the master concluded.

"To protect the butterflies."

There was a long pause—an overly long pause—that Nebu didn't break. Then Monlipèr continued.

"For the lamp to burn, it must be protected from the wind."

Nebu repeated, "From the wind."

"Yes, yes. It's what covers art that lets us see the truth."

He paused again.

"It's also what makes truth shine."

Suddenly Nebu remembered other very different things Monli- pèr had said the day he'd first arrived in the workshop. Why? Because his master had spoken of blindness that day as well. He had said that Nebu's European clothes blinded him. Wasn't he contradicting himself? The young man didn't insist. None of this was written down anywhere, so . . .

"Without its covering," the old man went on, "truth is furtive."

"Furtive," Nebu repeated without revealing any of the thoughts running through his mind.

"Yes, yes."

The young man was thinking about everything he had lived through, especially the girl by the riverside, her beauty, and how it had disappeared from his view. He thought about Ngungure's face after making love. He was quiet for a moment because he couldn't find the words to say what he wasn't thinking about, and he didn't want to lie either.

"So art is just an attempt?"

"Just an attempt," Monlipèr replied, "for no work of art is perfect."

This was just the beginning of a more complicated idea, so the master had continued: "Because art is the expression of our wounded humanity." But Nebu's ears were no longer open to hear the old man's maxims. His mind was clouded with his own thoughts, and in the chaos, another idea was rising up, fighting ferociously to tear him away from Monlipèr's philosophy.

"To see better, you must shut your eyes."

Yes, that's what the master said, and Nebu repeated, "Shut your eyes."

"Because art is the reflection of your most intimate dreams."

"Dreams," Nebu said, "intimate dreams."

"Yes, yes."

"Your dreams." Those words pursued him for quite some time. He repeated them again and again, measuring the weight of their possibilities until a truly frightening truth emerged: he didn't agree with his master.

"I want perfection, I do," he said. "A vision of perfection."

And he added, "I want to open my eyes to see."

Then, "I want to re-create what I see in my dreams."

Finally, "I want my dreams to come true."

The central precepts of his aesthetic flowed from his mind automatically, freely. That night he covered himself with his girlfriend's pagne before going to bed. Once again he dreamed of her. The scent of her body was stronger, his dream even more intense than before. Nebu dreamed the same dream several times. Sometimes it broke off and picked up again the next night. It took an even greater hold of him even while he was awake. He emerged from the labyrinth of his mind drenched in sweat, full of questions for his master. Only he was less and less able to speak honestly to old Monlipèr about his nocturnal possessions.

How so? He saw Ngungure much more closely than she had ever allowed. He didn't see just her face, but her nose, and not just her nose, but her nostrils. He saw his girlfriend separated into disparate parts, for soon he saw her hand cut open before him piece by piece, from the nails to her palm, from the palm to her wrist, from the elbow to her upper arm, and from the shoulder to her breast. He saw her breast rise in the juncture between her arm and her chest. He thought of Monlipèr's phrase "wounded humanity." It was a weighty argument. And Nebu realized that he had never really seen Ngungure. Don't emotions blind us to truth's brilliance? He realized that his girlfriend had always eluded him, and when he closed his eyes for the night, he dreamed of her even more intensely.

It was a stroke of luck, he thought when he woke, that he couldn't discuss Ngungure's nakedness with his master. But he was convinced that therein lay the secret of the artistic truth he sought, and that this set him apart from Monlipèr. One day Nebu saw a portrait of Ngungure among the photos Herr Habisch had displayed in front of his shack of surprises, and he thought of his dreams. He didn't react as children do, amazed to see friends' faces, or like those women, frightened when they happened upon pictures of people long dead. Nor did Nebu react like an artist who is searching for something new. He didn't thank his ancestors for sending him dreams of what photography could be, long before he had actually seen a photograph—before the arrival of the white man. Photography provided a practical solution to the theoretical problems he'd faced up till then.

Nebu had gone to Herr Habisch's to return the clothes he had bought and no longer wore. He wanted to trade them in for something more useful. Drawn in by the photos, he immediately knew what he wanted. The Swiss merchant refused to take back Nebu's clothes, however, and the apprentice's wages didn't leave him with much extra in his pocket. All the artist could do was plant himself in the middle of the kids and women crowded in front of the display of stiff faces. Looking at Ngungure's portrait, he was overcome with shame, and he glanced around, fearing that his private thoughts had been revealed to the pack, for the photograph of his girlfriend's face was a close-up, as only a lover could have seen her. It made public the forms that Nebu had only ever glimpsed in his dreams. The only difference was that this photo was in just two colors, black and white. And he'd never seen his girlfriend in just two tones.

When he left, he had a smile on his lips. What he had seen was forever inscribed in his mind. He smiled because, if he admitted that photography was technically amazing, he also realized it had its limits. It didn't achieve the detail of his dreams, but it did give him something he could say to old Monlipèr. That's why he wasn't disappointed when he returned to the workshop. He knew that it was up to him, and him alone, to recompose his girlfriend's face with his own hands, just as she appeared in his dreams. The furtive shapes of her beauty, the re-created beauty of a woman everyone had always said was ugly, that's what he wanted to capture in his art, what he termed his face of bliss, or his look of pure contentment.

"I want to capture that bliss," he promised.

There are stories that must be told just for the story itself, just for the story. This was one of them.

5

Getting Back to Ngutane and Bertha

That said, let's turn another page! Let's move on to the story about the young boy Nebu. Or that's what the doyenne said when she really meant the story of the young girl Sara. Her own story. Whew! In 1931, Mount Pleasant was filled with many lively stories, just as labyrinthine as those taking place in Foumban or in wartime Germany, although very different, too. As seen from Yaoundé, the world was still within reach, and everyday worries were pedestrian.

"Flowers." Ngutane's voice was insistent. "Flowers and not peace tree leaves. Not peace tree leaves, you idiots!"

Her outbursts were always met with silence. Wasn't she right? The sultan's daughter had had to lead two slaves into the bush to show them what she wanted, and still no luck. The next day again her voice rang just as loudly through the corridors.

"I said NO peace tree leaves! Don't you have ears?"

Two days later, it was "Flowers don't attract snakes!"

And again, Ngutane stressed, "Believe me, will you? Flowers . . . do . . . not . . . attract . . . snakes!"

Ah, Ngutane had lots of reasons for losing her patience. Another time Sara saw her scolding a foolish slave who the previous day had put warm water on the sunflowers Njoya so loved and had let them die, yes, die.

"What did you think you were doing?" Ngutane shouted. "Making tea?"

And that wasn't all.

"Where is your head?"

Was there anyone in Mount Pleasant who still had their head? Once, Sara heard a burst of laughter in the main courtyard; when she came out, she saw one of the sultan's wives dressed like a European. The woman wanted to make her ailing husband die laughing!

"Or make God cry," the doyenne added.

No need to say that these scenes at the invalid's bedside were the focus of everyone's attention. Enough people had crowded into the House of Stories that it was hard for anyone to remember who actually lived there. The house was enough of a puzzle that everyone thought they were in a poor, crowded neighborhood, and the house was strange enough that a kid like Sara could get lost, lose the thread of the stories that, one after the other, should have led her back to Nebu's body without making the impatient Bertha wait too long. Those fictional stories—told, repeated, or forgotten—those knots and all those abysses were captivating, even if the corridors where they were told were quite similar.

I could well imagine (who couldn't?) that Bertha's story was too tangential for a kid's ears. Especially because, for example, when the matron spoke of the birth of her son's artistic vocation, she got so caught up in the details that her audience was superfluous. Of course she wanted ears there so she could tell them about the meanderings of Nebu's artistic conscience; what she didn't want was a nine-year-old passing judgment. She was telling Nebu's story in order to make her own soul suffer again, to remind her body of the pain she had already experienced: to find a way to escape from the horrors of her past life. You could say that Nebu's story was as painful for her as childbirth.

Ah, Bertha didn't need an audience! Compassion is a mother's virtue, and she had none, especially when it came to the young Nebu. She raised her hand to slap the child when he came back late from the sultan's bedchamber. Did anyone think that the start of this woman's story would be the end of her violence? True, it had been a long time since she had last sent "her child" to bring back a whip from the courtyard. Yet she fell back on those outmoded methods one evening when Nebu told her he'd lost track of time. Bertha had heard better excuses from children before. She began to shout, "Are you trying to trick me?"

Once it caught fire, her rage would not burn out quickly.

"You're just like him," she said, her eyes red, "just like him!"

She was talking about the other Nebu, of course, the young man madly in love, the artist, the apprentice. As she repeated "him," pain lit up her eyes.

"Selfish," she said. "You're the most selfish child on earth!"

With these words she whipped herself into an ever greater fury, feeding the fire of her rage with repeated images of how Nebu had abandoned her.

"An individual," she went on, "a nothing!"

You try to tell Bertha that her story was raping a child's soul! Go tell her that for Sara, listening to stories at the sultan's bedside, now that he was awake, was far better than trying to follow the metamorphoses of a dead woman's face. You do that, the doyenne insisted, and then let me know if you can calm her down. Every story has its limits.

"You're no better than he was," Bertha insisted, "not at all!"

This time the boy she held in her hands didn't wait till the bamboo whip was lifted over his head.

"If you move," Bertha threatened, "I'll cut off your nuts!"

But Nebu didn't have any nuts.

"I say, if you move . . ." the matron repeated. "Nebu, get back here!"

The kid didn't come back.

"Nebuchadnezzar, get back here!"

Nebu fled, as far as he could. He knew the reach of the matron's anger. Her voice filled the main courtyard.

"My God," she screamed, "why did I give birth to such a rat?"

Several voices hurried to calm her down.

"That's how children are."

"Forget about it."

"My own children . . ."

Bertha didn't want to hear anything unless it was about her son, her own Nebu, about her own maternity. Nothing superfluous! She just kept screaming out her pain even louder.

"I'm going to teach him to respect what his mother says!"
All the voices agreed.
"Yes, you show him!"
"Hit him!"
"He needs it!"
"Do you want a whip?"
"That'll teach him to listen!"
"Nebu, where is the whip?"
"Children must respect their parents!"
"Hey, who took my whip?"
"You must teach him to love you."
"Teach him love."
"Where is my whip?"
"I'm sure your apprentice took it."
"Here, here's a whip."
"That's how children are."
"They wanted to hide my whip, uh-huh!"
"I told you I'd found your whip."
"Yaoundé," one voice said. "It's Yaoundé that's making our kids crazy."

It was a bald man with a bushy beard who said that, the menacing one who'd been so eager to find her whip. Nji Shua, the carpenter, whose beard always frightened the kids. He was known for his violent rages. No one called him by his Shümum name, Laponte, because he behaved like a brute. He whipped his apprentices till they peed in their pants, just for making little geometry mistakes.

That day, when Nebu came back to Bertha's, his ears burning and his eyes red with tears, the matron knew who had beaten him. She rushed to the door of Nji Shua's workshop, where the child told her she'd find his torturer. There she was, standing at the door of the man no one dared to look in the eye.

"Nji Shua," she shouted, "who asked you to hit my child?"
She was met with silence.
"Why don't you just slap me, too?"
Silence.
"Criminal," she cried at the door's persistent silence. "Assassin!"
She marched through the motionless courtyards.

"Is it bad luck or what?" she said to the few apprentices who stared at her, too afraid of the carpenter to show their approval of her actions. "He can't teach his own wives to listen to him and yet he dares to punish my son!"

Njoya's bedchamber was filled with fantastic stories. Paths that twisted and turned through unexpected lives, a paradise of surprises for children. All who visited would have liked to stay longer. Except Bertha; yes, all except Bertha. Yet one day her son went into the monarch's bedchamber and found him standing there—just standing there, not lying in his bed, Sara reported. The mute little girl she was back then was about to scream; she was ready to drop everything she was carrying. But the sultan gestured for her to keep quiet. Njoya wanted to surprise everyone. He always liked to catch his entourage off guard. Nebu played along, trembling as he completed the task for which he'd come: taking away the sovereign's excrement.

Some secrets are too heavy for a kid to bear; once outside, he coughed, and the calabashes he was carrying crashed down at his feet, feces covering the slaves lying before Njoya's door. Horrified, they stood up, but their anger was stayed when Ngutane's voice suddenly rang out. Rather than the shouts of a mischievous child, it was the voice of Njoya's daughter that filled the corridor.

"He walked?"

She had seen it with her own eyes, but still couldn't believe that Njoya had gotten himself up to stand by the window. She was asking the slaves, who stammered in their confusion.

"He walked?"

"He walked?" they asked back.

Njoya's smile was their only answer.

Ngutane wanted to know the details. "He really walked?"

Soon she opened the chamber's window and, putting her hand to her lips, let loose with the joyful cry of a Bamum woman: *"Woudidididi!"*

When she was sure of the truth, she ran through the corridors, her voice echoing in the main courtyard, announcing in tremolo the sight she had been awaiting for weeks, months.

"Alareni walked!"

Her voice multiplied her joyful cries.

"He's walking!"

"Fran Njoya is walking!"

"The sultan is walking!"

The echo of this cry that began in Njoya's bedchamber woke up not just Mount Pleasant, but also Nsimeyong and all of Yaoundé. The hundred people gathered at the sultan's doors, all those who had been waiting so long and so impatiently for a sign of life from their fallen sovereign, joined Ngutane in her celebratory cries. Some ran back to their homes, others came rushing out, all lifted their voices in a universal song.

"*Woudidididi!*"

The cry that took over Mount Pleasant on that tumultuous day of revelation didn't belong only to Ngutane, but to a country, a whole continent.

"He is walking!"

"He is walking!"

It was a long, strident cry that cut across the main roads of the stupefied city, rolled right down the hills like a landslide, and even grabbed hold of the fish in the river:

"*Woudi . . . Woudi . . . Woudi . . . Woudidididi!*"

6

The Audacity of an Apprentice
Before His Master

Back when he was in Foumban, Njoya never could have stepped into his palace courtyard and not found it full of action. Dozens of flutists, and just as many talking-drum players and poets singing his praises, turned each of his steps into another mythic tale. Telescoping trumpets, or *kakaki*, *algaita* oboes, and bells tried to outdo each other, providing a sound track for his walks. Despite all this tumult, he went along the streets of the city at his own pace. Sometimes he'd walk as far as the spice market, stopping amidst the thousand scents and the "*woudidis*" of the women amazed to see him, checking the prices of palm oil, paprika, chili, ginger, and bitter leaf as if he were a woman. He'd stop at a covered stand and ask the salt vendors about their wares as well as their families. He walked into the courtyards of houses, letting children come and tell him their names and their dreams for the future.

"What do you want to become?" he'd ask them.

"A master," replied one young girl.

"A weaver, like my father," said a boy.

"A potter."

"A calligrapher."

"An officer in the palace police."

Some children were too timid to talk. Sometimes one declared that he would rather be the sultan, which always made everyone laugh. Even Njoya.

"You must imagine your future if you want it to come true," he told them. "Don't ever let anyone else dream your dreams for you."

The children fell silent at these words of wisdom.

Then he'd ask, "What did I say?"

And they'd repeat, just like in school: "Don't ever let anyone else dream your dreams for you."

The sultan would smile and add, "Dreams are a basket of unending treasures."

And then, "You don't want a thief to steal them from you, do you?"

"No, Alareni!"

"And not your future either, right?"

"Yes, Alareni!"

"Why?" one child asked, seeming to grasp the invisible threat the sultan hinted at.

"Well, because the future, that's your gift to all of us, my son."

Njoya also reminded the children that every night they could dream the world anew and rebuild their future each day.

These ideas were far too weighty for them, but no one could resist the charm of his words.

"If you don't dream when you're children, what will you do when you're grown up?"

One of the sultan's favorite destinations was the Artists' Alley. Njoya loved to watch the artists at work. He became someone altogether different in a workshop, giving the blacksmiths and ceramists advice, speaking as if he were one of them; and he *was* one of them. He watched how their hands moved, the speed with which their feet set the machines in motion. He made suggestions about the choice of materials and colors, on how to use and combine them.

Monlipèr gloried in these visits to the workshop where he ruled. The old man went up and down the main street, more agile than any of the praise singers who busily surrounded the sultan, dancing in his shadow and ahead of him, adorning each of his gestures with an array of descriptions, decorating the sky with his magnificence.

It was during one of these visits that Nebu did what he should not have done; he leaped out of the frantic crowd and threw himself at the monarch's feet.

"I want to work at the palace, Alareni!"

Only Njoya's kindness kept him from being cut to shreds by the police and their cutlasses, for his sudden movement had broken all protocol. The sultan asked his riflemen to lower their weapons.

"I want—to work—for you," Nebu stammered.

Bertha's son spoke into the dust where he had thrown himself. His words were unintelligible. When he got back up, assisted by two guards who held him back, his braided hair was covered in the red earth of Foumban; he looked like a mystic. Nebu knew there was no precedent for his actions, but he also knew that only an extraordinary gesture could free him from the workshops of the Artists' Alley, from his master above all. Later he'd learn that it was because of his braided hair that the palace guards hadn't killed him. They thought he was an herbalist and were expecting him to describe his visions.

"He's just a madman," Monlipèr begged, waving his hands at the menacing guards. "He's my apprentice!"

Monlipèr was exaggerating a bit. Nebu had spent only two years in the master's workshop and already he wanted to move on. This wasn't how things usually went, but a necessary step in this case. The boy had learned all he could in Monlipèr's workshop, and as he grew less humble, he was increasingly unable to hide what was emerging in his dreams. And now work had begun on the sultan's new palace! This was an important project for any artist or artisan with ambition. Everyone working there had been chosen by the sultan himself or by one of his foremen. For once, Muluam and Ngbatu didn't seek to do harm with their indiscretion; filled with nothing but admiration for Nebu's hands, they now used all the superlatives at their disposal to prove that the palace was just the place for his talent to bloom.

Of course everything made in Monlipèr's workshops was destined for the palace, but those two boys had let Nebu understand that it would be different if he actually worked there. He would have the free rein all true artists dream of; a worksite of that size was the perfect place for him to test the limits of his audacity. For Nebu, it would also mean freedom from his two advisers, for he knew their darker side all too well. In truth, his actions had been triggered the day he noticed his two-headed snake adorning the palace entryway. Monlipèr didn't even tell me, he thought, feeling let down.

Clearly, he wasn't seeking full credit for the work, which he had been able to realize only as a result of his master's teachings, even if he had taken them as far as his imagination would go. It was a brilliant work, yes, the result of all he had learned from Monlipèr. In a way, the old master was right to present it as his own, even if it hadn't been made by his hands. It was the reflection of his ideas about art, even if seen from a perspective he hadn't really explored.

The influence of a dispassionate aesthetic was increasingly evident in the work produced by Nebu's hands, guiding their creation of sculptures like that one.

"It's mine," he had murmured.

An unknown feeling rose up in him, a feeling he knew was outrageous. Yet even after he returned home, he couldn't keep from telling his mother about it; she tried to temper his artistic sedition.

"It's mine."

After that episode Nebu stopped discussing aesthetics with his master. He just watched Monlipèr work, smiling at the master's ever-closed eyes and the "yeses" that peppered the old man's language. Bertha's son knew that his master could see only the vulgar side of reality. But you don't contradict your master; you just quit. The problem is that a slave can't do that. Joining a workshop meant accepting the master's unquestioned authority. Only he could free his apprentices—he or someone in a similar or even greater position. The boy's status prevented him from finding someone capable of freeing him in Foumban. The only option was to throw himself at the sultan's feet, as Muluam and Ngbatu had suggested. Nebu knew that he was breaking a thousand barriers and taboos. He was lucky. That day, instead of punishing him, Njoya heard his prayer and put him under the tutelage of Nji Mama.

In the palace, he met other artists, the best in the country and even in the world. There were Fulani, Bamiléké, and even Germans working on the new palace. Nebu was amazed by the ease with which these men reached heights he'd never dreamed of, making connections between things he had seen as unrelated. Sometimes he felt once again like a baby playing with clay, unaware that one drop of dirt can give birth to a man.

This is where he discovered the grandeur, no, the genius of Nji Mama and his younger brother Ibrahim, the sultan's two closest collaborators. People said they slept on either side of the monarch, that they were his "twin spirits." Some tongues hinted that Njoya preferred to turn toward Nji Mama as he slept. The two brothers were the only master artists who had accompanied the sultan on his trip to Buea in 1908, when he had tried to explain the symbolism of the Mandu Yenu to the Germans, who were very impressed by the sultan's dynastic throne. Their real mission was to observe the white men's tools, to see if their ideas could be used to further the ideals of Bamum art. Nebu had the good fortune of being apprenticed to Nji Mama, and he quickly learned that he couldn't hide any of his thoughts from his new master. "I know it's your work," Nji Mama said to him one day as they were passing by the palace's main doorway, which was adorned with the two-headed snake. "I know it's yours."

Of course Nebu didn't reply.

"A masterpiece," Nji Mama continued, caressing his goatee and bending his head, as he always did when he was thinking. "A real masterpiece."

Following custom, Nebu denied responsibility for the work and instead began praising Monlipèr. Nji Mama smiled. He was a man of few words, but everything he said was worth its weight in the gold the young man had used back in the Artists' Alley.

"Don't worry about it," the master added. "Even Monlipèr knows he's from the old school. He's proud of you."

Why did Nebu's cheeks grow hot all of a sudden?

Nji Mama reassured him. "There aren't many artists your age who've been accepted at the palace, did you know that? Very few young men take art as seriously as you do."

Thankfully, Nebu's urge to confess the thoughts that racked his belly was stifled by Nji Mama's didactic penchant for repeating himself: "Just a few young men."

Nebu kept walking, his shoulders bent. The master's words weighed on him like an elephant. Nji Mama went on to say that to be an artist, a real artist, he would need to sacrifice something.

"Something you really love," he added. "That's the truth in your art."

7

The Palace of All Possible Dreams

The construction of the new palace was thrilling. It wasn't the first big project undertaken by Njoya's artists, but the one that required all their talents. Like any other project, it brought challenges, pains, joy, and it was the largest ever undertaken in Bamum land or, according to the sultan himself, "in all of Africa!" Njoya truly wanted it to be a Palace of All Dreams, the amalgamation of all the best dreams ever dreamed by the best master craftsmen of his time.

Accidents occurred, of course. When a worker fell from the wall he was building, worry was written on everyone's face, even if the man didn't die. "An evil spirit pushed him," they said.

As the man remembered it, he had done nothing wrong, nor seen anything strange around him. Nebu remembered the words of Nji Mama. When an artist whispered to him that a worksite that big required a "great sacrifice" to attain perfection, he trembled. Bertha's son wondered, Have all the artists working here sacrificed something they love? He was afraid.

Yet the worksite didn't seem cursed to him. In his eyes, the shapes of the palace emerging from the ground were the materialization of a vision. He worked all the harder to bring forth his own dreams. His master had showed him that art is an ethos, and that was enough. Ngungure's happy face was the guiding principle of his work, and he was grateful for it. He finally understood that the road between dreams and death is the path of destiny itself, and also that art is a victory over fate. He wanted his art to bring life back into being, a true testament to love.

Death arrived in Foumban's courtyards in a very unexpected way. One day the palace couriers ran through the city announcing that the whites had gone to war. No one—not Nebu nor anyone else—thought the whole world was at war. Especially since the sultanate lived in perfect harmony with its Bamiléké and Fulani neighbors. Let them fight, Nebu thought. It's not our war.

He wasn't the only one to think so. Who would have believed that a war between whites, fought in lands beyond the borders of the sultanate, would be met with anything but indifference by the Bamum? Still, Njoya had sent hundreds of men to join the columns of German colonial soldiers, and there was word of similar recruitments in the English colonies and especially in those of the French, where the African soldiers, commonly called *tirailleurs*, were known for never taking the time to aim. But that certainly didn't impress the sultan's archers, quite the contrary. Nebu thought this talk of war was no more than rumors. No one in Foumban imagined that a war between whites could result in battles pitting armies of black men against each other. Nevertheless, all the Bamum helped the Germans dig trenches around the sultanate's capital and barricade entryways with sandbags; and all the Bamum smiled softly when the German officer explained it was "to protect us." Us?

One afternoon the *askaris*, who had always behaved disrespectfully in Foumban, were seen running into houses to hide.

"They're coming," shouted the soldiers, tearing off their uniforms so they could die naked. "They're coming!"

"They're coming!"

Everyone hid, but no one asked just who "they" were. The hardest thing, of course, was hiding Herr Habisch, as well as the missionary Göhring and his white companions. But it was funny, too, for it was the first time the Bamum had seen the merchant Habisch, known for his habitual arrogance, shivering like a baby. Even Fräulein Wuhrmann, so used to giving orders like a man, trembled with a fear similar to the one she so often inspired in the German school's female students. The world is falling apart, Nebu thought.

"They" didn't come that day. But no one forgot the panic "they" wrought. The Cameroonian campaign went on for a whole year before war actually arrived in Foumban. For Nebu, who'd been ordered to bring food to the hiding Germans, it was a revelation. He'd seen Herr Habisch filled with despair as never before. Surrounded by his merchandise, which now felt like a burden, since it kept him from fleeing, the Swiss merchant was giving away for free what he previously would have sold or traded.

Let me note in passing that this is how Nebu acquired the portrait of Ngungure that he never could have afforded. War does have its virtues! A plate of *kpen*, corn with peanut sauce, was all it took. Herr Habisch soon transferred his wares to Nji Mama's attic only to realize that "they" weren't ever going to come. Still, Herr Habisch didn't go back on his decision, but kept his goods stored away and, from then on, spent every night with his wares, much to the amusement of everyone in Foumban. That's where he was, surrounded by mirrors, jackets, shoes, and bottles of whiskey when the English soldiers finally arrested him. He didn't resist, but simply said, "You'll need me, too."

To which the British soldiers replied, "Don't be so sure of it, old friend."

"Never fear," Habisch announced to the whole city. "I'll be back."

Fräulein Wuhrmann told the soldiers that she wasn't German, but Swiss, so neutral. An English soldier corrected her.

"I'm sorry, love, but there's no neutrality in Africa."

Later she'd change her story, claiming to be Belgian. But the British officer for whom she traced her complicated genealogy wasn't listening.

"Are there any more Germans in the city?" he asked, his voice dripping with sarcasm.

The arrival of the English in Foumban had been announced by the sound of machine-gun fire. That was in December 1915. Njoya's reaction was the same as when the Germans had knocked on the door of his city in 1902, and again when Lieutenant Hirtler—yes, that was his name—had arrived in 1903. Njoya greeted them at the main entrance, accompanied by all his advisers as well as soldiers, bearing a plate of eggs. His soldiers were unarmed, and the sultan warned Foumban to show no hostility "to the new arrivals," since, he said, "this isn't our war."

The English, however, had a very different understanding of their arrival in a conquered city. They thought that filling the sky with fire, smoke, and the sounds of gunfire, destroying the walls of the palace under construction instead of accepting the greetings of the local sovereign, would establish their authority in everyone's mind and erase all memories of the Germans. At the sound of machine-gun fire—*ratatatatatatat*—a sound they'd never heard before, the inhabitants of the city ran to hide, scattering frightened chickens and dogs. No soldier fired back. Only two people were wounded. A woman fell as she ran, jostled by the panicked crowd, and a child stubbed his toe on a rock. Oh, I forgot: a dog was killed, too, squashed when one of the palace walls, brought down by an English grenade, collapsed on top of it.

The English soldiers came into Foumban following this apocalyptic display of their weapons, overturning calabashes and breaking chairs. They were blacks, some of them Indian. Their uniforms were different from those of the *askaris*. Five British officers led their columns. Njoya's men spent hours trying to convince the population of Foumban to come out from hiding and greet the new arrivals. Everyone set about cleaning up their courtyards, dusting off their clothes, and calming their crying children. The squashed dog was found under the ruins only much later. It was just a side casuality. I must say that the people of Foumban weren't yet aware of the butchery that, in the trenches of France, Belgium, and parts of the Ottoman Empire, turned human beings into dust and invented genocide.

The English arrested the hidden Germans and confiscated their weapons. To celebrate their victory, they drank cases of Herr Habisch's beer, wine, and whiskey. They scrambled the eggs Njoya had offered them and demanded the best food the Bamum had to offer for their soldiers. Like everyone else, Nebu saw the Swiss merchant come out of Nji Mama's attic, his hands on his head, a rifle pointed at his back. He looked like a madman, all covered with dust. He was joined by the missionary Göhring, his wife and son, and Fräulein Wuhrmann. They were pitiful. No battles took place in Foumban. Nevertheless, the chaos that arrived in Bamum land that day, scattering chickens, squashing a dog, and making children cry, will still be referred to in the history books as World War I.

8

A Colony, Postwar

"My granddaughter, will you let me finish?"

That's how Sara took the floor. The young people from Nsimeyong can attest to it: suddenly there was no way for me to interrupt the flow of her words, to tell her what I had found about her father in the archives. In truth, I was also happy to drink from her memory's endless river. It cost me nothing to be quiet for a moment. As for Sara, she emerged exhausted from the tunnel of her past. Still, she could have taken a short break and listened to me! After all, my research had brought me dramatically closer to her birth.

Of all the things that Joseph Ngono regretted when he got back to Cameroon after the war of 1914–18—this is what I wanted to tell the doyenne—the worst by far was the loss of his books of poetry. She wanted him to be a poet, didn't she? He had decided to "go back home," as he put it, anticipating that his country would not have changed in the slightest since he'd left. The colony had been divided between the war's victors, the English and the French, and his hometown, Yaoundé, was now under French occupation. For him, that wasn't the most important thing, oh no! Most important was that he get back to his homeland. As far as he was concerned, the new flags wouldn't change the scent of the ground after a rain. The country's earth was still red, just as rich as ever. Its persistent color let Ngono look back on his life in Berlin with distance and detachment. For him, the colonizers would come and go; Cameroon itself was unchanging.

The Ewondo lecturer hadn't imagined that the many years he'd spent abroad, in Germany to boot, would render him suspect in the eyes of the French. He realized all too late that he had opened up his mind to take in the breadth of the world only to come back to a country held captive by colonial mentalities; that he had left the streets of Berlin, fleeing from the threat of Adolf and other scoundrels of his ilk, only to come back to a camp. How could he have imagined that he would leave the warmth of the Landlord's house only to be interrogated once again by the police? Ah, when he arrived, Joseph Ngono was struck head-on by the prosaic colonial life he'd long forgotten. "Life in a colony is hell," he'd often say afterward, reflecting on what happened to him upon his return.

Ngono was no longer a native. That was the crux of the problem, especially for the colonial administrators who still saw him as one. How many times did he have to squelch his desire to shout back in their faces, to insult them, or, better, just to curse them outright: "*Ilang!* Asshole!"

Or to fight as he had in Berlin?

Against Adolf?

How many times had he wanted to shatter the mustache of a French colonial officer? Ah, from time to time Ngono made do with grumbling his foul insult: "*Ilang nuazut!* Your asshole stinks!"

Or even, "*Belobo lobo!* Invaders!"

What really surprised me was that he came back to Cameroon without his wife. I found no document suggesting that she had been blocked from entering the protectorate. It wouldn't have surprised me if I had—anything is possible in the colonies. The ex-lecturer married another woman, Sala, soon after his arrival in Cameroon. This woman first bore him a daughter, Sara, then a son, Carl. Ngono was distracted when the Catholic priest registered his daughter in the church records and didn't notice that he'd inscribed "Sara" instead of "Sala." When it was time to name his son, Ngono thought of his happy past, especially of his best friend, Charles Atangana. He decided to write the name with a *C*, like the English, rather than with a German *K*.

The two friends met up again later, in August 1923, and told each other about their very different experiences. They recalled happily how they'd traveled to Germany together on a boat registered to the Woerman company. "We were so young!" They remembered everything they'd done, especially their experiences with white women.

"I've changed," said Charles Atangana, smiling.

"Really?" Ngono replied, pulling a pack of cigarettes from his pocket. "Tell me." Joseph still saw him as a ladies' man. He hit the packet against the back of his hand and pulled out two cigarettes, offering one to his friend. Yet it was Ngono who had things to tell, for the chief saw right then that he was missing two fingers. As always, without rushing, Ngono described the details of his fight in Berlin, rekindling an intricate memory of Adolf and his bloody mustache.

"Me too, I have sad stories to tell," Charles Atangana confessed.

He told about losing his first wife, Marie Biloa, in a car accident just a week after he'd returned from Spain. "The very first car accident in Yaoundé, can you imagine?" He admitted that the accident had really changed him.

"I became an entirely different man," he insisted. "Monogamous."

He paused for a long moment, as if to make his reasoning more evident.

"Now," he went on, "I've decided to avoid bad luck."

Hadn't Joseph Ngono's whole life been just a succession of misfortunes? Sara's father opted to keep quiet and agree with his friend; he even "forgot" to tell him that he had also gotten married, and to a "white woman." He forgot a lot more things, our dear Ngono. But what does it matter? The two friends were together again, bantering in German, just for fun. That day, Nsimeyong echoed with the laughter of their reinvented friendship, the happiness of a complicity that had emerged intact from history's furious trenches. They met up again several more times, and on one occasion Charles Atangana left the neighborhood quite smitten with his friend's sister. Word had it that he was blind drunk, but so what? He had met Ngono's youngest sister, Juliana, who'd been just a "little girl with a flat butt" the last time he'd seen her, kicking a ball around in the rain as if she were a little boy. Today she had become "a beautiful woman of marrying age."

Charles Atangana was so happy he decided to run straight off to the church with his "dear Juliana" so Father Vogt could set a date for them to stand "before the Lord, our God." Joseph Ngono could only rejoice at giving his sister to his best friend; he agreed to be a witness at their marriage.

9

The Sultan's Soul Is an Open Book, Written in a Mysterious Alphabet

Very little of note happened in Mount Pleasant. The arrival of Ibrahim, Nji Mama's younger brother, shifted Njoya's perimeter somewhat. Although not part of the princely nobility, the Nguri, that man had, as he put it, abandoned the plebes and their foolishness. In short, that man, who broadcast his aristocracy through the tilt of his hat and his catlike eyes, infused new life into Ngutane's veins. It seemed that she chose her wardrobe just to garner one of his winks. Besides, the doyenne told me, the dance had returned to her steps, just as when she was in her glory back in Foumban. If until then she had found no partner who could keep up with her, in Ibrahim she suddenly had a man whose sense of style revealed a vanity beyond compare. And the master calligrapher was her childhood love, too. Sometimes, when the two of them entered Njoya's bedchamber, it was as if they were staging a play.

"Wow!" everyone exclaimed.

Of course rumors began to fly. After all, Ngutane was married to one of her father's ministers, who had stayed behind in Foumban. But Njoya had other things to worry about. With help from Ibrahim, Nji Mama, or anyone else, he began to move about, one step after the other, in the rooms where he was confined. Father Vogt's wheelchair had made a big difference, yes. Everyone, including Ngutane, raved about its practicality. All the sultan had to do was get out of bed. She'd push him along Mount Pleasant's corridors. The master artists had studied that chair until they were exhausted. Monlipèr had used all his talent as a blacksmith; Nji Shua had called on the spirits of his carpentry; even Nji Mama had joined in the artists' conspiracy. The seat the three of them had built together, however, proved dangerous for someone who was learning to walk again. The easy simplicity of the prelate's chair was far better than the magnificence of their rolling version of the legendary throne, the Mandu Yenu.

The three men weren't used to defeat, and tears ran from Monlipèr's eyes when Njoya finally chose the wheelchair that, according to the master, was an insult to the Bamum and their genius. It was a moment of triumph for Father Vogt, who spoke of God's will and paid more frequent visits to the sultan.

"God's grace is infinite," said Father Vogt, "for He is love."

He came to Mount Pleasant not only to check on the patient's health, but especially because the two had begun a conversation on faith and the washing away of sin, which the priest wanted to continue. If you'd told him that his arguments were just awkward reiterations of the same theses, antitheses, and syntheses of Christian conversion that the missionary Göhring had already exchanged with Njoya, he wouldn't have believed you. Father Vogt's hopes of converting Njoya burned all the brighter since the sultan, his interlocutor, was no longer the thirty-year-old who had played chess with Göhring in 1906, making him read and reread passages of the Old Testament translated into his language. And Father Vogt was convinced that Njoya was no longer the man who, back in Foumban, had had his scribes copy whole passages from the Bible while, unbeknownst to the German missionary, he wrote his own Book of Faith.

This was 1932, after all! This Njoya, living in exile, had looked death in the eyes, and, Father Vogt believed, no one could emerge unchanged from such an encounter, not even a sultan. The priest just needed to roll him along the corridors of his home in exile, through Mount Pleasant's courtyards, and soon the old pagan would shed the tears of his new faith. So great was the missionary's confidence that he had written in his circular #113 of the advent of a "triumphant future." His ambitious text concluded with the word "miracle." "A miracle has awoken the hills of Nsimeyong!"

So there they were, the sultan in his wheelchair and, behind him, like spirits, the brothers Nji Mama and Ibrahim. There they were, Njoya and Father Vogt, once again waging the battle of light against darkness or, as translated in the language of colonialism, the struggle between civilization and barbarism. Sometimes Ngutane listened to their exchanges (who else could referee such a combat?), even if only to protect her father from expending himself in useless arguments. Ah, isn't it a stroke of luck that Nebu was right there, glued to the sultan's side, even in the most private moments of his life? Isn't it a stroke of luck that he was there to fan the sultan's face in those moments of effort? That it was he who held a parasol to protect him from the sun?

Only once did the missionary look at him suspiciously. No one had told Njoya that it was the quick thinking of his shadow that had saved him from death. Nebu's silent eyes repressed his own story, pushing it down into the depths where no monarch ever strayed. Would it have been different had he spoken? The sultan's shadow has no need for a voice. No. The subaltern can't speak, and no one would have listened to him anyway. When the cleric suggested one day that the sultan leave his room for a bit of fresh air, Nji Mama intervened. He had understood Father Vogt's plan.

"The sultan can't be seen naked," he said. "It's forbidden."

How so? The ailing sultan is naked. It's that simple. Njoya's authority relied on restrictions. It was heightened by barriers similar to the thornbushes that surrounded the women's quarters in Foumban, where his wives lived. Even seeing him drink was forbidden. The right to look into his private chambers, his bedchamber, his bed, especially when he was weak and ailing, was a privilege possessed by some and not by others. Father Vogt knew that chance had brought him into a place where he had no right to be, but he wasn't content to leave it at that. He knew that his pale skin trumped all the restrictions built up around the monarch's body over a four-hundred-year reign. Colonialism had put the priest on a high horse, and he used that authority when necessary, his arrogance dictated by his certainty that he was following God's path.

For Father Vogt, Njoya was just a man, and what's more, a sinner. After all, hadn't Father Vogt himself, dressed in a doctor's garb, pulled him from the jaws of a certain death? How could anyone forget that the sultan's new throne was just the bicycle the priest had used to spread faith and sow miracles across Yaoundé? Ngutane was the only one who would occasionally interrupt his crazed sermons, under the pretext that her father was tired and had no more ears. Father Vogt would then bow out because in those moments she wore a face that no man (not even a white priest) would dare contradict. But even Ngutane couldn't assess the dizzying depths of the fatigue that had turned Njoya's body to rubber. The sultan wasn't just tired; truth be told, he was consumed by guilt.

Let's be clear: Njoya was pursued by nightmares. In his nightmares, he saw again and again Ngosso Din, the secretary and emissary of Manga Bell; Njoya had betrayed him to the Germans at the start of the war, an act that resulted in his being hanged for treason alongside his master.

Here is what had happened: having learned that war had broken out in Europe, Rudolf Manga Bell, the paramount chief of the Douala, who had studied law in Germany, wrote a long "Petition Addressed to All Cameroonian Chiefs." One short sentence summarized his arguments: "The Germans will lose the war." This wasn't his first petition, but it was the first that he hadn't addressed to the Germans. Manga Bell had long been in conflict with the colonial authorities. He had spent the months leading up to the war writing petitions to the Reichstag, the German parliament, and to German deputies; he had even sent his secretary, Ngosso Din, to Berlin to try to convince kindly ears in the German fatherland of the justice of his cause. These efforts had not produced the desired results; even the most fervent champions of democracy in the German parliament, the Social Democrats, had rejected his complaints. So for Manga Bell, the war was an unheard-of opportunity. In 1914 he turned toward Cameroon, sending emissaries inland, hoping to build a coalition of Cameroonian forces to chase the Germans from "our country." Ah, the famous coalition! To be brief, it never saw the light of day, and Njoya was the first to start digging its grave.

The sultan recognized the signs of his impending fall the day he saw his German friends in chains, at the mercy of the English. Then he thought of Ngosso Din, whose plans he had revealed to the Germans, and realized that he had rallied to the losing side. He also realized that he had betrayed the cause—which hadn't yet fully emerged from the mists—of what Manga Bell's envoy had called "our country," and "Cameroon" as well. Njoya hadn't ever stopped blaming himself for his fateful shortsightedness. Had he paid more attention to the news in the papers read to him, he told himself, he would have foreseen the German defeat as clearly as had Manga Bell. But he only actually read German newspapers, and one of them, the *Deutsches Kolonialblatt*, had announced in a big headline that Göhring read to him, *"Niederlage ist kein deutsches Wort"*: Defeat is not a German word.

With "ifs," anything is possible. In some sense, it was only logical that he adopt such warlike sentiments; after all, four hundred years of Bamum history had shown him that defeat was not a Shümum word either. What instinct could have whispered in his ear that the "invincible kaiser" and with him all his people were lost in a rather demented delusion? He should have taken Ngosso Din's predictions seriously, for Ngosso had been in Germany; he should have listened to the geostrategic analysis of his master Manga Bell, who had lived in Germany as well—then he wouldn't be in this place! Had he just looked beyond the borders of Bamum land on the map he himself had traced, he would have realized that to hold on to the colony, the Germans needed to fight the English to the west and the French in the east and in the south. He would have understood that only a miracle could let them win a war fought on so many fronts. Just looking at the Bamum map, Njoya could have foreseen what would happen in Germany. He had been blinded by his friendship with the Germans, that was the fact of the matter. The names of Ngosso Din, Manga Bell, and Samba Martin Paul were on his lips the night he collapsed in his bedchamber. They had come to him in a furious nightmare. History had proved them right: the Germans had lost the war on all fronts.

10

The Strident Echo of Names and Deeds

How strange the echoes of words! Even whispers are enough to awaken a sleeping infant. When returning to the matron's bedroom late at night, Nebu sometimes heard voices repeating old stories; sometimes, though, they told of real people's lives. They weren't exchanges among characters in a tale, but actual dialogues between people he knew. Not the whisperings of figures long gone, but of lovers united in exile. He heard the squeaking of doors opening after he'd passed by. He heard furtive steps behind him. Sometimes a woman chuckling in the dark. Sometimes he also caught the sounds of lovers. He knew that this licentious din was not born of his dreams. He also knew they were sounds children weren't supposed to hear, so he hurried on.

One day he stopped when he heard a burst of laughter at the end of a corridor. He looked up and down the passage, although he should have looked the other way. He saw a caftan and recognized the silhouettes of the master calligrapher, Ibrahim, and Ngutane. Nebu saw them disappear under the moonlight, complicit in their steps. He knew right then that he shouldn't have happened upon those secretive exchanges. He tried to convince himself it was just a dream, another bit of the endless reverie he'd been living since his arrival in Mount Pleasant, since his own face—a little girl's face—had disappeared into a multitude of rooms, a sea of words, and the uncertainty written on the faces of the banished men and women washed up there on the hills of exile. Yet the kid couldn't lie to himself that evening: "Just more stories," he said.

This time it was Ngutane, Nji Mongu herself, who was the protagonist. Nebu knew what kind of earthquake the echo of this adulterous love in exile would cause if revealed to the chattering mouths of the idle nobles. He knew what thunderbolts would be released in Njoya's bedchamber. Yes, how strange the echoes of words, the doyenne told me, especially in Mount Pleasant!

Listen, she went on, even Njoya's favorites, the ones he made love to the night of his attack, didn't understand who he was calling when he said the name Manga; how could they? Manga, that's also the name of the town where Njoya had met his first rival, in a very bloody battle from which he had emerged victorious. That was in 1894, years before the arrival of the first whites in the sultanate. Njoya had won that war thanks to an alliance with the Fulani of the north, who had taught him the art of cavalry. The alliance with the Fulani hadn't just secured his power, it had opened a new era for the Bamum; in exchange for their help, Njoya had given the Fulani permission to introduce Islam throughout his territory. It was then, when he saw a copy of the Koran, that the sultan fell in love with the chattering silence of books. When he saw the Arabic letters snaking their way across pages, he thought of inventing his own writing system. In short, Manga was the source of Njoya's grandeur.

How strange the echoes of places!

Really!

Could Njoya's two wives have known that Manga also named the site of his decline? Mata and Pena were too young for that story, too much in love with their man to feel anything but jealousy. Had they really studied his life, they would have known that this very word "Manga" was for Njoya as much an "open sesame" as a curse. At once storied—figuring in all the songs of praise sung about the sultan—and buried away in the shameful depths of his soul. The light of day and a silenced shade. Oh Mata and Pena, why, why didn't you see the depths of the monster that was swallowing up your man? For Njoya's body was attacked not by the forces of desire, but by the demons of history hidden in his veins: he, Cameroon's gravedigger.

"Ngosso! Samba! Manga!" he shouted.

And the two women thought he was lost in the antechambers of his climax when his body stiffened, his eyes grew fixed, his hand sank into the flesh of his own chest.

"Manga! Samba! Ngosso!"

Pena's voice awoke the main courtyard; she had thought that her husband was calling out for three other women to join their frolicking in bed. If the sultan needed those three ladies to pull him from his den, there was nothing she could do about it. Njoya had so many wives that even if you really tried, it was impossible to know all their names.

"Samba! Manga! Ngosso!"

Mata repeated her husband's cries.

"Manga! Ngosso! Samba!"

Njoya was also shouting. It seemed that the three horsemen of the past had suddenly returned, bursting into his apartments to demand the return of the lives he had betrayed, to remind him of this country, Cameroon, whose genesis he had delayed. They sent his wives rushing out into the courtyard of his home, the better to punish his scandalous shortsightedness.

Who, just who really could have known that the treaty between the monarch and his death was in fact a strange pact he had made with the burdensome guilt that was eating away at his soul like a ferocious worm? Who could have told his wives as they wailed in the courtyard that what was really causing him to suffer was something so private, so intimate that it wanted to stay hidden in the deepest recesses of his bed? Ah, if only Mata or Pena could have known!

How strange the echoes of names.

Really.

When Nebu entered the sultan's bedchamber on the day of his apoplexy, the monarch was still offering up those strange names and battling with devils. Slaves were running around, all convinced that the hour of final calm was knocking on the door of Nchare Yen's most illustrious descendant. So what pushed the boy out onto Nsimeyong's paths? How strange the echoes of names! That child, who began to run through the forest, rushing toward Father Vogt's church, envisioned, more than anything, his own liberation. By running away, he saved the sultan from a very spiteful story and transformed a little girl's suffering into the key to the salvation of an accursed monarch.

Njoya was caught up in a tornado from which even his most talented doctors couldn't save him, shaken by an explosion for which the sultanate's medical text, the *Nga Fu Nku Lap*, had no intelligent answer. He felt his body coming apart, ripped to pieces by the army ants of his best-kept secret. Torn from a nameless place where it had been entombed alongside the bodies of his shame, which were shrouded by nothing but his soul, Njoya's carnivorous past was eating him alive. Sitting in the wheelchair Father Vogt had built for him, Njoya knew that some calls for revenge never fade away. He had barely escaped. But anger's punishing flames would soon return, and once again he would have to face them alone. Maybe this time his body would prove too weak for the task. Yes, Njoya wanted to be saved from his past.

First from the catechisms of the missionary Göhring, and then from Father Vogt, he had learned that repentance was the only path to salvation. Yet—how could he forget?—it was Njoya's confession to Göhring that had alerted the German colonial forces, putting them on the trail of the budding nationalist conspiracy, for the pastor had repeated to the governor those three names the sultan had confided in him, one friend to another: Samba, Manga, Ngosso.

How strange, how strange the echoes of deeds.

"Can your God forgive the living for what they don't foresee?" Njoya asked, his struggle to speak tearing his face into a grimacing mask.

Father Vogt leaned his ear closer. Yet he had heard the question. He rubbed his beard and smiled, trying to take on an air of wisdom that his years in the tropics hadn't produced. Here is a man whose conversion won't be the result of the magic of sweets! A man whose suffering is a mystery! Clearly the sultan sought a way out of his torture, but what pained him so? Njoya didn't just want to be saved from his past; he wanted to be absolved of a future that was taking ever more unexpected turns, starting with Yaoundé, where he was exiled, which had been named the capital of Cameroon in 1921.

The history of his people filled his body. All he needed was to put just one foot in his courtyard to see it come to life, to see hundreds of people born anew—dancing, singing, shouting, ecstatic! Hadn't those thousand voices joined together to wail out those three accursed names and crush his body? Those people who filled his home, who had always filled his courtyard, would judge his actions. They all knew why Njoya was suffering; yes, he was convinced of that. Those evanescent storytellers, those who told of worlds of madness, were his paradise and his hell. That's why their stories, stronger than medicine, had swathed the walls of the room of his salvation. But didn't all those who had orchestrated a ballet of the dead in his quarters know the truth? The story of Manga, Ngosso, and Samba? Didn't the tellers of impossible tales know Cameroon's history? What was there to confess?

"Does your God forgive what the living can't forget?" the sultan started again, spitting out each word with difficulty.

Father Vogt thought for a moment before answering.

11

Are the French So Very Different from the Germans?

Let's head back to Foumban, fourteen years earlier, in 1916, for that's when the seeds of Njoya's doubt were sown. And for good reason. After nine months of occupation, the English left the capital of the sultanate in a military parade that woke everyone. A secret agreement with the French had persuaded them to abandon the city they had previously terrorized with their machine guns. Before leaving Foumban, the English officer offered Njoya his red pickup truck, the one he had brought to the city just a few weeks after his arrival. It all happened so quickly! Full of pride, the white soldier had shown the sultan his vehicle, telling him it was an example of King George's grandeur, "a model of British technological prowess."

It was, to be sure, a pretty old truck, but it had proved its strength on ungrateful hills and some wild paths. Njoya, of course, was happy to have a motorcar. Unlike the Fulani books he had leafed through and admired so long ago, or the Koran that he had immediately decided to imitate, the vehicle awoke in him the simple desire of possession. He didn't need his master engineers, not Monlipèr, the blacksmith, not Nji Mama, the architect, not even Ibrahim, the calligrapher. All he needed was to sit down on the machine's seat and move his hands and legs the way the Englishman had shown him. In his enthusiasm the sultan failed to question the reasons behind this sudden show of magnanimity on the part of a man who had previously taken such joy in humiliating him. Oh, Njoya ought to have wondered whether this car was his compensation for the Franco-British treachery!

But let's leave that aside for now, shall we?

To show his goodwill, Njoya greeted the French forces with a speech in which he promised his cooperation and, in a further gesture of appeasement, also offered them, as he had the Germans, a plate of fresh eggs. The soldiers who raised the tricolored flag sang the *Marseillaise*, forgetting that the crowds gathered to watch were by then quite confused about all these different flags and songs. The sultan wasn't wearing his ceremonial garb, something many interpreted as a sign of his displeasure. Things changed very little at first, except perhaps that the soldiers of the French forces (they all came from Congo) didn't pray kneeling on mats as those of the English had done. They weren't Muslim. Another important difference: the French commander didn't move into the building where the previous German and English officers had set up their headquarters. No one weighed the significance of this, maybe because the Bamum were blinded by the all-too-great similarity among the faces that paraded through their courtyards. Yet the rituals varied so greatly from one group of colonizers to another. Oh, if only Njoya and the rest of the Bamum had reflected on the differences among the French, the English, and the Germans!

Some among them were blinded by things entirely unrelated to the spectacles of the occupation. Nebu, for example, was so obsessed by his experiments in the workshops of the new palace that the soldiers and their uniforms, their anthems and their flags had no effect on him at all. The search for perfection was the only thing on his mind. And how! One day, however, as he was gazing out the window of his bedchamber, the silhouette of a woman heading up the street caught his eye. She was a slave, and therefore naked. But her face was Ngungure's. He closed his eyes and opened them again to be sure of what he was seeing. Bertha's son would have sworn it was true: she was the embodiment of all his dreams, the exact image of the only woman he had ever really loved.

"That's Ngungure," he exclaimed joyfully. "That's her!"

He stared at her intently, unable to believe his eyes. Oh! He saw the woman's head, her neck and shoulders, and her hands rising up to balance a basket of tomatoes on her head. No, it just wasn't possible! So he examined her legs and her feet. He watched her body as it moved, and he was captivated. He saw how her feet gripped the ground as she advanced so supplely, how her belly danced in rhythm with the slight movements of her silhouette. Just like Ngungure! Time and time again he had seen his beloved in his dreams, but never before had she appeared so perfectly. And yet he wasn't dreaming.

When the woman passed in front of him, he called out, "Ngungure." She didn't answer. He whistled; she didn't turn around. He didn't complain, though, quite the contrary.

Still as proud as ever! he thought.

Once again he looked her over from head to toe; his eyes alit on her shoulders, then rolled down to measure the volume of her behind. Nebu noticed that her buttocks moved in perfect symmetry, following the stately back-and-forth of her steps. He was amazed at how Ngungure's back called out to be measured by a sculptor's knife: in his mind he saw himself cutting it into two equal parts, split open from top to bottom like a papaya. She spread apart and scattered her seeds without slowing her pace. Yet the bright flash of her blazing flesh helped the sculptor as he hurried to reshape her scattered parts. Because, as he tapped on his own temple, Nebu was quickly recalculating the mathematical equations he knew by heart. He wanted to be sure that it really was his beloved, without disturbing the surprising rhythm of her apparition, without freezing—and thereby dissolving—the gracefulness with which she had offered herself up to him.

He was torn between the joy of having found her again and the terrifying thought that his discovery would erase her from his sight. He thought for a moment about the girl he had glimpsed on the river shore, the washer girl from Dschang, and he remembered how fleeting beauty can sometimes be. He did not want to lose his Ngungure again. He ran to his room and grabbed his sheet, which he wrapped quickly around his body. He threw one corner of the cloth over his left shoulder, as a Fulani woman would do, and wrapped his beloved's red pagne around his head. Then he set off after the woman.

"I'll be back," he said to his mother.

"Where are you going?" Bertha's voice asked from the backyard.

"I'm not going far," her son replied. "I'll be right back."

12

The Mathematics of a Woman's Body

Luckily for Nebu, his mother didn't protest. He realized only too late that he had forgotten his notebook.

"Argh!" he groaned. "I always forget it when I need it most!"

For a moment he considered going back to the house for it, but the thought of running into his mother dressed as he was made him keep going. He was happy that his woman's disguise allowed him to observe this newfound Ngungure freely, without being harassed by ill-mannered colonial soldiers. He wanted to capture her in movement. For a moment he was enchanted by the motions of his beloved's hands. Then it was her feet, then her shoulders. The perfect balance of the whole appeared to him, a synthesis that wrenched a cry of ecstasy from his lips. Yet he kept silent. Instead his eyes dived into the woman's steps, licking the footprints she left in the dust. He saw her place one foot on the ground, then the other, zigzagging slightly.

That's when his thoughts turned to animals. First, to a horse. Then a goat. Of course he thought of a cat, but also of a bird in flight. For this woman's behind was as harmonious as those that belonged to the animals he had seen trotting or taking off in flight. The elasticity of her steps evoked the voluptuous movements of a pigeon on the ground. And Nebu was reminded, as well, of a reptile's sinuous advance; he noticed the similarities between a gecko's slippery movements and the steps of his dear Ngungure along the red earth.

Nebu had never really paid attention to animals in flight or on foot. Nor had he ever dreamed of their movements. In order to concentrate on the shapes of the woman, he slowed her pace in his mind's eye, as a musician might with a new song, to better grasp the notes he had just heard. He promised himself he would study how animals moved later. On Ngungure walked, each of her steps adding to the languorous harmony, shimmering with the brilliance of a glowworm.

The sculptor was lost in his thoughts, comparing animals and humans, sounds and steps, bodies and music, when suddenly he realized that the woman had stopped. She greeted another woman. He noticed that the aura projected by her body at rest was identical to that of her body in motion. It was as if she were suspended midstep. She wasn't moving, but her body still suggested movement. Walking was inscribed in her stance, like one sculpture in multiple poses. The result was breathtaking. There it was, the unifying principle he had always been searching for, the magical number.

"That's it," he cried, putting his hand to his mouth to muffle his voice. "That's the formula!"

He watched the woman as she stood and walked, and at the same moment, his mind saw a statue perfectly still. His fingers were tingling. He wanted to shape his Ngungure, to sculpt her, re-create her right there where she stood. Because her body and her pose were perfection—of that he was sure.

"That's it," he mumbled into the palm of his hand. "The perfect body is the body of a slave!"

He had spoken out loud. Ngungure turned around. He tried to hide, fearing that his presence would be discovered too soon. He also didn't want to shatter the pose struck by the woman's body. Thankfully, since he was dressed as a woman, she didn't notice him. On the contrary, he was able to observe all the more closely how her shape shifted as she turned. The chiasmus of their respective gazes intrigued him, even though he didn't register it fully. Everything had happened so quickly, he had no time to dwell on this new mathematics of the body.

Ngungure soon left her companion and continued on; Nebu followed after her. They went by the baobab that marks the center of

Foumban, going down and back up the hilly paths; they passed by houses and the headquarters of the French official, Prestat; they turned several corners and soon arrived in the women's quarter. They crossed the iron market, where men paused in their work to steal a glance, grasping at the woman with their eyes as she passed. Then they went by the old palace, where the idle nobles gathered. Some people were shaving a neighbor's head; others were tuning their musical instruments or playing *ngeka*. Everyone was waiting for the sultan to appear.

Ngungure didn't speak with any of the noblewomen who sat in their courtyard cooling themselves with a raffia fan or chatting as they worked on their weaving. Nebu glimpsed several silhouettes inside the palace but quickly focused back on his model. A man greeted her; she responded with a bow. She hurried along, the suppleness of her body tracing identical shapes with each stride.

Nebu added this vision of her body's perfection to all the others he had amassed in his dreams. Everything was drawn so clearly in his mind that, had he sat down at that very instant, he could have reproduced it on a slate, just as Nji Mama did with the buildings he constructed: from memory. He would have set down the angle of her feet, her shoulders, and her hands as they delicately balanced the basket of tomatoes on her head. Bertha's son concluded that a body is but the sum of an endless array of triangles.

His face lit up with a smile at the thought of this mathematical beauty before him. Nothing was held back, each element revealed in turn, one after the other. What he saw, he saw in the immediate perfection of its presence. It seemed as if he could distinguish each of the woman's muscles as she walked, each of her bones, each of her nerves, and that he could calculate the exact length of each step, and each one after that. He could not hold back the elegy that burst from his lips.

A poem to Beauty.

"Woman," he began, adjusting his pagne, "you are my master."

13

A Man Revealed in a Burst of Laughter

"Njapdunke!"

Nebu never could have said whether he had crossed Foumban once, twice, three, ten, or twenty times. His path was dictated by that of the woman; the shapes of her body had captured his soul, his entire soul. He had entered the spice market without even realizing it. Roused suddenly by the scent of a potent blend of spices, he found himself surrounded by hills of peri peri, salt, ginger, onions, curry, and tomatoes in an endless array of colors. In fact he had stopped only because a woman with a yellow scarf wrapped tightly around her head had hailed his Ngungure by a different name.

She had called her Njapdunke. Yes, Njapdunke, the name of the sultan's deceased mother. At that very moment a treacherous flame sparked in the sculptor's belly, pushing a diabolical cloud of smoke through his lungs, cutting off his breath, and setting his nostrils ablaze. He automatically opened his mouth and quickly covered it with both hands. He squelched his breath by exhaling as hard as he could. It was as if, emerging from a long tunnel or surfacing from the darkness of a curse, he suddenly came back to his senses.

"Njapdunke," repeated the woman who had stopped the slave. She pointed at Nebu. "*That man* is following you!"

Nebu was paralyzed by those words: "that man." Just then the turbulent fire descended from his nostrils into his throat and took a quick turn around his chest before heading into his belly, whence it emerged with a force that opened his mouth and loosened his un-suspecting hands.

"Ah, ah, ah . . ."

He found relief in a powerful sneeze that shook all the spice stands around him.

"Ah-choo!"

The cloth he had tied over his shoulder in his efforts to pass as a Fulani woman came undone and fell at his feet. He bent down to pick it up, but the slave woman he had been following didn't give him the chance to cover himself up.

"Just what do you want?" she asked, staring him right in the eyes. "What do you want, you rat?"

As she spoke, she pointed her finger threateningly at his nose, all the while keeping her basket balanced on her head. Another woman with a shaved head abandoned her display of spices to join her. She spoke to the sculptor in a more conciliatory tone.

"Why don't you just leave her alone, eh?"

"*Woudidididi!*" cried the woman with the tightly wound scarf, drawing the attention of the whole market. "Here's a man who wants to become a woman!"

Lost as he had been in his own reflections, how could Nebu have realized that so many eyes were locked on him? He was shocked and confounded to discover the market's collective gaze. They were women's eyes—slaves' eyes one and all—peering from behind their merchandise. Never before had Nebu stopped in the spice market, and in that very instant, the captive nudity of its population para-lyzed him. Woken from his calculations of a woman's body in motion, he found himself surrounded by a hostile crowd. He was a man, the only man, and he wanted just one thing: to cover up his now naked body.

The women wouldn't let him be.

"You thought she was off to see her boyfriend?" they teased.

Nebu's body refused to obey any of his wishes; his repeated coughs kept stripping him bare. The women started making com-ments, trying to outdo each other. Each time he sneezed, they laughed and clapped their hands.

"God is giving you the punishment you deserve!"

But none of them knew just what Nebu was up to.

"Did you think she was cheating on you?"

"You don't trust her, huh?"

"Oh, men!"

The woman who had just spoken erupted in a strange laugh, covering her mouth with the palms of her hands and doubling over, like a rooster dancing around a hen.

"He-a-heeee!"

Her friends replied in unison: "Woooooo-hoo!"

The woman with the orchestral laugh turned toward Nebu and got right up in his face, as if the laughing chorus of women gave her a voice she wouldn't have had on her own. "So, you don't trust your woman?"

Her laugh united the crowd. Even the woman who had spoken to the sculptor in a conciliatory tone now mocked him.

"Just look at this man," she said to a few women who had stopped out of curiosity, now called as witnesses to masculine idiocy. "He's so jealous he can't even speak!"

"So jealous, let me tell you!"

"So excited that he can't let his woman go anywhere, right?"

The impossible collection of gourds filled with colorful spices that she balanced on her head had turned her into a walking perfume store. She was talking and huffing with laughter, all at once. Everyone followed her lead. A few women left, dragging their children behind them, shocked by the brutal language of the marketplace, but others continued to heap shame on Nebu with their foul words.

"It's typical, don't you see?"

"My husband is the same way."

"All men are the same."

"All men!"

"Allah!"

"They've just got one thing on their mind!"

All the women shouted together: "Women!"

"No," said the woman with the shaved head, "their *bangalas*!"

The spice market exploded in a single laugh. Some women were holding on to their neighbors' shoulders, others lifted their faces up toward the sun, slapping a leg or a knee or clapping their hands.

The woman Nebu had followed was laughing too. And how! Her face contorted with laughter, she abandoned him to the pack. She pointed an accusing finger at Nebu's head, wrapped in Ngungure's pagne. She was choking with laughter. Another woman tried to calm her down, calling Nebu a "crazy man."

"What a crazy man," she said, "dressing up like a woman to follow his wife! How crazy is that!"

"Have you ever seen such a thing?"

"What?"

"A man dressed up as a woman."

"Forget him," the shaved-head woman said to Njapdunke. "He's just like all the rest."

"Ah-achoo!" Nebu exploded.

The women no longer even noticed the explosive sneezes that prevented him from covering himself up. Their comments kept coming all the faster.

"Men are all the same!"

"All of them!"

"He's no different."

"All he has is just one little finger . . ."

"Just one . . ."

Never had Nebu ever felt so naked, never. He fled back home without his cloth. Still, he tried to retain the image he had captured of the woman, the formula for a woman caught mid-step that he had discovered in the chaos. He wanted to sculpt the woman of his dreams in the shapes of the woman he had observed. What did it matter if she was a bitch? He was determined to sculpt Ngungure in her form. He had just dreamed of Ngungure with his eyes wide open, and he didn't want to question the reality of what he had measured. He was freed from his dreams, and at long last, he could create. The vision of this woman on the street encouraged him, and the laughter of the market women infused his hands with the rage he needed. The infinite dream of reality filled his mind with a patience that had escaped him until then. That's how he became his own master, the master of his dreams. Nebu hadn't written his thoughts down in a notebook. But he would do it soon enough in the only statue he would ever produce.

14

The Survey of Pain

If life is full of coincidences, from the most incredible to the commonplace, it is also full of missed chances. While Nebu followed the slave woman across Foumban, Njoya, accompanied by his masters and their assistants, was crisscrossing the streets of his city to map its topography. Njoya had been pushed to undertake this task by the French colonial administration's increasingly evident arrogance. He had been surprised by the arrival of the new authority, which had moved into the sultanate before he'd even been told why the English had left. Some surprising details caught his attention, especially the signature on the official French response to his speech welcoming them, which informed him that the headquarters in Dschang, in Bamiléké land—the Bamiléké whom the Bamum had previously defeated—were now more important than those in Foumban, a city more than four hundred years old.

"If the French prefer the bush," Ibrahim had railed to all the notables, "let them go to Dschang!"

Yet Ibrahim couldn't help but see what was really going on: parts of the territory held by the ancestor Nchare Yen, pieces of land for which thousands of Bamum had, over the centuries, lost their lives, were falling into French hands without their sultan's consent. Njoya had been the one to offer land to the Germans, welcoming them into his city and his land. The English had imposed themselves with their machine guns. What about the French?

"Who do they think they are?" snapped an indignant Nji Mama.

"It's time to lay claim to our land," the sultan replied, "to map out our country."

With a team of a dozen people he explored all of Foumban's quarters and met with the landowners. The heads of the most important families were mobilized. Even the most respected slaves were called on to take part.

"The land is yours and no one else's," Njoya told them. "You know better than anyone the boundaries of your compound."

Naturally, he began with the gardens of the new palace. Then he moved on to the baobab, in the center of Foumban. The city's inhabitants took his appearance in their homes as an opportunity to air their complaints, to tell him their stories. And they had a lot to complain about—oh, yes, so many things to tell him! Accusations against the family chiefs, the Nji, against the whole noble class, the Mbansi. Hundreds of complaints about freemen, about men altogether, about forced labor, about the work done by noblewomen, not to mention their objections to new taxes.

"You should work," Njoya told the noblewomen, "if you want to pay your taxes."

"If it were only the taxes, Alareni," said a man, stammering respectfully but clearly distraught. "If it were only the taxes."

Njoya waited for him to finish; his neighbor cut in.

"Now we have to pay our slaves."

"Like any other workers."

"If you can't pay them," the sultan said, "well, they just won't work for you any longer."

"Mfon Bamum," an anxious man asked the Bamum chief, "do women now have the right to leave their husband?"

"They've always had that right," Njoya replied. "They've always had it. It's up to you to learn how to keep your wives satisfied."

And the sultan laughed.

Everyone felt relaxed around him.

"It's up to *you* to be your wives' lovers," he continued.

He stressed "you," staring right at the men. He had left his palace to draw a map of his country, and the land's voices were grabbing hold of his feet like mud after a rain. Everything was spiraling out of his control; the thousands of complaints that filled his ears signaled the slow but certain erosion of his land and asked him to fight against the storm brewing on the horizon. The more information he and his assistants collected, the more his ears were filled with complaints about land that had been lost. The ground's pain was a solemn call to action, one he didn't really want to hear, because he didn't want to challenge the French administration.

Nji Mama, whom Njoya had entrusted with the task of using all the collected information to sketch a map of Foumban, couldn't close his ears to the words rising up from the earth. His artistic soul, of course, was captivated by the chart on which he had noted, one after the other, the bits of information his assistants gave him; yet the city streets he traced on a large sheet of paper could not be kept silent forever.

"The map is speaking," he said. "The country is speaking."

Nji Mama imagined Njoya enthralled by this definitive picture of his country's capital. Oh, the master architect did everything in his power to satisfy the sultan's artistic urges. But he couldn't stem the flow of painful murmurs coming from the Bamum. No one beside the sultan could know that this map was the last desperate attempt to grab hold of a handful of earth under a torrential rain. The song rising from the ground revealed a dangerous void growing in its depths. The architect's pulse raced when he marked the location of the French headquarters in the middle of the map, writing beneath it in Roman letters, "Lieutenant Prestat." He stopped, read the name over repeatedly, and sighed heavily. He felt that this name did not belong on his map, not on Njoya's map. He erased it carefully and stood there contemplating his work's liberation, lost in his own thoughts.

15

A Woman Is a City, Unself-conscious

Nebu had been standing in front of the door to his master's workshop for some time. He wanted to tell Nji Mama that he had finally discovered the formula he'd been looking for and solved the equation that had obsessed him for so long. He wanted to tell him he'd found the solution to the mystery of how women move by adding up all the triangles that formed a woman, a woman with Ngungure's face. Then he saw the sadness in the old man's eyes and decided to come back later. That's when his stupid sneezing started up again.

"Come in," Nji Mama said, noticing his apprentice standing at the door to his workshop. "Come in, my son."

It would have been far better if only Nebu had been able to come up with a quick excuse. Instead, he just sneezed again.

"Do you have a cold?" his master asked, patting his shoulder.

Nji Mama's face was creased with worry on account of this sculptor. Nebu blamed the uncertain weather, the shift from the dry season to rain, the scent of the city's red earth, and what else? Still, he agreed to his master's suggestion that he drink some citronella tea.

"Ask your mother to make you some," Nji Mama insisted. "Herb tea soothes the throat quickly."

Nebu tried to change the subject, not realizing that his master was happy for the distraction.

"A beautiful map," the young man said after wiping his nose on a cloth Nji Mama handed him.

No word more astute than "beautiful" had come to mind.

"It's almost done," Nji Mama announced.

Together they pored over the roads, the location of the houses, the angles of the intersections. Nji Mama added other place-names. Two symbols marking the location of the palace and the baobab in the center of town gave a sense of perspective to the map, filling it with an unexpected breath of life. The Artists' Alley was nicely drawn. Nebu also recognized the spice market. His hand moved along mechanically, searching for his mother's house.

"Here's where I live."

"I know you live there."

His master's response was curt. Nji Mama had an ironic smile on his lips when he said "there," and he hadn't added anything to mark the spot where Nebu's finger lay. The young boy didn't have the courage to ask why. It would have been a stupid question. Why would his mother's house—that of a woman and, what's more, a slave—been important enough to deserve a spot on the historic map of Foumban? Was his mother's life worth the trouble? No one included such trivial details when they wrote history. Nebu knew it, and it made him sad.

"It's a very beautiful map," he repeated.

Nji Mama paused thoughtfully, his hand slowly caressing his goatee. Nebu didn't dare interrupt his silence.

"You know," the master began, "I saw you out walking the other day."

Caught off guard by the comment, Nebu replied without thinking.

"How did you know it was me?"

The words slipped out of his lips.

"Young man," Nji Mama calmly replied, smiling ironically, "I was once your age, too."

"Forgive me—Nji," Bertha's son stammered, his head sunk into his shoulders. "I'm really sorry."

His ears rang again with the spice market's laughter. He re-membered his disguise and lived through his humiliation once more. He didn't even know if he was apologizing for questioning the master's knowledge or for having walked clear across Foumban dressed as a woman. Just one question had him rattled: Does he really know everything? That question frightened him all the more because Nji Mama seemed to be able to see right through his soul. He had never lied to his masters. And now he couldn't keep quiet either.

"Yes," he said. "I was following a girl."

Nji Mama tilted his head to listen. Nebu told him about Ngungure and what he had noticed. The master was visibly impressed by the passion that lit up the young man's face and smiled at his timidity. He reassured his apprentice that his quest was legitimate, interrupting him only when the young man told him he had done it "for art, just for art's sake."

"You're exploring new terrain," Nji Mama conceded. "Entirely new."

Perplexed, Nebu suspected that what he had done with his muse, Njoya had done with the city itself. In fact, Nebu saw no difference between the fevered solution he'd found to the equations of a woman's body as she crossed the city—his logarithm for a body in motion—and the mapping of the longitude and latitude of Foumban's quarters. His master could understand this better than anyone else, he thought.

"I have all her measurements," he said. "Everything."

Nji Mama smiled.

"I have the triangles of her being right here in my head," Nebu said, touching his temple, clearly quite pleased with himself.

"It's crazy to follow a girl all the way across the city," Nji Mama observed. "Really crazy . . ."

He didn't add "and to dress up as a woman." But it was as if he had. Nebu wanted to explain that art's truth is found in the artist's nudity. That what he had done was no more ludicrous than getting lost in the city streets as you tried to note everything down so you could map it all out. That he could see the slave woman in his mind with just as many details as there were on the map spread out before his master's eyes. That he knew the latitude and the longitude of that woman's veins as well as the number of her heartbeats. That he had calculated the proportions of her bones and the weight of each part of her flesh. Finally, he wanted to tell his master that of course he wasn't trying to compare Njoya's map to his own vision and dreams of a woman. But he kept quiet. He wanted Nji Mama to understand that his vision of Ngungure was just as transparent as a survey. He didn't raise his voice, because he had no right to, and especially because he knew his ideas were outrageous.

The map before him was unique: nothing like it had ever been done before. It was Foumban! This map was the realization of one of the sovereign's dreams, Njoya's vision of the land of his ancestors. Nebu knew it, but his mind was filled with Ngungure alone.

"I can still see her now, just like . . ." he ventured.

Yes, Nebu wanted to say, just like this map. Nji Mama was listening, waiting for him to finish his sentence. The sculptor stopped, just shy of the fine line that separates genius and insolence; instead, he concluded, "like truth."

The master didn't interrupt him.

"Because truth is concrete, isn't it?" Bertha's son continued after wiping his nose once more.

Nji Mama didn't answer, for it wasn't really a question. Nebu knew his master understood even if he didn't interrupt. That's how Nji Mama was: a man of few words, but always a fatherly judge. Nebu didn't understand why there was such sadness in his eyes.

"You are still very young," the chief architect acknowledged, patting his shoulder once again. "Art is in your blood."

They looked at each other, and then Nebu lowered his eyes. The map of the city was spread out between them, and on it Nebu could have traced all the pathways he had followed behind the slave woman. The young man didn't know that his master had also left out the spot where the next group of Bamum would be put into shackles. The streets were like a network of twisting veins, and the map of the city was shaped like a beating heart. Nebu left his master in the silence of the exchange that followed their conversation. He slowly began to back up, turning around only once he'd gotten a good distance away. Suddenly the chief architect's voice echoed down the corridor.

"Don't forget the citronella tea," Nji Mama said. "Ask your mother for some."

Nebu saw him waving in the doorway.

"Yes, master," he cried, waving back. "I won't forget. Understood."

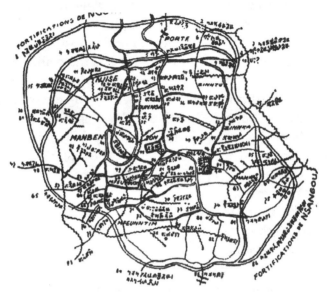

Map of Foumban drawn by Nji Mama in 1920. The location
of the French headquarters isn't given.

16

The French Officer's Mistake

It was the missionary Göhring who put an end to the Bamum practice of slaves walking naked in public. That was in 1911. He wanted to protect the son his wife had given birth to in Foumban, a boy named Njoya Göhring, in honor of his friendship with the sultan. Nansa Njoya—"Njoya the White," as people called the child—was starting to notice things and ask questions. The father did what any father would do if he had the power to alter reality to suit himself. Not many people remember that. What most do remember is an order issued by Lieutenant Prestat in 1920 that prohibited any clothing that didn't cover people from the knees "up to (and including) the breasts." People told me, moreover, that Lieutenant Prestat made that decision because he couldn't concentrate, was distracted by the sight of all those female breasts dancing in the streets, shopping in the market, sometimes lining up in front of his office, or even, on many occasions, coming right into his bed. Yes, I was told that the sight of so many naked women crowded his mind with images of fornication so clear that his written reports were filled with gibberish.

If his headquarters had been located outside the city, as the German and English headquarters had been, he would have cast a less nervous eye on life in Foumban. Ah, how to avoid the question? Maybe he would have had an entirely different idea of black women and slavery in general. Just one detail can change the course of history! According to some people, it was Madame Dugast who, despite her kindness, was behind the lieutenant's strictures; she agreed with him on most points, except for the closing of Njoya's schools and the requirement that all children attend the French school. In any event, women were on the front lines of the battle that soon broke out in Foumban.

When Bertha warned her son about the seamy side of love, even she didn't know that the whole sultanate would soon be caught up in the tornadoes spawned by something that would have been ignored anywhere else: someone trying to get a piece of ass. Did love have anything to do with it, really? Bertha was awakened one morning by a violent pounding on her door. When she came out of the house, four *tirailleurs* were pointing rifles right at her.

"Your son!" one of them shouted. Their eyes burned red with anger.

Terrified, Bertha stammered, "What?"

"Your son!"

The soldiers were in such a hurry that they provided no explanation. Two of them rushed into the house and came back out with Nebu, pushing him forward with their weapons. The young man's eyes were haggard. He sank down in the dust. The soldiers dragged him by his hands, feet, and hair. He struggled but couldn't stand up against four of them.

Bertha would have given her bones, her flesh, her soul, her life! She would have given everything, just not her son. The soldiers didn't know that. They didn't know what kind of mother she was; they had no inkling of the depth of her love. Yet it was love that threw her in front of their rifles, made her protect her son with her own body. It was love that made her run to Lieutenant Prestat, stand right in the path of his intimidating horse, and speak to him in a jargon she thought was French but was really a mixture of German, English, and French—in short, of all the European languages she had heard in Foumban, and which the officer took for Bamum. Sitting on his horse and stroking his four-day-old beard, he watched, silently distant, as the arrest took place. His uniform was dirty, his shirt gaped open, exposing his chest. His white hair was blowing in the breeze. His stony silence encouraged the violence of the soldiers, who pushed Bertha away, the better to chain up her son.

Isn't colonialism a good thing? Prestat thought, chewing on a stick and spitting out the splinters. Tell me, isn't it a good thing? There you have it: the portrait of this man, old enough to be happy not to have died an unknown hero, decorated but dead, poisoned in the trenches of the Marne or Verdun. He had survived the worst of the butchery because he had opted for a career in the colonies, and now he had become the most important voice in this four-hundred-year-old sultanate. Yes, that's him, Prestat, Lieutenant Prestat, an officer whose career had been stalled by a colonialist asshole who didn't understand his brusque style of governing and had exiled him to the hinterland. A man given free rein to rule as a Lord of the Tropics! Yes, that's him, almost ready to retire and still only a lieutenant, a man who felt the virtues of old Europe weighing on his balls while his heart beat with the fervor of a Napoleon in exile, and who marched across this conquered land to free the people so they could enjoy the pleasures of a constitution and a civil code!

Yet writing laws, even democratic ones, meant breaking with age-old customs. For the good of all, someone needed to grab hold of those traditions and tear them to shreds, since, after all, "you can't make an omelet without cracking a few eggs." That was Prestat's motto; he didn't see his omelet-making mission in the same sneaky way Göhring had, for example. The missionary had been able to use his friendship to convince Njoya that many of the customs handed down from the ancestor Nchare Yen were inhumane, even cruel; the English had passed through the sultan's city, apparently staying out of his business and even, in the end, giving him a car; Prestat, on the other hand, was convinced that the place needed a firm hand, a ruler inspired by a love of progress and democracy. It needed a Man of the Law capable of inspiring respect, or else any laws he'd proclaim wouldn't be worth the paper they were written on.

Let's take slavery, for example. Didn't Lieutenant Prestat himself order that "as of today, December 15, 1920, no one will work anymore without pay in Bamum land"? Had the Bamum immediately complied? No. What about matrimony: Hadn't he decreed that polygamy would henceforth be abolished in the sultanate? Hadn't he announced—and his word made it law—that "to set an example, he would begin with Njoya's six hundred eighty-one wives, who"— as he explained in his report—"would henceforth have the right to sleep with whomever they wanted if their husband didn't call for them"? Had the sultan separated from his excessive number of wives? Ah, we can understand the lieutenant's impatience, can't we? After all, isn't colonialism a good thing?

Claude Prestat, lieutenant of the French army, chief administrator in Foumban: sitting in his headquarters under mosquito netting, he could include "liberty, fraternity, equality" and anything else he wanted in his Bamum Declaration of Rights; he could have calligraphers copy it in bright letters and post it all over the city, including on the palace doors. With one swift move he could tear apart the Bamum Book of Laws, the *Lewa Sun Sun pa Funfun manten ne Mfen Njweya ka let mi a yet mun nera, mbu a pu na*! And of course, the same Prestat, betrayed by his girlfriend, now trampled the very same progressive laws he had just promulgated! He could come with his Congolese *tirailleurs* and arrest the son of a bitch who had screwed his girl, and that's exactly what he was doing.

The woman in question was the slave Nebu had followed one day for purely aesthetic reasons. She had retraced the sculptor's steps, going backward along the path where he had followed her, searching everywhere in Foumban for him. She had found his house and, rather than calling his name, had knocked three times on his window and waited. She had waited and knocked again. When Bertha's son opened the window, he saw her face and remembered his madness from two years before; he remembered the spice market's laughter and his master's mocking smile. He shook his head in disbelief.

"What do you want?" he asked.

The woman didn't reply, but smiled and lowered her eyes. Nebu didn't push for an answer.

This time she was dressed.

Maybe she's converted to Christianity, he thought, shaking his head once more.

Christianity was very popular among the slaves and women. If Foumban's nobles and freemen were turning toward Islam, which gave them the right to take, or keep, multiple wives, Christianity was mostly a religion of slaves who couldn't even afford to get married. There were exceptions, of course, first among them Mose

Yeyap, that son from a good family whom Fräulein Wuhrmann and the missionary Göhring had convinced to join their church, to pray alongside slaves, and even to marry one . . .

But let's get back to Nebu, for the young man was no longer used to seeing women let their pagnes fall in front of him. Time had tempered many of his impulses, if not all of them, and his talent had made him an enigma. So why didn't he just slam his shutters in Njapdunke's face? Was it because, like any man, he had nothing against a quick adventure? Who can say that he didn't see complications lurking behind this brazen woman's face, who? Yet the flesh is a curse, at least according to Bertha. Flesh can suddenly come back to life, especially in a young man who has spent too much time in his palace workshop calculating the proportions of women without being touched by a single one. No need for metaphysics here. It was simple: Nebu needed to get laid.

17

The Audacity of the Flesh

One year after Nebu had followed Njapdunke across the city, an act had been proclaimed that officially released Njapdunke from slavery; at the same time, however, she'd been led right into Lieutenant Prestat's bed. There had been a lot of gossip about her move, but Bertha's son was deaf to Foumban's rumors, as well we know. Njapdunke had previously belonged to Njoya's mother, whose name she bore. Her rise into the spheres of power explained her arrogance, and Nebu hadn't forgotten that she had previously called him a rat. Her foul words reminded the sculptor of the vocabulary his mother used to describe his father, the language of his friends Ngbatu and Muluam. Why do lower-class people always cover themselves with muck? In Nebu's mind, Njapdunke was dressed like a European because of Prestat, that was all. So he asked her, "Aren't you the white lieutenant's woman?"

Nebu saw her eyes flash defiantly.

"What of it?"

"That's just what I'm asking you."

He smelled a trap. Njapdunke knew it, and so she told him something sure to make him fall like a man whose head is controlled by his stiffening penis.

"He can't get it up," she said when Nebu asked why she had knocked on his window. "He can't get it up."

She assumed a look of abject humiliation, as only a neglected woman can. Wasn't that the worst part—that she had to come looking in the streets of Foumban for a man who could get it up? How embarrassing! It wasn't bad enough that she had been born a slave, did she have to become a whore? After all, wasn't she a woman, too? And a Bamum woman at that? And Nebu, wasn't he a Bamum man? Njapdunke admitted that the lieutenant gave her things, lots of things, and bought her the most extravagant dresses.

"Like the one I'm wearing," she said.

She opened her hands, spun around with her arms spread so Nebu could see the brightly colored, ostentatious dress she was wearing.

"It's from France," she added. "From Paris."

Bertha's son didn't react.

"Do you know what the French call it?" she asked.

Nebu didn't.

"They call it *haute couture.*"

Saying the French words "*haute couture,*" she smiled. Then a shadow fell over her eyes. She didn't lack for things, she explained, her voice cracking, but for action.

"What can I do with these useless outfits?"

She didn't need clothes, but a man, she continued, stressing "a man." You should have seen how she stared at Nebu when she said that. With those words she seemed to break down the window that framed the sculptor's face, freeing *a man* hidden behind it. And that wasn't all; with a strange smile, she added that she needed "a *djo* as crazy as you." She recalled out loud how Nebu had followed her across the streets of Foumban "that day." She recalled how he had looked at each part of her body, capturing details she knew were inscribed in his dreams.

"It's crazy, isn't it?"

Nebu's voice was gone.

"Don't tell me you've changed," Njapdunke went on.

She felt that, in the young man's mind, her clothes were as transparent as her body had been on that day.

"Do you think I've forgotten?" she asked.

Of course she had realized that day that his behavior was a sign of his love. Putting her hands on her hips, she asked him again, "Do you think I don't know?"

Yes, she had heard about the statue Nebu was creating in the palace. Who in the city hadn't heard of it? But she knew, yes Njap-dunke did, that the statue had the shape of her body. She had come to the artist's home, she continued, still smiling—and she empha-sized "artist"—in answer to a call that his timidity prevented him from making and that had burst out silently in his art.

"You love me, don't you?" she suddenly asked.

"What?"

The conjugation of the verb "to love" woke Nebu like a bucket of cold water on the face of a sleepwalker.

"You love me," Njapdunke continued confidently. "I know."

"You?"

"But you don't want people to know, right?"

"What?"

"Tell me the truth."

"The truth?"

She had knocked at his window, she said, because Foumban would have been scandalized had she been seen at his door. Prestat wasn't a violent man; he was violence personified. In short, he was the Man. Everyone knew that. But they wondered if it was the result of demented tropical dreams—nightmares filled with ven-omous snakes, dangerous crocodiles, nosy rats, cockroaches, and mosquitoes—or if, perhaps, it was drinking too much alcohol in the sun and avoiding the shade that produced such colonial characters. No one knew for sure. Some believed that it was the lack of sex. Only a good fuck can calm an irascible man, they said.

To avoid any misunderstanding, let me quickly add that these aren't the reasons why Njoya had given the girl to the lieutenant when he arrived in Foumban; it was because custom required it—ah, our famous customs! And the girl in question, Njapdunke, learned only after she'd gone into Lieutenant Prestat's bed that the reason for the Man of the Law's infamous anger was, in fact, his impotence.

"And the truth is, Nebu, you can get it up."

It was her way of skirting an embarrassing situation and making sure the sculptor understood what she meant.

Nebu was listening. He didn't need Njapdunke to praise her own beauty, he could see it. And even if he had forgotten, his hands would have shown him the way around her womanly body, for, oh yes, they still knew the dimensions of her skin! Knowing that this perfect body—the body he had taken apart and put back together repeatedly in his dreams—was going to waste made him angry. He wanted to pull this woman off the street and peel those degrading clothes right off her. How many times after this did she come knock on the artist's window? Over how long?

One month? Or two?

One thing is certain, even if Nebu didn't give a fuck (no joke), the sculptor wouldn't be the first artist in history to sleep with his model. So why was there such a fuss? His story had a flavor no one could make the women at the spice market give up; they immediately recognized the man who'd disguised himself as a woman. The story was imbued with the scent of those tales the idle nobles ate up, and they knew Njapdunke, too. This rumor had the hot pepper bouquet of delicious gossip, the succulence of braised fish in tomato sauce. Soon the whole city knew the story of the woman who knocked on the sculptor's window, and they recognized the young man whispering from behind the shutters. People smiled. No one allowed themselves to tell the betrayed man the dirty story of his knocking girlfriend, oh no! Many women opted instead to come to the boy's mother, urging her to remind him to be prudent. And that's how Bertha learned of her son's secret exploits. Trembling, she lectured him, talked to him about love. Ah, she said, the Bamum talk a lot! Was he trying to bring about his own death? This time—though it's hard to believe—Nebu obeyed her.

Never was a mother happier! If only such a story could be forgotten. Njapdunke's belly soon got the silent mouths talking again, giving new life to the winded tales. Her belly began to chatter in those places where all the people had fallen silent. And in the heart of the uncharacteristically quiet spice market it revealed the story that every woman had decided to keep from Lieutenant Prestat. Njapdunke's belly grew. It grew and grew, defying Nebu's mathematics. It grew so much that the women of the city had to hide the future mother. In one of their kitchens, Njapdunke gave birth to a little boy as dark as a shadow, with the sculptor's face—a baby whose first sign of life was a satisfied chuckle.

A man's humiliation can have the dimensions of a suffocatingly small kitchen. It can be as broad as a courtyard. Lieutenant Prestat's humiliation was the size of a sultanate, more gigantic than an *iroko*, a teak tree, in a clearing. It was amplified by the centuries-old baobab in the center of Foumban, which matched the height of his colonial ego. His humiliation was mythic: it had silenced a market full of women but made a newborn burst out in laughter. The child's laughter echoed through all the alleys, streets, and passages, all the houses and bedrooms of Foumban; it came through the history of the old city and woke up the chief omelet maker from his worst nightmare, the face of an infant howling with laughter. It filled him with a burning desire to "kill the son of a bitch who did this to me."

Or rather, no: "To kill the bitch who made a fool of me."

After a little more thought, no, better to commit suicide, those vile creatures don't deserve a bullet.

Kill the child?

Kill the son and the mother and silence the nursing baby's guffaws? For silence was the only thing that could bring peace back to the horrified streets, to the horrified world. The women of Foumban were not unaware of Prestat's anger. Terrified by the universe's uncontrollable laughter, they sent the mother and child to a distant exile. Njapdunke left behind her a bit of doubt and mostly a question: Where had she gone? She also left behind an imprudent accusation of rape that she thought would clear her name entirely, but which sent the Man's soldiers flying to Nebu's mother's door, encouraged in their quest for vengeance by a silent and devious informant, Mose Yeyap, who recalled quite clearly the lover's long braids. That's how Lieutenant Prestat arrived in Bertha's courtyard, his body consumed by an unbroken anger, his tin soldiers marching ahead of him.

18

The Newborn's Mirth, and So On

Even if the firsthand accounts of this period are lacking in women's voices, what version of events could be closer to the truth than the scar left on Bertha's neck? The report written by Commander Martin, Prestat's superior, then based in Dschang, uses a euphemism to describe the lieutenant's actions. It invokes an "error of judgment." A recounting of the events as they happened are found only in Njoya's memoirs, the *Saa'ngam*, although it was Martin himself who translated Njoya's book into French. "Two pages were cut out," he mentions in a note, "undoubtedly because they mentioned living persons still occupying important functions in the country." He wrote this in 1949, the height of the French colonial reign in Foumban, leaving us thirsting to know who, yes, who culled those pages, so important for our story, from Njoya's book—and especially, what that person was trying to hide.

Here's what we know: the previously mentioned report tries to massage the truth underlying the shame, for it takes Lieutenant Prestat's version of things, exaggerates parts, and then lays out an elaborate theory of colonialism. According to Prestat, the girl—who had been given to him by Njoya upon his arrival in Foumban and whose accomplice he had arrested—was the sultan's secret agent. She had tried to poison him with a dried fish head, having obtained the poison from a palace artist known as Nebu—the sultan's evil hand—whose braided hair marked him, "according to local custom, as a master herbalist." As soon as Prestat had eaten the poisoned meal served to him by Njapdunke, he had felt his lips burn. He opened his mouth, stuck out his tongue, and his eyes turned red. His breathing grew strained and his heart raced. He was only able to prevent his entire body from exploding because he had the presence of mind to drink a whole barrel full of water.

"Have you ever eaten Bamum cooking?" my friends from Nsimeyong asked; they recognized the description of the after-effects of a hot, spicy meal.

How right they were!

But Lieutenant Prestat didn't buy it; poison was the only possible explanation. How so? The report continues, quoting many slaves who, when questioned, confirmed that the poisoning cook was following the sultan's orders. Martin didn't note that the aforementioned slaves were brought in by Mose Yeyap, a man motivated by his own ambitions. It's true, the woman Prestat accused had been the slave of the "despot's" mother—as he put it—and she was named after her. Poor Prestat, what a mistake it had been to hire her to work in his house, yes, what an "error of judgment" to have taken in that woman, clearly already "in the employ" of the sultan!

Njoya wanted to kill Prestat, the report went on, because Prestat had been moved by the condition of the lower classes and intended to do something to bring "democracy to the sultanate." He had opened his ears to the little people, his heart to the Wretched of the Earth, and he had worked to bring about the "emancipation of all the slaves and women in Bamum land." "Isn't colonialism a good thing?" the lieutenant asked. "Doesn't it represent the opportunity for those who are now last to become first tomorrow?"

Of course, once Nebu was arrested, Prestat had him tied to the baobab, but that wasn't forbidden, and he had done it only in order to extract a confession from him, just as he hoped to extract the truth from the city that kept his secret—so these stubborn people would tell him where he could find the poisoner and, eventually, the name of the man behind it all: Njoya. "Progress and democracy can't be stopped by one man alone," he insisted.

Nebu came through the ordeal with his teeth clenched. No, he didn't say a word. He didn't cry either. Or call for help. Why would he have called on Njoya? "The native is a child. He understands only one language," that's how Martin's report concludes. In the darkness of Africa, Lieutenant Prestat did not want to force a young man to cry, but rather to demonstrate France's infinite justice to all, so that no one would ever forget, but always remember.

"Nothing personal," reads a note added in pen at the bottom of the page.

Who wrote that? Prestat? Martin? How to know? It remains that Lieutenant Prestat was not punished, for "France must not lose face," as Martin concluded. Prestat left Foumban two years later, having reached retirement age, for "while his intentions were rather good, his heart was too sensitive to the fate of society's most vulnerable classes."

When the soldiers arrived with their prisoner in the center of town, all of Foumban gathered around them. Old folks, women, men, children, animals: everyone was there. Not just Bertha; all the women from the spice market were up in arms, all the mothers horrified. Oh, everyone was terrified! The *tirailleurs* used their rifles to shove away the hands of the distraught city as they feverishly tied the sculptor to the trunk of the baobab. What Lieutenant Prestat ordered them to do, they did, without delay.

"One!"

"Two!"

"Three!"

"Four!"

"Five!"

The whip rained down on Nebu's back.

"Six!"

"Seven!"

"Eight!"

Who was counting? The spice market. Who was counting? The granaries. Who was counting? The houses. The kitchens. The hundreds of people gathered in the courtyard of their collective humiliation. The hearts of the Bamum who had taken the boy's story as their own. The bellies of all the women who had thought they could keep him hidden. The baobab whose sap had become the young man's blood. Who was counting? The hair that had grown on the sculptor's head for seven years, grown and grown, now braided itself around the tree of misery; his hair reached up and grabbed hold of the tree's branches, hugging the sky, the better to stifle his torment. It is said that Nebu received as many lashes as there are branches on a tree, but who was counting?

"Nine!"

"Ten!"

Yes, who was counting? The flesh of a man, of a son, but especially that of a mother, of all mothers; each mother felt the hippopotamus-tail whip through her belly, cruelly sealing her fallopian tubes. Who was counting? Those men, yes, who felt their blood and their sperm run dry. The weakened loins of everyone there, especially Bertha, who threw herself on her son and was lashed, once, twice, three times on the neck. Who took the blows of a whip so violent it bit into her flesh and tore at her bones before letting go. Who was counting? The old master, Monlipèr, his horror-struck eyes open wide because he had never before seen such a thing, who threw himself in front of the soldiers, covering mother and son with his own body, offering his face to the men with the whips, letting loose with a slew of proverbs and begging them to stop, only to receive his full portion of lashes, too. Who was counting? The whole country was begging the soldiers with the whips, asking them to stop, to stop before it was too late, to stop in the name of God! In the name of the black race!

"This is my son," Bertha said. "Don't kill him!"

His body was covered in blood.

"My son," said Monlipèr.

The soldiers were deaf to their tears. The silent approbation of their lieutenant, or at least the nickering of his horse behind them, dictated their actions and encouraged their busy hands to keep going. They knew Lieutenant Prestat would sentence each of them to make up for any lashes they failed to administer. Those soldiers knew that in this country, where they, too, were foreigners, they could count their blessings that they were among those inflicting the pain. That's what you call being on the right side. When Monlipèr threw himself down before their happy hands and grabbed hold of the whip they were using to lacerate Nebu's back, they let him have the final blows meant for Nebu.

"Who do you think you are, old man?"

That's what one of the soldiers said.

"Who?"

"Vermin!"

"Monkey!"

The fourth soldier finished the master artist off. "You are nothing!"

"Yes," repeated his fellow *tirailleur*, "you're just a burro!"

The word "burro" would have applied to the *tirailleur* if he weren't wearing a uniform and if he didn't have a whip in his hands. Whipping an old man had left him quaking in his bones, but he knew that all the laws around there were worth nothing compared with his tricolored uniform. He had stopped believing in proverbs the day the French colonial administration had given him a rifle. Was it Monlipèr who saved Nebu from death? Or were the vengeful soldiers just tired of making him suffer? What is clear is that different versions of the story were told. The old engineer paid dearly for his courage; when the list of people to deport from the sultanate was set by Lieutenant Prestat's successor, four years after this incident, in 1924, his name was right there.

"Don't you have a mother?"

Monlipèr's question echoed off the pain that had torn open Bertha's neck.

"What kind of people are you?"

His words made Prestat's blood boil, for the lieutenant knew what danger he faced, alone in such a big city, practically a prisoner in the heart of a sultanate, where he understood neither the verbal gestures nor the body language. The old man's questions were echoed in the mood of the gathered crowd, which had fallen silent but struggled to restrain itself.

"What kind of men are you?"

Isn't it surprising that it was Nbgatu and Muluam, the two friends Nebu had met in the old man's workshop, who ran to help their master to free the miserable sculptor from the baobab? No one else had the courage to undo what a colonial officer had done. But they couldn't just leave an unconscious, beaten man to die in the middle of town. What was it that held back the usually quick hands of the Bamum? There were those who remembered that years before the French arrived, even before the English, during the German colonization, the boy's father had hanged himself from the baobab where Nebu now suffered. They talked about fate closing a vicious circle. Thankfully, Nebu's companions had shorter memories. The present, the chaos of the present alone, dictated the logic of their actions.

"He's our *djo*," they said, meaning, our brother.

Bertha cried out to the heavens; Monlipèr held her son's body. The old master spit blood, cursed the earth. Njoya arrived too late. He had been alerted by a strident rumor echoing across the city and was informed of what happened by his couriers. He had rushed to the site of the crime accompanied by his scandalized entourage, including Nji Mama and Ibrahim. The whole palace had followed, in fact. When he arrived at the foot of the baobab, Prestat and his men had already left. The monarch's horrified face met the wounded eyes of the woman holding her son, unconscious and bloodied, in her arms, cuddling him like a baby. Njoya's ears were filled with the people's grumbling, which grew into shouts that were useless in the face of disaster. This wouldn't be the last time the sultan would come out on the streets of his city without everyone bowing down respectfully, without praise singers lifting up their many voices, without the sky brightening in hopes that his reign would last for a century. The drama that played out that day in Foumban had transformed him into just another inhabitant in his sultanate. Everyone knew that he, Njoya, was the French lieutenant's real target.

NJOYA AND MOSE

ᚦᛚ ᚼ

For one may rise, and fall the other may.
—Dante, *The Divine Comedy*, Paradise, Canto XIII
(translated by Henry Wadsworth Longfellow)

1

In History's Chattering Poor Neighborhoods

While Sara went on with her story about the whipping, I noticed for the first time that her face was beginning to show her age. Her eyes were wan. Her hands and feet trembled. Her voice grew difficult to hear, a whisper. It was as if her throat had been eaten up by the story, by her own story. Or maybe, having spoken for so long without interruption, she was just losing her voice. But it was also because she felt each of Nebu's lashes on her own body. Yes, it was as if the whips of the Congolese *tirailleurs* tore into her legs, flowed through her veins, and brought her heart to a stop with a strangled cry; as if her own forgotten past had come back to life, horrific blows tearing into her flesh. Reliving the life of that boy she had agreed to become when she was offered Bertha's swollen breasts to suckle, she had unleashed the hell of the matron's life in Foumban.

There was a cost for opening herself up to the artist's fate. Nebu's lacerated body had left Sara without a voice—suffocating from his torment. She finally understood the pain of a mother's bleeding heart. Had she been a mother herself, she also would have wished to give birth once more, just to alter his fate, to invent another, better life for him, because life in a colony is cursed, as we all know. Yet Sara followed another path. She accepted Nebu so that the mother would come back to life and smile at her once again.

"She never hit me," Sara said, her lips still trembling with emotion under the weight of her silent cry, her eyes red with pain. "She never hit me. Never."

"Now I know why," I answered. "How long were you her son?"
Her reply was slow to come.

"For as long as she shaved my head."

I took her hands. Her palm was covered in sweat. She shivered again.

"Do you want to do my hair?" I asked.

My question didn't surprise her, even if she opened her eyes wide, as if I were joking. Far from it. It seemed to me that any distraction would be welcome, would help her to find her way back to life after that painful tale.

"Careful," she added. "I'm not a hairdresser."

"I know."

"I'm just an old-fashioned woman," she warned me, smiling now. "Just an old woman."

"I've straightened my hair, dyed it, cut it short, had bangs and everything else you can buy. Today I can tell you that I've become a fan of old-fashioned hair."

Sara burst out laughing and wiped her nose with a corner of her *kaba*.

"But," she added, "how would I know that?"

I sat between her legs, putting my head into her hands. I felt her warm hands smoothing each part of my hair. She hadn't asked me how I wanted the braids. If truth be told, I hadn't just given her my head to do; I also wanted her to reshape my soul.

"I'd prefer braids," I suggested anyway.

"At your service, Madame," she replied in French.

"Why not the style of 1932?" I suggested jokingly.

"Okay," she replied seriously. "Style 1932."

"Easy to remember?"

"Let's wait and see."

While Sara had been talking, the crowd around us had grown bigger and bigger. My friends from Nsimeyong who dreamed only of New York and whose days dragged under the weight of boredom seemed interested by the hidden history of their neighborhood, by the life of this girl dressed as a boy, the girl hidden in the old lady, and the boy taken in hand by the women of a spice market. They made numerous trips to the National Archives for me, photocopying the texts I needed to figure out Sara's story. Their diligence left me speechless time and time again. Even the birds from the Internet café broke off their searches on husband.com and joined in our hunt for stories; Google became their favorite site. Often they came back angry, telling me that an essential manuscript written in Lewa characters, a register of capital crimes, an important circular, or an indispensable report had been abandoned in a dusty file, half eaten by rats, or drowned in the waters of idiocy. What my dear friends really couldn't understand was why the ruins of Mount Pleasant, which they now gazed upon hungrily, had been left to rot. By uncovering layer after layer of the House of Stories buried under Nsimeyong, Sara had turned their limping lives into limitless fountains of potential. Their future had been stolen, and they learned that their past had been as well. They didn't hold back their blame. "Can't the state do anything right?"

It was Arouna who asked that question. He had naturally become the leader of the group, always the most passionate, the most energetic, far smarter than his swagger of a wannabe gangster from the Bronx would suggest. I told him that the Cameroonian state, although built on a foundation of negligence, incompetence, and much more (corruption, nepotism, dictatorship, and everything else that a banana republic can come up with to sink its future), was the offspring of the historic betrayal that produced Njoya's violent nightmare: the betrayal of the association of chiefs that the sultan had refused to join in 1914, which he had exposed to his friend the missionary Göhring, thereby causing the death of Manga Bell, Samba Martin, and Ngosso Din.

I suggested to Arouna that the aborted nationalist roots of the Cameroonian state might be what were haunting the sultan, provoking the nightmares that were the true source of his suffering.

"He had a different vision of our country."

"What vision?" Arouna asked.

Perhaps, I explained, Njoya wanted the sultanate to become a state within the state, because the very strange history of the Bamum had always run counter to what we would today call "the Cameroonian national identity."

"So Njoya really was just a collaborator?" asked a provocative voice.

"Collaborator" raced through the electrified crowd like a red-hot bullet.

Arouna seemed to be waiting for it. "Isn't resistance another form of collaboration?" he asked everyone.

"You're joking!"

"If you resist, you've already accepted the premises of a battle," he continued. "It's not the same as ignoring it, right?"

"Go on."

"Which means, you get swallowed up . . ."

"By what?"

"By a battle that's not your own."

"And then?"

"You get pulled into a war you didn't start."

"What do you think?"

"No one can win that kind of war, my brother, that's what I think."

"What do you mean?"

"The winner is the one who sets the rules," Arouna concluded. "The others are just collaborators."

He seemed to have grasped the logic behind Njoya's chaotic life; for him, the sultan was, you might say, a precursor, a Cameroonian before the letter. He met the irritated faces of his buddies, none of whom could muster arguments strong enough to shut him up. I felt a silent nationalism boiling up all around, the heartbeats of an elemental force. I didn't come to Arouna's defense. How could I? He didn't let anyone else speak anyhow. Yet, I wanted to ask him, wasn't Mount Pleasant—in a way—the realization of a new consciousness, since the voices heard there came from all corners of the earth to create the sultan's memoirs? Maybe it was Njoya's fate to be uprooted from Bamum land so he could give birth to a different country, a different Cameroon there in the capital of the country that had banished him. I told my dear friends from Nsimeyong that their buddy's argument held water. Njoya never would have wanted to be consumed by greater forces—not race, nation, continent, or the First World War. Arouna and I were bombarded with a thousand questions.

"What are you talking about?" one voice called out. "Wasn't Njoya Cameroonian too?"

"An African?"

"A black man . . ."

"Yes or no? If yes, then he had to . . ."

"Then he couldn't . . ."

"Then how did he dare . . ."

I was smothered by all these obligations that define an authentic black woman, a true African man, a good Cameroonian. I would have liked to ask my friends: okay, what if Njoya didn't want to be covered in any of that shit? But I also didn't want to offend them. They lived in a world of superficial evidence, when to my mind, the sultan was all about listening, doubting, searching.

"The books tell me that he was Bamum," I answered. "That's all."

Njoya knew that, I added, from the genealogy transmitted to him by the many voices of his people; he wrote down those tales and compiled them in his book, the *Saa'ngam*, so that everyone would know and none would forget. "Your country, not mine," he might have said to my self-styled nationalists.

"Listen," I shot out, "what do you want? The man gave his eldest daughter, who was Muslim, a Christian first name: Margaretha— the same name as Göhring's wife, no less. And he even called the missionary 'his brother'! If the English had stayed in his territory after they'd arrived in 1915, the sultanate would have been administered with Nigeria. Would that have made any difference to him?"

Some of the young people thought it would have made a big difference because it would have been to his advantage. And they didn't stop there: they said Njoya wouldn't have died so soon had the English been in charge in Cameroon! I was dumbstruck. My impassioned interlocutors had discovered in the archives that the Germans had been chased from Yaoundé not by the French, but by the English, who captured Ongola on January 1, 1916. So, they asked, shouldn't we, as Cameroonians, be concerned with such details?

"What contract did the English and French sign behind our backs allowing the French army to occupy a land it hadn't conquered?" one boy asked.

I couldn't answer that. Arouna, who had surprisingly switched camps and joined his friends, also asked, "What made the Western states put Yaoundé and the rest of Cameroon under the wrong mandate?"

Looking at his friends, he stressed "wrong mandate," and I realized he was still trying to see which way the wind was blowing. His words unified the group in a shared sense of indignation.

"Why didn't the League of Nations ask us which side we wanted to join?" an indignant voice inquired.

"With the English or the French?" another boy clarified.

"Which would have been better?" I asked him.

He couldn't reply. In fact, Arouna didn't give him time to.

"So why didn't the League of Nations ask us whose colony we wanted to be?" he asked.

And then he added, "What if we wanted an entirely new system, like the Germans after the war?"

"Why wasn't the Cameroonian diaspora, people like Mandenga, invited to send in their suggestions?"

A thousand questions! My friends from Nsimeyong looked at me, they looked at Sara and waited for us to reply. Whoever tells a story is responsible for it, that's what I learned that day. I told them what Njoya himself had declared when the English soldiers entered his defeated city: "Their war, not ours."

Arouna jumped. "Didn't I already say that?"

"Yes, my son," Sara conceded, "but then you changed sides."

I burst out laughing despite myself.

"I'm always on Cameroon's side," he answered irritably, turning back to his friends.

"The sultan's position was clear," the old lady explained. "Njoya always needed to be the one holding the reins of his own story, that's all." His story—from the depths of Foumban to the palace of the German governor, Ebermaier, to the English occupation and the somber years of the Franco-English contract, right through his exile to Mount Pleasant in Yaoundé—it all shaped Cameroon. He had never really traveled, only a few kilometers, but the triangle formed by his steps had grown into a country, a unit. The whole universe had barged into his bedchamber, bringing its conflicts and its lunacy. That's how he perceived life; he tried to make sense of the discord and madness and give it meaning in the many books he wrote.

"So, was he an egotist?" Arouna demanded. "A tribalist?"

"A free man," Sara replied.

"Free?"

"A free mind imprisoned in a black body."

The young folks of Nsimeyong didn't understand what it meant to be free when you were caged up, when you lived in a colony, when you obeyed French orders, when you lived in a world that escaped you.

"Yes, free to make the wrong decisions," the old mama said, "but responsible enough to pay for those choices with his life."

"He wanted to own the world," Arouna asked, "without being owned by it?"

"To speak of the world . . ."

". . . without being spoken for by it."

The young folk of Nsimeyong were enthralled by Sara's story, and their endless discussion pushed the doyenne to continue her tale, exasperated that they understood so little of it.

2

In Yaoundé, Rain Is No One's Friend

November is the rainiest month in Yaoundé. But in this city, the rain has very strange habits. It can fall every day for a week between one and four in the afternoon. It falls with the precision of a Swiss watch but never forgets the cruel vivacity it owes to our proximity to the equator. Accompanied by a wicked wind, it twists trees, destroys houses, tears off roofs, and fills the Mfoundi River. When it rains, water takes control of the city. Those who live in the valleys take refuge in the hills. Colonial civil servants, officers, and doctors; merchants, palm wine tappers, and shoemakers; the unemployed, the prostitutes, catechumens, and nuns: everyone stops working because the city is shaken to its very soul by the thundering of the water falling from the sky—plop, plop, plop—and sinking deep into the ground's viscous arteries. Some take shelter under verandas, their shirts wet, pants rolled up to the calves, sandals in hand. They chat with the strangers next to them, and together, they curse the gods. Dogs shake themselves off, rousing horrified men and women. Roosters and hens stand on one leg, their heads buried beneath a wing. Only the ducks strut about proudly under the rain. Those ducks! They puff out their breasts as if showing off medals of honor, drinking down the water in crazed gulps.

The wind's clamor drowns out the voices. Rushing through windows, the wind opens them with a violent gust and then brazenly shuts them. Slamming doors when it wants, the wind scatters leaves across the ground and whips through the people's stupefied souls.

The rain comes through the straw roofs, drenching lovers in their beds. But the rain also fills the calabashes people set in their courtyards to collect drinking water. Children turn their open mouths to the sky so drops fall directly down their throat. Others hold their hands like cups, quickly filled by the sky. Some just strip off their clothes, running, jumping, shouting, dancing, and playing naked under the singing rain. Sometimes, too, you'll see a man walking under the rain, his head covered with a large banana leaf. A rivulet of water flows down his back, marking his path as he stomps through the puddles. Sometimes it's a woman struggling to control her multicolored umbrella as the wind tugs it away. The woman doesn't walk, she dances under the storm. She dances like a Mami Wata, and the men in their shelters, captivated by the lascivious movements of her body, laugh and talk loudly together. Under the veranda's protection, they can do nothing but chatter.

"Idiots," the woman shouts at them. "What are you looking at?"

"Your calabashes, Mami Nyanga," a man replies shamelessly, "your calabashes."

"Your *uhuhu.*"

"Your *koukourou, ma ndolo.*"

"Your *nyama nyama-o.*"

Meaningless onomatopoeias, you know how men are. Their eyes are always too big and they're too happy to talk when they've nothing to say. They laugh and talk so much because the rain has left the walking woman transparent and silenced their voices. But rain in this city can also be cruel. Who has forgotten the day it tore the zinc roof off a house and tossed it across the neighborhoods? Like hens at the sight of an eagle, everyone ran to hide, except for one child who wasn't sufficiently alert to the danger of the suddenly emptied courtyards and continued chasing his ball. The flying metal sheet decapitated him as the people screamed, unable to react, and his head rolled off after the ball he'd had so much fun playing with. Yaoundé's rain can't be what it is without awakening the scent of the earth, no. A possessive perfume, with an inebriating scent. It floods in through the nose, permeates your clothes, intoxicates the mind, and enchants the air even as its water turns paths into muddy tracks and poor neighborhoods into swamps. When it rains, it's as if the rain awakens the Essingan, the titular spirit of the city's seven hills, ordering him to march on Ongola, the city center, to join the forces of oppression and thunder down its vengeful and unjust anger on the valleys.

It was on one of those especially rainy days that Njoya recognized Nebu. Mount Pleasant was crowded that day. Not wanting to get wet, people had run for cover under the sultan's roof, and the men and women who'd come from afar to tell the monarch their life stories were stuck there, too. Everyone's eyes were turned toward the sky's madness. People were grasping onto windows and doors, insulting the rain that had covered their best clothes in mud and upset all their plans. With pale faces they took cover under verandas, their eyes still filled with the whispering of the sky's punishing spirits, distracted only by the unbelievable decision of one man who, after running through the storm for a long time, sought shelter under a roof only to realize that he was already totally soaked and so set off again on his marathon. These people took up all the covered spaces while the rain falling from the roofs drummed an endless tom-tom in the hollows of their souls, a tom-tom that shook up the universe just to make it stand still. This time it wasn't the sultan's fall that had stunned everyone all around and brought life to a halt. Everyone just accepted the only choice the rain offered the capital's inhabitants: to wait, wait, and wait some more. For when it rains, water becomes the sultan of Yaoundé; it becomes the paramount chief of the capital, and what's more, yes, it becomes the country's high commissioner!

Njoya had been up for a long time before Nebu arrived. The boy's delay had left the monarch's pages speechless. Bertha's endless story had kept him leashed up, it must be said. He had run through the rain, jumping in puddles and making his way along the overcrowded corridors. His efforts hadn't managed to make up for lost time, however, because the matron hadn't let him go until she had said the last sentence, the true ending to the story of the sculptor and the violent Lieutenant Prestat. So when Nebu came into Njoya's apartments—through the back door, for he was feeling guilty—he was met by the masklike faces of the slaves who, in their whole lives of servitude, had never seen anything as scandalous as a shadow arriving late. Ah, my children!

Just then a threatening voice welcomed him. "You are late."
That was Nji Mama. The master's eyes were red with anger.
"You are late," he repeated.

Nebu lowered his eyes, as was expected, and kept his hands
clasped in front of him. Nji Mama's anger took on a new form as Nji
Shua encouraged the master architect to "give a lesson to that little
delinquent."

"Show him."

Everyone would have approved had the master architect whipped
Nebu, for he was clearly at fault and deserved to be punished.
There was a time when a slave would have been chased out of the
palace for arriving late, but Nebu didn't know that. It had been the
only way to ensure the sultan's safety. Who knows what kind of plot
a late arriver could have cooked up during his lost time? Oh, of
course, that was a long time ago, even if for Nji Mama it wasn't the
rain, but the city itself, Yaoundé, or rather, no, the French, who had
done away with the laws to which the Bamum had been accustomed, leaving nothing but chaos behind. That day, Nebu had once
again crossed paths with Nji Shua's whip, and he stifled his urge to
call for the matron. He knew that there was no escaping from punishment now. What held back the woodworker's hand this time,
however, was a voice coming from inside, a cavernous voice that
echoed across the somber corridors and, with a terse order, put a
halt to the masters' anger: "Leave that child alone!" said the voice.
"Don't touch him!"

It was Njoya's voice; he appeared in his wheelchair. He was
dressed rather lightly, his posture more than ever suggesting a defeated fighter. His eyes darted around furiously. That was the first
time he really saw Nebu. And what he saw was pitiful. The boy was
trembling as only a tropical rain can make a child tremble. Fear had
dissolved his flesh and his bones, fear of the whip.

"What's going on?" Njoya asked.

His voice cracked even more because of his apoplexy. Nebu
would have responded, but he couldn't speak. Rather ashamed, the
two masters kept quiet.

"Don't be afraid, my son," Njoya continued.

Ah, if Nebu had spoken, his sputtered excuses would have called back to life the whole history of Foumban; he would have told the sultan about his suffering mother, the story of the whipped mother, the mother who hoped for her son's rebirth, determined to give him a better life than the accursed existence he had suffered. He would have evoked Nebu's tragic fate, the son, the young man, the artist who had felt the whip's lashes deep in his body, without crying, without calling for help from the sultan or anyone else in the universe, because his soul had been consumed by pain.

"Come here," Njoya said. "Tell me what happened."

Nebu knew that words alone could never fully express the suffering of the whole country that he had swallowed, a tale that had left his head shaved in a sign of unending mourning. His eyes looked for the words that could tell of the breadth, the odious, silent breadth of the grieving world, and of its tragedy, which had locked the sultan away in his bedchamber.

"Nebu is mute," Nji Mama interjected.

He whispered in Njoya's ears, and right then, the old mama told me, she saw Njoya's eyes open wide, pausing in their dance. That's when she realized he was cross-eyed.

"Nebu?" he asked, after a long pause.

His encounter with this boy of the shadows had left him stammering.

"Yes, Alareni," Nji Mama replied, "the boy is mute."

Njoya opened his mouth to speak, but tripped over his own words and fell silent. He was struggling, yes, struggling with the vocabulary of his memory, which eluded his tongue. Nebu's frightened silence had opened the abyss in which the sultan had been imprisoned, and suddenly it was as if the men who had been caring for him had never really faced up to the truth of his long decline. It was as if, for the first time, all of them realized that their sultan had really fallen. Njoya soon pulled himself together, took a deep breath, then turned and rolled his chair back toward his room. Nji Mama, Nji Shua, and everyone else raced after him. For a moment the boy just stood there, frozen by the events he had caused and by how the utterance of his own name had revealed a great man's handicap. A blow on his back roused him, reminding him that the day's rhythm wasn't dictated by the late arrival of a shadow.

"To work," Nji Mama's voice ordered. "To work!"

3

The Limits of Anti-French Sentiment

Mount Pleasant had received its ration of water. It had rained for a whole week on the neighborhoods where the natives lived. Housing had been destroyed, the Mfoundi River was swollen. The white neighborhoods, on the other hand, had stayed dry, even gotten some sun. Only the wind and the scent of the earth reminded everyone of the alluvial segregation, which was especially meaningful for Nji Mama.

"Know that here, even the rain supports the French," he told his younger brother when Ibrahim arrived in Yaoundé. "Here, even the rain is unjust."

The chief architect had never gotten used to Yaoundé. Some people cannot live in exile, Njoya's architect among them. He suffered. Without the sultan, he would have already finished his business, gathered his family, and returned home to Foumban. For him, Njoya's illness was the logical consequence of his stay in a foreign land. He blamed the weather, but also the ground and the rain, not to mention the capital's skies. Forgetting the nightmares that filled his sovereign's nights, he saw the high commissioner plotting behind the clouds and in the depths of the ground, controlling the rain and the fine weather from his palace in Ongola. The official's visits were too rare; his neglect of the sultan, after issuing the orders that had chased him from Bamum land, was in Nji Mama's eyes enough to convict him. In fact, everything pointed to him for one simple reason: he was French.

"They want to kill the sultan," the chief architect told his brother the very day Ibrahim arrived in Mount Pleasant.

And he was categorical. Anger lit up his eyes.

Ibrahim shook his head. "Nji, aren't you exaggerating this time?"

Ibrahim knew that Nji Mama's anti-French sentiments long predated his exile and that his complaints about the weather in Yaoundé were just a new variation on the theme. He also knew that his brother respected France—the birthplace of many artists, he'd been told—even if he still had many other grievances against the French.

"Let's do something," Nji Mama murmured, his wide-open eyes searching for a possible solution. "We must do something!"

"Like what?"

"I don't know . . ."

Nji Mama's face was lost in a despair Ibrahim had never seen before; he kept repeating, "I don't know, I just don't know—"

"Listen to what the doctor says," his younger brother interrupted. "That's what we should do."

"You're joking?"

It seemed that Ibrahim's suggestion had relit a fire in his brother's eyes where there had been nothing but ashes.

"Nji, you want the sultan to survive, right?" Ibrahim continued, holding his elder brother's hands.

"What do you mean?"

"Well," Ibrahim begged, "listen to the white man."

"Do you want to kill him?" Father Vogt had asked Nji Mama one day, having lost patience with the architect's hostility.

That was during the episode over the wheelchair, which Nji Mama had opposed until the end. Father Vogt had understood that it wasn't just about the chair. But his words had crossed a line. That Nji Mama would become his own sultan's murderer—ridiculous! As for the chief architect, he couldn't hold back his indignation. And to think Father Vogt was French on top of it all! "Alsatian," the priest would have replied. "I am Alsatian, my dear friend."

That would have just confused Nji Mama even more, satisfied as he was to have found in this overly zealous prelate the enemy he needed. Like everyone else, of course, Nji Mama had perhaps wondered why this French priest sometimes spoke to the sultan in German, the European language Njoya understood best. But in the end, the architect would have assumed it was just a trick to convert Njoya. The Alsatian had once before explained the globally explosive ramifications of his nationality, but that day, it must be said, Nji Mama hadn't been listening.

In Mount Pleasant, in any event, Father Vogt was the perfect target for all the master artists who detested him. When Nji Mama realized that he'd never convince Ibrahim either, he turned back to Ngutane, but he had to admit once again that she really enjoyed pushing her father along the corridors of Mount Pleasant in Father Vogt's chair. In short, he remembered our Nji Mongu's delightful discovery of European fashion—and of Ibrahim.

"Now you are both talking like them," Nji Mama said one day to Ibrahim and Ngutane, and like them, he was serious.

It was the nocturnal whispering of those two that gave him the pretext he needed to express his disapproval publicly. No story is ever kept quiet for long in Mount Pleasant. Soon some storyteller would make it his own, seasoning it with the salt and pepper of his imagination. That's how Nji Mama got wind of the love between his brother and Njoya's daughter.

"Do you want to kill him?" he asked the lovers.

Nji Mama now held the stronger hand. He could go on the offensive; his arguments would carry the day. He knew that hearing about his daughter's dalliances would be the end of the sultan.

"After all you've done," he asked Ngutane, "do you want your father to have a heart attack?"

There was no room in the master architect's heart to understand a diva's loneliness. He had no patience at all for her search for happiness. For him, a woman was a child, and Ngutane needed to have a more dignified childhood, for she was Nji Mongu! If her version of this affair went unheard, it's because Nji Mama squelched it. Ibrahim calmed his elder brother's anger and kept the maniacal flames of his anger from reaching the walls of Mount Pleasant. But from the corner where he was contained by his guilt, the calligrapher couldn't argue his case too strongly. So Njoya's daughter suffered alone for a shared guilty passion.

Ibrahim warned Nji Mama. "You'll destroy everything if you talk to the sultan. Is it really necessary?"

If Ngutane had, in any event, long thought about returning to Bamum land, the unexpected revelation of her love affair gave her the push she needed. Ibrahim liberated her from the vicious circle in which Njoya's decline had trapped her. Only Ibrahim had wings broad enough to reach the heights where she had hidden her wounded heart, you could say. One push from him, and she fell like a bird. To think that Nji Mama failed to see that with her departure, the story of life in Mount Pleasant was coming to a close!

4

All Roads Lead to Foumban

When Ngutane arrived in Foumban, she found a task so urgent she forgot her troubles at once—and how. When Ibrahim explained the situation to her, he had downplayed the volcano boiling there, not wanting to upset the ailing sultan. First some background: when he was in Foumban, Njoya had encouraged the slaves to enroll in the German school, which was now French. In other words, he had sent them away from his own school, which was of course quite popular but couldn't accommodate everyone at once. Everyone wanted to learn to read the pictograms he had invented, but Njoya, a systematic man, had opted to educate the nobles first. He chose to start from the top, his dream being that once instructed, the ruling class would spread the knowledge that he wanted accessible to all: freemen, slaves, and the numerous captives in the sultanate.

The Germans hadn't upset his plans, but after the French banned the sultan's school, the nobles suddenly found themselves in a para-doxical situation. The curriculum they'd followed in Njoya's school had been invalidated; the knowledge they'd accumulated over years spent studying mathematics, drawing, law, medicine, agriculture, and other fields was now useless. In just one night, the cream of the crop of Foumban's best schools had been transformed into a band of illiterates. They ran to the French school and found the first rows occupied by slaves or captives. This created extraordinary situations. The oldest students in the elementary classes were all from noble families. On top of that, these students were punished when they skipped school: French school was universal and obligatory!

A truly shameful situation that soon became outright pitiful, for the noble students received awful grades, of course, even when they made an effort. Those young men who had sometimes worked for years as scribes, copying manuscripts for the sultan, who had mastered Njoya's various alphabets—the Akauku, the Nyi Nyi, the Mbima, and sometimes even the Lewa alphabet that the sultan had invented—earned the worst grades in French composition because they were forced to write in the Latin alphabet they'd just learned. It didn't help any that the sons of slaves burst out laughing when one of those nobles sitting in the back of the class didn't understand a thing about the simple arithmetic taught in French. And it was even worse when, in the dictation exercise of one of these newly illiterate students, there were twice as many mistakes as there were words. When a small child, the son of a Bamiléké captive to boot, laughed right in the face of a member of the Mbansi secret society because he couldn't conjugate the French verb "to be" in the past tense, the long-repressed anger of a class used to giving orders exploded. A resounding slap on the disrespectful boy's left cheek, however, awoke the anger of the boy's mother, who, thanks to Madame Dugast's lessons, had smelled the sweet scent of emancipation. The years of French education were bearing unexpected fruits among the Bamum.

That's how things stood when Ngutane returned to Foumban. She joined forces with Madame Dugast, and together the two women visited each of the villages in the sultanate, informing the nobles of the need to listen to them if they didn't want to lose the coming battles. Yes, they needed to convince those wounded men that this wasn't a repeat of the story of Lieutenant Prestat fifteen years later! How could they forget about Prestat?

"The battle lines have shifted," Nji Mongu told them.

But they weren't convinced until she added, "This is our war."

Madame Dugast advised them not to keep their daughters at home when they sent their boys to school—"if you don't want them to become slaves tomorrow."

Ngutane realized, however, that Nji Mama's anti-French convictions had deep roots already and that none of her speeches—or the spectacle of her friendship with the woman she happily called "Idelette"—could change that. She also learned that the rumor of her father's assassination by the French in Yaoundé had spread like a weed, sowing the seeds of anger everywhere.

"The French are killing him in Yaoundé, aren't they?" some asked her. "Thankfully, Madame Dugast isn't like them."

Ngutane would have asked them what Madame Dugast was like, but they didn't even let the sultan's daughter tell them about Mount Pleasant. Their daily gossip had already crafted Nsimeyong's true story, and Nji Mongu's mouth could only confirm what they already thought they knew.

"First they made him sick, right?"

"They made him lose control of his hands."

"Unable to speak."

"What about his legs?"

"Crippled him."

"Then they gave him a chair on wheels."

"So he'll never walk again."

"Just sit there like a dead man."

"More dead than alive."

"So he'll die."

Everyone in Foumban was consumed by this belief, and even today it still burns strong. This fiction made the fresh news that Ngutane brought from Yaoundé seem like nothing but lies.

"But he'll outlive them!"

"Yes, he will!"

The nobles held their breath, fuming mad. Things were no different in Foumban, they said. They had seen how the French administration was doing everything—*everything*—to destroy the dynasty that had ruled in Foumban for four hundred years. They had seen—no lie—the French build up their power to challenge the authority the nobles had always held in the palace. They had seen the French create new positions of authority and give them to slaves, who had no shortage of arguments against the reigning elite. Now the elite were no more than judges whose opinions no longer mattered, whose authority to register births, marriages, and deaths had been revoked. They were Tangu, who had seen all the other members of their secret society exiled; teachers of Akauku writing who had been chased from the palace, where the library was found, and were now considered illiterate; the police of a palace devoid of life and, worse, forbidden to bear arms. They were praise singers in a time when nothing deserved to be praised, genealogists of a family whose power had been suspended. All these nobles, whose endless rants filled Ngutane's days and nights, were wounded, yes, wounded. They looked to the sky and saw nothing but birds of prey and no one there to protect them. The sultan was gone.

"They want to kill him, tell us the truth!"

So the nobles sat in the courtyard of the half-built Palace of All Dreams, and nothing happened in the city to challenge their pessimistic views. They had seen how the most important decisions had been wrested from their hands, from the hands of the founding families; they had seen their slaves become masters over the Bamum. Because they didn't want to obey orders from their own captives, they gathered in the palace courtyard and killed time with gossip, raffia wine, and games of *ngeka*. What else could they do? Even the sultan's ears had been locked to keep out their advice. And that wasn't all, one of the men insisted, his eyes aflame.

"From now on, they want the sultan to be elected!"

The nobles around him exploded. "Elected!"

It was a rumor spread by the men who were working with the French, which the slaves had applauded, of course. It was only a rumor, to be sure, but the French often circulated their decisions that way, to see how the people would react before signing decrees and sending the police to arrest those who failed to comply.

Mose Yeyap was the one who usually circulated the French rumors. During the sultan's exile he had set himself up as the spokesman of the oppressed. He had managed to isolate the sultan's representative, Fompouyom, by mounting sordid plots that made him unpopular. A man of many masks, who switched easily from a Fulani *gandoura* to a European three-piece suit with a top hat and spectacles, Mose Yeyap had positioned himself in the center of all the most important decisions in the sultanate and no longer hesitated to go by the European version of his first name, Moses. No one could explain the reasons behind his arrogance, even if in the Evangelical Church of Foumban—a legacy of the German missionaries, where he, as one of the first to convert, was the most influential member—he continued giving sermons on the innovations brought to Israel by Moses's revolutionary laws. Holding the position formerly held by Pastor Göhring, whom the French weren't in a hurry to replace, he often preached about the Exodus of the Jews from Egypt's hell, pontificating on the liberation of the slaves from Pharaoh's chains.

His regicidal enterprise was helped along by the many episodes and books of the Old Testament that the sultan's scribes and copyists had translated; he could enrich his incendiary sermons with verses written by Njoya's own men in a language everyone understood. If in the church Mose used his faith to convince the slaves that he was their Man, outside, his position as translator helped tip the balance of power in his favor. His noble birth and his family name destined him to be one of the sultan's councillors, and of course he'd never forget that. Nji Moluh, Njoya's heir, had of course attended German and French schools, but he had refused to bow down and had gone into exile with his father. To top it off, he was Muslim. As a result of all of this, Foumban was open game, especially for the pretender!

Ngutane peppered Mose Yeyap with questions.

"Elected? Have the French lost their heads entirely?"

Mose kept an even tone as he answered. "They elect their president, too, you know."

The calm look on his face annoyed Njoya's daughter.

"We aren't French."

"So what?"

Oh, Ngutane, had she gone to one of the French schools that had popped up in Bamum land (not the one where her friend Madame Dugast taught, it goes without saying), and had she read what the children studied, she would have known that the sultanate now had a new genealogy that wasn't rooted in Nchare Yen's bravery, nor in the waters of Rifum; she would have known that the children learned that their ancestors were "the Gauls," whose strange mustaches were shown in the pages of their reader, *Mamadou et Bineta*!

And she would have known that there was no role for her father in the future written in the books from which the children memorized and recited passages so happily.

"A sultan is not a president," she told Mose Yeyap.

"Things change."

"Do the English elect their king as well?"

Ngutane had understood that the battle for Foumban would be difficult. But she hadn't anticipated such perfidy. She had heard about elections in Nigeria, where, they said, it had been suggested that the Yoruba elect their king, their *alake*.

"The French aren't the English," Mose replied.

"Ah, so explain it to me."

"The march of democracy cannot be halted."

"What do you mean by that?"

"We aren't in Nigeria—"

"Believe me," Ngutane interrupted at last, "even France is just one province in the world."

But did Mose Yeyap even want to listen? With his calculating mind, he already saw himself running in an election against the leader of the sultan's family—once the sultan had died, if not sooner. He dreamed of such an election. He certainly couldn't force the Bamum sultan to abdicate, but it no longer seemed impossible. Circumstances had forced the German kaiser, whose photo and W-shaped mustache had previously adorned Njoya's walls, to abdicate in 1918. The end of their monarchy had shaken the Germans, who, as Mose knew, hadn't seen it coming either. For him, the pathways of change were strange. Sometimes democracy was ushered in by machine guns, cannons, and grenades. Yes, sometimes it arrived at the end of a military occupation. Still, an election, and nothing but an election, would justify its bloody means. If the future could conjure monsters, he told himself, it could also open the doors to paradise.

"A paradise of gangsters," Ngutane protested once more.

But Mose Yeyap didn't listen to her. He was convinced that she had a "prewar mentality," meaning before the First World War. She hadn't yet understood that to win an election in occupied Foumban, what mattered wasn't your position on a genealogical chessboard or the way the ground stuck to your feet, but the number of votes in the ballot box and, of course, the support of the French colonial administration. To become a leader in post-1916 Bamum land, what mattered most was being friends with the French. That requirement excluded Njoya and his legitimate heirs. Mose Yeyap had popular support, thanks to his position in the Christian church and his defense of the slaves, a support that, he knew, would put him in power in any democracy. He didn't need to listen to the sultan's daughter. In fact, history was moving against her. If an election were organized, with democratic-style campaigns, the slave vote—which he had wrapped up—would far outnumber the Mbansi nobles and the freemen. In short, Mose Yeyap already saw himself the newly elected sultan.

"The world is changing," he said, smiling broadly as he chewed on a kola nut and spat. "The world is changing very quickly."

"And some are hoping it will just come crashing down, huh?" Ngutane retorted.

Ah, she was a master of irony!

5

The Writer's Creation

Meanwhile, in his room in Mount Pleasant, Njoya was battling with his body. He was battling to break through the barriers to his memory and his actions. Ibrahim held his right hand and taught him how to write again. Father Vogt had prescribed a number of exercises for the sultan to do each day to strengthen his muscles and had stressed the importance of drawing. The priest hadn't been able to convince Njoya to worship his white God, but his arguments had sufficed to awaken the artist that, since the onset of his illness, had been slumbering within the sultan. So he spent hours in his bed or armchair, holding a slate, his two faithful aides by his side; the ink dripping from the piece of wood between his fingers made him look like a writer.

If Nji Mama and his brother Ibrahim had forgotten that Njoya was recovering from a dangerous apoplectic seizure (could they ever forget that?), they would have thought that the sultan was frozen, just waiting for the inspiration he needed to create the seventh version of his writing system, which was, really, his most impressive work. What left the two masters speechless was that when he really did begin to write, the monarch jumped back to the birth of his intellectual project, reworking an older version of his writing, using once again the pictograms he'd abandoned long before. Memory can be a real curse, but it is also a testament to life. The two men were dumbstruck when Njoya dragged his hand across the slate and wrote, in the Lewa alphabet:

That was his name. They stared at each other when, after a similar effort, the sultan dug further into the past for the name of his ancestor Nchare Yen:

It was as if, through the flesh of the words, the sultan had invoked the spirits of his land, asking for their help to restore his crumbling authority. If Ibrahim had told him that the ancestors had fallen silent when faced with the sultan's tragedy, this historic truth would have wiped out his sovereign's efforts. Not all truths are good to say. Yet Njoya wanted his chief calligrapher to stay by his side. He wanted Ibrahim to mentor him in the cryptography of his pain as he sought to use the gracefulness of his fingers to rebuild the strength of his whole body. Ibrahim had previously supervised the composition of the *Saa'ngam* when they'd been in Mantoum; he had orchestrated the work of the scribes, the copyists, the calligraphers, the illustrators, and the miniaturists. Who better to be at Njoya's side in those moments when, once again, thousands of storytellers filled his belly with their tales? When his fingers were impelled to produce letters, who better to guide them? And when his memory of painful things came back in malevolent nightmares, who better to help distract his mind with healing arabesques? Who better? If writing reinscribes life on earth in furtive blots of ink, Njoya's battle against the forces that had defeated his body was waged primarily on the surface of a slate, by means of pictograms he hoped would bear fruit.

The whole of the universe resided in his words, but more than anything, they concretized the memory of his life's events. He wrote one word after another, one figurine after another, one story after another, revealing anew in his writing the sinuous fullness of life. Yes, he saw the world take shape again before him; he saw the new palace he had built, where he had not yet lived, take shape on the hills of Nsimeyong, not through the accumulation of bricks, but of words. He saw the House of Stories in whose corridors he was imprisoned connect with the Palace of All Dreams, letting him know he was free. For when he wrote, Njoya was free, free and sovereign! From his bedchamber in Mount Pleasant, he was free to wage war against the infamous forces that had spread their miasmas across Foumban. He didn't even need to hear the echo of Mose Yeyap's felonious voice.

Holding his writing tools firmly in his hands, Njoya battled for his survival, convinced that he would win by beginning to write the history of the Bamum once again: *Here again is the book of the history of the Kings of Rifum.* The year was 1932, the seventeenth day of the month of March: the day he awoke. According to all the history books I've been able to consult, Njoya had only another fifteen months, two weeks, twenty-four days, and twelve hours to live, so I can tell you this now: it was his most loyal servant, Nji Mama, who would oil his body and return it to the earth of Foumban that he missed so terribly, burying him alongside his mother, Njapdunke, who was seated and waiting for him. But that, of course, the chief architect didn't yet know.

6

Mose Yeyap's Manifesto

Even today there are many in Foumban who still believe that Njoya's battles began in 1920, in the time of Lieutenant Prestat and Njapdunke. The profound wound that event left on the soul of each person in the city is still as painful as the scar Bertha bore around her neck. However, Captain Ripert, who in 1922 took the place of the irascible lieutenant, had decided to let the fire beneath the Prestat affair burn out by itself. This man—whom people remembered most for his seven identical outfits, in the same cut and beige color, which led everyone to believe he never changed his clothes—would also have liked to disappear, humbly, beneath the silent piles of paperwork. In fact, Ripert would have been quickly forgotten by the Bamum had he not had his own episode with the sultan, one that discouraged all those who had hoped Prestat's replacement would have better or, as Nji Mama put it, "more civilized" manners.

Yet when he arrived in Foumban, Ripert took the dusty file he found on the table and read the reports in just one night, eager as he was to open new chapters. His attention was tripped up by some of the names written in large letters, but no matter. One of those was Monlipèr. Ripert soon happened upon that man's name again; during his tours of the city, it seemed that "Monlipèr" was the most popular name among the artists. Mose Yeyap explained to him that in Shümum, "Monlipèr" meant "teacher," adding as well that the Monlipèr referred to in the text was probably Nji Kpumie Pemu, the chief of the Artists' Alley. Mose continued, although Ripert hadn't asked, adding that the young man whipped two years before was working for that same Monlipèr at the time of the incident with Lieutenant Prestat. The new French commander cocked his head.

Maybe that's when the captain concluded that Nebu must have learned to dream dangerous dreams from that man. Mose Yeyap, very chatty that day, also mentioned Nji Mama's name, which Ripert hadn't recalled, because it hadn't stood out in the confusing mass of Bamum names all beginning with Nji. Ripert hadn't given much thought to what his translator told him, but did he really need to think about it? A Cartesian, as all French colonizers pretend to be, he had seen a logical chain linking cause and effect and had drawn the necessary conclusions, though he didn't yet voice them. The red line that connected Nebu to the sultan seemed quite clear: it had already been traced in the report found on the table. Prestat had, in fact, stressed the details of his poisoning by his maid, Njapdunke. He had written in large letters the name of the man who had given her the poison (Nebu), the names of those who had plotted his poisoning (Monlipèr and Nji Mama), and of course the name of the man who, in his palace, pulled the poisonous strings (Njoya). He hadn't forgotten to wrap it up by warning his colleague about fish heads. Captain Ripert didn't need any additional arguments to convince him that here all the omelets were made with the same ingredients, but his first decision was to remove Monlipèr from his position in the Artists' Alley. Maybe he would have gone even further. All evidence suggests that Nji Mama was beyond his reach, since the chief architect worked in the palace. No need to say that from then on, the worksite of the Palace of All Dreams became the officer's main target.

Ripert's rather surprising second decision was to promote Mose Yeyap. He had hired Mose as a translator because his name appeared several times in his predecessor's report, each mention more flattering than the previous one. In French, and in a style far livelier than Prestat's listless prose, Mose Yeyap had told him the story of the fish and the poison, of the palace and the sultan, of dreams and lovers, of the public whipping and the girlfriend. Amazed, as he couldn't stop repeating afterward, "that a black could speak our language so well," Ripert had put the Artists' Alley under the translator's control. It was Mose's first promotion in the ranks of the French administration, and it came just after he'd been hired. It had been facilitated, of course, by testimonials, each as flattering as Prestat's, as well as by a letter of recommendation from Madame Dugast describing him as a trustworthy man "who in 1915 had gone to Douala, at his own expense, to welcome us." Madame Dugast had also written in her letter, "He's our Man"—with a capital *M*.

Nebu was never invited to the French commander's headquarters. Maybe Ripert had concluded that the sculptor was just a small footnote in his Book of Accusations. Only Nji Mama was summoned to answer some "routine questions." The master emerged from the French commander's office totally changed, convinced of the truth of the assertion we've already heard, which at that point he only murmured: "They want to kill the sultan."

Of course no one believed him. He repeated the phrase again and again, repeated it so often that it was finally lost in the silence with which everyone from then on took note of Captain Ripert's decrees.

"He only asked me questions about the sultan"—that's what Nji Mama confided to those who came to ask him for the truth.

Replacing Monlipèr would not be easy: Mose Yeyap could perhaps translate everything the French said into Foumban's multiple languages, but he'd never be respected by the artists and artisans, not to mention the apprentices. He wasn't of the same stuff. Giving him control of the Artists' Alley was like putting an army in the hands of a praise singer. Mose knew he would need to impose his authority on a world that was foreign to him, and no doubt hostile as well, but he didn't refuse the promotion. Instead he ran to borrow several books from the French school and quickly learned the basics of Western art. Then he invited all the artists to what he called a "very important" meeting. That day he dressed in his best *gandoura*. With the French commander at his side, he declared that a myopic tradition was limiting the potential of Bamum art.

"From now on, art is free," he announced. "A new era has begun for Bamum art, my dear friends!"

Captain Ripert agreed.

"Have you ever thought of becoming your own masters?" the translator continued amidst the general silence. "How can you declare yourselves artists when you submit your creative powers to an authority figure? Times are changing, my brothers, and art must reflect those changes. In fact, it is through art that the upheavals of our times find their best expression!"

Mose Yeyap knew those words would hit home with these artists.

"You are the eyes in our head, the guardians of our imagination, the conscience of our people. You hold the roots of our future in your hands. In your hands, you have the truth of our condition, for you see what we cannot and you hear what is hidden from us. Your hands have the extraordinary power to give a name to our era! Even the sultan doesn't have that power!"

Though everyone was already listening attentively, they all jumped at the word "sultan" and then listened even more closely. Muluam and Ngbatu, for example, felt a new power surge through the tools they held in their hands, and they weren't the only ones. Behind them, the deposed master, Monlipèr, commented sarcastically on the words of the new chief of the Artists' Alley. This time he wasn't blind to what was going on. In another corner, Nji Mama grumbled along with him.

"The artist must represent the changes taking place across our society," Mose Yeyap continued, "and in doing so, each must choose sides in history's battles."

"Aha," said Monlipèr. "What camp are you in, then?"

"You artists cannot remain neutral! You have been thrown into the Nshi River, and you must swim if you don't want to sink. Of course, you haven't been locked up in a madman's tower, but still, you must free yourselves from the authority of your master even if he's the sultan!"

This time the word "sultan" sent a wave of flames through the gathered artists. Such outrage had never before been felt among the Bamum.

"There you go!" said Monlipèr.

Having cleared his throat, Mose Yeyap was starting another subversive phrase when he was interrupted. "Do you mean that now our art must serve the white captain?"

The disgust with which the voice pronounced "white captain" had been lost on no one. The question was followed by a tumult, from which Ripert would have recorded many comments insulting the French administration if only he understood Shüpamum. He demanded a translation of the chattering, but his translator had mastered the art of liberal translation whenever necessary.

"They don't believe," Mose said, moved by inspiration, "that art is free in Europe."

Then Ripert laughed. "Tell them," he added, following up where Mose Yeyap had left off, "that Europe has produced great artists! Talk to them about the grandeur of the French artists who decided to listen only to their own inspiration. Talk to them of Gauguin and Delacroix . . ."

Even if he peppered it with the names of Gauguin and Delacroix, Mose continued his tirade about artistic freedom in his own way. His gestures grew more emphatic. He seemed to be boxing an invisible but dangerous foe.

"The best artists," he said, "are those who have freed themselves from the authority of their master and who obey only the laws of beauty, for beauty cannot be governed—"

"Does that mean," Muluam interrupted, "that we can create works of art that oppose the sultan . . ."

"Answer him," Monlipèr shouted from behind the young man. "Tell us the truth, you palm rat!"

Mose knew he was on dangerous ground, but he also knew he didn't have to answer impertinent questions, especially those from the apprentice of the man he had replaced. Yet Muluam hadn't finished his question. Ngbatu did it for him: ". . . or against the white man?"

This interrogation by a tandem of voices unleashed a din that forced Mose to move on to his conclusion. There was too much chaos and too many whispers. For the first time, the Artists' Alley was caught up in a strange fever. Even his French master looked in surprise at the inflamed crowd.

"What are they saying?" Ripert asked.

Mose Yeyap hesitated.

"Will you translate what they are saying?"

The tumult had overtaken the crowd. In truth, what could Mose have said? He had provoked a generalized anger, less because he had asked the artists to work according to his new rules than because he had reminded them that the palace had grown too poor and was no longer able to buy the works they produced. Njoya had always sponsored the artists; he was the one who had built the alley for them. It had been constructed long ago, when his demands for works of art had grown so much, requiring the efforts of so many hands, that the artists employed had needed to set up shop outside the palace walls. The sultan needed decorations for the palaces in and around Foumban destined for his wives, and he needed numerous gifts for his growing number of interlocutors. What he couldn't give away, he sold in stands that he opened in neighboring lands. This artistic flowering was possible only because of the stability of his reign. The arrival of the Germans, followed by the English and now the French, and the restrictions they placed on his trade had diminished the demand for works of art.

The last and most important order Njoya had made—can you believe it?—was a gift intended for the German governor, Ebermaier, in 1908. Later he had commissioned a new Mandu Yenu, but only after the Germans had confiscated the original throne. Who among the artists could fail to see that the palace's power was waning? Gone were the years when even the land of the Bamum reserved its best fruits to satisfy the palace's life of luxury. Njoya's income had been greatly reduced when the German colonizers had placed limits on his lands, his trade, and the work of his subjects. They had confiscated the best land in the sultanate for their banana, palm, cocoa, and coffee plantations, paying Njoya only a small dividend. Today, on Ripert's order, the sultan lived on an annual pension of a mere eighteen thousand francs. Even if he was still the only one who owned a vehicle in Foumban, and even if he maintained his prestige in the colony in other ways, in reality, Njoya no longer had the means to be the sole patron of the Artists' Alley. Clearly, when Mose Yeyap gave his impassioned speech on Bamum art (Nji Mama called it the Manifesto for the Prostitution of Bamum Art), colonialism had already bankrupted the palace of the Bamum sultan.

Yes, Njoya's position as patron of the arts had sometimes been seconded by the nobles' love of fashion, which kept many jewelers and sculptors busy. However, since fashion is a fickle supporter of the arts, the alley's masks and decorations fell out of favor after Herr Habisch opened his store in Foumban. The noblewomen wanted nothing but his gold chains; and Swiss watches, which enthralled them with their ticktock, were soon found on their wrists. Only a few remained faithful to the art of the alley's master jewelers. One might say that with his speech, Mose Yeyap landed the last blow on an already bowed back. And you'll recall all the elegant women of Njoya's court leafing through Herr Habisch's *Quelle* catalog and placing orders for things they certainly would have previously gotten from the Artists' Alley. Perhaps many of the noblewomen were genuinely overjoyed by the death of Bamum art. As for Ngutane, she recognized that this death in some sense foreshadowed her father's.

The artists—well, they didn't need anyone to explain the situation to them. They experienced it in the changes to the orders they received. They kept destroying more and more unsold sculptures in order to make copies of those sold by Herr Habisch. In fact, when Mose Yeyap gave his speech, the artists of the alley had already learned to bend to the desires of new patrons, artificially aging their sculptures "to give them an authentic look." They had to, if they wanted to survive. Monlipèr was one of the few, even the only one, to resist money's subversive influence.

"So does this mean we should also sculpt prostitutes instead of noblewomen?"

There was no end to the questions.

"Should we sculpt in mud rather than gold?"

All these debates, of course, had happened before Ibrahim's hands-off approach allowed the workshops to produce what tourists wanted, which created work for everyone and killed the artist in each. Mose Yeyap saw that the workshops were stagnating. That's why he could only smile at Muluam's and Ngbatu's questions, which he knew were inspired by old Monlipèr. He understood that these voices of dissent were the last-ditch effort of a frustrated, already defeated group to salvage its dignity by throwing itself into the dying embers. The old man was condemned, and his art along with him. Was the translator too impatient for the birth of the new?

Would he have preferred to hurry along its arrival? Had anyone asked his motivations, he would have sworn it was his love of Bamum art, even though many thought he was driven by political ambition alone. The truth is certainly somewhere in between.

"What are they saying?" Ripert demanded.

"They're discussing what I just told them," Mose Yeyap replied.

The white man didn't insist.

7

How Can One Be Both Black and Fascist?

How could I forget what Arouna and his friends found in the archives? In 1922, the year of the events in Foumban, in the same month, September, and on the same day, the eighteenth, when Mose held forth, and just a few hours apart, a confrontation between two close friends took place in Yaoundé. This dispute is the first actual memory Sara has of her father, and the old lady was categorical: the friendship between Charles Atangana, the politician, and Joseph Ngono, the poet, couldn't have continued on a high note. They were too different to forever be arm in arm. Their only regret was that their personalities clashed during a wedding, particularly since it happened during the celebration for Atangana and Juliana Ngono.

It all started in the house of the young couple, whom Joseph Ngono had just honored with a speech in their language after they'd been sermonized and blessed by Father Vogt. It all started, yes, when the couple was still dressed in their festive clothes: the chief in his handsome tuxedo, a black top hat on his head and a long Cuban cigar in his left hand. Joseph Ngono was also wearing a tuxedo, borrowed but just as black, his handicapped hand in his pants' pocket. Juliana was standing, dressed in white, waving her gloved hands, asking everyone to calm down, just to calm down, good Lord, to get a glass of wine, a beer, or something else instead of tearing each other down with awful, cutting words.

What had happened?

Charles Atangana's voice had suddenly exploded: "One might say, my brother, that you have become one of those fascists."

In the calm that followed his insult, which made everyone fall silent, he tilted his nose and stood tall, waiting for Ngono's reply and puffing on his cigar.

Fascist? Ngono thought.

He immediately remembered Adolf with the mustache, and the echo of that hoodlum's violence rang again in his ears. He thought about his hand, which he could no longer lift up in a salute without feeling ashamed because of the two missing fingers. He saw again Berlin's police station, where the police had asked him the same question over and over for hours: "Are you a Marxist?"

Ah, those policemen knew nothing besides that one stupid question!

Why Marxist? he had wondered then.

And now he was a fascist?

Here are the facts: Joseph Ngono had said that it was time "in our country, for blacks to organize, to march on Ongola, the city center, and proclaim the Republic of Cameroon." He had added that it was time, "high time," for Cameroonians to realize that the days of colonization in their country had ended when the German administration had come to an end—that since then, they were free, "totally free," as free as the Germans, for example, who hadn't waited for anyone's permission to declare themselves doubly republican and de facto to bury the monarchy that had governed them until then and led them into the hell from which they had just managed to escape. Cameroonians were free, too, Ngono had said, free to vote for whomever they wanted as leader, to elect the president of their choice, the chancellor or sultan or whatever they wanted, "free, even, to elect a demon if we want, because we are free to make mistakes and responsible enough to pay for them."

"But my dear friend," Charles Atangana had replied, this time in French, "we're not in Germany here!"

Ngono didn't see what that mattered.

"We are already a republic!" Charles Atangana continued. "Don't you know that yet?"

"You mean a colonial republic?" Ngono asked. "How can a republic be colonial, my friends?"

This time he had spoken not to Charles Atangana, resplendent in his tuxedo and enjoying his cigar, but to the many faces gathered all around.

"A colonial republic?" he repeated with a loud laugh. "The French are making a joke!"

"No," Charles Atangana interrupted. "The French Republic, my dear friends. We are French citizens."

Ngono's reply cut to the point.

"But we aren't French."

This abrupt sentence had been met by total silence. Charles Atangana might have asked, "Are you German, by any chance?" and the discussion could have turned into a mudslinging fight. For who didn't know that Joseph Ngono had spent two years in an internment camp following his return from Germany, falsely accused of "collusion with the enemy" because he was returning from there; that despite his diplomas, his training, and his experience, his radical positions had brought him nothing but sorrow. He was out of work. Everyone also knew that Charles Atangana had changed the spelling of his first name; and most important, everyone knew he had vowed never to repeat the years he'd spent in exile in Mantoum among the Bamum.

Who didn't know that it was he, Charles Atangana, whom the French used to introduce cocoa into Southern Cameroon, to replace the peanuts that until then had been the region's real source of revenue? All that was needed was to look out the window and see the immense cocoa plantation he'd created "to set an example." The French had quickly forgotten the German friendships of the man who'd hidden German officers in his compound in Yaoundé until 1916, when the English arrived in the city. The French had quickly forgotten, as well, that the chief had followed his German friends to Guinea, to Fernão do Pó; that he had defended them before numerous European tribunals long after they had lost the war. Ah, but *the people* knew all the details of Charles Atangana's life, and there was even this song:

> *Charles Atangana, the war is over.*
> *Hey, Charles Atangana, the war is done!*
> *The cannons will fire no more.*

So run away fast! Why do you stay?
All of you, Ewondo, come run away!
Come run away fast, dear brothers!

Who didn't know this song summarizing his position during the war? The French high commissioner had turned a blind eye to the chief's "little mistakes" because he used the "impressive strength of his voice" to convince the Ewondo to cultivate cocoa, as the colonial administration encouraged them to do. Atangana, who had been looking for a chance to regain the power he had begun to taste under the Germans, didn't pass up this chance to return to his city, Yaoundé, riding in a carriage. Yes, people knew the source of his present wealth—and its cost. They knew that Charles Atangana employed hundreds of workers from his own ethnic group on his plantations, imposing harsher work conditions than those found on colonial plantations, forcing them to work like slaves. They knew that sometimes his men whipped those who hadn't paid their taxes, hunting them down in the bush when they ran to hide and bringing them back to the city in chains. They also knew that all this zeal was his way of making the colonizers forget about his German sympathies. Besides, hadn't he been chosen by them because he was the most vulnerable?

On that wedding day, it was evident to everyone that despite the history shared by Charles Atangana and Joseph Ngono, their lives crashed into each other with a violence rarely witnessed in history, scattering bits of their shameful past around the living room. Suddenly they were no longer friends, and even less brothers-in-law. Their honesty was limitless, and the only real tragedy was that they had chosen to bare their souls on such an occasion.

Juliana Ngono intervened once more, but not even she could stop her brother from saying what was on his mind.

"*Anti Zamba ouam*, my God, why don't you men just drop it?" she shouted. "Do you want to kill each other?"

Behind her, voices rose up in support.

"Yes, drop it."

"Come have a drink."

"Yes, some wine!"

"Red or white?"

"A beer!"

"Two bottles of beer."

"Isn't there any palm wine?"

"Real palm wine?"

"No raffia wine?"

"What about my beer?"

"We've got beer."

"Corn beer?"

"Banana beer?"

"What about *arki*?"

"My beer, you bastard!"

"*Arki* is illegal."

"Forbidden."

"By who?"

"Why?"

"*Akié*, ah, my brother, do you want to drink or fight about politics?"

Even drinks weren't exempt from the battle!

Juliana Ngono called to her husband once more. "Charles, come, let's dance."

She walked out through the unending circle of voices. But the chief didn't follow her. The quarrel between Ngono and Atangana wasn't the kind that dissolved into banter. It needed to go on to the bitter end, even if that meant one of the fighters would end up losing his head.

"As for me," Ngono went on slowly in order to give more weight to his words, "the day I was born, I was Cameroonian."

"How do you know?" Charles Atangana cut in.

That answer sent a ripple through the crowd. The chief went on, weighing each of his words, suggesting that Ngono might be taken for a fascist.

Why fascist? Ngono wondered.

Ngono was flustered by Charles Atangana's choice of words. In the insult he read the threat of a denunciation. News of Mussolini's march on Rome had reached the protectorate, making the French officials with whom his friend spent his days feel uneasy. The

French were afraid it would give ideas to the colonized, especially those who read the newspapers, ideas of "unifying the black race." That's what they meant by "fascists." For Ngono, on the other hand, it was the tumultuous years he had spent in Berlin that inspired what might have been the proclamation of the Republic of Cameroon.

Had Charles Atangana asked his friend on which side he stood when Germany twice proclaimed its republic (an event that had clearly inspired Ngono), that would have been a reasonable question. But a "fascist"? Ngono remembered heated discussions in Berlin, in the House of Exile, with friends of all stripes, surrounded by kids playing, laughing, and crying. He recalled how Mandenga, who never stopped dreaming of getting off the boat back in Cameroon with his whole family, was ready "to do something." And Ngono recalled the question so often put to him: "But to do what?" Ngono also recalled the day when, in a moment of real despair, possessed by the contagious bad mood that losing the war had provoked in the Germans' minds, he had cried out, "We were defeated!"

The Landlord had looked him straight in the eyes and replied, "We haven't even begun our own war, my son, so how could we have been defeated? Look at a map of our continent," he said, pulling him over to a large map. "The only names you'll find there are also over here in Europe. Look, here you have the French Sudan, the Belgian Congo, German Kamerun, or rather, the French and English Cameroons, as they now say, Portuguese Mozambique. Look, there's even a little Spanish Guinea! The only thing we're missing is a Swiss Nubia! And where are we Africans in all of that? Do you believe that we have stopped existing because of it? You see, the colonizers' mistake is that they always imagine Africa without Africans, like on this map. Don't make the same mistake, for the day will come when we Africans reinvent our continent! And on that day the world will awake to the sound of our proud children's cannons!"

That's how Mandenga the Landlord talked. His eyes aglow with the vision of a colonial apocalypse and an African future.

"But why count on others?" he added. "It's up to us to defend ourselves!"

These distant memories echoed in Ngono's mind while, in the country to which he'd returned, he heard Charles Atangana talking about a French Republic that included "us," and it was as if this time Atangana were saying "We are defeated."

Ngono looked at his friend, who, after tagging along behind his German companions, today claimed French citizenship. Ngono smothered a laugh that had suddenly gripped his chest. *He can't understand me*, he realized.

Several people had gathered around these two verbal combatants. No one dared to jump into the breach, and even Juliana Ngono had shrugged her shoulders, signaling her defeat, for her husband had turned to her only to ask for another glass of wine. This time it was Ngono who announced he was thirsty and asked if Charles Atangana wanted to have a drink with him. When each man had a drink in hand, the man of the day rose, turned toward his friend Joseph Ngono, and said, "My brother."

"So where were we?" Atangana asked, taking a big puff on his cigar.

To his great surprise, Joseph Ngono replied, "Go dance with your wife. It's not worth continuing."

Charles Atangana couldn't have agreed more. The sounds of a cakewalk pulled him from his seat. Soon he was waddling around the living room, his exaggerated duck steps entertaining the crowd. People knew, though, that the spirited discussion was only deferred. One or two voices called out to Joseph Ngono as he passed, "Congratulations, my brother." But his mind was elsewhere. Whose wasn't? Maybe the people who were congratulating Joseph Ngono were doing so because he had really pulled something off by marrying his sister to the most flamboyant and unpredictable man in the protectorate.

For everyone there, the future was more of an opening than a battlefield. Never had Ngono longed so much to be by himself and smoke a cigarette. He didn't slam the door behind him when he left the happy crowd.

8

Judgment Day

December 1932. There are stories that need to be told—for the one who's listening, and only for the one who's listening. Everyone could see how Mount Pleasant's thousands of stories had transformed the sultan. He had regained weight, looked good, and was asking for more. His face glowed as he hungrily breathed in, like an exotic perfume, the things people told him, and the sparkle of his wit cheered his visitors. This was especially true when he listened to a story he had already heard a week or a month before. Njoya enjoyed it best when he knew the story's ending. Some people were surprised by this need for repetition, but others took his good humor as a sign. He had been imprisoned in his apartments for two years. The monarch's ears had drunk down the many voices that had come from all around Cameroon, all around Africa, yes, from all over the world to bring him the firsthand accounts of their lives. The strength of his voice had quickly returned, but not the precision of his hand. His fingers still lacked the dexterity they had before his illness. Njoya did his best to offset his failing health, to escape from his soul's traps. For example, he demanded more and more from his memory. And so, in addition to the spicy stories inscribed in his Book of Time, he also reconstructed his body's own genealogy. Writing was his best medicine, letters the real components of his health. A slate would decide the outcome of his final battle with his body, and Ibrahim, the master calligrapher, was sure he would win that battle as well.

Njoya began writing to overcome his apoplexy, but writing soon took on a different meaning. The shapes, the letters, and the silhouettes—which he first scribbled absentmindedly, then out of boredom—soon became systematic studies. They became images, faces. Because memories return to us through a filter, he soon discovered the limitations of his visitors. He realized that they told each other their stories and, short on inspiration, often returned to those they had already told. They rehearsed before telling them to him and often chose those he'd enjoy the most. Maybe the masters had edited out the more licentious ones that they didn't want told to him. What Njoya quickly understood was that his entourage wasn't worried about his salvation. What they wanted, quite simply, was his health. So when Father Vogt suggested that he had perhaps heard all the world's stories, but not yet the Story of Stories, it goes without saying that the excited sultan lent his ear, his curiosity piqued by the voice with which the priest had made his promise.

"It's a story that contains all the stories you have already heard," the prelate said, smiling and scratching his head. "Then it brings them to their logical conclusion, for it's the story of salvation."

Njoya was surprised that Father Vogt had waited so long to tell him this story. Wasn't salvation what he had always been looking for? But Njoya wasn't the only one who'd been waiting for this conclusion, the moment of its realization. The bearded priest had long been waiting as well. The next day he washed and ironed his cassock. It gave him an air of respectability that the city's dust had always conspired to deny him. His nuns followed behind him, carrying the tools required for the sacrament, ready to collect the fruits of what would clearly be a lengthy confession. Twenty young boys walked behind them, singing. There was no sign of mirth on the faces of those children dressed in white: their priest and his Church had so often postponed Judgment Day that they were truly ready for its arrival. Each choreographed step was taken with the gravity of a scene prepared long before.

"Judgment Day?" I asked.

"Oh yes," Sara replied.

All of Mount Pleasant, all its ears, had gathered together. If anyone had looked into the courtyards, the houses, the kitchens, and the beds, no living soul would have been found. Everyone was there, men, women, children, and animals; all eyes and ears were washed, rinsed, and open to hear the words that would come out of the mouth of the miracle-making priest. Hadn't Father Vogt made, right before everyone's eyes, a rolling throne that had been nothing but a blessing? Ah, the high commissioner had made his excuses, using the pretext of some pressing work, but in Mount Pleasant, no one really expected him to come. Father Vogt alone was a bit disappointed, but, oh well! He snapped at his nuns, using a tone that here only husbands use to talk to their wives. But in any event, everyone thought of the nuns as his wives.

"Give me the Gospels," he said.

It was a huge book, bigger than the one the missionary Göhring had used in Foumban, its pages red with the dust of Nsimeyong, or perhaps from being read too often. When the priest raised his right hand, the catechumens stopped the song that had accompanied each of the priest's gestures up to then and immediately intoned the Ave Maria, their faces frozen and their hands clasped in front of them. It wasn't just about the sultan, no; the fate of all of Cameroon would be decided that day, in this courtyard where a hundred had gathered to witness the ceremony in silence. Sometimes Father Vogt opened an eye to assess the effect of the scene on the pagan congregation, knowing that the smallest things can bring unexpected results. He knew that Göhring had worked to save the souls of all these people; he had read the Old Testament to them, to Njoya in particular, and the sultan had had most of the stories of that book translated into Shümum—to add to his own library, it must be said. Father Vogt knew how well the story of Moses had been received among the Bamum slaves, although no one had told him the real reasons behind the rather surprising choice of that story. It was easy, he imagined, to make a patriarch like Njoya appreciate the flavor of myths.

"Here is the story of Nji Shua," Father Vogt declared, clearing his throat several times and looking at the sultan.

He opened his Book of Miracles to the right page, the first one in the Gospel according to Matthew, and read the genealogy of Jesus, whom he had strategically renamed Nji Shua. Of course, when he heard his name, Nji Shua, the master carpenter, beamed with joy.

Several of his apprentices weren't listening, and he cuffed them on the head. Father Vogt read several passages, then looked up to gauge the effect of his words on the crowd. He gestured with his hands as he spoke, acting out the characters' roles. He didn't fail to include Bamum names in the story, to make it easier for everyone there to understand. Of course, he was used to giving a little nudge to help constipated miracles along, but this one was, to his mind, the most daring of his career.

Father Vogt preferred not to imagine how the pope would react to this even if he was convinced that the Catholic Church would understand his motives. Besides, Pope Pius XI had never been to Africa. The prelate didn't merely give God a familiar name—he called him Nshi, after the river everyone knew, the life source of the Bamum—Nji Shua's disciples were also given names everyone recognized. People were heard crying out in joy because he'd just mentioned the name of a copyist or a miniaturist, a ceramist or a weaver. None of them had ever imagined that their uneventful life would one day be part of a great tale. At other points people heard tears, laughter, or a long murmur because, like an actor who can't resist playing to the audience, Father Vogt couldn't keep himself from hamming it up. All the listeners had recognized their names in the tale when they realized that the only one left unmentioned belonged to the man whom the father had come to convert first and foremost: the sultan. After inserting Njoya's entire entourage into his tale, the priest turned back toward the monarch, setting in motion the next phase of his elaborate battle plan.

"What happens to Nji Shua?" Njoya asked, impatient to know the rest.

"He is betrayed."

A shock wave ran through the crowd.

"What?"

"Betrayed?"

"Yes," said the priest, taking a deep breath. "Betrayed."

Njoya smiled and hit his cane on the ground. He recalled his discussions with the missionary Göhring, the only white he had ever called his brother. He saw once more the night of his confession, which he had never gotten over: Manga, Samba, Ngosso. Yes, the

sultan had been in power for too many years not to know that
Father Vogt's love story could only end with betrayal.

"By whom?" he asked, for that was the only possible surprise.

"Who dared . . ." an indignant voice added.

There, Father Vogt didn't use a familiar name; he stuck with the
story's original. The fire he'd lit in his listeners' eyes would have
burned the traitor to ashes if he'd singled out someone in the crowd.
He looked around slowly, articulating each of the syllables as he said,
"Ju-das."

"Judas?"

"Yes, Judas."

"Judas what?"

"Judas Iscariot."

"Who is this Judas Iscariot?" the listeners asked each other, as if
talking to strangers.

"Point him out!"

"He's a character in the story," said Father Vogt quickly, raising
his hands. "Just a man in the story."

Everyone felt reassured. A man with a name that ugly could
only be a traitor, they said. The crucifixion was an easy part of the
story to tell. Father Vogt knew it by heart, of course, and he elabo-
rated it dramatically, hammering each of Calvary's nails into his listeners' hands. The horror he saw traced on their faces, he had
planned it all out, right down to the silence that followed the end of
the Passion. He closed his book, wiped his burning mouth, bowed
before the sultan, took time to catch his breath, and then disappeared into the crowd. The fate of Nji Shua would make its own
way into everyone's soul overnight. The smile on Njoya's face gave
the priest hope that maybe, this time, he had reached his goal.

The night was calm. But the next morning Mount Pleasant awoke
to women crying and children running every which way in the corridors.

"He's dead," voices shouted.

"What?"

"He is dead!"

"Who?"

"He is dead!"

The men rushed into the surrounding woods, where they found the body of the carpenter, Nji Shua, crucified on the branches of a eucalyptus. No one shuddered. Not even Njoya, for he had been convinced by the Story of Stories. With the zeal of the newly converted, everyone waited three days, staring at the face of the dead man, who, they were certain, couldn't fail to rise from the dead and complete the already mythical tableau of his suffering. There were even some so zealous that they swore that Nji Shua's beard had gone white; others insisted that hair was growing in his bald spot. All these rumors contributed to turning his cadaver into a legend. The wives he had treated so badly during his lifetime declared him a saint.

Everyone was disappointed that Father Vogt didn't come back to finish his story now that the hero's crucifixion had taken place. If they failed to understand why the priest, instead of rejoicing, was so unwilling to witness his Judgment Day in person, they refused to believe the tale told by the catechumens, who said they'd found him in the church, damning the population and offering up curses that the children wouldn't complete: "That son of a . . ."

"Nji Shua won't rise from the dead," someone said after the fourth day. "He won't rise."

It was the familiar voice of someone who'd always looked upon the French skeptically. The chief architect hadn't even gone to see the body of the man with whom he'd built so many buildings. He just pronounced the final words: "He will not rise."

"Wait, Nji, you'll see," people replied. "A dead man doesn't run away."

"Does that mean he can rise?" Nji Mama asked.

Some argued.

"The white man is strong," they said. "Why don't you accept it?"

"If someone is stronger than you are, just carry his bag."

"It's only been three days and one morning since Nji Shua's death."

"And one morning."

"Not even four full days."

"Not even four days."

After the fifth day, when the colonial police came to

investigate—alerted by the stench of the body people refused to bury, which had filled the whole city with its asphyxiating miasmas— a woman accused everyone of having interrupted the miracle. It was the dead man's third wife.

"He just married me," she said. "How could he be dead already?"

"Go take care of your children," people replied. "Now you are a widow."

"I'm pregnant."

"Well, you're free to find another father for your child."

Ibrahim announced the news to his brother.

"You were right," he said. "Nji Shua is truly dead."

The carpenter's tragedy had as many public repercussions as the priest's humiliation. By using Bamum names for his story, Father Vogt had lifted the violent master, who whipped his apprentices and wives, to an unparalleled height. Suddenly the possibility of becoming a saint had appeared before Nji Shua, along with the promise of a paradise he had already forgotten about. Who would spit on the beatification? There was only one thing he had to do, and it required courage. Nji Shua, long accustomed to living the life of a villain, had clenched his teeth and accepted that he would die like a hero. His apprentices didn't refuse the nails he distributed; they had been waiting a long time for a chance at revenge. Ah, Nji Shua didn't even cry out when they pierced the palms of his hands and his side. Being crucified was the only good thing that could still happen to him in this life.

Yet the crucifixion of Nji Shua also marked the beginning of the end of Mount Pleasant. Who would agree to live in the shadow of a master who hadn't been brave enough to live his life to the end? The memory of his life was as shameful as that of his death, and it soiled a whole other story that hadn't yet been told. Their collective effort to wipe his face from their memories was a failure. The dead man was buried under the tree where he'd had himself killed, like a dog. Even the tree died soon after. It wasn't just that Father Vogt's miracle didn't take place; he had dragged the colonial police right into Mount Pleasant's courtyard, and that evoked bad memories of far-off Foumban. Each person recalled the dramatic start of Njoya's exile and the upheavals of the French administration. No need to say that the time for revenge had come for Nji Mama. He had always looked at the priest with suspicion, but had never thought that vengeance would taste so sweet.

"I told you," he repeated to anyone willing to listen. "I told you not to trust that man."

There weren't many to contradict him. Even his younger brother kept silent.

Njoya heard the story of Judgment Day differently. The tragedy of the man who had taken a curse upon himself and asked to be crucified to satisfy his deep need for salvation reminded the sultan of the illusory depths and false promises of tales. Njoya was disappointed, but he was certain that the dead man hadn't just written another version of his life, he had put an end to stories altogether. After this, no other story would make any sense. There were no more delicious stories to listen to or interesting folktales to tell. Each sentence was clichéd, each word tarnished by blood's purple ink. The idea that the only thing possible after this story's conclusion was that every story come true filled the sultan with sudden happiness. Even the drying up of words in the mouths of storytellers and the false promises of stories seemed unimportant in light of his ecstasy. That day, he got up and walked without his wheelchair. He had come through the world's stories and discovered that the only thing that remained was the palpable reality of the present, all stories being but the prologue to life.

"I am emerging from a very long dream," he said when he reached the main courtyard and the sun's caress. "A very long dream."

He hadn't staggered.

9

The Virtues of a Drawing Well Done

Over the long course of his ailment Njoya had understood that his body was his true master. He had become the slave of his flesh and bones. If the invention of a writing system was due to his will to give form to the world's multiple voices—much as he had done with the Shümum language, drawing on the other languages spoken around him—his grudging memory, his trembling hands, and his feeble body had taught him that now, in his chambers in Mount Pleasant, he had reached the end of a long path. The only thing left after the end of so many stories was to retrace the route of his life. To begin everything over again, he thought. To live it to the fullest.

Faced with the thousands of names of people whose stories had been told to him by hundreds of voices, he finally understood that he had been allowed to contemplate the infinite variety of life in order to notice that in each section, however small, the universe's dramas play out. After Nji Shua's failed resurrection, he opened his eyes and saw fragments of unfinished stories floating in the air like butterflies. Stories taking the place of religion, each offering identical promises of bliss. What made him sad at the high point of his newfound joy is that Nebu erased his slate after each storytelling session. Njoya had tears in his eyes thinking about those thousands of lost stories.

He recalled how he had remained motionless when listening to the stories that had given him the most joy, and how he'd almost succumbed to those that had threatened to wipe him out. He wanted to explore the world of sensations again, to come back to life; he wanted to become an animal, a two-headed snake that shifted at will between two destinies. He wanted to become a lizard that lost its suddenly burdensome tail. He wanted the power to take apart his nightmares by chewing them patiently; yes, he wanted to chew on the story of Ngosso Din, among others, to chew on it calmly so he could swallow it at will. He wanted to become the master of his memory and, like a cow, rekindle the memory of feasts from the midpoint of his life, to digest and savor them anew. Yes, he wanted to hold the beauty of words immobile before him.

Njoya recalled how he had invented his writing system. He recalled asking everyone around him to draw life's most important things. Nobles, free men and women, slaves, children, blacksmiths, sculptors: everyone had set to work diligently and summarized their lives on a slate. They had all brought to life the encyclopedia of their experience, the well-considered dictionary of their dreams, their wisdom and their fantasies, their hopes and the facts of their existence, the arts and trades common in the sultanate; and they had drawn it all on many slates. Njoya remembered how he had all those slates washed and then had drunk down the collected water. Then he had fallen asleep.

Never before had his belly hurt as much as that night of his epiphany. He had called his shadow ten times during the night to help him go to the bathroom. And when he finally closed his eyes for a few hours, holding his behind with both hands, a dream had unrolled the encyclopedia of life, broken down into minimalistic forms. All the forms of the world were encapsulated in his mind in distinctive figurines. Was he in a trance, still dreaming, or already awake when he wrote down the first pictograms of his Lewa alphabet? He no longer knew. He who had eaten death and life and, in his body, transformed them so he could bend them to his will, he was the happiest man on earth. Because his dream wasn't dead. He had kept it alive in a book, a *lerewa*. He wanted to retrace the path of his life, but this time in reverse. The joy the past gave him transformed his awakening in Mount Pleasant into a promise. After the fiasco of Judgment Day, Njoya still hungered for the quest promised by Father Vogt, for the story that would save him from the tunnels of his thoughts by capturing the essence of ephemeral beauty. He still thirsted for that one story that would give his body back its full powers, as his alphabet had previously done for the universe's forms. He knew, yes, he knew that his work couldn't stop at the borders of Foumban; the storytellers who had visited him in Mount Pleasant had opened the windows of his life to the universe. He had always needed a translator to understand the surprises of the world that were revealed in their stories, but this time he wanted to relive the ecstasy by listening to them differently—in all their purity.

He looked at Nji Mama, who had participated with him in all his experiments in Foumban. The chief architect, the man who had been at the origin of each of his inventions and who had first seen through Father Vogt's ruse, had nothing to say. Njoya didn't insist. The truth was that exile had had a devastating effect on the imagination of the illustrious master. Wounded in his soul, all his certainties unsettled, robbed of his greatest artistic project, the Palace of All Dreams, Nji Mama had let rage cloud his tormented eyes and anger take possession of his hands. The shadow of his boubous and the familiar sound of his sandals in the corridors were still anchored in Mount Pleasant's memory, but he was now only the silhouette of the man he'd been in Foumban.

Njoya also turned toward the master blacksmith, Monlipèr. The old engineer, though he had once built a printing machine for the sultan, was silent. The two masters were like baobabs planted in flowerpots. The growing roots would ultimately destroy the pot holding them. Yaoundé seemed to have dried up their spirit. But Ibrahim, the youngest of the council, smiled. He was that plant that only needs new soil to come back to life.

"Alareni," he proposed, "you have been writing all this time."

Njoya listened.

"Maybe now you should draw."

Draw? Where could Njoya begin? The faces of all his visitors crossed his mind. He recalled that they were as different as life's surprises. Some were as black as ebony, others had the fair complexion of Arabs. There were some, like the Nubians, who were so black they looked blue. Visitors like Father Vogt were white. Some were tall while others were short, even though they were grandparents. There were fat ones, too, as well as others who were thin. Where to begin?

If someone had told Njoya that what he was composing, with his trembling hands in the half-light of his bedchamber, were the fragile forms of a nation that he hadn't yet named because she hadn't yet been born, perhaps he would have just laughed, for his quest aimed most of all to give a face to shapes that had become invisible and that were, moreover, too diverse to be truly unified. Was it worth the trouble to give them a name too? Ibrahim made him understand that an image would be closer to life's thousand faces than thousands of words would be, and that the face of a mother portrayed the infinite stories of maternity much better than a flood of words. Ibrahim became his guide, unleashing the waterfall of his words, for the master calligrapher was right. Njoya recognized it. Yes, why not draw?

"Why not draw?" he said, smiling broadly.

This was the first time the sultan took the artistic advice of the younger brother over that of the elder. In fact, Njoya's teetering body had already accustomed him to sharpening his eyes. He retraced the path he'd followed when inventing his writing system, this time backward. He went from letters to syllabograms, then to phonograms and pictograms. He did it in response to the request of the young master, who had already seen him draw shapes using the letters of the Lewa alphabet. Rather than a failed scribe, Njoya became an alert illustrator, and he began to look at the shapes he traced on his slate with surprise. Instead of taking beauty apart with his words, he discovered it in its original form. He let it flower like a frail daisy amidst a passel of leaves.

"The eye is essential," the monarch said, exultant.

Nji Mama didn't understand at first, but Ibrahim was the master of these sessions.

Njoya continued. "The ear comes second, in fact."

One day he turned around and looked at his shadow, who, standing behind him, was fanning his neck; he looked at Nebu as if he had never seen him before. The boy started.

"You say my shadow is mute?" he asked.

That's how the lad became the best story Njoya ever drew, and how Sara became the sultan's model. By chance—but is it really just chance?—she became the prototype for the remarkable voices floating all around.

10

The Sultan's Calculations

Foumban, 1922. Never had Nebu felt so much pain in his body, never! Confined to his bed for weeks, he couldn't even move a hand. He couldn't move his feet. It was as if he were condemned to take on the sultan's suffering in his own body, but eight years earlier and in his own way. Isn't it sublime that God invented mothers? Bertha flooded her son's suffering body with love. Because, in his suffering, Nebu had become once again the son that women had torn away from her, the son she could love to her heart's content. "All of this because of a girl," she murmured, hot tears running down her cheeks.

Nebu didn't answer.

Bertha refused to remember the *tirailleurs*' whipping hands, or Lieutenant Prestat's vengeance, for that matter. For her, it was only the logical consequence of a chain of events that began with Ngungure. Had her son looked the other way when that bitch called him, he would have avoided the anger of the Frenchman and his soldiers—that's what she told herself. Her mother's heart was categorical. It beat with a systematic hatred for all girls, a hatred that was nothing more than the other side of her limitless love for Nebu, a hatred that would later transform into another sort of love. For the moment, the only thought in her head was, That whore!

Bertha's face was a mask of disgust because, when she looked at her son's suffering, she saw Ngungure's face. Her lips trembled

when she thought of her grandson whom "that girl" had torn away
from her, and she spit. To think that all the market women had come
together to help birth the child! Bertha's hatred was as focused as
Nji Mama's rage at the French, whom he blamed for the bad weather.
For the master, his apprentice's woes, even his beating, were just
the start of a litany of complaints he kept to himself, grievances that
were sure to be followed by more misfortunes, all originating in
Paris. With the methodical focus of the man of science that he was,
he counted out one by one the atrocities committed by the French
against the Bamum, and his mouth twisted open, as if trying to set
off a cry for justice in his soul.

Of course Ibrahim had also been shocked by Prestat's bestial
violence, but he had put his hopes in the new face of the French
administration, Captain Ripert—especially since he had aligned
himself with Madame Dugast. If women—white or black, German,
French, or Bamum—had had a voice at the table in those days,
maybe colonialism would have worn a different face. Maybe it would
never even have existed at all. That's what Ibrahim thought: love,
not war, would rule the world. And women were a calabash filled
with love, etc. To his mind, it was possible to take a moment of dreadful suffering as a promise of future happiness, and maybe that's why
he paid several visits to Nebu and spoke to him of conciliation. No,
Ibrahim wasn't a fatalist, but hadn't the time come to look for paths
toward peace, especially after the episode where that boy had
almost lost his life? Was Ibrahim a wet rag? Far from it! Nor was he
a coward. But he had lived long enough, and in the company of
whites, to know that there are fights worth avoiding because they
aren't necessary. "They are like women, you know," he said. "Always
jealous."

The voices of Bertha, Nji Mama, and Ibrahim summarized the
differing opinions that crossed paths in Njoya's ears, in some sense
canceling each other out. The sultan didn't complain to the French
administration about Prestat's violence, no. Maybe the group around
Ibrahim convinced him of what he needed to do. The monarch accepted the suffering of one of his artists with a father's stoicism; yes,
he accepted it, and took responsibility for the sculptor's care. Nor
did he intervene when the French administration decided to replace

Monlipèr as the head of the Artists' Alley. Then, as well, his authority had been publicly called into question, but Njoya politely ignored the provocation: "I'm not that crazy."

After all, Mose Yeyap was "his son," as he said. And after all, it was he, Njoya, who had taught Mose to write in Foumban's first Shümum school. And again, it was Njoya who had advised Fräulein Wuhrmann to take Mose under her wing when he was just an adolescent, who had allowed him to marry a slave and had let him continue the work of the Christian church after the Germans had been chased from the sultanate. Yes, Njoya had closed his eyes when, in his zeal, Mose had begun to convert the palace slaves—including the slave of his mother Njapdunke—to Christianity!

It wasn't a big deal if Mose Yeyap had become the Man of the French. After all, Njoya himself had sent his own children, including his daughter, to European schools. No one had forced him. "Losing a son" had never worried Njoya. Each child is a unique adventure. On the contrary, he was convinced that he had given "his son" the best opportunities life could offer. So he wasn't afraid of losing power when the Artists' Alley was put under Mose's control, even if the French administration saw it as a weakening of his prerogatives. The son in question, Mose, came from a very influential family, and in any event, he was destined to take his father's place among the palace councillors. "Time will resolve all misunderstandings," Njoya believed. "Common sense will prevail."

After the whipping, he sent two of his personal doctors to Bertha's house and ordered his wives to cook their best meals for the wounded man and his mother. As for Monlipèr, Njoya found a new position for the deposed master. He had always wanted to give other duties to this amazing blacksmith who had once built him a machine to grind corn. This time he gave him the task of building a printing press. From then on, they spent their nights working on plans and imagining shapes and figures. In fact, Njoya was convinced that work, and work alone, could wrest him from the chaos that was spreading its stench over the territory. More than ever, his workshops became his refuge.

The sultanate's largest worksite, and the one that meant the most to Njoya, was still the Palace of All Dreams. The monarch put all his remaining energy into it. Alone in the ruins of his emerging dreams, he found the silence that life's cacophony deprived him of. And it was the only place where he could retreat with his masters away from the arrogance of the new colonial administration. His dream was to silence the world, and especially the French, with his works, with the grandeur of his building projects. He hoped in that way to triumph over their small-mindedness, to shut their treacherous mouths for good. "The largest building in Africa," that's what he called his new castle, then under construction, and he was impatient to see the look of surprise on the faces of the colonizers, who had made his life so difficult, when they saw the extent of his talents.

Common sense will prevail, he thought.

In secret, Njoya hoped that the French would finally bow down before him, full of respect, as had the Germans, who used to shout *"Donnerwetter!"* at each of his projects. He hoped they would recognize the strength of his vision, and when his Palace of All Dreams rose up to the setting sun, they'd simply say, "Fran Njoya."

"Alareni."

"Master."

"Master."

Again and again: "Master."

11

The Awakening of the Artist in Pain

1922. A woman's body appeared to Nebu in all the perfection of its shapes, in the full harmony of its features and the poetry of its song. It appeared to him in the bliss of an equation. Was it the body of his dreams? Yes. Was it Ngungure's body? How to know? He never again saw the face of the woman who inhabited his dreams, since his dreams were now composed of disjointed shapes that he reconstructed when he awoke. Night after night the faceless woman returned to his ailing soul. She appeared so often that finally he began to wait for her on the borders of sleep, impatient, even in his trepidation, to dream his dreams.

Art is an elixir for an ailing soul. Bertha's son began to sculpt again because the faceless woman appeared less and less as his health improved; because, as he healed, the shapes that led him to ecstasy began to vanish. He wanted to keep dreaming of her. The less he suffered, the less the woman of his dreams filled his nights and the more he felt the need to bring her to life with the power of his hands. When Nebu began his statue, he couldn't even get up from his mat. That's why he started with the feet that he had observed so carefully.

Instead of using wood or bronze or stone, as he had been taught in Monlipèr's workshop and as he had done in his workshop in the palace, the sculptor used clay. The softness of the earth is a balm for a wounded body. He sculpted the woman's feet with precision, applying the techniques he had learned from his masters and the art he had devised while following and observing the slave woman and others in the street. Beginning with the feet was also the most prudent way to proceed because his mother wouldn't wonder if they belonged to a man or a woman but would simply be overjoyed that her son had found the strength to work again.

Nebu began to sculpt again because he had discovered that pride is an antidote for defeat.

"They didn't defeat you," his mother swore when she saw him working. "They didn't defeat you."

Her eyes were shining.

"They don't have that power," her son replied, a smile on his lips. "On the contrary, they just made me stronger."

He paused.

"Suffering has given me even more inspiration."

Nebu finished the feet of the statue with all the love he had amassed in his dreams and with all the love that his mother spread over his body. It was apparent to him that the statue he was working on would be a testament to love. His mother was happy to see his work because she didn't yet know he was sculpting a girl's feet. It amused her to pretend that her son was sculpting himself legs so he could walk again, as he did in his dreams. For Nebu, the faceless woman could only be Ngungure.

Bertha was saddened when he announced that he was returning to his workshop in the palace. The mother was saddened, but the artist knew that there is no worse censor than a mother. In the palace under construction, amidst the community of artists working to bring their visions to life and whose compositions were all blended together in the Palace of All Dreams, Nebu could let his statue's legs grow according to his spirit.

He needed to work on the sculpture lying down, for his body was still too weak to stand for long. Even in this position he was able to give the body of his sculpture the behind of his dreams, "as round as two calabashes." When he finished the back of the woman, he noted the voluptuous reaction of the artists, and he paused. If only his colleagues could polish their language as well as they polished their materials! From his years in the Artists' Alley, in Monlipèr's

workshop, and especially from Muluam and Ngbatu, the sculptor
knew how foul a goldsmith's language can be.

"*Djo,*" one of the artists said, "you still want some?"

Everyone burst out laughing.

"You haven't had enough clit?"

"Enough pussy?"

"And we all thought the French had cut off your penis!"

"So you still have your balls?"

"Leave him alone," a friendly voice piped up.

Dirty jokes were the only way these souls, so focused on material beauty, could have fun while they worked. It was their way of
keeping their dreams alive amidst life's garbage. A way to remember that their work aimed to make life's ugliness bearable.

"He's sculpting a girl to avoid masturbating," said a miniaturist.

"What do you mean?"

"That he's going to screw his statue?"

"God is great!"

"Have you ever heard of such a thing?"

"What?"

"A sculptor screwing his own statue."

"*Djo, djo, djo,*" a voice continued, "masturbating next to his
statue, that's understandable, but screwing it . . ."

"He is crazy."

The man who kept talking about "screwing his statue" was a
middle-aged weaver. Was it Nebu's lying-down position that inflamed his mind? His own rugs were more traditional, only symbols
in elaborate patterns. Nebu smiled; the weaver was from the old
school, Monlipèr's school. He didn't even bother to answer the insult.

"Another girl?" a calligrapher said in surprise. "Are you looking
for bad luck?"

"Why don't you forget about girls?"

"Haven't they made you suffer enough?"

Some artists defended Nebu.

"Do you want him to make only animals, like you?"

"Spiders?"

"Two-headed snakes?"

"Leopards?"

"Horses?"

"Men on horseback?"

"And that's all?"

"Leave him alone!"

Never had a community of artists been so electrified by a work of art. The painters stopped working; they stared at Nebu's work, their mouths gaping open. The portraitists were stunned into silence. They had made hundreds of portraits of the sultan, his family, and his lineage. They had used their best techniques to depict the potential of the human body. They knew where the shadows fell and where light should be placed to give the most realistic effect. But in the presence of this sculpted woman, they suddenly measured the imperfections of their mathematical calculations. The weavers also stood speechless before Nebu's mastery. As for the miniaturists, who could have convinced them that their figurines were still worth anything? The calligraphers, they were as dumbstruck as the scribes.

The more the statue took shape, the more faces glowed and the more tongues loosened. Each one could clearly see a woman taking shape, and not just a woman: a woman in motion. And not just a woman in motion: a woman in harmony with her silhouette, a woman whose chest hung just as it should to heighten her beauty, a woman whose behind was "as round as two calabashes"; it was the woman all Bamum men had always dreamed of. The perfection of her body awakened the desire of the artists, who all wanted to make love to her, yes, to possess her, yes, to screw her one after the other. That's what really made them all chatter on as they stood there around her. This woman awoke the man slumbering in each of them and made them bow down at her feet, their open mouths yapping out their adoration. Only a few artists, the eldest among them, could wrest themselves from the strength of her charms. But they, too, were stupefied.

The youngest artists were simply incapable of keeping their mouths closed as they felt the hardness growing between their legs. They didn't care that in the very heart of their chattering, Nebu was lost in the most enigmatic of silences. The men were agitated and their language smutty because they saw in Nebu's work the creation of a master, a new master, and because this creation took hold of their bodies and unsettled them as no work of art ever had before.

"Master," one of the miniaturists finally said. "Master."

He was the first to renounce the trashy talk, transforming it into an exclamation. The congregation echoed him.

"Master."

"Master."

The cacophony converged in this one word. Nebu hadn't even completed his creation. He still had the woman's head to do. He spent days and weeks working on it, for he wanted it to correspond perfectly to his vision. He didn't want to reproduce Ngungure's face, for he assumed that the face of a woman known to be dead, whose bloody head was still present in everyone's mind, would have chased all the artists from the palace. He didn't want to reproduce Njapdunke's face, because the pain of losing her was being replaced, bit by bit, by the pain of never having seen the son she had taken away. Nor did he want everyone to burst out laughing at the sight of Njapdunke's face, since as everyone remembered, she had been Prestat's woman.

And his mother? She was a slave. Nebu didn't want his statue to be looked down upon. So he decided to compose a face at the intersection of the three women he loved so much, and in such different ways. The eyes he took from Ngungure because they were the eyes that had captured him, chained him up in a House of Passion. The ears he took from his mother because Bertha was the one who had truly listened to the story of his suffering from beginning to end. The mouth he took from Njapdunke because his hands still remembered its sweetness clearly. The nose he took from his mother because Bertha's nose was as sweet as a mango, etc.

Rather than signing his artwork with Nji Mama's name, Nebu drew a gecko eating its tail, a tattoo he had first drawn on Ngungure's belly. With this head, the statue of the woman became so perfect, so much a woman, so precise that you could have recognized her children if she'd had any. You would have known her social status by the sway of her hips as she walked. A woman sculpted from among all the possible Bamum women, she was *the* woman every man hoped to see emerge from life's monotony and walk into his courtyard. But most of all, she was the woman Nebu had never, ever stopped dreaming about.

She was his love.

When he said "done," the sculptor heard a clamor rise up around him. The artists were applauding. Each one showed his respect. All looked at his finished work and it was as if a silent prayer dictated the movement of their eyes. They walked around the statue, shaking their heads. Some took Nebu's hands and smiled happily. They wanted to touch the fingers that had brought such beauty to life before their eyes. When Nji Mama came to see the work that was creating such a commotion in his workshops, he could only repeat what everyone else had already said: a new master was born.

"I knew it," he added. "I always knew it."

Nebu had asked his master to wait for his work to be finished. He didn't want to be distracted by the judgment of an eye he respected so much. And now it was a triumph, it was triumph itself. Nji Mama's joy burst forth when he welcomed the new master into the ranks of those few men, that select number in Foumban who had been ennobled because of their talent and called *Nji*. A man of very few words, Nji Mama didn't intone a hymn of praise, as the other artists and masters had done. His eyes alone expressed his joy, his eyes that were usually so clouded. Then his face lit up, and the master burst out laughing. The master laughed because of the excellence before his eyes. Everyone laughed with him because everyone understood that Nji Mama's laughter translated the enchantment each one had experienced.

Even the chief architect couldn't wait to see the eyes of his colleague Monlipèr explode at the sight of the statue of love. Everyone knew the old master would laugh as well, the laugh of a philosopher, the laugh of an old man. No one wanted to miss his words. But everyone wanted to hear his laugh echo through the workshops. Maybe he'd raise his hand and declare that Nebu's statue was "the crowning achievement of Bamum art." Would those words have even sufficed, would they have been accurate enough to describe what the sculptor had done? What about "the pinnacle of the creations of all the masters"?

Nebu was the pure product of two of the best workshops and

two of the most respected masters the Bamum had ever known. Wouldn't the reference to tradition diminish his feverish talent? Why not talk of a "work of genius"! For in fact Nebu was a genius, yes, the resurrection of the best sculptors of Nok, Ife, and Benin. The reincarnation of the masters who had carved the House of Granite in Zimbabwe. The renaissance of Africa's true artistic genius, which had transformed Egyptian stones into pyramids! That's what amazed everyone. What would the colonizers say? Yes, what would the French ethnographers say? Does it matter? To me, yes, and what's more, their dubious comments are public: "Copy of a photograph most certainly seen in the display of a Swiss merchant who had previously opened a shop in Foumban"; "A poor imitation of European realist art."

Why are you surprised? The arguments put forth in the archives are always the same when it comes to the locals. It's always so evident. Yet, what would the sultan say? What about Njoya? What would he say, he whose eyes were used to beholding grandeur? Nji Mama was walking on air, but also full of gratitude. He would bring the new master to the sultan's attention; he would be the one who whispered in Njoya's ear, when he introduced Nebu, "Alareni, here is a new spirit."

"*Donnerwetter!*" the sultan would say when he saw Nebu's statue, and everyone around him would agree.

This would be the third time Njoya would meet the sculptor. The first time, Nebu was a slave; the second, the sculptor was half dead. This time Njoya would free him from the obligation to dress in ways that marked him as an apprentice and as a slave. Bertha's son no longer appeared to be one or the other with his long, untamed goatee and hair that flowed down his back. The monarch would make him a respected master, a *Nji*. No one was surprised that Nebu was the only one not enthralled by his historic creation.

"That's how true artists are," Nji Mama observed. "Always skeptical," he added after a pause.

12

Artists in Politics

If Njoya had told himself that bringing Monlipèr back to the palace would resolve some of the conflicts shaking up the Artists' Alley, he had underestimated the outrage caused by the replacement of the old master by a man the artists called a simple talker—a man in the pay of the French, to boot. Artists and artisans came several times to tell him that the best workshops had been left to the rats and to inform him of the planned death of their furnaces. These complaints saddened the sultan, who greatly valued the arts. He reassured the complainants, asking them to follow the orders of the French administrator, who, no doubt, he added, wanted to get them to do their best work, just through different methods. He also asked them to respect the initiatives of Mose Yeyap, who was, after all, a son to him.

Njoya also knew moments of doubt and instants of rage—the latter being more frequent. What was most important to him was to avoid any public conflict, especially at that moment, when his mind was entirely preoccupied by the construction of his new palace. It was the thirtieth year of his reign, and never before had he quarreled with the whites who had passed through his lands. The fact that he had survived two colonial regimes reassured him. It hadn't been easy. He had even maintained the peace in his country in 1914, when people said the whole world was at war. As for Ripert . . .

When, in defiance of all protocol, Muluam and Ngbatu came

once more to lay out their grievances against Mose Yeyap, Njoya asked them to calm down and go back to work. He advised them to follow the directives of their new master because that was what apprentices were supposed to do. He then told them that the roads of art were long and that the best way to become a master was to avoid politics and to work, work, and work some more. He took the example of Nebu, whom he knew to be the friend of these two fellows and who, after being dragged to the center of town and beaten almost to death by soldiers, had still mastered his anger, transformed it into beauty, and become the youngest master ever among the Bamum.

"He could have gone mad, right?" Njoya added. "He could have gone mad."

"Yes, Alareni," the two apprentices replied pitifully.

"But he didn't."

"No, Alareni."

"Follow his example," the sultan concluded, "and common sense will prevail in the house."

"Imitate the masters," he added.

Njoya couldn't really turn a deaf ear when these young men expressed a fury that boiled in his veins as well. Looking at them, he saw his own youth. One day they'll understand, he reassured himself. They'll understand that keeping quiet doesn't mean being a coward.

Njoya believed he'd put the affair behind him when the two apprentices left, bowing deeply, walking backward, and murmuring words of praise and thanks.

"Master."

"Master."

"Alareni."

The next night, Foumban was awoken by the shouts of a terrified woman. Mose Yeyap had just barely escaped from the cutlass of a man who had forced his way into his house and terrified his family, although no one was hurt. The Man of the French had fled through the bush and spent the rest of the night hiding in his employer's office.

This attempted murder created a wild commotion. Never

before had the city seen such crowds gathering in the night. Even the threat of the First World War hadn't ignited such passions in the people. Foumban had been shaken by the shouts of Mose's wife, who thought her husband was dead. And in the confusion, Muluam's phrase was repeated again and again: "They want to kill the sultan."

The apprentice sought to distract the crowd from the failed murder by conjuring an imaginary one, an assassination that everyone feared would happen.

"They want to kill him!" shouted Mose Yeyap's wife.

People repeated the words that Muluam carried from courtyard to courtyard: "They want to kill him!"

"They want to kill Fran Njoya!"

"Mfon Njoya?"

"Mfon Njoya."

Muluam said that with his own eyes he had seen the sultan held prisoner in his palace.

"Can we accept that?"

He had seen Njoya weakened, yes, he had seen him naked.

"Naked?" people asked.

"Yes, naked."

"That's unacceptable!"

Muluam said that it was Mose Yeyap who wanted to see the sultan dead. He wanted to take Njoya's place with the help of the French, who had made him their Man. His control of the Artists' Alley was only the start of an elaborate plan, for since when in Foumban had one ever seen an artists' cooperative run by a talker—"just a talker"?

"When?" a voice asked from the shadows.

"Never," everyone replied.

Riling up the pack in the dark of night, Muluam had become that voice of accusation whose strong echoes rolled up and down Foumban's hills, gathering in valleys all over Bamum land. Meanwhile, Ngbatu galloped through the city's alleys, spreading his friend's cacophonous rage through all the compounds. Soon scores of torches signaled the movement of an agitated crowd, and the voices, gathered in courtyards, rose up in a stormy rumble. Captain

Ripert did not intervene. He had no way to stop such gatherings in the night. The few Congolese soldiers posted to him were barely enough to ensure his security and that of his small hut against such an upswell.

That night no one slept. Not even Ripert, huddled in his office, a rifle in his hands and big beads of sweat rolling off his brow. When he opened the door of his shelter in the morning, it wasn't just hundreds of men who had overrun his courtyard, making Muluam's and Ngbatu's words of rage resonate through the night. His terrified eyes counted two . . . no, three . . . no, four thousand people at least.

Let's be very clear: the entire population of Foumban had gathered before the captain's office, even if Ripert later minimized the incident in his report so as not to give the impression that the French administration (that is to say, he himself) had been defeated. Muluam and Ngbatu's plan had worked. They had mobilized the workshops' artisans and apprentices, who had spread out, whipping up anger across the land. They had repeated the phrase Muluam had grafted onto the maniacal shouts of Mose Yeyap's wife: "They want to kill him!"

Everyone understood: "They want to kill the sultan!"

Nji Mama's opinion had prepared the terrain for the hurricane now unleashed. Every man who was a man, every woman who was a woman—everyone had felt the threat run through their flesh. They wrested themselves from bed and rushed toward the palace.

No one asked "Who?"

Because everyone knew what had been going on for too long, no one asked "Why?"

Because everyone knew what was happening in Foumban since Prestat's arrival—no, since the English had entered the city, leaving one dog dead; no, since the Germans had appeared in Bamum land. The conflict that had begun more than twenty years before had taken an overtly violent turn. For a long time, far too long, patience had been the Bamum response to the underhanded European encroachments. Every time the sultan had asked his best soldiers to lower their weapons, they had obeyed: every time. They had obeyed "so that common sense would prevail" but had quickly realized that they were in fact defenseless. They had been fooled.

Several times Njoya's guards had caught young men and turned them over to the Europeans, who forced them to work like slaves on their plantations. The sultan had even asked his soldiers to fight in wars that were not their own and to defeat people that had never been in conflict with the Bamum, each time as a "sign of his friendship" for the Europeans. Never had his efforts resulted in greater peace for the Bamum. On the contrary, the sultanate's foundations had been weakened, its most important achievements destroyed. Its inhabitants impoverished.

Anger flowed through the veins of each woman and each man who had abandoned their beds that night to answer Muluam's and Ngbatu's cries; they all found themselves in front of Captain Ripert's offices in a gathering of thousands of angers, small and large. The nobles had their recriminations, which differed from those of the women and of the slaves and, of course, of the captives. The captives had their own reasons to be angry, wholly unrelated to the motives of the nobles or the freemen, etc.

Some members of the crowd complained about heavy taxes, the head tax that was slowly crippling large families. Others talked about being forced to build roads or lay railroad tracks, or about the coffee and cocoa plantations where they were put to work. Others still deplored the lessening of their power after the whites arrived and began giving authority to their intermediaries—who were all slaves, to make matters worse. Students complained that the education they'd received in Njoya's schools had been devalued, their diplomas no longer guaranteeing any job because only those who had gone to European schools got posts in the French administration.

Ah, what hadn't they inscribed in the Book of Rage!

Some voices, crazed voices really, raged against the sultan, accusing him of being a coward and a traitor who didn't give a damn about the suffering of the Bamum and was selling the country's future to the rats. All these voices in the night: if you listened closely, you could sense how they were working against each other, ready to fight each other, even to the death. It was only by chance that history had found, in the person of the zealous translator, the match to light all these different fires. And these voices—contradictory voices, curious voices, angry voices, vengeful voices, irritated voices—were all unified by Muluam's one cry: "They want to kill the sultan!"

They joined in Ngbatu's urgent demand and amplified one another: "We want Mose Yeyap gone!"

The only thing Captain Ripert could do when confronted with these voices, which grew louder and louder as day dawned, was to summon the sultan. But Njoya's arrival didn't resolve the problem—on the contrary. Mose Yeyap suddenly emerged from his hiding place; he saluted the sultan, executing an awkward series of incomprehensible gestures, at the end of which he tripped slightly and knocked the sultan's cane from his hand. The chaos grew. A hand (was it Muluam's? Ngbatu's?) tore the translator's hat from his head and threw it on the ground.

At that very moment a rifle was fired.

The sky froze.

Let's put it this way: Captain Ripert, who had just come through his longest night, during which he'd been worked over by maniacal mosquitoes; Captain Ripert, whose mind had not stopped imagining all night long the whole range of violent acts native hands could inflict upon him, who had seen unfolding before his eyes all the scenarios he'd read about in colonial travel tales; yes, Captain Ripert, who recalled what he had read in the reports of his predecessor Prestat, who had clearly warned him about the "Bamum people, and the natives in general," Captain Ripert emerged from his insomnia with trembling hands and a transparent soul. The service weapon he held in his hands confronted the hundred rifles the sultan's soldiers had brought when they answered the night's call.

Yet Captain Ripert's frayed nerves are not to blame for this affair, nor is his fertile imagination, even if it multiplied his visions of death by mutilation and even nightmarish images of cannibalism, topped off with scenes of women's breasts going wild. What is clear is that a fuse was lit in his mind that caused his better judgment to go up in smoke, making him think he was in real danger, ordering him to lift his rifle and fire a warning shot into the sky. Aware of the fact that if armed conflict broke out, he'd be whipped into mayonnaise, he didn't mean to kill anyone. He didn't want to hurt anyone. He wanted to send a warning to the agitated crowd, a warning that he translated himself so everyone would understand:

"Calm down or else . . ."

"Or else what?"

In the heart of the chaos that had been brought to a halt by his rifle shot, rare were those who heard him finish his sentence:

"I'll kill your damned sultan!"

No, no, and no. Njoya wasn't taken hostage by a frightened captain. A French official is not a terrorist. The great French Empire that spread over three continents and on which the sun never set— "Eternal France"—had no need to take local kings hostage! That's ridiculous! That Congolese *tirailleurs* pointed their rifles at a crowd, four-fifths of which was unarmed, including women carrying children on their backs, was just an aberration. An exception that confirms the rule.

"Calm down," Ripert repeated, "or I'll call for reinforcements!"

Dschang was only a hundred kilometers away, and many more *tirailleurs* were stationed there. But for years the administrative post in Foumban hadn't even had a car at its disposal. In order to carry out his threats, Captain Ripert would have had to count on the freshness of his best horses, and it would have taken them a whole day or even two to complete the mission. Oh, the captain was clearly far from the calmest head in this gathering of men who were used to salvos of gunfire during the annual celebration of Nguon, at dances and other ceremonies, and who hadn't even dropped to the ground after his warning shot.

"We want Mose Yeyap gone!"

That was Ngbatu.

"We want Monlipèr back," Muluam added.

The crowd chanted, "Monlipèr!"

"Monlipèr!"

People stamped their feet and roused the sky with their inflamed mouths:

"Monlipèr!"

"Monlipèr!"

"Monlipèr!"

13

Who Killed the Artist?

All the tales of that demented day are in perfect agreement on one point: it was Captain Ripert who fired the one gunshot that everyone heard. Some testimonies stress that he shot into the air. Because his rifle was a Berthier 8-mm carbine, a 1906 model that the French army was still using in the colonies, I can say in all confidence that the bullet—shot at a speed of 2,300 meters per second by a rifle that could hit a target at a distance of 3,500–4,500 meters—would rise up to a certain altitude before falling back to the ground, pulled down by the indomitable laws of gravity. It also follows quite logically that the speed of Ripert's bullet would be reduced during its fall because it would be propelled by gravity alone and, most of all, because it would have been slowed down by wind resistance. That bullet wouldn't pose any real danger to anyone, and the possibility that it could kill a man is next to nothing. The only damage it could cause would be a bump on some unfortunate soul's forehead.

More than three thousand people clearly saw the French captain take his rifle, point it at the sky, and shoot: kaboom! That those assembled later said instead that it was "the French," in the plural, who had tried to kill the sultan is certainly linked to the nature of the anger that had clouded everyone's judgment since Nji Mama had leveled his accusation—the anger that had pushed shadowy hands to try to assassinate Mose Yeyap and had brought together the crowd in front of Captain Ripert's office. "A rush to judgment," the historian would say. Yet I know, yes I do: the objectivity required for the analysis of the actions of the colonial officer is the same as for any reading of the actions of Njoya. It is one hundred percent certain that the sultan wasn't in his palace when Ripert's shot flew through the sky. Ripert had summoned him to his office, counting on the presence and authority of the sultan to get him out of an explosive situation.

Njoya's entourage would without a doubt testify that the sultan was right in front of Captain Ripert when the trigger was pulled, and I am sure that some would have happily taken truth serum, if that practice hadn't been forbidden by one of Lieutenant Prestat's decrees. Yet no one was called to testify, not one of the three thousand mouths who were gathered in front of Ripert's courtyard when he sat down to hatch his report. And what remains in the archives are the conclusions of the stressed-out captain, who declared that only Njoya could have killed Nebu: yes, that's what he wrote: "killed Nebu."

A pretext serves many ends, but first and foremost it provides a way out of a difficult situation. And this is where objectivity is replaced by illogic. Of course, colonialism isn't logical. After Ripert's rifle shot, it took a lot of goodwill for everyone in the surrounding crowd to be convinced that the sultan was still alive and that no one, not even Ripert, had tried to kill him. Still, the captain would have had to make a certain number of promises to finally clear his courtyard and find a way out of this crisis. The first thing that everyone was asking—or, rather, demanding—was the replacement of Mose Yeyap. Captain Ripert wouldn't do that; for him, replacing an unpopular official would have been a sign of "weakness." According to one of the directives there on the French officer's desk, the French Republic should never show any "sign of weakness," especially not "in front of any natives"—that was the real crux of his problem.

Ripert wasn't a man to ignore directives. So he refused to listen to the sultan's suggestion that he replace Mose Yeyap with Ibrahim, who was beloved by the Artists' Alley. What's more, Ripert refused to ask his *tirailleurs* to lower their weapons and return to their barracks. Too many refusals for a man in such a weak position! Once again, he threatened to call for backup from Dschang, and even from Yaoundé. He ordered the sultan to make his pickup truck available to the French administration to smooth out that process. In the face of such an obvious bluff, the crowd didn't give up its demands, which were repeated by the twin mouths of Muluam and Ngbatu.

The Man of the French needed to leave, yes. So then Captain Ripert accused Njoya, said that he, yes, he, Njoya, was behind all this confusion, that he was pulling the strings. Captain Ripert declared, yes, that he would hold Njoya responsible for anything that happened in Foumban that day, as if that hadn't been the sultan's responsibility since his birth! As if, "for common sense to prevail," Njoya hadn't himself cleaned up the trash that had piled up in the streets of Bamum land since the first white had set foot there. The situation was so ridiculous that the sultan would have burst out laughing if he hadn't known how much his laughter would have added to Ripert's humiliation. What Njoya knew was that the cost was going to be high this time, especially if measured in terms of Ripert's nerves: they were a purse it would be best not to stretch any further. That's why he decided to word things differently and speak to the captain in a friendly way.

"I didn't ask them to come here," he said, his conversation with Muluam and Ngbatu still fresh in his mind. "In fact, I asked them to put up with Mose."

Captain Ripert didn't believe him. How could he? Mose's translation didn't help any.

"Liar!" shouted the French officer.

Mose didn't translate the insult; it would have just riled up the Bamum people all the more and to no good end. Never before had they heard their sovereign called a liar. But of course, very few people here, none really, had read the reports of the French officers, who often used such language in reference to their sultan.

"How can I ask them to leave," Njoya continued, "when I didn't ask them to come?"

He might have added that he was in the same position as Captain Ripert, but he didn't have the chance.

"Tell them to leave," Ripert threatened, "or I'll send you into exile!"

Yes, that's what the colonial officer said, and this time Mose Yeyap translated: "exile."

There was no law in the Indigenous Code that advised shouting threats of exile in the face of a sultan. But wasn't Captain Ripert himself the law in person? Moreover, he wouldn't have hesitated to sign such a decree, right there, in front of his office, in front of everyone. He wouldn't have hesitated! Martin, his boss in Dschang, would have covered for him, "so that France not lose face." Njoya knew very well that in an occupied territory, the smallest are really the big men, and that the decision of a subaltern colonial officer means just as much as that of the high commissioner. For years he had avoided conflict with the Europeans, and now suddenly he found himself caught in the middle. He called the two leaders of the protest movement, lectured them publicly, and asked them why in the name of Nchare Yen did they want to sow disorder in Foumban?

"Chaos is already in the house, Alareni," Muluam replied. In his anger, the boy had forgotten the ritual gestures of politeness he ought to have made before the sultan.

"You no longer respect my orders?" Njoya demanded.

Neither Muluam nor Ngbatu replied.

"Do you want someone to die?"

Ngbatu was quicker than his friend. "Alareni," he said, "we just want Mose Yeyap to go!"

He turned and faced the crowd of apprentices behind him. "Isn't that so?"

The thousands gathered replied with one voice, "We don't want him anymore!"

Muluam stressed, "Alareni, we all want Monlipèr."

He emphasized "we all." The crowd chanted, "Monlipèr! Monlipèr!"

In vain. Captain Ripert still wouldn't accept Ibrahim, whose name Njoya had put forward as a replacement, for the reasons we already know. France, etc. Yet he knew that the French colonial administration couldn't make an ad hoc decision while under siege. It took him several hours to convince himself, and it was really against his own will that Ripert finally emerged from his office to read the decree recognizing a new authority in the Artists' Alley. People whispered, but didn't applaud. For what Ripert wanted in exchange was a gesture of goodwill, to "show the French administration, etc." He demanded that Muluam and Ngbatu be thrown into prison for "attempted murder," "destruction of property" (Mose's house), "inciting rebellion," "disruption of the public order," and several other dreadful offenses. Njoya didn't contradict him, no. Even in the palace, his court would have condemned the two fellows, accusing them of disobeying the sultan's orders. Taking advantage of this start of a dialogue, the Bamum spread out their list of complaints: lower taxes, lifting the limitations placed on the authority of husbands over their wives, suppression of forced labor, etc. The French officer interrupted their fervor. He demanded that all the men be disarmed before speaking to him. That was met with a lively protest, and the list of their complaints grew even longer; but the captain reminded the proud Bamum riflemen that carrying weapons had already been banned by the Germans and the English, and so was illegal under the French.

"Illegal?" they shouted in surprise. "Are the French really Germans?"

"What do you mean, illegal?" one man shouted. "Since when?"

"The sultan never banned our rifles!"

"Who do you think you are?"

"Will the French ensure the sultan's safety?"

Et cetera.

At the end of this rather long day Captain Ripert had met the crowd's most pressing demands and gotten its two most inflamed advocates off the streets. No more than that. What people didn't know is that he had committed to memory the faces of all those he'd seen inciting riot, for he mentioned their names in the report he subsequently wrote and sent to Dschang in order that it be forwarded to High Commissioner Marchand in Yaoundé. Mose Yeyap gave him the names of these subversives, and the translator added that they were, for the most part, apprentices of the deposed master Monlipèr, which made Ripert's next decision all the easier. In truth, he had already made up his mind when they announced the death of a man on the worksite of the new palace.

"Will this chaos never end?"

Ripert jumped on his horse, rushing with the alarmed crowd to the Palace of All Dreams.

And that was just the start of it.

14

The Equation of an Assassination

Here is what had happened: the crowd that had gathered in front of Captain Ripert's office was dispersing when an out-of-breath slave threw himself at Njoya's feet. The man's face was dripping with fear, and his hands were waving madly.

"*Wombo-o,*" shouted the slave, "he's dead!"

"What?"

"He is dead!"

"Who?"

"*Wombo-o!*"

When the sultan, his entourage, Ripert, and his *tirailleurs* arrived at the palace, they found Nebu's body smashed on the ground, surrounded by pieces of the statue he'd been working on. A very strange death, yes, a very strange death! The sculptor was entirely naked, and his penis still standing. By all appearances, he had fallen from the window of the Palace of All Dreams with his statue. The palace workmen surrounded him, stunned. They were pushed back by the voices of the sultan and Captain Ripert, who both wanted to see for themselves before believing what had happened. So, for the fourth time Njoya met Nebu, but this time Bertha's son was dead.

"What happened to him?" the sultan asked.

And Captain Ripert asked, "Who killed him?"

With a policeman's quick eye the Frenchman measured the dimensions of the wall from the window to the ground. His question demanded an answer, but as it emerged from his lips, it was cut off by the shout of a mother exploding in the heart of the crowd. It was Bertha. She threw herself on the body of the son she had loved so much but hadn't been able to save. She beat her breast, revealing to everyone her body splattered with Nebu's blood, her mouth open to the sky to release the pain in her belly caused by the amputation of the most important part of her life.

"My son!" she cried.

All the women around her repeated her cry.

"Our son!"

"My son!"

"Our son!"

"Who killed our son?"

"*Wombo-o!*"

Bertha's body was clothed in pain. Her hands were lifted up to the sky, and her endless cry tore the universe with a tremolo that left no eyes dry. Njoya couldn't contain himself either at the sight of this genius sculptor whom he had elevated to the status of *Nji* just a few months earlier. The sultan cried. Monlipèr, Nji Mama, Ibrahim, all the city's masters, and several others were also devastated by this great loss. The crowd gathered around the suffering mother and cried with her.

In fact, the whole sultanate was devastated by the artist's death. All of Cameroon—what am I saying?—all of Africa would have cried for such a loss! All those who had been alerted to what had happened in the Artists' Alley, who had come together to vent their rage with their collective demands, now had an actual death before them and one specific question on their lips, a short one: "Who killed Nebu?"

The French colonial administration—Ripert himself—had never looked sympathetically on Njoya's plans to build his Palace of All Dreams. It had always wanted to put an end to work on the site; pushing the sultan into bankruptcy was one way to do that.

The death that took place at the palace gave the captain the pretext his bosses needed, just as the protest movement that had shaken up the Artists' Alley had inspired him to write a vitriolic report that tied it all together. He demanded that everyone clear away from the site of the drama. He was heard. The tearful mob carried the artist's body into the distant neighborhoods. A hundred hands rushed to console the mother who had seen her son's body lying broken on the ground.

Back in his office, Captain Ripert quickly wrote a thirteen-page report to his superior in Dschang, a report that ended with a practical solution and a scandalous accusation that he hadn't had the guts to formulate out loud in front of Nebu's body. The conclusion: "We must do something."

By "we" Ripert meant the "colonial administration," which in Foumban meant Ripert himself, of course.

As for his accusation, it was just as clear: "Njoya is behind all of this disorder."

That was the sort of conclusion and accusation that Commander Martin in Dschang didn't need to read twice. He had been waiting for them. High Commissioner Marchand, on the other hand, might have sent a dispatch from Yaoundé asking "Why?" Martin would then have sent him a sketch of the palace under construction drawn by Nji Mama, the sketch Ripert had attached to his text to bolster his accusations. (The captain had confiscated it as proof that Njoya's construction didn't respect the minimum standards set for the protection of workers.)

However, the sketch of the palace, covered with notes written in Akauku letters, would have neutralized Ripert's accusation had it arrived on the high commissioner's desk, even if it was meant as important evidence in support of the captain's claim; Marchand would have sent it on to the Ethnographic Museum in Paris for "more analysis," and from there, the plan would have been sent on to the learned colonial administrator in Senegal, Delafosse, in order that he "determine if it were the product of an authentic indigenous intelligence."

Such is the administrative route the report accusing Njoya would have taken. The Palace of All Dreams would have been mentioned in a scientific article on Bamum writing and Njoya's creations, on which Delafosse was then working. It's useless to say that such an article wouldn't have changed Ripert's decision, for on that day his anger caused by the death at the palace was limitless and his will to bring French justice to bear could not bend before science.

Had a Bamum master artist told him what was evident to everyone's mind—that Nebu's death was the sacrifice required for the
construction of the palace to progress unimpeded, yes, that the sculptor had to die so that the worksite would from then on move ahead
smoothly—Captain Ripert would have shouted, "Superstitions!"

His Cartesian logic governed his thoughts, like the mechanism
of the double-barreled rifle by his side, and his decision to "be done
with the sultan" was so firm that it had the abstract clarity of a coor-
dinate plane:

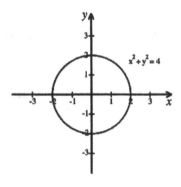

With the variables:
$x^2 = $ *Nebu's death*
and
$y^2 = $ *Njoya's palace*
The result could only be:
$4 = $ *Njoya must be banished from Foumban.*

Had the artisans drawn attention to the artist's nakedness, Ripert
would have explained that some slaves still went about the streets
dressed only in a loincloth, despite the orders of his predecessor
and of the Germans before them. The "strangely erect penis" of the
deceased sculptor wouldn't have made him change his mind. On the
contrary, had anyone evoked the statue of the woman in movement
that the sculptor had just completed, suggesting the possibility of
an artistic metaphysics, Ripert would have burst out laughing. If
anyone had even said that the statue was so perfect that once completed, it was only logical that it come to life, "stand up and walk,"
the captain would have been amused by "all this foolishness."

The doyenne's theory was that Nebu's father had come back from the dead to kill his son. The Dog's anger was logical, no doubt: he wouldn't have been the first murder victim to rise as an assassin and then happily return to hell. That was what Sara thought, at any rate, and I tend not to contradict her. Foolish or not, this is what happened, according to the testimony of the slave who announced Nebu's death to Foumban's stupefied crowd. The man had heard a repeated noise coming from Nebu's workshop that sounded like a couple making love. When he went to look (an action he confessed with no little shame), he saw the sculptor's behind moving rhythmically between the legs of a woman. He smiled, of course, and headed off, "satisfied," for Nebu was, and these again are his words, "still the right age for that kind of thing."

"Artists always have women in their workshops," he added. "Don't they?"

How could he have known that the woman in question was a statue? He thought, on the contrary, that it was a model.

"Artists always sleep with their models, don't they?"

Soon he heard the cry that typically marks the culmination of that sort of artistic practice.

"You wouldn't have imagined that he'd take flight, right?"

Evidently no one in Foumban had ever seen a man take to the air. The slave's description resonated in the ears of the artists who had worked alongside the sculptor and knew the strange voluptuousness his statue had aroused in them when they'd seen it lying on the ground. All were happy that they hadn't responded to the urge to "screw the statue" that had rushed through their veins: "That could have been me."

The slave's tale had a very particular echo in Bertha's suffering ears. Once again she saw her son tied to the Devil's curse. The matron clenched her fist harder and harder, this time never relaxing. The woman she had wanted to kill for so long had been turned into dust when the statue had fallen with her son from the fourth floor of the Palace of All Dreams. Bertha blamed herself for not taking action sooner.

"I should have killed her before this," she sobbed.

Little did it matter that she was talking about a statue. "That girl killed my son!"

"There was no way to know that she'd kill him, right?" asked the slave when he reached the end of his horror story.

"How could we have known that she was a spirit?" the frightened artists wondered.

And their eyes recalled the statue of the woman with the "behind as round as two calabashes." They dissected "that woman," who was now a vampire to them. Her beauty no longer awoke their dirtiest thoughts, their highest words of praise. Perfection never goes unpunished, they told themselves, these men of wisdom. Nebu had invoked a goddess, the Goddess of Beauty. She had come and struck him down! She had killed him, then disappeared like all the other women who, in different ways, had made him understand the devastating meaning of love. That's what the artists thought, with tears in their eyes.

"How could I have known the Devil would come back?" Bertha asked in despair. "How?"

She was thinking of Ngungure. Who else? The matron only ever thought of "that girl"! Yet in a certain sense it was the perpetual return of that same girl into her boy's life that later gave her the will to give birth to Nebu once again, even if only by telling of the twists and turns of his life, because for her, there was no doubt: the Devil had killed him. Who would have had the courage to tell her she wasn't being rational? Who, yes, who?

As we already know: colonialism isn't logical, either. So all these accounts, each as wobbly as the next—from the slave's tale to the thoughts of the artists about the Nebu affair and all the various other versions of his death—did not find their place in Ripert's terse prose when he sent the completed report on to his bosses in June 1924.

For Ripert, who hadn't witnessed the fall, there was only one person who could have killed Nebu: the sultan. Just as there was only one person who could have gathered such a crowd at the doors of the offices of the French administration: Njoya.

How could Ripert have guessed that for many in Foumban, and in many of the versions of the young man's death that blamed the French, it was more likely he, Captain Ripert and none other, who had killed Nebu. And those who lent their voice to the commu-

nity's disgust spread word throughout the region of this new conspiracy: they had clearly heard one shot, just one gunshot, which
had been fired by him, Captain Ripert.

"Listen," they said, "Ripert's vicious bullet did exactly what the
French administration wanted. After flying up into the air, it zigzagged and turned back down the street that leads from the Artists'
Alley to the center of town. It flew past the spice market that, thank
God, was empty, and drilled through the women's quarter, then the
palace's main courtyard, which was, thank God, deserted; then it
entered the palace through the main door, going up the forty-two
steps to the fourth floor, through the door of Nebu's workshop, which,
unfortunately, had a hole in it, and with its speed remaining at 1,623
meters per second, it had pierced the sculptor's heart—rather than
just giving him a bump on the head—and pushed him out the window with the statue, whose hand he was holding just then, thereby
putting an end to a fragile life and reducing the pinnacle of Bamum
and African art to dust!"

"What a loss," everyone cried. "Oh, what a loss!"

That was Nebu's destiny, they thought. It was the high point of
his travels, of his search for perfection; and in perfection, his search
had ended. Everything had begun and ended with a woman.

"O the misery of life!" the artists cried, looking at what was left
of the dead statue. "He fell into your hands, and he is dead!"

Had I been there—me—Bertha, I would have probably said to
the dead sculptor, "You! You who never expressed pain but only
love, look at the cloak of suffering under which you were crushed!"

"Killed!" repeated a voice in the crowd.

And another, "Yes, killed by a French bullet!"

Of course thousands of voices repeated that truth.

"Truth?"

My friends from Nsimeyong would have sworn to it: "The distance covered by Ripert's bullet is well within the limits of an 8-mm
Berther carbine Lebel. Logical, hmm?"

Yet the French officer, he didn't want to listen to such un-
Cartesian accusations. His decision was supported by the power he
had to write his own version of Nebu's death in a report, his ulti-
mate weapon, which he would send to Dschang by soldiers on

horseback. In his report, Captain Ripert wrote his conclusion in red capital letters and underlined it several times: "IN ORDER FOR PEACE TO BE FINALLY RESTORED AMONG THE BAMUM," he insisted, "NJOYA MUST BE EXILED."

He added a strongly worded warning against any reliance on the version of events written by the sultan in the *Saa'ngam* and against the very different conclusions drawn by Njoya. He also warned future historians who might discover the monarch's version, because, he said, "in his treachery, Njoya has invented a writing system just so he can hide his thoughts and actions from us."

His "us" meant, of course, the "French administration," and he added as appendices to his report examples of this writing. I think what he couldn't foresee is that Martin, his boss, would be so impressed by Njoya's Akauku figurines that he'd spend the rest of his life trying to understand the sultan's pictograms, an epiphany whose crowning moment came with the patient translation of the Bamum memoirs. Ripert, who was in Foumban, never evolved at all. In his report he even added, "Njoya has treated himself to a car to humiliate the French administration in the eyes of the Bamum people," and concluded, "Njoya is a two-faced man."

Did he mean that Njoya had the gift of being everywhere at once? Oh, he certainly wasn't suggesting that the sultan's power was so great that he could be both in front of him in a crowd of more than a thousand and, at the same time, in his palace killing the sculptor whom he had promoted to the rank of *Nji* just a few months earlier. Maybe Ripert only put into writing the threat that he had already articulated out loud, because whatever a colonial officer has already said in public will sooner or later become a decree from the colonial administration.

Deafened by the noise of all these stories, speculations, theories, and likelihoods, no one suspected that Nebu himself felt defeated when he finished his statue, that he had failed as an artist to bring Ngungure back to life, even though he had re-created her in a perfect statue. So no one suspected his despair at having achieved artistic perfection only to discover its limitations. Had the theoreticians of his death thought about it, they would have understood that in his suffering, the sculptor had decided to follow his beloved to the kingdom of death and to throw himself out the window of the Palace of All Dreams alongside her. For death is the limit of art, isn't it? Yet how could people have thought about suicide? And why should they have? After all, and here the French officials and their adversaries in Foumban would certainly agree, a Bamum man simply couldn't kill himself for a reason like that.

15

The Multiple Faces of Powerlessness

Njoya had never felt as powerless as on that day, when faced with Ripert's accusation; nor had the Bamum. In their reports and declarations, Prestat, Ripert, Martin, Marchand, and other colonial officers had called him all sorts of names. "A despot."

The Bamum had put up with it.

"A man who doesn't respect human life . . ."

They had put up with it.

". . . who keeps hundreds of women prisoner in his harem."

They had put up with it.

"A Negro king who controls the life and wealth of his subjects."

They had put up with it.

"A tyrant."

They had put up with it.

"A multiple polygamist."

They had put up with it.

"A slaver."

They had put up with it.

"A rapacious potentate."

They had put up with it.

Even "a black," they had put up with it. But "a murderer"?

The Bamum had thousands of responses for that. Yet everything they had to say was suddenly meaningless in the face of this bald accusation. They proposed thousands of theories for Nebu's death, but all their explanations were shot down. They had filled the palace's main courtyard with their surprised faces, but it was as if the space had remained entirely empty.

"Njoya, a murderer?"

They had a tragedy on their hands, and even their tears were as weak as a rain in the dry season. Foumban—no, all of Bamum land—was crying for the dead artist and soon discovered that the land's most ardent defender was toothless. When the mourners spread out through the city, carrying Nebu's body, when they gathered in Bertha's courtyard to mourn the sculptor as he deserved, all that remained among the debris at the Palace of All Dreams was a profound silence.

Back in his office, Ripert had signed a decree forbidding any sort of public assembly. Even the children knew better than to cry. Lizards no longer lifted their inquisitive heads to the sky. Dogs no longer barked, no. In the deadly silence that clothed the city, had you listened carefully, you would have heard only the throbbing of an undercurrent of rage. It was the fury of a city, of a world some four hundred years old, of an ancient continent, of a timeless universe that had been trampled and had silenced its ire. It was an anger too large for a burning body. This fire had taken hold of Njoya's body—foreshadowing his fall, yes, his fall—its flames searing his body, licking his chest, veins of fire inflaming his heart, ready to consume him whole, like a mad volcano.

The sultan hadn't yet fallen victim to his treacherous body. He could no longer control his hands, that was all. They trembled, trembled. Suddenly all his inventions had become useless, yes, useless. His life had no direction. When he, now a wreck, returned to his palace, when he walked into the artists' workshop—the dead artists' workshop—he was slapped by the silence. In this place once so full of life, he was confronted by the absence of the young man he had met only four times and yet who had shown him the grandeur of what Bamum land could create. He suddenly evaluated the infamous price of all his compromises. It was as if his own son had been killed. With his cane, he struck the wall.

"Shit," he shouted. "Shit!"

Everyone froze; Njoya had never used the foul language of slaves.

"Shit!" he said again.

The sultan couldn't control his tongue, couldn't stop his hands. His cane fell on the weaver's loom.

"Shit!" the weaver cried.

Njoya's mouth was creased. It could only come up with the same word, which he repeated endlessly. Had he shouted, had Njoya exploded, the sultanate would have understood. His hundreds of wives would have understood and his children, too. Looking on silently, everyone there knew that their land's fate had taken a tragic turn. Had he cried, the sultanate would have found a container for their sovereign's tears. Even his ancestors would have supported him.

"Shit!" said Njoya, striking a figurine.

He was destroying the work of his own artists. He threw out their manuscripts. The thousands of words in the palace library flew away. Calligraphers and miniaturists saw him coming and hurried to protect their work. With books hidden beneath their arms and on their bellies, they snuck away from his frenzy. Even today, the books they saved from the palace are scattered throughout Bamum land, hidden in boxes, stashed under the beds of the inheritors of that night of unequaled defeat, far from Njoya's endless wrath.

The sultan's cane came down on backs, but the wounded artists didn't cry out, their suffering bodies too busy protecting the work of their hands. They would have preferred to die in order to save their art. Alas, an anger that doesn't reach its target can only be self-destructive. It is born in the gut, takes hold of the throat, and, smoldering, dissolves all words. The body becomes its prisoner, for such a rage is like a strangled sneeze. The chaos that was unleashed in the palace workshops was the reflection of Njoya's silence, which had let disorder spread through Bamum land since the arrival of the first whites in 1902. Violence lives in powerlessness—it was twenty-two years of powerlessness that defined the trajectory of the sultan's cane.

"The rats!"

Suddenly his eyes fell on Monlipèr's printing press. Instead of protecting his work, the old master had sought to calm Njoya. Let's forget the usual titles, the master said to himself. This time he called the sultan Nji Ma Yuam.

Njoya didn't respond.

"Mfumbaam."

The old engineer knew that those two names that had been given to Njoya by his grandmother always made him smile. They were his own praise names. This time, however, they had no effect.

"Menkulashun."

This was the name given to Njoya by his father, Nsangu. It did nothing to calm the sultan either. The master blacksmith tried proverbs.

"Fran Njoya," he said, "even during rainy season, the river keeps its name."

That didn't work either. So the old man moved on to stories.

"Menkulashun," he began, "do you remember what the lion did when he was hit by an arrow?"

"What?"

The master began with a series of sentences, each repeated by the chorus of his colleagues, who rushed to join in, each adding his own bit: Nji Mama, Ibrahim, Nji Shua . . . It was a folktale.

"Shut up!" Njoya ordered.

The sultan spoke to them as if to apprentices, and his voice echoed through the silence of the whole palace. Who would have dared to say another word? An anger that has grown for as long as Njoya's, an anger as vast as the suffering of the Bamum couldn't be calmed by verbal tricks alone. It needed to re-create the destruction that the Bamum sultan had always refused to see "in hopes that common sense would prevail"; in order to be calmed, his anger needed to reinvent the chaos of life these past years in Foumban. It needed to find release in the crack of a thunderbolt, like the one that had struck the baobab that had stood for hundreds of years in the center of town. Yes, it needed to give voice to the silence of all the conscripts Njoya had torn from their families and given to his colonial friends for their *njokmassi*, their forced labor projects. Born of impotence, this supreme rage needed to be lived out fully. The masters cowered like children before his violence.

"Shut up!" Njoya shouted in their silence, again and again. "Shut up! Shut up!"

It was as if he were speaking to spirits, as if his crude and violent words, as well as his destructive cane, had all been roused by history, by the story of the three Bamum youths who had been under his orders and, by his fault, taken prisoner, suffering because of his bad judgment.

"Ngbatu! Muluam! Nebu!"

But also it was as if instead of their names, Njoya was calling "Samba! Ngosso! Manga!"

And then "Ngbatu! Nebu! Muluam!"

History doesn't lie. It just keeps repeating itself. The sultan's spare words were a hammer, a hammer raining down everywhere, as far as the eye could see: "Samba! Ngosso! Manga!

"Manga! Ngosso! Samba!"

Njoya's hammer broke everything in its path, everything. Soon it rose up over old Monlipèr's printing press. The machine had filled the master with immense pride, even if it hadn't yet produced the desired results. It was the fruit of several years of work by the best blacksmiths in the region. It was the precise, detailed work of a nearly blind master. This machine had undergone many changes, but Njoya's real vision, that the thousands of books in the Library of the Future would be produced by simply rearranging letters, had remained intact in the minds of all those who had worked to realize the project. The printing press was the pinnacle of the sultan's intellectual project, of his work as a writer. It was supposed to occupy a place of honor in the Palace of All Dreams, the grand salon; from there it would spread History, providing a new center of gravity and reproduction for all the world's tales. But now this limitless printing press was suddenly offered up for sacrifice, emptied of meaning.

At once, the machines Njoya had built, all his machines, appeared to him as the private ailment that had made his heart always accept compromises. Art became the umbrella of his unhappiness, the wall he had built around his existence to forestall his own death, and writing was transformed into a cowardly bargain. Writing—isn't it a way of fleeing from the complexity of life to hide in the aseptic realm of alphabets, in the magic of words? Letters draw us into a putrid dance: a dance with zombies! Writing compensates for life itself; it is disengagement, child's play. Njoya realized that his experiments with pictograms and phonemes, with syllabograms and words, with tales and histories, with lives and dreams—all those experiments that had led him from anecdotes to a printing press had been possible only because, from the very start, he had given up when confronted by History's forces. And these forces were now tightly clenched around his neck. He had abandoned his people and taken refuge in the workshops' promise of eternity.

Death was revealed to him in the form of the Invisible Book he had always been writing, and the printing press became the most vicious component of his own political resignation. It became the most visible sign of the factory of shame he was building within his Palace of All Dreams. Writing became Njoya's real nightmare and the printing press its foulest feature. So he lifted it up with all his strength, stood silent for a moment while all around him his master craftsmen, the master artists, and their apprentices were frozen in the sharpest of silences by the unexpected sight.

"Shit!" cried Njoya.

And he smashed the machine on the ground.

Metal pieces scattered around him by the thousands. He raced out of Nebu's workshop. It was as if this one definitive, determined, barbaric, inhuman act had wrung his anger dry. The stunned silence of all the artists was heard throughout the city, rushing through the alleys, into houses, and flowing into the Nshi River along with pieces of the word machine and the tears of Monlipèr, who had leaped toward his machine but had been unable to prevent its destruction. Now the old man collected bits of debris, and with his trembling hands he tried to put the lost printing press back together. The despair of the master craftsman could only flow into a larger river, the much larger river of tears Bertha shed for the son whose shattered bones he had previously tried to mend.

To the tears of the old man were added those of all the Bamum, beginning with the tears of all the artists who were unable to complete the phrase that would have expressed their suffering. Those men cried because their master was crying, and he cried because somewhere in the city a mother was crying for her dead son. "What a loss!" everyone said. "What a loss!"

For posterity's sake, this is how Madame Dugast described the suffering of old Monlipèr in her book, *L'Écriture des Bamum*: "He is now a man with a white beard, but he still cries when telling this tragic story." I never understood why Njoya didn't come out of his palace to express his rage for everyone to see. For many people, his withdrawal was an enigma. There are those, however, like Nji Mama, who were convinced that Njoya was mourning his own loss. In truth, however, the sultan was mostly angry with himself for not having sufficiently defended the Bamum. He was drowning in guilt and in a heavy feeling of remorse that would surface again later in Yaoundé and knock on the doors of his soul.

Just a few months after these events the population of Foumban was again woken up by exclamations coming from the palace. People jumped out of bed and gathered in the main courtyard of the Palace of All Dreams.

"*Wombo-o!*"

"Again?" some said.

This time the city's inconsolable voices weren't mourning a virtuoso of the human form. Nor were they crying over the destruction of a mechanical marvel. On the contrary, it was the departure of a great man that left them aghast. Njoya's red pickup truck was parked in front of the palace gates, where the still-silent crowds had gathered. Besides the driver, there were seats for four others: the sultan; his favorite wife of the moment, Ndayie; and his collaborators, Nji Mama and Ibrahim. Nji Shua, Nji Moluh, Ngutane, and the other children were sitting with the servants in the back, where bunches of bananas were usually piled. The Nguri followed on foot. That day, the pickup truck and its convoy weren't yet leading Njoya and his entourage to Yaoundé. First they made a stop, a very long stop, at the sultan's residence in Mantoum, for this was only the beginning of a ten-year exile that eventually, in 1931, would strand the sultan on the green hills of Nsimeyong, in Mount Pleasant.

What Ripert had once uttered as a threat had in the end become an administrative decree. But that was nothing special—at least not in a colonial territory.

16

The Smoker's Conversations
with His Solitary Cigarette

In 1922 Foumban struggled to maintain an illusion of peace; Yaoundé as well. Leaving the wedding of his sister earlier than any brother-in-law would have, Joseph Ngono was drunk. He was so drunk that he fell down several times as he was walking off. What's happening to me? he wondered.

So he hit his head with his hand, trying to wake himself up. Then he heard a voice say, "You are lost too!"

"Me?"

"Yes, you too."

It was his shadow speaking to him. He had come back to Cameroon to realize that a dominated country can never be the home of a free man, that he couldn't call his country a French possession. He had realized, much to his horror, that the only place where he had really been free was wartime Germany. And that Cameroon under French occupation didn't deserve to be at peace with itself. This country needed to be shaken up! That night in the capital, on that road devoid of people, empty of life, he felt his heart beat for the House of Exile back in Berlin. There, he believed, everyone would have understood.

Yet that thought frightened him.

"Where is your home?" his shadow asked.

Ngono knew he was being ridiculous, yet still he shouted, *"Ilang!"*

In his borrowed, badly fitting tuxedo, with his bow tie undone and his talking shadow, he was the perfect target for the colony's first police squad—he knew that. It would have been the high point of his disgrace, the real fall of an obscure angel—to be arrested in the streets of Yaoundé for public drunkenness and convicted by the colonial police. Yes, his brother-in-law, Charles Atangana, would have slipped a word to his friends (why not to the prison director himself, Monsieur Poubelle, with whom he was on very good terms?), but at what price? Joseph Ngono then thought about Dr. Mult, who had always supported him in Germany. Rather than keeping silent like that kindly professor, Charles Atangana would have taken the place of Joseph Ngono's argumentative shadow and asked, "What were you thinking? Where do you think you are?"

Joseph Ngono wouldn't have answered, because he already knew at least one thing: he wouldn't come out of this battle a winner either.

Because he wanted to avoid a humiliating, bare-assed defeat, when he heard a motor coming up behind him, he jumped into the chief's cocoa plantation and hid. Once in the plantation, he began walking, past cocoa tree after cocoa tree. It was an endless plantation, the same tree, the same height and width, spread out all around. This monotony made him spew out the last thought he wanted to tell his friend: "Only superfluous people could plant this shit everywhere."

He could vomit, oh, Ngono could cry, do anything he wanted in this plantation of Charles Atangana's, no one would have heard his voice. He could have insulted those trees, spit on their uniformity. He could have asked them if this was how they imagined Africa's future: the infinite reproduction of the same old shit. Yes, he asked them what used to grow there before them, if they had inherited the memory of the land where they were planted. The trees couldn't answer. He went on, asking them if they knew who had lived before on this spot they now occupied. If they knew whether those people, whose lives they had displaced, had been happy to see their future peanuts destroyed, those peanuts with which they could at least have made spicy sauce. He asked the cocoa trees if they knew they were the product of the forced labor of thousands and of the empty dreams of just a few: "People so empty that their seed is superfluous."

He paused, looking for another way to put it.

"Superfluous seed," he repeated.

He liked those two words: "superfluous seed."

"Superfluous trees planted by empty minds and captive hands."

And then, "Superfluous time inhabited by superfluous characters."

He could have gone on, Ngono. In his indignation he didn't notice until it was too late that he was lost in their jungle. Maybe it was the alcohol that made his feet so heavy. Soon he felt the kilometers weighing on him. Yet he was still in the same spot, amidst the same cocoa trees, in front of the same tree. He decided to keep walking, to keep going through the middle of the cocoa plantation, but then he found himself back in front of the tree he'd just left.

"Shit!" he shouted. "Is there no way out of here?"

Had anyone told him that he was lost in a labyrinth, he would have burst out laughing. For Joseph Ngono the construction of a labyrinth was a sign of intelligence, generosity, playfulness, happiness. Here, all he saw around him was systematically planned misery, vacuity, "superfluous emptiness."

"I am lost in the superfluous," he said.

But this time he laughed, for even the thought seemed stupid. Still he continued.

"I am imprisoned in emptiness . . ."

He paused, entertained.

"In a prison of emptiness."

His smile had become a laugh. He repeated the word "emptiness" several times, and each time the word ricocheted off the surrounding trees: "Empty. Empty. Empty."

Suddenly Ngono wanted to urinate. With his legs splayed so he wouldn't lose his balance, and holding his penis with both hands, he emptied his urine on the roots of a cocoa tree. He pissed and pissed and pissed. He leaned on the cocoa tree to keep pissing, looking up at the overcast sky. It was as if he had a huge bucket instead of a bladder. When he finished, he took a deep breath and spit on his urine. He searched his pockets and found a pack of cigarettes.

"Empty," he said once again.

There was just one cigarette left in the pack. He studied the lone cigarette, and it was as if it had the crumpled shape of his soul. He wanted to talk to the cigarette, to ask if it would agree to take the place of one of the fingers he'd lost in Berlin. His smile grew wide when he found a packet of matches. Ngono lit his last cigarette, inhaling hungrily, then let the smoke out through his nose. He looked at the match burning his fingers and then at the empty cigarette pack.

"Emptiness and more emptiness," he said.

Everything amused him. He took a long drag on his cigarette, inhaled, and let the smoke out in small puffs. He didn't want to waste the smoke he felt filling his body. The match, on the other hand, was burning out quickly. It had formed a circle of light around his hand, but soon that miraculous light burned out as well. So he lit the cigarette pack on fire. The matches burst into flames so bright it made him jump. The light turned the surrounding trees into a wall. He saw the cocoa trees dance, then twist and turn into shadowy forms. The fire wasn't strong enough to reveal the actual faces of the spirits around him. He wanted to save the shadows. He felt his heart speed up its beat. He was happy! The fire of his happiness would soon burn out as well. The embers were burning his fingers. He tossed the pack on the ground only when he couldn't bear the pain any longer, and he watched the flame slowly die out. How sad when night again covered the world!

Does emptiness always win? he wondered.

Now the only light came from his cigarette.

17

The Cocoa Tree of the Mysterious Path

It was the faces of his two children that pushed Ngono to try to find his way out of the cocoa plantation. In the depth of the night he suddenly saw Carl's fragile eyes and Sara's delicate smile. This time the lights didn't disappear. On the contrary, it seemed evident to him that only his children made this empty country livable for him; they filled it with their lives. He felt that Cameroon was a nation and his children its population. This country was the only thing they had. And if he, Joseph Ngono, wanted to live here, he owed it to himself to become their child. The idea of becoming the child of his children made him smile in the half-darkness. So he'd have to live his life backward, he thought; from the very end to the beginning, back to front. The end is also a beginning!

"My life has been too scattered for me to live it in just one place," he remarked.

A phrase took hold of his eyes: "The world is my country!"

And Ngono burst out laughing at that idea.

"I can only be condemned to solitude," he noted. "My country is too vast."

He paused again, inhaled deeply the warmth of his cigarette, and released puffs of smoke into the night.

"The world is my country," he repeated, "not a family!"

This time it was images of his imprisonment in a camp upon his return to Cameroon that came to mind. What hurt the most was the

word "family." The reverse side of wandering is solitude. Had he
ever loved his wife Sala? It was she who had given meaning to this
life he'd dragged all over. He saw meaning in the faces of the two
children she had given birth to. An accumulation of friends' faces
followed those of his children, but also an assortment of missed opportunities, of casual friendships and families he hadn't had. He
had been on the road for his whole life, Ngono, looking for a country that had continually escaped him. He had followed uncertain
paths that led him nowhere. Today, imprisoned in the darkness of a
cocoa plantation, he listened to the rhythm of his own soul, and the
sarcastic shadow he had always tried to escape revealed itself to
him, his companion in unending misfortune. For the first time since
his return to his native land, for the very first time, he thought of his
German wife and was covered with shame.

What happened to her, to Hilde? he wondered.

He thought that she had probably had children too.

Maybe she didn't remarry.

When had he stopped thinking of her? Had he ever loved her?
Life's ugliness brings out the worst in men. Was he capable of love?
Had his suffering made him inhuman? Did he really detest the
whites? Had he become a racist, too? Was he a fascist, as Charles
Atangana had suggested? Joseph Ngono trembled at the thought
and recognized that he had been hurt by his friend's slur. There are
limits, even to vocabulary! But he hesitated at the thought that Hilde
had perhaps really loved him. Maybe she had kept her faith in him,
as women often do, "somewhere in their most private parts." That
thought terrified him. He thought of his sister. Juliana has a husband now, he said to himself. Maybe she loves him.

He, however, had never looked on his friend Charles Atangana,
now his brother-in-law, with as much contempt as he did that day.
Images from the wedding ceremony ran through his mind, and that
reminded him of one thing he had never had himself—the thing
the Landlord hadn't failed to surround himself with back in Berlin,
even as he dreamed of his far-off country—a family. Even Charles
Atangana had a wife now, and a new family. What about him, Joseph
Ngono? He hadn't actually married the mother of his children. He
hadn't even officially recognized them as his own. He had spewed

out his bitterness in a political argument with his friend; he had gotten dead drunk to forget that mistake; and now he was laughing at his own bad behavior. Was it jealousy? he wondered.

He saw himself standing in the shadows while his friend was surrounded by light.

"That bastard," he said in Ewondo. "He's always walking on the sunny side of the street!"

Joseph Ngono burst out laughing at this image of his relationship with the chief. Yet he was also surprised by what it revealed about his personality: jealousy. Still laughing, his eyes took in the trees around him, his gaze lost along the infinite rows of cocoa trees. There's the truth of a happy family, he thought suddenly, the plantation of a happy home.

What he saw around him was ugly. Joseph Ngono couldn't deny it. Behind the smiling face of Charles Atangana he saw this sordid plantation, the battered faces of thousands of people he didn't know who had sacrificed their lives, their health, and yet who were also friends, brothers, sisters. Those people, he saw them in chains, sitting alongside the road, waiting to work in Charles Atangana's plantations. They were Ewondo, from his friend's ethnic group. He saw them weeding the chief's cocoa plantations, paid almost nothing, treated worse than the whites would have treated them just so Charles Atangana could have the most extravagant wedding in the colony. And it was his own sister's wedding too! Joseph Ngono realized that it is impossible to know the actual price of happiness and to remain happy. Sadness enveloped him. He realized he had finished his cigarette. He threw the burning butt down in front of him and watched it trace a red line in the somber air.

Was it his silhouette that he wanted to flee most of all? He couldn't know for sure; it was dark now. He walked across the plantation. He walked, bumped into trees, and kept walking. He was no longer drunk, but the clarity of his mind didn't help. He wanted to be inebriated. Yet it was enough that he was lost. He felt dizzy, and the trees still weren't revealing their secret to him.

He sat down under one, closed his eyes, and began to dream. He thought of his childhood. Wasn't that the only time when he could say without hesitation that he had been happy? He saw himself, naked, kicking a ball around in the rain, and he thought of Carl. He suddenly saw that his children were living the same life as he had. They had nothing new to tell him or to offer him, for their present was his past. He imagined that their future would be his present, and that thought made him very sad. We are all prisoners, he thought.

He turned his inflamed eyes on the cocoa trees. They, more than anything else, imprisoned his future. He wanted to cry out, to insult someone. But who? The guests at the chief's wedding might have heard his voice. He cried out. No one answered. His voice ricocheted off the trees and came back to him confused. Maybe the music drowned out all other noise, or maybe it was joy that left everyone deaf. Happiness is egotistical. He closed his eyes and decided to sleep. The scent of the earth combined with that of the cocoa plantation filtered into his mind. He woke with a start, coughing. He opened his eyes wide and realized that he couldn't breathe. Smoke was everywhere. He understood too late that after he'd tossed it, his cigarette butt had set the grass beneath the cocoa trees on fire. The trees in front of him were already caught up in the mad flames.

"*Scheisse!*" he cursed in German.

What had made the fire spread so quickly? I wondered, truly surprised. Grass in the dry season? Or had his vengeful urine transformed into petrol? In his raging despair, had Joseph Ngono urinated fire on these trees? How was that possible?

"Shit!" he cursed again.

Sara informed me that her father had no petrol with him when he left the wedding party. How could he have? Wind carried the coals across the plantation, the doyenne said. How could I contradict her? The twin hills of Mvolyé and Nsimeyong played Ping-Pong with the fire, she added. And then she told me that her father had already understood that he had the power to change his life, that his friendship with Charles Atangana also brought him great satisfaction. Joseph Ngono's intent was not to commit a criminal act, she stressed, and even less a revolutionary one. He had lost his illusions and discovered a happiness defined by her, Sara, and her brother. Yes, if he was already an idealist, a dreamer, a Marxist, a nationalist, or—what else?—a poet, he would have emerged from his friend's plantation a changed man: he would have emerged as a family man.

However, with the plantation where he'd found illumination on fire, he was in danger. He had only his clothes with which to fight the flames. He took off his clothes and tried to fight the flames with his tuxedo. Sadly, the fire spread with a speed fueled by Yaoundé's dry season. Joseph Ngono fought the fire and shouted for all he was worth. He shouted and fought the flames. His jacket caught fire. He threw it away and, holding his breath, ran toward the center of the plantation. Even in his despair the trees didn't show him the way out. Soon he was again faced with the deadly yellow fire. It was as if the flames had joined forces with the lines of identical trees to build a suffocating and rancorous wall that blocked his way, leaving no chance for escape.

"Help!" he cried. "Help!"

No one answered.

"Help!"

The voice repeating his cry was just the crackle of the branches and leaves from the fire all around him, taking hold of the universe with its fury. Hope can't be quantified, only its results. Oh! Joseph Ngono once again opened his mouth and shouted for all he was worth, but all that came back to him was the melodious echo of his own voice. The flames had started in on a song he knew. A song as deep as the song of death. A hymn sung by a chorus of trees. He heard verses that he could understand even if he no longer knew all the words. It was a love song, a song of unhappy love. It was the lamentation of a lost country, a song so sublime and so poignant that Ngono had tears in his eyes. Yet he sang the fire's song, replacing the words he couldn't recall with names of his own choosing. He began with those of the people he had failed to love. He called for his German wife, Hilde, and then the mother of his children, Sala. He called his children, Sara and Carl, and his sister, Juliana. He even called out the name of his friend Charles Atangana.

One by one, Joseph Ngono recited the names of the people he held in his heart. He named his father, his mother, his grandfather, his grandmother, and the ancestral spirit of Yaoundé, Essignan. He continued with all the Cameroonians he knew. He called for the

Landlord in Berlin: Mandenga! Mandenga! Mandenga! Tears ran down his cheeks. Ngosso Din, he didn't forget him, even if he'd never met him; then his boss, Manga Bell. Samba. He called for all the Cameroonians of the diaspora that he knew. He said the names of the members of the traveling theater group that had taken up his years during the war. He called out the name of Theophilus Wonja, his wife, Martha, and their four children. Louis Brody—whose girl-friends scattered across Germany were too many to name, and who couldn't even count all the children he had, "because that brought bad luck"—he called for him as well, and then Martin Dibobe, who worked for the railroad company, who was never available for meet-ings and always cursed "the white man's work." And who else? Yes, who else, who else did he call? He even said the name of that woman from South-West Africa whom he'd met one day in Frankfurt, but maybe she was from Rhodesia. He thought he'd forgotten her long ago, Nyasha, and who else? He called all the people close to his heart, the people he called his family, as if only they, whom he'd failed to love as he ought to have, could still save him from the flames that day.

"Help me," he begged. "I don't want to die here!"

18

The Cocoa Spirit

Here is what Sara told me: her father had reached a level of awareness such that he wanted nothing more than to be a happy father. I couldn't ask her how she knew that, just as I couldn't ask her how she had known the details of his thoughts when he was trapped inside a cocoa plantation. I knew that she had told herself this story over and over. I imagined that like any orphan, she had told herself the story of her father's death so often that it had become true. And with good reason!

"Show her some respect," I advised the young men of Nsimeyong.

"In a certain way," Arouna interrupted, "we all invent our history, don't we?"

"As long as it makes us happy," I replied.

Sara wanted her father to have changed. Who would have refused her that? Some questions remained unanswered, questions that my friends from Nsimeyong only asked me later.

"Do you think one cigarette can set a whole cocoa plantation on fire?"

How could I know?

"Do you think urine can burn like kerosene?"

There I wanted to say, "Go ask Sara!"

They didn't stop.

"Do you think wind can carry fire?"

"What do these city boys know about fire?" the old mama would have responded, chortling as only Cameroonian women can.

Whatever the explanations and theories, the fact remains that
Ngono's efforts didn't save him. The people celebrating at the chief's
were alerted by the yellow glow of the flames that lit up the sky, and
not by the shouts of a man trapped by his own death. Or rather, no,
it was Sara, still a young girl, who said to her mother, "Mama, fire!"

And pointing at the courtyard with her finger, she showed her
mother, whose thoughts, like those of all the other adults that evening, were elsewhere.

"Fire?" repeated her distracted mother.

"Isn't that a fire?" someone else looking out the window asked
at the same time, but then, too, the dancing crowd didn't listen.

"A bushfire!" shouted a man who burst in suddenly.

Only then did the whole crowd awaken.

"A bushfire!"

"Fire!"

"The plantation's on fire!" cried another man.

"Fire!"

Then the dancers were caught up in a wild commotion. Everyone ran to the door. Husbands forgot their wives; children, including Sara, were left inside the house. Dancers trampled on one another
because some had heard that it was Charles Atangana's house that
was on fire. When the crazed crowd ran toward the cocoa plantation
with water to put out the flames, it was already too late. The confused guests found everyone in the neighborhood fighting the fire,
wearing themselves out in a fight that was lost from the start.
Yaoundé had only one fire truck, and that day it arrived too late. In
fact, the firefighters arrived in time only to write down in their
report that the cocoa plantation that "Monsieur Charles Atangana,
Paramount Chief of the Ewondo, had planted on his property to
lead his people by example into a new era of progress and prosper-
ity, had been reduced to ashes."

"A criminal act?" the white officer in charge asked.

His eyes scanned the guests.

"Do you know who did this?"

How could the chief's guests have answered? If Charles Atangana hadn't intervened, the *tirailleurs* would have arrested everyone, guests or not. The chief was crushed, of course, but he wasn't

defeated. He knew that the cocoa project had already gone too far to disappear in flames. The French government had invested millions and millions of francs, and already cocoa trees were popping up all over Southern Cameroon. The destruction of his plantation was a desperate act that, in the chaos of this brightly lit night, could only make him laugh.

"Only a madman could do that," he told the French official, "only a madman."

For Sara, however, her father wasn't a madman. On the contrary, she told me, the fire had spread so quickly only because hundreds of people had joined in his rage. Guests from the chief's wedding had come out to pour petrol on the flames instead of water, she told me. Sara suggested that some of them urinated on the cocoa trees. Too many people didn't want cocoa in their lives, she confided. That's how the enormous fire on the hilltops of Nsimeyong lit up the whole capital.

That fire is Sara's first real memory, her very first memory of her father.

"The fire killed him," she concluded.

And sometimes at night she still heard his voice calling them, calling her and her brother. When she told me this story, it was as if she could still see him burning in the flames. Tears ran down her cheeks, and she looked at me sadly, for I couldn't save her "poor Ngono" either.

"His body nourished our land," I said, trying to console her.

Sara smiled.

I could see the fire from that long-ago evening burn in her eyes once more. Yes, it was as if she had become her own father. The members of her ethnic group, ordered by Charles Atangana to replant cocoa trees on his property, refused to set foot on the accursed field. Some said they had seen a man walking there at night, as if trying to find his way between what remained of the trees. The man was reciting names.

"A madman?"

"No, a dead man."

"Dead dead?"

"Dead dead."

The workers said that the dead man had called their names, too.

"Our real names."

"Even the names of our wives."

"Of our children."

"It's a spirit."

"That plantation is damned."

Of course Charles Atangana burst out laughing. Still, the laugh of a chief, however paramount he may be, doesn't make a cocoa tree grow. So he hired Bamiléké workers. He had good memories of them from his exile in Dschang. He paid them a reasonable wage and added health insurance to their salaries, something that in all those years had never before been mentioned in the colony. It was an offer those men couldn't ignore. The vision of money persuaded them to leave their native plateau en masse and to confront Yaoundé and the curse of the pyromaniac spirit. But this time it was the ground that balked.

Or maybe the Frenchmen's seed wasn't any good.

The cocoa trees still didn't grow.

"Bad seed," cursed the workers, albeit under their breath, "bad cocoa!"

They also said, "Damned cocoa!"

For a long time people talked about the burned-down plantation that refused to bear fruit, refused to repeat the cycle of infamy. If the city already told itself a million stories about the paramount chief, this only added to the man's mystery. The story of the spirit in his house was well known. In the pocket of his flamboyant jacket Charles Atangana kept a key with which he locked the haunted room, everybody knew that. Why else would he have a gold chain hanging from his jacket pocket, people wondered, if not to lock up the spirit of the fire and to keep him from burning down his house?

Joseph Ngono's calcified body was discovered only much later. The story of his wandering spirit spread through the capital. People said he'd been sold out to the French by "his own brother," Charles Atangana. His death coincided with a time when workers on construction sites and factories in France began to demand better salaries. Even those who didn't know the story of the spirit talked about a man who had died on a plantation, "in a fire" that nothing had been done to prevent. That tragic end reminded the wretched of the injustice of their own condition.

There were some who were impressed by the salary Charles Atangana promised his workers, a salary that, any way you looked at it, was far above the pittance their white boss gave them—even if none of the chief's workers had been paid yet. Sara recalled that there had been revolts here and there in the protectorate, protests in the streets of Yaoundé. People were demanding the same salary as the whites. Soon they demanded the same pay on all the cocoa plantations, and then on all plantations, on all worksites. And, finally, the same working conditions for whites and blacks. In the end, the protestors were demanding nothing less than equality and freedom.

The doyenne also recalled that her father's spirit inspired the words of the rebels when they faced the *tirailleurs'* rifles. The discovery of Ngono's body had transformed Charles Atangana's cocoa plantation into a cemetery. No one wanted to go near it anymore.

"Superstitions," cursed the chief.

Aside from his colonial friends, he was the only one to think that. Even the French officials couldn't convince the recalcitrant population, or the land, to resume work producing cocoa. In the end, Charles Atangana had no other choice but to abandon his field to the first taker. Only foreigners could be convinced to build homes there. So first he gave a part to the Catholic missionaries when one of them, a priest, knocked on his door bearing the conviction that he "could make miracles in this bush." Charles Atangana asked him just one question, "Can you also chase away spirits?"

"The Divine Spirit will inhabit this place," he said, "and make this a land of miracles."

A fervent Catholic, the chief understood the prelate's words in religious terms and answered, "Amen."

He named what remained of his property "Mount Pleasant"; perhaps he hoped that name, which he'd heard once on his travels and was a happy reminder of his wanderings, would conjure away the curse. Did the chief invite Njoya to the capital so he could help him in his final attempt to convince planters from the west of the country to conquer the cocoa spirit, hoping they would obey an authority they'd known back in their villages? Why not? In any event, his friendship was always two-faced.

So in 1931, when Njoya agreed to leave his retreat in Mantoum for Yaoundé, when he agreed to drive his red pickup truck to the City of Seven Hills and take up residence there with his entourage on that bit of land Charles Atangana so graciously offered him, he was the one doing his friend a favor. But the sultan didn't know that he was bringing a painful chapter to a close. The rest, as we already know, is Sara's story.

19

Sublime Reveries on a Tour Through the City

Even though Charles Atangana's car had, in the meantime, become a constant presence in Mount Pleasant's main courtyard, the children had never gotten used to the noise of its motor. Each time, they announced the Cadillac's arrival with their happy voices and enchanted its departure with their shouts, songs, and dances. Running in the dust that the machine kicked up, waking up the houses, shouting along with the motor's noise, they transformed Charles Atangana's appearances into an unending party.

This time the chief had come, as he said himself, "to take the sultan out." It was high time, Sara realized. After two years of reclusion, it was time for Njoya to get out of his house, out of Mount Pleasant's alleys, out of the main courtyard, out of the walled community, just to breathe in the city's air. Besides, the sun was shining regally, like a ripe orange unpeeling in the sky. There was no longer any reason to stay cloistered, no. Charles Atangana had trouble believing that Njoya hadn't seen anything of the capital in all the time he had been there. He took it personally. "I will show you my city," he declared.

Njoya had done the same for him in Foumban, when Atangana had visited him there, before his exile. In fact, the idea of a walk outside was what really excited the sultan. He was more than happy to escape from the labyrinth of Mount Pleasant, even for an instant. Still, "Where are we going?" he asked.

His expectant eyes were bright.

"Into town," Charles Atangana announced with a broad smile.

In Foumban, it would have taken at least an hour to dress the sultan. It would have taken even longer that day to dress this man who'd been handicapped for so long but had lost nothing of his natural vanity. Njoya demanded light clothes. He chose a black and red *gandoura* himself, one in the Bamenda style.

"Perfume!" he ordered. "Perfume!" Even though he was already wearing perfume.

"We're just going out, right?" he asked with concern.

"That's all," his friend swore. "But after two years, that's enough of an exploit, isn't it?"

"Just a quick tour?"

"We'll leave the moon for tomorrow!" the chief joked. "No photos today, no surprise visits. Just a quick tour."

He and the chief took the Golden Car. Nebu, the shadow, was sitting in the back, between the chief architect and Ibrahim. He held the sovereign's cane. The price Charles Atangana had to pay to have the sultan sit next to him was separation from his "dear Juliana." But it was worth it. "Just for today," he said, full of good humor.

The sultan's guard ran behind the car. The excursion looked like a parade. Sara confessed that she had never been in a car before. That her first experience took place in a procession, wasn't that ideal? Because the chief's car drove along slowly, she had the impression that cars always went slowly. The golden Cadillac was well known in the city, and the convoy never crossed through a courtyard without people turning toward it and shouting with joy. Truthfully, they were all excited by the sound of the automobile and by its song, so new here! Their curious eyes added a sort of dignity to the procession. Several people joined in, marching alongside for quite a while.

Njoya had always loved going down into his city, into Foumban.

"Is there a market here?" he asked his friend.

Charles Atangana did not hesitate.

"Not just one!"

He began to count, using his fingers on the steering wheel.

"There is . . . the shoe market, a . . . coal market, a spice market, of course, a fruit market, a women's market, and so a men's market . . . a . . . clothing market . . . a . . ."

His pride that Yaoundé had not just one but a whole slew of markets to show his guests from Foumban was visible. He had used all his fingers and still kept counting.

"Did you know we have galleries now?"

He realized that his friend didn't know what a gallery was. He added that it was a "white man's market," but that didn't help. The chief himself had seen a gallery only once, in Paris.

"Well then," he concluded, "let's go to the gallery."

From Mount Pleasant, that meant crossing through Plateau, going past the French military base and the post office—in short, going into the white part of town. When the car reached Plateau, it became clear that this excursion by the two chiefs would be a historic event. People gathered around the procession, forcing it to stop. They didn't disperse, even when Njoya's men tried to force them back. Charles Atangana was in his element. He reached out with his hand and waved. The people waved back gleefully. It was as if the city were touching its Miracle Maker.

How different from the 1920s, when these same people had been overjoyed by the burning of his cocoa plantation! The crowd is a very naïve child. Ten years had passed, ten years, and Charles Atangana was once more the paramount chief. It was obvious in the gaze of all those people who had lined up along his path, drawn there as if by magnetic force. It was hard to imagine there was a greater authority in Yaoundé, or that it would be the French high commissioner, Marchand. You would have thought the country had stopped being a protectorate and that Charles Atangana had become its president!

When the chief stopped later in front of a shop, Njoya felt sad. It was painful to him that he couldn't just step out of the car and walk by himself in the street. Here in Yaoundé, he knew he had a freedom of movement he never would have had in Foumban. But for his body, ah! Charles Atangana soon returned, a newspaper in his hand.

"News from Germany," he announced, getting back into the car.

He knew the news would interest his friends. Germany was the secret they shared. So he read the headline: " 'Adolf Hitler Is Named Chancellor.' "

"Lieutenant Hirtler?" asked the three Bamum with one voice, their eyes wide open.

"Don't ask me," Charles Atangana replied, shrugging his shoulders. "Me, I've already left that country behind."

The tone of his voice translated his feelings well. The subject was closed for a moment. But just for a moment. Njoya hadn't had a newspaper for quite some time; since Ngutane had gone back to Foumban, in fact. He realized how much he missed her. Her vitality always made up for the sluggishness of his feet. Still, he recognized that she was doing invaluable work in Bamum land. He knew she had galvanized the people in a way that his representative, Fompouyom, and even his heir, Nji Moluh, had been unable to do. He had received a letter from her recently, in which she told him about the success of her campaign for the schooling of the nobles and added that her own children had already been admitted to Madame Dugast's elementary school. Ah, the sultan thought, the most important thing was that she be with her family, with her children. That's where she needs to be, he added.

Today I can say this: the future was coming quickly. Soon Ngutane will come back to Yaoundé, divorced, having left her husband, who, in her absence, had become an "infidel" and taken a fifth wife. She will marry Ibrahim, her dear "Ibrahimou," whom she has loved since childhood. She will be the scribe's fourth wife. And that's not all: Madame Dugast will for once forget her distaste for polygamy, which always chilled her love for "everything Bamum." She will happily bless the marriage of "her best friends in Foumban, and offer them a special gift from Europe": an Atmos clock, made in 1928. For years that wedding will set the standard for fashion.

Back to the moment at hand. Njoya's eyes didn't, in fact, see such a complicated future ahead. They had fallen on the photo of the man in a dark jacket under the newspaper's headline. Is that or is that not Hirtler? he wondered.

Thirty years had passed, and his memory played tricks on him.

Have the Germans accepted this? he also asked himself.

He recalled how angry the Bamum had gotten when that stupid German officer, Lieutenant Hirtler, had sat on his throne; that was in 1903. Distant photos of a distant life, he thought, and handed the newspaper to Nji Mama. The life all around him was livelier. The cries, the laughter, the sunny faces, the theatrical gestures—all made Njoya happy. And then all those blacks dressed in Western clothes! Men going about on bicycles. They pedaled fast, zigzagging through the pedestrians, unaware of their graceful movements. The sultan thought he recognized Ngosso Din in the crowd. He looked again, but it was someone else. Soon he also thought he recognized Nebu, Muluam, and then Ngbatu, before realizing that the city was just playing another trick on him. All these people walking or riding or moving toward a dream, or maybe a nightmare that no one could foresee. They were like cats chasing their tails endlessly, turning their shadows into a circle until they fainted.

"Read this," said Ibrahim's voice from the back of the car. "President of the Assembly, that's what Göhring has become . . ."

But Njoya didn't want to listen anymore. If we're to live with it, the past must be dreamed anew. But what about the future? The easy life in Foumban, where lazy pages sat in front of the palace, was a distant echo of the bouquet of life bursting out in this metropolis. It was as if the whole country offered itself up jovially, in a shadow dance, to the sultan who had come back to life. In front of a pet store, a black woman in extravagant clothes caught the attention of the Bamum men. Nji Mama saw her first.

"That one, she's something else," he whispered.

He was talking to his brother, who had shut himself off from the world by reading the newspaper, but his words alerted the three other men. The woman was holding a brightly colored umbrella over her head, and with her free hand she was pulling a dog, a particularly ugly creature that refused to budge and was barking terribly. None of the men in the car had ever seen such a pooch.

"Is that a rat or a dog?" Nji Mama asked.

Ibrahim answered, "Go ask the woman."

"Is it a dog or a man?" Njoya added, with the same good humor as the two brothers.

The three men burst out laughing. The paramount chief, too. Then he looked in the rearview mirror. Only Nebu hadn't reacted. The little boy was clutching his chest.

"Don't you want a dog like that, Sara?" the chief asked.

20

The Surprising Blindness of the Polygamous

"Sara?" repeated the three Bamum.

In Mount Pleasant, everyone knew her as Nebu. Since she had no voice, she couldn't contradict the name that the matron had given her. What's more, at the end of Bertha's thousand tales, hadn't the soul of the lost son immigrated to the girl's body? Hadn't the dead man from long ago come back to life in this belly that had digested his torture in one story after another? For two years, Sara's body hadn't betrayed her secret. The hot stone with which Bertha flattened her breasts had done its job, you could say, but it was also as if the little girl's decision to give Nebu another chance had suspended her development. Even at twelve years of age, she still didn't have breasts.

Meanwhile, Njoya had taken her as his model, keeping himself busy by drawing the features of her face. Until then, he'd gotten only as far as the shoulders. He had struggled with this portrait of a shadow—it was the first he'd done. The definition of the eyes, the nose, the mouth, and the ears had given him the most trouble. That the boy had feminine features had helped him a bit, since that made him stand out. Isn't beauty found at the intersection between total opposites? But Njoya just couldn't finish Nebu's portrait, despite all his efforts. His hands were weak, of course. Or was it his mind? Who could have told him that it was the abyss of Nebu's body that escaped him? That it was the boy's hundred faces that disconcerted him?

Ibrahim had encouraged him, revealing with a thousand words of praise the precision of his lines and sometimes even holding his hand and pushing it along, but to no avail. The sultan had structured the boy's body around the face, which he had reduced to a few simple lines. He believed he had finally captured its essence when his friend revealed something unbelievable to him: The young boy he had spent his days drawing was actually a girl? The shock he felt was that of an artist who has for too long remained blind to his model, only suddenly appreciating his essential beauty.

"You're joking!"

It was Nji Mama who answered.

All eyes turned toward Sara.

"You are . . ." the master architect stammered.

"A girl?" his brother concluded.

Sara nodded. Nji Mama and Ibrahim had to hold themselves back from pulling down the boy's clothes to reveal the young girl who had hidden herself for so long. How had she done it? There, in the middle of the lively city, among the most fervent voices of the central market, the surprised men were frozen inside the car, their eyes fixed on the silent girl.

"A girl?" Njoya repeated.

"Don't tell me," Charles Atangana interrupted, speaking to the polygamists who surrounded Sara, "that you don't recognize the scent of a girl?"

He was so surprised by his friend the sultan's dazed reaction that he could only laugh. Sara's revelation was just too comical for that monogamist; he couldn't believe that Njoya's six hundred and eighty-one wives hadn't taught him to recognize a woman.

"Don't tell me you didn't know either," he insisted, addressing Nji Mama and Ibrahim, "despite all your wives."

"A girl!" Njoya repeated.

And he remembered all the times Sara had seen him naked. Nji Mama recalled, as well, the law mandating that the sultan's shadow be a boy. Never had he been so wrong. He also remembered Nebu's shivering face the day the boy had arrived late to work and entered Njoya's life as a model. Ibrahim recalled only the drawing sessions, and he, too, remained as still as a statue. As for Sara, she wasn't shocked at all. For her, Nebu's story was over. Not because she had lived to the end of her character's fate, but because a few days before, she had gotten up and discovered spots of blood on her mat. She had run to Bertha, thinking it was Nebu's tragedy that was making her bleed. The matron had burst out laughing and told her it was something she'd have to live with from then on.

"It's your own blood," she said.

Sara still couldn't understand. Bertha continued, "Now you are a woman."

Sara knew that her development could only signal the matron's defeat. Yet that day she saw no sign of surrender in the matron's eyes. In a certain sense, the belated mother had, by telling her story, liberated herself from her accursed life, from the suffering of her soul; now she could accept someone else's daughter for who she was. A very belated liberation, the doyenne confided to me, for Sara was no longer a young girl, and then the palace laws were rather strict: the onset of a girl's period marked the end of her stay with the matron; it was the sign that she should be sent to the sultan's bedchamber. The matron's farewells provoked Sara's compassion, and because of that compassion, Bertha looked upon the girl with loving eyes. It was a love that Bertha and Sara had both been searching for up to then. The matron accepted it, even if it had arrived through an unexpected doorway. She kissed the new young woman and said her name for the first time. "Sara."

She repeated Sara's name several times, as if she were inventing her own liberation on the foundation of someone else's. That day, Bertha left Mount Pleasant.

The capital swallowed up the rest of her story.

So we return to Charles Atangana and the Golden Cadillac.

"That's my brother's daughter, don't you remember?" said the chief.

How could Njoya have remembered? He was rebuilding his memory step by step, one story after another, and it had taken him two years to regain the agility of his fingers, as well as the liveliness of his eye. He had realized that even if he had found his mind's vitality once more, he still needed to breathe if he wanted to really live. Women were fighting all around the automobile, their faces smashed up against the windows. They wanted to show these luminaries the wonders they had for sale. The guards, overwhelmed, pushed them away, but couldn't silence their voices:

"Onions?"

"Tomatoes? Tomatoes?"

"Chief! Chief!"

"Salt?"

"Do you want hot pepper?"

"Oranges?"

"Cheaper!"

"The cheapest in Yaoundé!"

"In Cameroon!"

"In the world!"

The market's rich voice grew louder and, in a gust, swallowed up the vehicle in which a secret was being transformed into the beginning of a woman's story. Because in the silent interior of a car, surrounded by those women, Charles Atangana began to tell Sara's story. There in the center of Yaoundé, with his words he peeled away the layers of the still-silent girl as if she were an onion, even as the women outside waved the spices they wanted to sell in front of him. That's where he revealed to Njoya the girl he had once offered him as a present. It could happen no other way, for Nebu's story was that of a girl, as well as of a city. It was the story of the capital of a country that revealed itself in its hidden truths, in the woven pathways that echoed to the four corners of the earth and shocked the world, distant and threatening, in order to distill its own limitless perfumes.

How could Njoya have lived in this city for so long without catching a glimpse of its stories? The faces of all those women in the windows, yes, all those faces, contorted by words but rendered mute by the windowpanes that Nji Mama and Ibrahim had closed tight. Didn't all those faces suddenly reveal the infinite variables of this singular story that was taking shape on the chief's lips? The essential joy of this place that had brought the sultan back to life: How could he, Njoya, not have felt it for so long?

"I have been blind to life," he said.

"No, dear friend," Charles Atangana corrected him, "you were sick."

"And you have begun to see again," added Ibrahim.

Nji Mama added his words to those of the others: "To hear."

"To talk."

"To smell."

"To walk."

"To live."

Looking at Nebu, Njoya now saw a girl, a girl dressed as a boy, who shivered as she turned her face toward him and timidly smiled. The sultan loved what he saw and smiled back. For now he could finish the incomplete portrait without hesitating, drawing the torso of the girl, the smiling girl. Yes, Sara was smiling, and her smile transformed her body into happiness. What Njoya discovered—the doyenne there in her courtyard was sure of it—was the beginning of her own story.

The only problem? It was the chief who was telling the story to his friends. She wouldn't have had the courage, or the right, to speak up herself, even if the sultan hoped she would.

"Her name is Sara," Charles Atangana began, looking at Sara in the rearview mirror and smiling at her as well.

Sara was pure joy.

"What else can I say?" the chief continued, then paused thoughtfully.

He started with the end, which was also the beginning. He told the story of his friend, Joseph Ngono, and how he had survived the racist thugs in Berlin, then died in a cocoa plantation, "back in his own country, right where Mount Pleasant stands today."

"It's still not a closed case," he said, "but it'll come."

He paused.

"Yes, it'll come, even if it takes twenty more years."

He revealed, however, that the case had gone cold because High Commissioner Marchand had concluded, after reading the reports of his officials, that Joseph Ngono had died in a fire he'd set himself.

"It's just not logical," insisted Charles Atangana.

The paramount chief didn't want to believe that "his brother" could have set fire to his cocoa plantation.

"He can't have done that to me."

Then he said that he couldn't hold back his tears each time he thought about it; he felt responsible for the death of Joseph Ngono, who had left the wedding reception without telling anyone. Yes, the chief admitted that he hadn't yet found the right words to console his dear Juliana, his friend's younger sister.

"Your father was my brother, do you know that?" he asked Sara in their language, still looking in the rearview mirror that showed him only the girl's face.

Speaking to the sultan, he added, "We were like this."

Saying "like this" in French, he pressed his two index fingers tightly against each other on top of the steering wheel.

"She grew up with her uncle," he said. "Owona. But I always hoped she would come live with us."

He fell silent.

"You are my daughter, do you know that?" he continued in Ewondo. "But I also wanted you to live with my friend here."

After thinking for a moment, he corrected himself. "With my brother here, you know?"

Sara hadn't stopped smiling. After all, what did he know, Charles Atangana? If she had told him that several souls sparkled in her body, would he have believed her? Still, Sara smiled because she realized that he was looking at her in the rearview mirror; but when she looked in that mirror, what she saw was her own face. The chief looked at her with love-filled eyes. Like Njoya, who hadn't stopped looking at her these past few days as he was drawing her portrait so badly, could he decipher the tangle of her features? Ah, Sara didn't have the right to interrupt him and to speak for herself, in her own voice, in the midst of these men. If she had told her story, however, if she had opened her mouth in that car, she would have told the story of a mother of shadows, whose name Njoya certainly wouldn't have known, even though she had trained the majority of his wives. Sara would have described how, even though she was just a little girl, she had transformed Bertha's once terrifying grip into the embrace of a truly loving mother.

But Sara also would have told how she herself had invented this maternity by consenting to become the son Bertha had never stopped searching for in girls' bodies. Sara would have told how she had listened to a story that wasn't meant for a nine-year-old girl, just to awaken the breathless mother in the body of a menopausal woman. And the story of that mother would have been Nebu's, the master artist the sultan surely would have remembered with horror. Sara knew that the sculptor's story would have brought tears from all the men around her. Would they have had tears on their cheeks as well if she'd told them the story of her own life, after the death of her father in Charles Atangana's model cocoa plantation? Would they have cried if she had told them the story of her mother, Sala, whom she'd never seen again? Or the story of her brother, Carl, who had come to visit her only once and then to say, despite his young age, that he wanted to become a *tirailleur* "because then he could kill whomever he wanted, including Uncle Owona"? The chief would have certainly exploded in anger if she had revealed the truth about whose hands had set fire to his plantation. Or, rather, he would have said that he had always known.

"I always knew that he was," he'd say, "that he was a . . . piece of shit."

Sara smiled, but in truth, she was the one in tears. Was it because in this suffocating market the spices strangled her with their menacing odors? Was it the silence of all those women waving outside the closed windows? Or was it the thousand and one stories of the world that had come together inside that car, in that city? Suddenly a force took hold of her stomach, her lungs, her throat, her nose, binding them in one treacherous flame. Sara stiffened, opened her mouth, and with one hand, one foot, searched for support; she grabbed hold of the car seat, of her own knees and the knees of Nji Mama and Ibrahim, and then her own chest; she opened her nose wide to suck in the oxygen missing from the car, then closed her mouth and opened it once more, violently this time, and produced the sneeze of the century: "Ahh . . . ahhh . . . ahhh . . . aaatchoo!"

Ibrahim's newspaper went flying. When Sara reopened her eyes, the whole world's frozen face was fixed on her. Her monumental sneeze had made the Golden Car jump twice. The women all around stopped dead. The girl wiped her eyes and her nose with the back of her hand, astonished by the silence her voice had created. The men watched her closely.

"*Akié*," Charles Atangana finally asked, holding out a handkerchief. "Do you want to swallow us all up or what?"

He was smiling.

EPILOGUE

卦 弓

This is not a story to pass on.

—Toni Morrison, *Beloved*

Untitled

History is a House of a Thousand Tales. It's a compound with many bedrooms, courtyards, corridors, passages, doors, and windows; a labyrinth, yes, a zigzagging concatenation of memory's chains, but also a house of several floors; an agglomeration of whispers, murmurs, gossip, anecdotes, cries, jokes, and laughter; a perpetual reminder. It's a school for the young and a projection of dreams; a banquet for zombies—the insatiable masses—and a balm for us all. It's the only real judge of our errors and our successes. A cruel master that stands before us. History is our only future. It is easy to imagine a past world, where a reified African would meet a white man, reified as well, in a tragic duel, in a battle for life or death, the first armed with an arrow, the second a cannon! How naïve to put one's feet into the colonizer's chains, to take up once again the struggle of the native man, even though we were born and raised independent. But what about the overwhelming wave of nausea that rises up within at the sight of this continent running blindly into the devil's hands, or when History rushes headlong into tragedy's camp. Sara's story reminded me that when the thunder of the First World War awoke Europe's capitals with its mad songs, its destructive hymns also echoed in several African cities.

Blessed are those who understood, in the flames of 1914, whether in Foumban or in Berlin, that they were entering not civilization's great house, but the corridors of mass murder. The millions who died in the trenches and on the battlefields of that world war left behind other souls, both black and white, forever wounded. Blessed, too, are those who in 1933, whether in Yaoundé or Paris, in Foumban or Berlin, had sufficiently clear vision to predict that their future was conjuring a huge furnace, much larger than the one from which they had just escaped. Those few, the chosen people of a story of madness, be they Njoya, Ngono, Atangana, or Bertha, knew that they were poised between two worlds, and not the two worlds evoked by history books, no. After listening to their tales, I can say that they were caught between a truly bleak present and a future bleaker still. That opaque fate, they shared it with the colonizers who had come into their cities and into their lives, whether they be Wuhrmann or Father Vogt, Prestat, Göhring, or Hirtler; but alas! they found no language sufficiently humane to relate their shared fate. Whatever the case may be, as they entered such an uncertain future, waking up in the ruins of their destroyed homes, holding in their hands the rare instruments they had invented—alphabets, pictograms, drawings, reports, books, statues, etc.—with which they sought to transform their fears and their dreams into figurines of lives, they were touched by the fire that hardens the bricks of the present. Their story is the flesh of our quivering earth.

I left Cameroon before Sara told me what happened after she'd been plucked bare in the Golden Car, right in the middle of town. I left Yaoundé with Nebu's story more or less complete in my mind, but with Sara's only just beginning. The young men of Nsimeyong accompanied me to the airport. They, too, carried the story of the old mama in their bellies, and I had seen for myself how much it had changed their lives. Arouna told me he had decided not to marry me after all. That made me burst out laughing, for we had become friends.

"Didn't I tell you I already have a husband?" I asked him.

It was his turn to laugh.

"You too, you are a labyrinth," he answered, disappointed that I hadn't told him this at the outset.

"You never asked me," I reproached him.

"You haven't even told us your story," he suddenly remarked.

"You never asked me that, either."

"Is he American?"

"Who?"

"Your husband."

"Well . . ."

Two months after I got back to the United States, I found an envelope from Cameroon in my mailbox, an envelope covered with stamps. It held two letters, one of which was an extremely beautiful text written in Njoya's Lewa pictograms, and the second was a letter in French signed by all my friends in Nsimeyong. I started with the letter from my friends because it was easier to read. They told me that Sara was dead. The whole neighborhood had buried her with dignity, according to Bamum customs, even though she was Ewondo. But they also told me that Nsimeyong had decided to build a memorial in her honor, to transform the two stones that remained from Mount Pleasant into that house of which she had been the last surviving memory. By doing so, the letter informed me, the poor neighborhood hoped to "attract tourists." Even in the dust that collective letter brought from far away, I could smell one of Arouna's financial schemes.

But the letter went on to tell me that Sara had been given a burial befitting the neighborhood doyenne she was. And here I had tears in my eyes. I suddenly saw her again, surrounded by hens in her courtyard in Yaoundé, sitting with her feet crossed; I saw her take a pinch of tobacco and swallow her sneezes so she could tell me the story of her life. I even felt the warmth of her fingers transforming my head of hair into that old-fashioned style that made her laugh and thrilled me to no end because it was the revelation of her life. I still felt her breath on my shoulder when she was braiding my hair, and I recalled how Sara pulled me toward her, whispering in my ears the most astonishing—or really the most unbelievable—bits of her story, safe from the indiscreet ears of the neighborhood and my friends. I saw Sara braiding my hair, grabbing my head, section by section, and keeping my whole mind alert. I was transported and, at the same time, submerged by the sky of that unending reminder she had inscribed on my head in the structured beauty of a cornrow braid (which had made many black women in the United States stop me on the street to ask who had done my hair). I ran to the bathroom, looked in the mirror, and there behind me I saw Sara, winking conspiratorially. I closed my eyes and kept looking at her. This time she smiled.

"What do you know?" she asked.

"Nothing," I replied.

"Always nothing, always nothing," she repeated, laughing and holding a pinch of tobacco in front of her nose. "Don't you learn history where you come from?"

She meant "in the United States."

How to answer? Sara! Ah, Sara!

Her voice was still in my ears, her voice that had told me the most incredible stories in the simplest way; still, I couldn't hold back my tears when I translated her letter. It was the story of her life in Njoya's chambers after her public revelation. And she told of this new life with details I wouldn't have thought possible, with an honesty that, I finally understood, was her way of finishing with the House of Spirits that Mount Pleasant had in fact always been for her. But her letter ended with a sentence that made me fall right down:

. . . and then—do you understand?—I became the sultan's wife.

Acknowledgments and Sources

This novel places onstage very well-educated Cameroonians and Africans: true citizens of the world, in fact. If it is anachronistic to imagine that Seneca had received a doctorate, a certain level of erudition is certainly necessary to understand his writing. Owing to the twists of African history, however, the writer of this novel—who was educated and has published books in French, English, and German—had to come to terms with his own illiteracy when he discovered Njoya's library: a library that is open in the city where the writer was born, Yaoundé, and which holds the very heart of Cameroonian and African literature, even if it has been erased from their contemporary literatures. To enter into conversation with this library's world of pictograms, phonemes, words, letters, and books, to bring the Lewa and Akauku alphabets back to life, and to be faithful to fiction's truth, I needed to change the destinies of many characters and many dates as well. May the descendants of these illustrious characters understand and forgive me!

The books used in the preparation of this novel are too numerous to be cited here, for this is not a history dissertation, but a work of imagination. That said, Tardits's *Le Royaume bamoum*; *L'Écriture des Bamoum* by Dugast and Jeffreys; *Die Bamum-Schrift* by Schmitt; Delafosse's article on Njoya's secret royal language, as well as Geary's pictographic research, especially her *Mandu Yenu: Bilder aus Bamum*, which she published with Ndam Njoya; Tuchscherer's research; and

Les Dessins bamoum, in which one can see Ibrahim's drawings, were all troves of information. The digitized colonial archives of the University of Frankfurt and the University of Southern California, the German cinematographic archives in Berlin, and the Centre national de la cinématographie in Paris, as well as various websites, allowed me to see what the world I was searching for could be. It was all brought to life by a photographic exhibit put together by the students in my course Tropical Germany, at Vassar College in the United States.

I will never be able to thank Barbara Koennecker enough for having insisted on the idea of Njoya; Chris Abani, for having facilitated certain things; Nyasha Bakare, for having traversed the hallways of the writing of this text, first in English, in a manuscript she patiently read, and then in French. My thanks, as well, to Konrad Tuchscherer, for his truly unique enthusiasm, his historical knowledge, which he so generously put at my disposal, and for providing the prints of Lewa writing that I use in the text and those of Akauku writing found at the start of each section—writing systems on which he worked with Nji Oumarou Nchare and Jason Glary. Finally, Laure Pécher! You were the one who really believed in this project!

This is a book about books, and so an homage to all of Africa's ancient libraries, its forgotten hagiographers, and especially those who worked in obscurity during the long era that is described so poorly by the term "colonialism." But it is, above all, an homage to a unique book, a marvelous collection of memories, that was begun in Foumban around 1908, its final version completed on Monday, June 19, 1921, in Mantoum, Cameroon: Sultan Njoya's *Saa'ngam*.

Baltimore, 2006–Princeton, 2015

Translator's Note

Translation is necessarily an exchange between languages, times, and individuals; this project has been possible only because of the generosity of those who helped me follow the conversations of Sara and Bertha to their enchanting conclusion. I want to express my immense respect for Patrice Nganang; his combination of aesthetics and engaged ethics is inspiring. I first learned of Njoya and his library when Patrice gave a talk at New College of Florida in 2007; thank you, Patrice, for this opportunity to explore the pathways of Mount Pleasant and the ambiance of Njoya's court. Chris Richards and Miranda Popkey of FSG were tremendous supports through the editing process; my thanks to them for their patience and their eloquent advice. Hector Kamden Fonkoua, of the University of Bayreuth, kindly responded to my questions about Cameroonian idioms and forms of address. Caroline Reed and Theresa Burress of the Jane Bancroft Cook Library helped locate sources for quotations in the novel. A grant from the New College of Florida Faculty Development Fund allowed me to focus on this project in the summer of 2014. Any errors in the translation are certainly mine, but I give my thanks to those who helped me in my efforts to reflect the novel's scope and its love of words.

Mount Pleasant is primarily a novel about interpersonal connections—connections through stories and art, language, love, and home. I am so grateful for the love and support of my family: for my husband, Uzi Baram, and our children, Jacob, Miriam, and Ben.

CPSIA information can be obtained
at www.ICGtesting.com
Printed in the USA
LVHW042303210722
724001LV00001B/87